Murder Is Just the Beginning

by

Carol Kravetz

CHAPTER ONE

The sleek, silver 2017 Jaguar XE rumbled slowly along the alleyway, the wipers working periodically to clear flecks of snow off the windshield. Its front passenger tire clanged noisily over a manhole cover, rudely disturbing two cats fighting for scraps from a Deli's dumpster. They both screeched their disapproval before disappearing into the frigid night, neither one victorious in finding anything in the way of substantial nourishment to feed their pitifully thin body.

The driver inched the car forward towards the turn onto the main road, some twenty yards ahead. For the first time in a long time, his mind was ticking over in a calm, rational manner. He'd certainly had a lot to think about over the last few weeks, particularly the last couple of days. Although loathe to admit it, he'd been more than a little bit apprehensive, scared shitless, if the truth was known. But now, if anything, he was more curious than he was concerned because, according to his contacts just a couple of hours ago, the death toll still stood at three. As he contemplated that fact, he quickly corrected himself. The *murder* toll now stood at three. He would find out in a matter of minutes if the number had risen to four within the last 24 hours.

Within seconds, he pulled up almost alongside where he wanted to be. Stepping out of the warmth of his brand-new car, he carefully negotiated the slippery sidewalk and thought, not for the first time, that winter in Massachusetts was a blessing only for those who enjoyed snow and winter sports. He enjoyed neither.

His breath plumed out in front of him as he approached the newspaper-vending stall. Wind moaned balefully between the buildings and whipped up snowflakes and debris from the litter strewn street. It was 5:30 in the morning and he was safely assuming that the vendor would have received delivery of, and had put out ready for sale, today's papers, including the *Boston Globe, USA Today,* the *New York Times.* And, of course, the local papers, the *Bathville Record* and the *Bathville Post.* He could have been in the comfort and warmth of his own home doing this, he hated reminding himself. He could have done what millions of people did each and every day, he could have gone online and checked out any of the newspapers' websites. He could have used any electronic device he wanted: his Smart Phone, his Tablet, his laptop, even his PC. But no, any of those devices had built in hard drives and systems that could be tracked and traced in the hands of a law enforcement officer trained in searching for incriminating evidence, including most frequently visited websites.

Extracting a couple of dollar bills from an overstuffed Gucci leather wallet, he passed the money to the sleepy-eyed vendor and picked up the fresh copies of the *Record* and the *Post.* While waiting for the newspapers to be slipped into a cheap plastic bag, he cast his eyes over the selection of magazines and let his gaze rest for a long moment on the adult section. No, he couldn't treat himself, he decided. He had more pressing business than ogling the assets of young ladies, most of whom were probably young enough to be his daughter. Not that *that* particular detail bothered him. On the contrary. Maybe tomorrow, if he found what he was looking for in the newspapers he would indulge in one of his favorite pastimes, he promised himself.

Gruffly thanking the vendor, and waving away the loose change, he shuffled back to his Jag, ignited the engine and turned the heater up full blast. The few minutes he'd been out in the biting cold, his cheeks were already numb. January in Massachusetts, a swell time of year, he definitely didn't think so.

He was home within fifteen minutes. His cleaning lady wasn't due until around 9:00, so he had plenty of time to read every page of both newspapers in relative peace. His friends and business associates knew he was a night owl and he felt confident enough that they would respect his wishes that he shouldn't be contacted until at least late afternoon. But even if the phone did ring, there was always voicemail on his land line or his cell phone to pick up the message.

He put on a pot of coffee and while it was brewing, he took a quick shower to cleanse his body of the stale cigar and cigarette smoke aroma that seemed to be clinging to him, picked up from his trip to his very own night club just a few hours before. He usually went to the club late in the evening and stayed until early morning, just to oversee - and often browbeat or intimidate the staff - what was going on. He simply didn't want to miss anything and certainly didn't want to be taken advantage of. If the barman helped himself to even one drink without paying for it, or the dancer skipped off the stage five minutes early, he made sure their pay was docked and often did that without an explanation. His staff was too scared of him to question his motives.

He loved his club, The Blues Haven, had owned it for several years now and it was thanks to its patronage and quite a few shady dealings here and there that he could afford the Jaguar, this large five bedroom, 3 and a half bath home in one of Bathville's more exclusive areas, the trips to Europe or St. Kitts or Hawaii whenever he wanted and, of course, the extensive and escalating monthly medical bills. God, he hated having to pay those medical bills, but they were a necessity and a constant reminder of the promise he had made to his dying mother several years previously. She had been the only woman in the world he had ever truly trusted and adored completely, and the only woman in his life he had never used or abused. She was now long dead, though, pushing up daisies in an elaborate gravesite in a cemetery on the outskirts of the city. She had just wanted him to look after himself and he tried to do just that, but those damned bills…Oh well, *someone* had to pay them and if not him, then who? He had never married and had been an only child and, to his knowledge, had no extended family, not even a cousin or two, waiting to come out of the woodwork anytime soon. He was completely alone, which suited him fine.

After his shower, dressed only in fleece lined leather slippers and a warm dark blue bath robe that just about covered his ample 290-pound frame, he poured himself a cup of coffee, left it black but added three sugars and carried it and the two local newspapers into his study.

The *Record* was always the more informative of the two newspapers and certainly seemed to cover the city's news and events with more decorum and liveliness, thanks to the team of superb writers and editors. He set aside the sports section to peruse later, scanned the front page for the listings and turned to page 3 for what he was looking for, the Death Notices. Bathville, although less than an hour's drive from Boston, had a fairly decent sized population of 425,000 so he wasn't surprised to see that since the previous day, there were at least 20 new deaths listed, in alphabetical order.

The name he was looking for wasn't there. As soon as he realized that, he expelled a long breath, not even aware he had been holding it. So, the murder toll remained at three. For now.

There was a section in the *Record* titled "Local Up-Dates", on page 2 and he turned to this next. And there, right on the bottom right hand column, he found the information he needed. All he'd had to do, of course, was phone the hospital, or even visit the hospital, but he preferred not to have anyone either recognize his voice or recognize his face. Besides, hospitals these days were so scared of lawsuits, they never gave out patient information to anyone anymore, even if you could prove you were a family member.

The up date was short, but told him all he had to know. "Gloria Ho, 23, of Blackwell Apartments, Kirkland Road, Bathville, who was found beaten to within an inch of her life in her apartment 3 days ago, remains in critical condition at Bathville General Hospital. Doctors are imploring relatives, friends, or eyewitnesses of the attack to please come forward to assist the police in their investigation."

That was all there was, but that was all he wanted. He didn't want the girl to die but he certainly wasn't going to be held responsible if she did. Because Gloria Ho worked at his club as a waitress, and because the 3 murder victims had also worked for him, the police had already questioned him extensively. Two days ago, he had spent most of the morning and part of the afternoon being grilled at the 7th precinct but he'd been released after his alibi had proven him innocent of both the involvement of the murders and Ms. Ho's beating. He certainly didn't want to go through an ordeal like that again. The cops had come too close on too many occasions on that day to finding out the truth, but he was relatively certain all his answers, with the help of his alibi, had thrown the cops off his scent. Now all he had to do was keep it that way.

Settling back to enjoy his coffee, he picked up the sports section.

The Bruins had had a big win over the Maple Leafs the previous night, cause for celebration indeed.

It was enough to put him in a good mood, so good, in fact, that when his cleaning lady arrived a couple of hours later, he immediately beckoned her out of the kitchen and, with a gleam in his eye, a gleam she had witnessed many times since the commencement of her employment with him, she set aside her mop, allowed herself a resolute, internal sigh of acceptance and went to him. She had long ago been able to swallow her revulsion of him, but it hadn't been an easy task. He was just always so demanding, had even roughed her up a little bit when she had been foolish enough to slap away his roaming, unwanted, clammy hands on occasion. He had made it perfectly clear he owned her and she knew that if he didn't pay such good wages, she wouldn't even be here in the first place, never mind let him use her for sex. But money talked a universal language, even to a cleaning lady who was an illegal immigrant from Nicaragua, a single parent to three growing children and therefore someone who really needed the extra dollars just to make ends meet. She figured that if she kept giving him the sex he craved, it would help him keep his mouth shut and not report her to Immigration.

Moments later, as he felt her tongue work its magic on him, he decided that the real thing was always much better than using pornographic material to jerk off to. And he was, after all, her boss, which meant she had to obey his wishes if she wanted to continue receiving a handsome weekly paycheck.

He had to admit, though, it gave him a great deal of satisfaction and glee being able to control her like this. As long as he kept dangling the threat of the INR in front of her, he could keep it just like this for as long as he wanted.

CHAPTER TWO

Winter was toying with the citizens of Massachusetts. February had started out relatively mild, compared to the freezing, bitterly cold January. Lazy snow flurries added only a dusting to the snow banks that lined the roads and sidewalks of city and village alike. A couple of times, it had even been mild enough to rain.

Then, in the wee small hours of the fifteenth, winter came back, with a vengeance. It was all too reminiscent of the Polar Vortex of the previous year that had produced sub-zero temperatures, ice and snow storms, severe wind chills and heavy freezing from Canada all the way down to even the southern United States. This time, the temperature plummeted to the low twenties, the wind picked up again, producing bone-numbing wind chills and, to add insult to injury, a major storm that started life as a heavy rain system, rolled up from the Carolinas and the further north it tracked and met the cold temperatures, the precipitation turned to snow. By the time all was said and done, the storm had dumped up to fourteen inches of the white stuff in most areas of New England, before making its exit off the Atlantic Coast just south of Bar Harbor, Maine.

Bathville was located right on the shores of the Atlantic Ocean but being in such proximity to the sea didn't spare it from receiving a foot of snow after the last flake had fallen from the black sky, just before dawn started to break.

City workers were out in their plows, clearing the streets for the commuters. The roaring salt trucks, trying to keep the slippery roads from freezing over and becoming even more dangerous, followed the plows. More snow was forecast for noon and it was a pretty safe bet that most, if not all, schools in the area would be closed for the day.

It was 6:15 and still dark out when Paul Cameron stepped out of his apartment. He greeted the fresh blanket of snow with a wry shake of his head, but at least the superintendent had been out already to shovel and salt the pathways and the parking lot. Dressed as he was in blue jeans, a chunky royal blue sweater, a heavy denim fleece lined jacket, a scarf and warm gloves, Paul initially didn't feel the cold until he stepped past the shelter of the building. Then the icy blast of the north-westerly struck him full in the face worse than a hand slap and, pulling his scarf up around his ears and also using it to cover his nose and mouth, he bent his head and hurried forward, with some difficulty, to the parking lot, hoping and praying he wouldn't have to dig his car out.

He was in for a pleasant surprise. The wind may have been bitter, but it was also strong, and it had drifted the snow in some places to about four feet high, while in other places, it had swept the ground almost bare, showing patches of concrete or dead, brown grass here and there. Paul's car was completely snow free around the tires, which was good because he was already late for where he was going.

Undeterred, he started the engine, turned the heater on full blast and went back outside to clear the snow and ice off the windshield and remaining windows. By the time he had finished, his cheeks and toes were numb but when he got back into the car, at least it had warmed up sufficiently to stop his breath from billowing out in front of him every time he exhaled.

Fifteen minutes later, he pulled up outside the back entrance to Pete's Gym. He hurried inside to the warmth, stamping his Nike sneakers to get the snow off and thinking a nice cup of hot chocolate or coffee would go down well round about now. He had skipped breakfast, he was starving and he needed some internal central heating to get him going.

He was assaulted with the familiar smells and sounds of the sprawling, two story brick sports complex: The sharp odor of chlorine from the pool, the tangy scent of sweat from exercising bodies, the faint, intermittent *thwack* of the soft rubber balls hitting the walls in the racquetball courts, bouncy, energetic music from the direction of the aerobics or Zumba or Pilates or spin class halls and the whirrs and grinds of the exercise equipment being put to use by men and women of all shapes, sizes and ages.

The storm obviously hadn't been enough to keep them all an extra hour in their beds, not when they were looking for the perfect, beautiful, muscle-toned body.

Paul went into the main exercise room. Sure enough, all the bicycle, rowing, stair-climber and treadmill machines were being operated by a score of sweating, panting people. He knew only some of them as a nodding acquaintance. To them, he was just a guy who came in several times a month, not to exercise, but seemingly to pick up his friend. Nobody knew what he did for a living and certainly nobody cared.

Paul spotted his friend at the speed bag in the far corner of the large room and walked over to him. "Hey partner," he greeted cheerfully. "Nearly through?"

It seemed that Dave Andrews was intent on beating the living daylights out of the poor, defenseless speed bag. He took one last almighty swipe at it and grinned broadly at the man who had just called him partner. "I have fifty crunches to do, then five minutes of a gentle stroll on the treadmill to cool down and a few cool down stretches. After that, I'm all yours."

Paul nodded and watched in semi-amusement as Dave walked over to a workout bench, wiped his sweaty face with a towel and proceeded with his crunches. Never having been one for overly rigorous exercise himself, Paul stayed in shape by playing an occasional game of basketball, racquetball, going for a five-mile jog once or twice a week or by leading an as active as was humanly possible sex life. In the winter months, he played hockey for the Bathville Blazers and he got a lot of his exercise in the rink at games or at practice. He never had been able to understand his friend's need to punish himself in a grueling ninety-minute workout two or three times a week. Exercise should be fun, not exhausting.

He ambled over to Dave, straddled the bench and sat down at his feet. "You know," he started lightly, "there *are* easier ways of getting in shape."

"Oh yeah?" Dave didn't even break his careful rhythm, he carried on with crunch number eight that segued perfectly to crunch number nine. "It's too cold and snowy outside to go jogging, in case you haven't noticed."

"That's not what I meant."

"It wasn't?" Dave was all innocence, but he couldn't hold back a mischievous smile. "Oh yes, yesterday was Valentine's Day. The day for lovers, romantics and hornballs like you. So how did it go with Cindy last night anyway?"

"I got her into bed."

"On your *second* date? Cam, you're slipping."

"Well, let's just say it was worth the wait. And let's just say that she's never going to have an experience like that again with any other man. How was *your* Valentine's evening? Did you do anything that would make me proud?"

"In a manner of speaking. I managed to scarf a whole heart-shaped box of chocolates all by myself. That's why I've been here since 5:00 this morning, instead of the usual 5:30, to burn off those calories."

"Chocolates? In a heart-shaped box? Why would you even buy yourself such a thing? Unless…" Paul raised his eyes hopefully. "Unless you bought them to give them to a lady, only you chickened out at the last minute?"

"Not even close. I was in the store getting milk and the chocolates were on the counter. I couldn't refuse. I know, I know, impulse buying, but they were fairly decent chocolates so I'm really not complaining."

"Oh." It wasn't the answer Paul had wanted and disappointment clouded his eyes. Then he adopted a casual look. "Say, last night, Cindy was telling me all about this friend of hers. Judy, her name is. She sounds really cute too, blonde, blue-eyed, legs up to her throat and down again. She's twenty-four and apparently she measures 36, 24, 35. Maybe we could double date sometime. Interested?"

"Nope."

"Dave, come on -"

"I'm counting, Paul, shut up. Twenty-one…twenty-two…"

Paul waited as patiently as he could for Dave to reach 50 and when he did, Paul tried again. "Did I tell you her name's Judy? She's a nurse, drives her own car, has her own apartment, I hear she likes to work out too…"

Dave lay back on the mat, then raised himself up on his elbows to catch his breath. "I told you a long time ago I was through with women. Maybe one of these fine days you'll realize I mean it." He sounded neither pleased nor displeased to be having this conversation, but it was obvious he had heard it all before and he was bored with it. He spied a free treadmill and bounced up quickly to claim it before someone else did, also giving him opportunity to get away from Paul and the subject Paul brought up three or a hundred times a day.

Paul watched with an inward sigh as Dave punched in the program he wanted on the treadmill. Judging by the determined, fixed look on Dave's face, the matter was closed again, but Paul, who for a long time now had been trying to coax his friend to go out on a date, even a double date, wasn't prepared to give up so easily.

For some reason, Dave had very deliberately and even apparently quite willingly, imposed a life of celibacy upon himself over a year ago and Paul, who reckoned Dave had suffered enough by now, was determined to get him to change his mind. Once or twice, when the circumstances had been right, Dave had nearly weakened too, but he had an iron will coupled with a very stubborn streak and nothing, or nobody, could ever get him to change his mind once it was very clearly made up.

One thing Paul was suitably impressed by was Dave's willpower. Hordes of women had literally presented themselves on a plate to Dave, but he had always managed to turn each and every one of their advances down. Paul, who adored the members of the fairer sex, wasn't so sure it was something that he would ever be able to do.

It was easy to see why Dave was so appealing to the opposite sex. As raven haired as Paul was fair and at six foot three only an inch taller, he had a lean, muscular frame and his exceptionally handsome features were only made all the more attractive by the ever-present pout he had on his lips, or the broodiness he usually carried in his very dark blue eyes.

To a stranger he could appear mean and moody, often even intimidating and abrupt but being the strong silent type was just the image he liked to portray. Very few people had seen him in his true colors that he did such a good job of hiding from the real world. He had an incredible sense of humor and he delighted in teasing Paul to death most of the time about anything he could think of. Paul, whose sense of humor was just as wicked, always gave back as good as he got, and the two men shared a relaxed friendship that was certainly never dull, and which was also built on mutual trust and respect.

Dave's downfall was his temper. It wasn't unusual for him to lose it very easily, even over a very simple matter, but Paul had long since gotten used to it over the four years they had been together, and it was now second nature to tune himself out from his friend's ranting and raving until he knew, by a kind of radar instinct, Dave had calmed down again. It was yet another example why the two men got on so well together because Paul was the pacifier of the team, the easy going, nothing ever bothered him type.

Dave's temper tantrums were balanced on the other side of the scales by a genuinely caring and extremely generous nature. He was kind, almost even too kind, some people would think, which would only succeed in hurting his feelings when he found out what these people were thinking. But he usually didn't care too much. He liked to give and that was that and the beauty of his generosity was, he never ever expected anything in return.

The two men were extremely close and had been practically since day one of their working partnership as detectives in the 7th precinct of the Bathville Police Department. They were each vastly intelligent, excellent at their jobs and each man complimented the other beautifully simply because they were so compatible, even with all their wildly different outlooks on life. Paul was completely at peace with the world, Dave often gave the impression he felt the world owed him one, but that was just the way they were.

To a casual observer, they were two career driven, self-confident, incredibly handsome, tall, muscular bodied young men, one with blond hair and blue eyes, the other with dark hair and blue eyes. They didn't seem to have any egotistical mannerisms, or any rivalry, just a real camaraderie that was pleasant and usually entertaining to watch.

After his stint on the treadmill and his cool down stretches, Dave retired to the locker room for his shower. Paul was waiting by Dave's locker when he came out, his hair slick and tousled and a towel fastened around his trim waist. "Wonder what the Captain has in store for us today?" he mused as he removed the towel and finished drying himself off. "Hope there's nothing new brewing, it's too cold to work outside today. Too snowy, too wintry."

"You big baby," Paul – who was Brooklyn, New York born and raised and therefore no stranger to the winter climate – sympathized.

Dave hailed from Las Vegas, Nevada and, although his white winters had been few and far between, it was the damp cold of the east coast he still found hard getting used to. "Get bent, partner," he returned smoothly. He glanced at the clock and when he saw the time, he stepped into his shorts and hurriedly finished getting dressed.

"Are you going to leave your car here until later on?"

"Sure, why not? Pete doesn't mind, he knows who it belongs to and I know he'll keep an eye on it for me." Dave pulled his thick winter jacket on, zipped it up and headed for the door with his gym bag slung over his shoulder. "You parked out back?"

"Yup, usual spot."

"Okay, I'll see you there in a couple of minutes, save you having to drive all the way round to the front to get me. I just need to throw this bag in the trunk and get my gun and holster."

Paul went back to his car, whistling cheerfully to himself. It was past 7:00 now and still pitch dark out. The wind was howling mournfully as it stirred up the snow, which looked the color of a rusty nail in the light cast off from the orange overhead parking lot lights. Shivering, Paul was just about to open his car door when he felt something hard suddenly being pressed between his shoulder blades. He knew immediately what it was too, he owned one himself and therefore knew it intimately.

It was a gun.

CHAPTER THREE

On the day that would commence the countdown to a permanent change in Paul Cameron's twenty-six-year-old life, there he was, in the freezing cold of an early winter morning, with a gun pressing into his back. He could be only moments away from serious injury, or even death, but he knew enough through experience that the best thing to do right now until he'd fully assessed the situation would be to keep his calm.

"Hey, buddy," he said with just the right element of surprise. "What's going on here?"

"Shut up," hissed his attacker, a male. "Don't say another word or else I just might be obliged to shoot this here gun I have aimed right at you."

Paul inwardly groaned in impatience. "Yeah, I can feel it," he said, ignoring the warning to shut up or else. "What do you want from me?"

"Your money and your car."

All the money Paul had on him at the moment amounted to about forty-three dollars and he would give that up, no problem. His beloved car on the other hand? Never. He tried to twist his head around to get a look at his assailant, but he was stopped abruptly when the gun was raised from his back and pressed in against his right temple. "You don't need to do this, pal," he said as amiably as possible. "You're making an awful big mistake."

"I said shut up. Give me your car keys. Now!"

Whoever this was, he was obviously an amateur if the shaking of his voice was anything to go by. He sounded like a kid too, a youngster no older than his mid-teens, but one nonetheless who might be high on crack or PCP or whatever the drug of choice on the streets and in school playgrounds was these days. He was speaking directly at ear level to Paul, which meant he was at least as tall as he was, but Paul couldn't see a shadow or reflection on either the ground or the car window that could tell him what kind of build the kid had.

Paul hated these sorts of situations. He hated having to try and reason with someone who probably didn't even know what planet he was on and Paul knew that if he tried to surprise him, whatever the kid was high on, or if he was coming down from it, a surprise attack could make him over-react and possibly make him trigger happy too.

The last thing Paul wanted or needed was to start his day with a gaping bullet hole in his gut or his back or his head.

Paul wanted to stall for time to give Dave a chance to appear. "Look, man, take it easy, okay? I'll give you the keys in a second, but just…" He was cut off when his attacker whistled harshly through his teeth.

"Jesus Christ, what sort of a car is this? What shit you got in there?"

Paul knew what he was referring to. Although not a police issue sedan, he used his personal car for work and it was equipped with a police radio and an emergency beacon, among other things. However, despite the evidence, if he blatantly confessed to being a cop, he may as well kiss the world goodbye. "Look, it's not what you think, it's not as it seems, it…"

There was an audible sigh of irritation. "You're a cop, aren't you? A stinking, lousy, sonofabitch cop."

No sense in denying it now, Paul thought. "Well… umm… now

that you mention it…"

"Just my luck!" There was a moment of irritated silence as the kid contemplated how to handle the unforeseen turn of events. And then, "Okay, okay. Seems like there's a change of plans about to happen. I'm just going to have to take you with me. Yeah, that's what I'll do, take you with me."

"Be reasonable, man. If you hurt me or take me or my car, you're not going to get very far. My partner is right inside the building, he's going to be here any second, but if you just take off now, he'll not hurt you and neither will I."

"Yeah, right."

"You have my word."

"Pig's honor, huh? I know all about that, it ain't worth shit."

"I mean it, man. I'll even still give you the money you asked for. Here, my wallet's inside my jacket… let me reach in and get it."

"How do I know you won't be reaching for a piece instead?"

Oh God, Paul thought*, a piece? The kid had actually said* a piece? *Too much watching crime shows on TV.* A huge blast of wind whistled past them, skimming fine, powdery snow from the tops of the snow banks, and Paul instinctively shivered. "Because my gun is inside the car. I'll even let you frisk me if you don't believe me." He didn't receive any response to his invitation and he started to get impatient. "Come on, man, I'm freezing my nuts off here and I'm sure you are too. Let me get my wallet out, I'll do it nice and slow and you can watch me the whole time. Have we got ourselves a deal?"

"No, no deal. You're a cop, cops don't know how to make honest deals."

"Okay, man, whatever you think of us, I'm sure it's perfectly justified but I mean what I say. Hey, I value my life, I don't want to play no hero cop, but I do want you to have the chance to run now, before it's too late." The kid's gun was still digging into his temple, but Paul reckoned that if he was really serious about shooting him, the kid would have done so thirty seconds ago. With that in mind, Paul managed to retain his cool.

The only thing on this mind now was, what on earth was keeping Dave? He should have been here by now, they were running late for work and one thing Dave hated was being late, so he should have been here minutes ago… unless he had stopped to talk to somebody and had forgotten the time, or maybe he had left something in his car and had back-tracked to get it, or…

The early morning sky was at last starting to lighten to a dull shade of pewter when Dave appeared from the building. There was just enough light for him to see the predicament Paul was in and, crouching down, he ran up to the passenger side of Paul's car without either Paul or his attacker having heard or seen him. The wind was whipping away any words that they might have been saying to one another, but Dave knew by Paul's very stance he was on the receiving end of an armed robbery. There was no other reason that Dave could see why Paul had chosen to wait for assistance; although he could easily have overpowered the kid, guns talked loud and clear.

Taking a silent count of three, Dave pulled out his gun, slowly stood up and released the safety catch, the sound making a loud click in the morning air that had chosen that moment to still. He was standing directly facing Paul, but deliberately in the kid's blind side and he coughed almost politely. Dave smiled benignly when the kid's head jerked towards the sound of the cough, but he was most amused at the look of confusion that came over his face. The unexpected onset wasn't enough for him to take his gun away from Paul's head though and, although he couldn't see that the kid was now looking at Dave in a state of bewildered surprise, Paul didn't intend on making any moves until Dave gave him the signal it was all right to do so.

Dave didn't really believe the kid was going to be using the gun, on Paul or on anyone else. He was too shaky for starters, Dave didn't think the safety was even off the gun and the surprise he'd just received should have been enough for him to pull the trigger. But it hadn't, not that either Dave or Paul were prepared to take any unnecessary risks.

"Just can't leave you alone for even a minute, partner," Dave stated affably, then swiftly trained his gun on the attacker. "Drop the gun, kid. Now."

"You drop yours instead," came the incensed retort and Dave rolled his eyes in exasperation.

"I *hate* when they say that," he remarked in wonder to Paul. "Don't you hate it when they say that?"

"Yeah," Paul dutifully agreed. "Sort of puts you in a stalemate situation, doesn't it?"

"Sure does and I hate stalemate situations too, they really tick me off. What's he after anyway?"

"My money. My car."

"Your car?" Dave shook his head at the attacker. "Oo, big mistake, man, *big* mistake."

"Who gives a shit? Back off or else this pig gets it."

It was then that Dave noticed the kid move to finally release the safety on his gun. Dave had grown tired of the game anyway, it was too cold to be standing here exchanging pleasantries. "No, see, I don't think so." With a barely noticeable nod at Paul, he deliberately fired his gun into a snowbank behind the assailant and Paul, who was the only one who had seen the nod, seized the opportunity to knock the gun from the now startled kid, overpower him and have him handcuffed, all in one swift, well-practiced move.

While Paul politely shoved the kid into the back of Paul's car, Dave took a few moments to locate the entry hole in the snowbank where he had fired the bullet. It had travelled through the impacted snow and ice but had come to a stop a foot or so in and once Dave had located the casing and wrapped it carefully in a piece of cloth he pulled from his back pocket, he joined Paul in the front of the car.

"Now that that's over with, I'm absolutely starved," Paul stated as he pulled carefully away and entered the rising stream of traffic traveling slowly on the snow packed street. "Shall we do breakfast?"

A little while later, when they were halfway to the station, the car radio crackled and seconds later, their superior's voice boomed over the airwaves. "Bravo Two, come in, Bravo Two. Cameron, Andrews, either one of you two jerks awake yet?"

"Ah, the master's voice," Dave said dryly and picked up the mike. "Yo, Cap, so nice to hear your friendly tones so early in the morning. How's it hanging?"

"Cut the crap, Andrews. What's keeping you two? I need you both down here, like ten minutes ago."

"We're already on our way. We would have arrived five minutes ago, only we sort of ran into a tricky situation."

"What, long line-up at Dunkin's coffee shop this morning?"

"Nope, nothing like that." Then, with a grin at Paul, Dave added, "Well, if you really must know, at McDonalds there was."

"Andrews!"

"Just kidding, Bob, honest to God, it was just my little joke to try and brighten up your morning for you. Sheesh, some people can be *so* touchy, don't you think? What's the matter, sir, did your favorite donut get stolen by someone else before you got the chance to -?"

"Shut up and give me your ETA."

"ETA?" Dave glanced at the dashboard clock and then outside to see where they were. "About ten minutes."

"Make sure that it is."

It was actually closer to thirty minutes, partly deliberately, of course, before they arrived at the Captain's office. The traffic had been slow moving the whole way from McDonalds to the station, they had taken their time booking their perpetrator, throwing him into holding, then logging themselves in and treating themselves to a cup of coffee in the canteen and finally Dave having to give a full reason to the Desk Sergeant on duty on why he had fired his gun that morning. It helped save a huge discussion when Dave, slightly smugly, retrieved the casing from his pocket and presented it to the Sergeant, who took it delicately, looked at him silently for a long moment, then waved him impatiently away. They reckoned they had made the Captain wait long enough when they knocked on his door, strode inside without waiting for the command to enter and sat down in front of his desk.

"Sit down," the Captain ordered without looking up from his

paperwork. He finished what he was doing, threw his pen down and scowled at them both. "Took you long enough."

"But seeing that we're now here…" Paul prompted, completely unconcerned.

Captain Bob Hamilton was a big man in his early fifties. He had light brown hair, deep brown eyes that twinkled naturally when he was in a good mood, which was often, a ruddy complexion and a hefty waistline. He stood at six foot five in his bare feet and tipped the scales at three hundred and ten pounds. Despite his bulk, he was amazingly light-footed and actually quite graceful. He was a fair man, not given to tantrums or unreasonableness, he was well respected by his workers and superiors alike and he ran a well-oiled ship where things seldom went wrong.

He had gained the respect of his superiors because of a little plan he had masterminded some sixteen years back. His dream was to let younger officers make it to the rank of detective as quickly as possible, his reasoning being that sometimes a younger eye was sharper and more receptive than an older eye. Experience counted, certainly, but so did enthusiasm and unsuppressed intelligence and he truly believed there were a lot of officers all over the United States who were being held back from their true vocation in life simply because the powers that be in the Government dictated they were a little green behind the ears.

And then, while still honing the finer details on his program, on September 11, 2001, the horror of all horrors happened, when terrorists flew passenger planes into the Pentagon and the World Trade Center, taking the lives of many civilians, firemen and police officers alike. US citizens cried out for better protection and bigger police forces and the then President George W. Bush promised to deliver just that.

After several years and a lot of wrangling and pleading, Captain Hamilton had finally been granted the go ahead to make his dream a reality. He had thought up, all by himself, a tough entrance exam and, although the response from all over the country had been overwhelming, he was only allowed to take on two new recruitments into his own precinct. Most of the candidates, men and women alike, did better than average on the written exam, some were disqualified on the physical part but at the end of the day, after what had seemed like an interminably long period of eight or nine years going through interviews and a strict process of elimination, the two successful candidates had been picked and they were sitting now in the Captain's office.

But the Captain's biggest fear initially was how well they would perform once they were out on the front line. Gaining almost perfect marks on the exam was one thing, getting down to the actual nitty gritty of police work was another matter entirely. He couldn't end up with egg on his face because of two young men he had been willing to take a chance on, he would lose the respect of his peers and superiors and receive, possibly, a nasty rap on the knuckles for having wasted X amount of dollars of Government funds.

His first meeting with Paul and Dave had buoyed his spirits and restored his confidence. Dave was the senior of the two by five months and, like Paul, had done the required criminology course in college, graduated top of the class at the police academy and then each had spent exactly three years working the beat in their respective hometowns. They had come to Massachusetts at the tender age of 23 but they were mature for their age, instantly likeable and obviously quite intelligent. It helped that they were prepared to grab on with both hands to this new career opportunity and, after solving their first case with unstoppable energy, excellent ideas and a sharp, pleasing flair, the Captain relaxed, sat back and accepted with good grace the congratulations from the people above him who were no longer dubious of his long-awaited dream.

Then, about half way through the first term of the Obama administration, Government funding for his project was no longer made available and he'd had to put his plans for future recruitments on ice.

It took about another five years, but after a lot more haggling and pleading his case with the powers that be, the Captain was, at last, granted the permission to take on two more officers to be made into detectives within the 7th precinct in Bathville.

Which was how Paul's life was going to change.

CHAPTER FOUR

"I have a new assignment for you," the Captain began in a matter-of-fact tone, "and this one's a real breeze. In the middle of March, I'm taking on two new officers and I want you to show them the ropes. And yes, that's an order."

Paul and Dave glanced at each other in surprise. "Why us, sir?" Paul asked.

"Because I reckon you're the best qualified for the job. After all, you two were the original – and so far, the only – applicants to be given this opportunity, you know the drill and you can teach the new officers everything you know on making the transition from uniformed cop to a detective."

"Opportunity?" Dave repeated. His eyes suddenly lit up in genuine pleasure as he had just put two and two together. "You mean you've received the go ahead to renew your program? That's great, Bob, a real bonus for you. I know you had just about given up on ever being able to re-start it again. So, what's the plan?"

"The first thing they'll be doing when they arrive is they'll be going on a course at the academy. They've already done their criminology degree… passed with flying colors too, the both of them…so, obviously, the next step is the academy. I've been assured by their commanding officer that they're both very bright individuals but because of the nature of the program and because they're to be recruited as detectives, I want to see if they really are suitable for that sort of work. Also, they have a lot to learn about how police work is done over here, which is another reason why I'm sending them straight to the academy."

"Wait a minute," Paul interrupted, "what do you mean, "how

police work is done *over here*?" Where are they coming from?"

A smile spread slowly over the Captain's face. "They're flying in from Ireland. Er, excuse me, I believe the correct name for their country is *Northern* Ireland."

"Northern Ireland?" Dave cried. "I thought you were keeping your program open for American applicants only? How come, after all this time, the Government suddenly lets you renew your program and then gives you the go ahead to take on foreigners? It doesn't make sense. How did they even know about this program over on the other side of the ocean?"

"A couple of explanations. Their superior, Detective Inspector Billy Clarke, has a cousin who works in the Dallas P.D. Clarke was over visiting his cousin, he heard of my program being in operation several years back and made inquiries when he got back to Ireland to see if it was still available. When September 11th happened, as you know, security in the States took on a whole new meaning. Everyone was on form to protect and serve this country. But now, sadly, security just doesn't get the funding it deserves anymore. Probably through his cousin again, Clarke heard the program was up and running again, and by pulling a few strings and calling in a few favors, he managed to sell the idea to our Government that who better than two officers from Northern Ireland, where security is always at the maximum level, come over here and help out where they can with what they know about security. The officers in question took a preliminary exam and their marks were outstanding. Impressed, the US Government made them take the exam you both took and again, the results were almost perfect. It's no crime applying for immigration from one country to another anyway and when they learned they were accepted, the officers applied for their Green cards, had Clarke speed up the process with whoever he knows in Immigration and once the Green cards were issued, they put their house on the market, sold it and booked their plane tickets."

"So," Dave said slowly, "what all this boils down to is, you're taking on two new men from overseas, giving them the same opportunities you gave Paul and me and in the meantime, you want us to baby-sit them? Seems too easy if you ask me. What's the catch?"

"No catch. And oh, by the way, who said anything about them being men?"

"They're *women*?"

"Top marks, Andrews. Now I know why I knew you were detective material."

But Dave would not be appeased. He had been in such good humor that morning but now, as he was always able to do, he let his mood do a one-hundred-and-eighty-degree turn, his infamous temper bubbled to the surface and he glowered angrily at his boss. "Forget it, Captain," he snapped. "I will *not* be chaperone to two broads from a pinhead country like *Northern* Ireland." Already, he had conjured up an image of two girls built like tanks, who probably had to shave the whiskers off their chins at least twice a day and who probably drank Guinness straight from the keg too. "That is an absolute insult to my intelligence."

Captain Hamilton knew all about Dave's reticence towards women and he had half-expected this sort of reaction from him. He let Dave have his little tantrum, then he said smoothly, "It's not meant as an insult, Andrews. On the contrary. But like I said, it *is* an order, so you really have no choice in the matter."

Dave thumped his fist on the Captain's desk. "This is so unfair. Why are you doing this to us? Don't you know we'll be the laughing stock of the whole department?"

"I hardly think so. Paul, you're being very quiet. What do *you* think?"

Paul glanced uneasily at Dave, who was glaring right at him, challenging him almost, to dare take the Captain's side. "Well, I, er, I'm flattered to be asked, of course," Paul said diplomatically, "but surely you don't need us to look after the new recruitments. Surely if they're capable of leaving one country to come live in another, they know how to look after themselves."

"Oh, I'm sure they do. But you two are the best team I have, and I want you to give me another good team by teaching these new officers everything you know, at the same time maybe learning more about security yourselves. After all, these officers have been raised in a country where terrorists the likes of the IRA walked amongst ordinary folk in the grocery store every single day, and, okay, so maybe the IRA has supposedly laid down their arms and the country is trying to keep the peace, and maybe the IRA, going for peace or not, is not quite in the same league as Bin Laden and his minions were, or certainly nothing like today's ISIL, but they're still terrorists, responsible for many innocent lives being lost. These women have worked under threat from terrorism for the whole of their working lives." The Captain shifted his cool gaze back to Dave. "Any other objections?" he asked, knowing full well Dave had.

"Why did you let them come to this precinct anyway?" Dave said with a barely concealed sneer. "I can understand you wanting to keep them in Bathville, but there are eight precincts to choose from, why not put them in one of the others instead? And I *still* can't understand why you would let foreigners take the positions. Look at the unemployment figures for Christ's sake, Americans are clamoring for jobs right and left, and you just overlook them? I'm sorry, I fail to see the justice in that. Does the Commissioner even know about this?"

"Of course he does. Who do you think gave the approval for them to be accepted in the first instance?"

"Then the Commish needs his head looked at – just as much as you do. Who the hell's paying for all this anyway? The department? The tax-payers?"

"If by "all this" you mean their airfares and the cost of getting their personal items shipped over, the two ladies in question are paying for all that themselves. Their salaries will be paid in the same way all of ours are. Like I said, they'll have their Green cards, so they're legally entitled to work in the United States and therefore legally entitled to get paid. I know you're required to be an American Citizen to become a cop in the Commonwealth of Massachusetts, but we have been given permission from the Governor's office to waive that requirement. I have them down for a four-week course in the academy at New Braintree and depending on how they make out -"

"Wait a minute, *four weeks*?" Dave's expression darkened even more. "I thought it took twenty-five weeks to go through the system? No matter how good I was way back then, I still had to do the full course, as did Paul, as did all of us."

"You're right, it does take twenty-five weeks to get through the academy, but if you had let me finish, I would have gone on to say that if, after that four weeks is up, and I feel they're not ready to hit the streets, I will be insisting they remain in the academy until I am certain they are capable of proving that they can handle themselves accordingly. Because they've already had extensive training in their own country to be a police officer, I was able to get the rules bent a little and they won't have to reside at the academy through the week. Nor will they have to be there at 5:30 every morning, they're scheduled every morning for 8:30 sharp and can leave around 4:00 in the afternoon if they've met the requirements for that day. They stay later, of course, if they haven't. After they leave the academy, no matter how long it takes, I think it would be best if you all worked on their first case together and -"

"Wait a minute," Dave interrupted again. "We're going to have to work with them too?"

"Of course. That going to be a problem?"

"What do *you* think? Paul and I work together, just us two, nobody else because that's the way we prefer to do it – and I certainly don't appreciate being forced like this to work with someone else." *And females into the bargain,* he added into himself.

"Well, sorry about it, Officer Andrews. The decision has already been made and it is out of my hands."

Paul, ever the peace maker, wanted Dave to calm down so he started asking a few questions off the top of his head to give Dave a chance to do just that. "So, what are the mystery ladies' names anyway?"

"Catherine Edwards and Krista Nolan. They are 25 and 24 respectively, unmarried and no dependents."

"And just why do they want to leave their own country?"

"The political situation and ever ongoing religious bigotry in

Northern Ireland have played a large factor in their decision. Even with the so-called cease-fire, it hasn't gotten any easier for the security forces over there. Unfortunately, the old beliefs and hatreds between the Loyalists and the Nationalists seem to be raising their ugly heads at an alarming rate again. I believe the two ladies in question are of opposing religions but that hasn't stopped them from becoming very close friends and they're each eager to try for a new life in a new place."

"Loyalists? Nationalists?" Paul asked.

"Loyalists are the population who wish to remain loyal to the Queen and remain part of the United Kingdom. Presumably predominately Protestant. Nationalists want Northern Ireland dissolved as a country and returned to Southern Ireland. Presumably predominately Catholic." The Captain lifted up a couple of manila colored files. "These are their dossiers," he explained. "You're free to read them over when and if you wish. Everything's explained, all you might want to know, like their medical history, including the physical tests they have just completed to ensure their admission into the academy, their evaluations by the Immigration Service, their status and performance rating within their own police stations. Any questions you need answering go ahead and ask."

Dave reached over and snatched one of the files from the Captain's hand. He scanned the first page without really taking anything in, then threw the folder carelessly back on the desk. "This blows," he stated, "this absolutely blows. This is good enough reason for me to hand in my resignation." With that, he stood up, glared one last time at the Captain and strode from the office, banging the door behind him on his way out.

After his friend's stormy departure, Paul inwardly sighed. "Guess he forgot to count to ten, didn't he?"

"So, what else is new? What the hell's his problem anyway?"

"Damned if I know. I think he's coming down from a sugar rush." Paul was thinking about the box of chocolates Dave had mentioned earlier that morning, but he knew the Captain wouldn't have a clue what he was talking about. "I really don't know. I'll go talk to him in a few minutes, give him time to simmer down."

"Do that and find out for me why he's being so unreasonable about all this. You'd think I'd asked him to do something completely horrendous the way he's acting."

"Yes, well, you know how he is, hates his routine being changed. He's a creature of habit, always was, always will be. I'll be out at my desk if you need me, assuming this meeting is over."

"It's over, for now."

Paul only remained at his desk for ten minutes before he decided to go in search of Dave. He looked all over the four-story building and was just about to give up when he realized the first place he should have looked should have been the target practice area, located way down in the bowels of the building, beneath the basement garage. Sure enough, there Dave was in one of the stalls, firing his little heart out at a target that was positioned as far back on the line as it would go.

Grabbing a set of ear protectors, Paul approached him, waited until he finished the clip, then tapped him on the shoulder.

"What are you doing down here, Big D?" Paul asked casually.

"Practicing, what does it look like?" Came the terse reply.

"What do you need to practice for? You're already the best

marksman the department has."

"Yeah? Thanks, but there's always room for improvement. Now, unless you want to get deafened, either leave or put those ear protectors back on." Dave started to reload his gun, but Paul stopped him by laying a strong hand on his arm.

"Come on, Dave, talk to me. Why is this bothering you so much? What's the big deal about having to look after two females? It could be a lot of fun, you know, it will certainly be interesting, different and it will-"

"Shut up, Paul, I'm not interested in what you have to say."

"So, what are you going to do? Disobey the Captain's orders? Quit, like you threatened to do? What?"

"I'm tempted to quit, believe you me, I'm tempted. But why should I give up my career for two females who probably aren't worth the agro anyway?"

"Does that mean you're going to do it then?"

"Seems like I have no real choice in the matter, does it? Captain's orders *are* Captain's orders after all, so who am I to try and argue with the great white master? Only thing I want to know is, whatever happened to good old freedom of choice, huh?" Dave impatiently shrugged Paul's hand off his arm and angrily finished reloading his gun. He took aim at his target again and kept firing until his gun was empty. Each bullet had hit home exactly where he had wanted it.

Paul waited patiently while Dave brought the target up for a closer inspection, commended him on his dexterity and decided to let the matter drop for the time being. "I'm heading back up to the office to finish the report on that kid who jumped me this morning. How much longer you going to be here?"

"For as long as I want to be." Which translated into Dave would much rather be left alone right now and Paul nodded he understood.

"Okay, you know where I am if you need me."

But Dave was no longer listening, he was already reloading his gun again, his lips set in a thin, hard line, which meant it would be a long time yet before he would be even close to simmering down again.

Paul walked away, puzzled as to why Dave was acting like it was such a big deal when really, it wasn't. He didn't mind his new assignment, in fact he was already looking forward to it even though he didn't yet know about the impact it was going to have on his life. But he did know he had his work cut out in getting Dave to accept it.

That night, as they often did, they went out for a beer together. Dave had calmed down somewhat but it had taken him the rest of the morning and well into the snowbound afternoon for him to reach his usual frame of mind and Paul and the Captain wisely had not broached the subject again.

But now, seeing it was just the two of them, Paul reckoned it would be safe to try again and, as was his usual way when it was about something important, he plunged right in. "Do you feel threatened or something by what the Captain has asked us to do?"

Dave looked at him in genuine surprise. "Threatened? Why in the hell should I feel threatened?"

"I don't know. Maybe because they're women?"

"Why should that make a difference?"

"Because you won't even date one anymore, never mind work with one unless you absolutely have to."

Dave chuckled, obviously finding that remark very amusing. "I'm not that bad, Cam. You make it sound like I'm afraid of women or something."

"I know you're not afraid of them, but I do know that you don't particularly like them."

Dave's expression shifted subtly, and he looked moodily down at the bubbles foaming out of the top of his beer bottle. He erased them with his thumb and looked at Paul in cold bitterness. "You *know* why I don't like them. Any woman I've had in my life has caused me nothing but pain or trouble."

"But that was a long time ago, partner. You shouldn't bear a grudge against two women who are going to be strangers in a strange land. And you shouldn't have them branded as the enemy until you at least meet them and see what they're like. Not all women are bad or out to hurt you and the sooner you get over that stumbling block, the sooner you'll be able to start leading a normal life again. And yes, that includes dating and sex and romance and the whole nine yards. What do you intend to achieve with this celibacy rap anyway? You want to die an old man with your pecker all wizened up and about to drop off through lack of use?

Dave rolled his eyes. "Oh Jesus, you really know how to paint a pretty picture, don't you? Look, just give it up, Paul. If I ever intend dating again, you'll be the first to know. Until then, don't ever mention it again."

"But Dave, don't you understand something? People are starting to ask questions about you. The same people are even starting to think you're gay."

"And I really give a shit about what other people are thinking about me. I'll start seeing women again when and if I feel like it, not because I have to prove a point to people who have no right poking their nose into my private life anyway." Dave took a healthy swig of his beer, stifled the rising gas in his throat and pointed a warning finger at his friend. "Kill the conversation. I'm bored with it. Again."

Paul groaned in despair. "You know what your problem is, Andrews? You're nothing but a stubborn jerk."

"Yeah, I know, I do my best to maintain that reputation."

But Paul, although he thought he had, really hadn't ever seen just how stubborn Dave could be. Over the next few weeks, he would.

CHAPTER FIVE

On February 22nd, Paul and Dave were assigned a homicide case that was very time consuming and at times even seemingly impossible they were ever going to get it solved. As a result, they put in a lot of overtime and, claiming she could no longer handle his hectic schedule, Cindy broke it off with Paul.

Used to receiving rebuttals like this because of his job, Paul accepted the split and her reasonings with good grace, if not with a little regret. Cindy was a nice girl but just apparently unable to deal with dinners and other dates being broken off at the last minute. She claimed she really did understand that he was very dedicated to his job, but she also managed to tell him, not without a little sarcasm, that his job wasn't going to keep him warm on a cold winter's night.

With no new love interest to occupy what little spare time he had, Paul devoted his all to the case and on March 5th, the day before his twenty seventh birthday, he and Dave finally placed all the pieces of the puzzle together and solved the case, coming up with a motive, a murder weapon and the murderer himself.

A few days later, they were presented with a case regarding another homicide but this one was drugs related, even more time consuming and had to be handled delicately to ensure no mistakes were made.

On March 15th, they had it all but wrapped and on the 16th, they achieved their goal. In the morning, they were in the station at their desks, preparing the final report when Captain Hamilton appeared at his office door.

"Cameron, Andrews," he called. "My office. Now."

Glad for any excuse to get away from the dreaded paperwork, Paul and Dave arose and went into the Captain's office. Inside, they saw the Captain had two guests, two ladies who were certainly quite pleasing to look at.

Paul beamed them both a friendly smile. "Hello there, ladies."

Dave barely acknowledged them with a nod.

Captain Hamilton walked back round to his side of the desk and rested his bulk on his chair. It groaned and creaked with familiar knowledge of the weight sitting on top of it. Aware all four people were looking at him for either an introduction or an explanation, he fixed his most professional and courteous smile on his face and gazed at Paul and Dave.

"Gentlemen, let me introduce to you Cathy Edwards and Krista Nolan. Ladies, Detective Dave Andrews and Detective Paul Cameron at your service."

It took only a second for the names to register in Dave's mind and he just about managed to conceal a scowl. So, the women from Northern Ireland had arrived. Terrific, he didn't think so.

"Which one of you is which?" Paul asked.

"I'm Krista," she answered with a hint of shyness. "And you are…?"

"Paul." He offered her his hand to shake, which she did and when the contact was broken, he could still feel the warmth and strength she had conveyed with the simple, time-honored gesture. He shook Cathy's hand too, his smile rich and honest and his eyes twinkling softly with welcome and good humor. "And you must be Cathy. It's a pleasure to meet you both, particularly when we've heard so much about you.

Welcome to the United States of America."

"Thank you," Cathy said warmly and looked expectantly at the one called Dave to see if he was going to greet them with a handshake or a smile. Her own smile faltered when she received neither and, immediately losing her momentum for a friendly introduction, she retracted inside herself in the way she sometimes did with strangers, to let Krista strike up an ice-breaking conversation.

But Krista, who usually talked a mile a minute and had a true talent for talking to strangers as if she'd known them for years, had chosen this moment to keep her mouth shut.

Aware of Dave's reluctance to participate in any kind of a greeting, Paul folded his arms across his chest and sat on the edge of the Captain's desk, retaining his relaxed smile to help put the ladies at their ease.

Paul simply couldn't get over Krista and Cathy's appealing good looks – every image in his mind's eye he had built up of them was totally wrong. They were quite beautiful, he would even be prepared to use the word *stunning* because that was certainly what they were. As Captain Hamilton droned on in the background about something or other, and as Dave retreated into his moody little shell of indifference, Paul sat and quietly assessed the newcomers, finding he was quite enjoying the show.

Krista was tall, about five nine, and slim, probably weighing in at about one hundred and twenty pounds, but she was definitely filled out in all the right places and she carried herself with a naturally comfortable air and graceful poise. Her hair was very dark, almost as dark as Dave's, and fell down her back in a thick, layered sheath with the bangs at the front short and feathered. Her complexion was creamy and flawless, her cheekbones high, her nose pretty and feminine and her lips, which fronted perfectly straight white teeth, were full, sensuous and inviting. But her *piece de resistance* had to be her eyes. Almond shaped, clear green, flecked here and there with tiny gold specks and fringed with long, thick eyelashes, Paul suspected they had lured many a man under their spell… just as they were doing to him right now, he realized with a jolt. *And* she hadn't even being looking directly at him, nor seemingly was she even aware of his appraisal…

For distraction, he quickly switched his attention to Cathy. She wasn't as tall as Krista, only about five four, he guessed, and she probably tipped the scales at around one hundred and ten pounds, making her quite petite but perfectly rounded where she should be. He liked her hair, it was dark with a lot of hints of auburn and it stretched all the way down her back in a tumbled mass of curls and waves, giving her a wild, gypsy-like, free spirited appearance. Her skin gave off an untainted peach glow, her nose was perfectly sculpted, her lips generous, her chin strong and determined and when he lifted his scrutiny to her eyes, he was in for a pleasant surprise. They were blue – make that *very* blue, he quickly corrected – and the lashes that framed them were long and in abundance.

Both women could hold their own in the looks department, that was for sure and he fell in love with their accents too when they started asking the Captain questions regarding their itinerary for the next day.

A few minutes after the initial introduction, the Captain suddenly stood up. "Please excuse me, I have something to take care of on the third floor. I'll be back in a little while."

Left alone, an awkward silence descended upon them and it was Paul who started the conversational ball rolling. "What made you ladies want to come to the U S of A? Unless…I'm sorry, is that too personal a question?"

Krista quickly shook her head. "Oh no, we don't mind that you asked. We needed a change of pace, basically. We both love our chosen careers and didn't want to give it up, so we decided to try our luck in another country. Thanks to our former boss finding out about Captain Hamilton's program, we wanted to offer our services against terrorism and we jumped at the chance to come here. We only arrived yesterday so we haven't really got our bearings yet, but Captain Hamilton took us on a guided tour of the city this morning and most of what we saw looked really nice."

As Krista filled Paul in with where they had been that morning, Cathy did what he had done and quietly assessed him and Dave. She knew she was looking at two of the most ridiculously handsome men she had ever seen, two men who would look quite at home in a jeans commercial or a razor blade commercial, or even on a catwalk, doing the male model bit. She couldn't help but wonder if they were the sort of men who *knew* they were gorgeous but the more she remained in their company and read their body language, the more she didn't think that was the case.

With Dave, she had to admit she was a little intrigued. She couldn't understand why he was so quiet or why he seemed to have a permanent scowl stamped on his features, nor could she understand why his amazingly dark blue eyes were giving nothing away except a silent instruction that everyone keep their distance from him.

Dave's attitude and appearance were in such sharp contrast to Paul's. Paul was being very friendly, perhaps to make up for his friend's muteness, he seemed attentive, charming and eager to offer his services towards Krista and herself. Whereas Dave's eyes were cold, Paul's were warm and quite appealing too and, despite his honey blond hair, his eyebrows and lashes were much darker and therefore all the more noticeable.

But all that aside, Cathy couldn't deny the two men exuded sheer animal magnetism and a raw sexuality that could be dangerous if ever she chose to explore what they had to offer. Not that she ever would, the last thing she, and Krista too for that matter, wanted was to get romantically involved with anyone just yet. First, they had to get themselves established both in a home and at work, then they had to get accustomed to a new culture and only then, when they felt comfortable and settled, would they even consider exploring a new relationship with any man.

Aware there was a lull in the conversation, Cathy pulled herself out of her meandering thoughts and back to the present. "Are you both from Bathville?" she asked, hoping to draw Dave into the company.

But Dave ignored the question, so Paul had to answer. "No, I'm from Brooklyn and Dave is from Las Vegas, out west. We've been here for nearly four years now and we love it. Don't we, Dave?" He turned to his friend with an innocent expression, deliberately dragging him into a conversation Paul knew he didn't really want to be a part of.

After a second, Dave said curtly, "Yes." And that was the end of the conversation as far as he was concerned. He had promised himself a long time ago he wouldn't be even remotely friendly to the two girls when they reached Bathville's fair shores and now that he at least knew what they looked like – absolutely gorgeous in a way he had least been expecting, definitely not the type to shave the whiskers off their chins –

he was more determined than ever to keep their relationship at a cool and professional distance.

"I must say," Paul continued, with a slight frown in Dave's direction, "it really is wonderful to have you ladies here. As I heard the Captain tell you earlier, Dave and I have been assigned the task of looking after you, you know, helping you out with lifts, showing you around, that sort of thing and I'm certainly looking forward to a welcome change in my routine. It will be a pleasure to help you both in any way I can." He shot Dave a cool glare. "In any way we *both* can."

Neither Krista nor Cathy got a chance to respond because just then, a man popped his head around the office door. "Andrews, telephone call, line two. Sounds important."

Dave glanced in his direction. "Thanks, Jim, I'll take it out at my own desk."

Paul watched his partner leave, then he turned to the two girls with an apologetic smile. "You'll have to forgive my buddy, ladies, he tends to be rather shy at times and short on the conversation department too. Once you get to know him, you'll find he's a really nice person."

"I'm sure he is," Cathy said dryly, clearly unconvinced that someone who seemed so rude and standoffish could actually be nice.

Paul excused himself to see if Dave's phone call needed his attention too but when he got out to his desk, he saw Dave wasn't even on the phone anymore. In fact, all he was doing was the crossword in that morning's edition of *The Bathville Record*. Paul studied his profile for a long moment and then said as casually as possible, "So, what do you think?"

"Of what?"

"Of Cathy and Krista."

"Oh…them…all right, I suppose."

"All *right*? Dave, they're gorgeous, even you can't deny that."

Dave threw the newspaper down. "So what if they are? Still doesn't mean I have to fall at their feet and tell them that."

"Are you going to even be cordial to them?"

Dave broke into a broad grin. "Of *course*," he said enthusiastically.

Paul's eyes narrowed in suspicion. He hadn't failed to hear the underlying sarcasm in Dave's voice. "In that case, you won't mind if I ask them out for a drink tonight so all four of us can get better acquainted?"

"Ask them out if you want to. Me, I can't go, I have people to do, things to see."

"You have nothing planned, Dave. You told me so this morning."

"Something came up." Dave picked up the newspaper again and put a frown of concentration on his face. "Hmm, let me see, eleven letters for what a graphologist would study."

"Handwriting," Paul answered curtly and, no longer wanting to be around him, returned to the Captain's office.

To make up for Dave's apathy, he invited the girls out for lunch and, while getting to know them a bit better, by the end of their meal, he had come to the conclusion they were very intelligent, very sweet, very funny and entertaining. Krista was a great conversationalist once she got started, Cathy was more shy but certainly just as friendly and witty. Cathy was more cynical while Krista greeted everything with good humor, but they certainly worked well together, had an obviously mutual trust and high regard of one another and shared the same devil-may-care outlook on life.

They accepted his offer for the drink that night and when he took them back to the station and entrusted them into the Captain's care again, his only regret was that Dave had missed out on an enjoyable lunchtime.

One lunchtime wasn't the only thing Dave was going to miss out on.

CHAPTER SIX

Doctor Warren angled his pen light into his patient's eyes and found the pupils responding, but only barely. At least it was an improvement on the way she had first come into hospital, when the EEG had registered only the merest of brain wave activity and her pupils had been fixed and dilated.

She had been in a coma ever since she had been brought into the Bathville General Hospital, almost eight weeks ago. She was of Asian lineage, pretty and had possessed a body that had obviously been well taken care of. But her face was now recovering from a mess of broken bones and bruised and battered skin. Her nose had been broken in several places and it had been a nightmare to try and piece the cartilage back together to give it some semblance of normalcy. Her teeth had been shattered, many ribs cracked, broken or chipped, her kidneys had been severely damaged, her spleen ruptured, her left lung punctured, her right arm broken in three places and, as if that wasn't enough, she had massive internal bleeding.

And yet, despite her serious injuries and the subdural hematoma that had resulted in her coma, she was still alive and still hanging on.

Doctor Warren was in his early thirties, unmarried and had unruly blond hair, green eyes and a slightly overweight build that didn't look too bad on his six-foot seven height. He wasn't considered handsome, but his features fitted together in a comfortable way and what he lacked in looks, he made up in personality. He was sweet natured, even-tempered, capable of bringing out maternal instincts in any female over twenty just by a smile alone and he wanted only three things out of life: To become a successful plastic surgeon, to see the Boston Bruins and the New England

Patriots win the Stanley Cup and the Super Bowl respectively in the same year and to watch this young woman pull through completely from the horrible injuries she had sustained.

He couldn't understand why he was so intrigued with this woman. He knew it wasn't – or at least he didn't *think* it was – a sexual attraction he held for her but something about her tugged at his heartstrings every time he looked at her. Maybe it was just her lying in limbo in a hospital bed, looking peaceful and vulnerable, with no real clue to her condition. Maybe he just felt sorry for her because he guessed she had been quite pretty before the broken nose and damaged cheekbones and teeth. Her whole facial structure had had to be rearranged and, although the repair job had been performed to the best of his ability, his expertise wouldn't have restored her beauty completely.

Whatever the reason, Doctor Samuel Warren looked in on her often, sat in with her when there was no need to and quietly willed her to hold on and to recover so he could find out more about her.

He recalled the day she had been brought into Emergency, on a cold, snowy day in late January. A team of paramedics had wheeled her in on a stretcher, stating her injuries, her colossal blood loss and her impossibly low blood pressure. She had flat-lined twice in the ambulance on the way to the hospital but each time she had been brought round and Samuel, who wasn't even on duty in the ER and had only been down there to pick up a raffle ticket for a nurse's son's second grade jumble sale, reckoned that if she had been pulled back from the brink twice, she could do it again. Where there was life, after all, there was hope.

Although he had carefully kept tabs on his patient after her multiple surgeries, he had still been surprised to find her in one of his wards almost a month later, after being moved from ICU. He hadn't given the order for her move, but the Chief Resident had pleaded her case rather well, that the patient wasn't getting any worse and might respond better to stimulation if she was in a less intense environment like ICU. In a semi-private ward such as this, the patient had shown only minimal signs of improvement, but Samuel had taken it upon himself to take extra special care of her.

And *still* he didn't know why.

According to her chart, her name was Gloria Ho. A perfectly ordinary name. Her address was in a rather dodgy area of Bathville, which didn't mean she was a bad person, just someone who was a bit down on her luck. Her family was listed as dead and whether that was true or not, Samuel didn't particularly care.

But whoever had done this to her, whoever had raped her first, beaten her up to quite literally within an inch of her life after, had done so with fists and boot-clad feet and some sort of a blunt instrument like a baseball bat or a hammer. A boyfriend maybe, or a husband or some stranger to her who had pounced on her while she had been entering her apartment and had mugged her for whatever little money she may have had on her.

Samuel frowned as he realized his memory was letting him down. According to the police report, she had been pounced on while going into her apartment, but her wallet hadn't been touched and, even though the apartment door had already been opened, nothing inside had been stolen, or even trashed. The entertainment system was still there, likewise the flat screen television and DVD player and even a home computer. He remembered with sadness being told that the police had found a few books on a home college course about accounting. Obviously, Ms. Ho had wanted to better herself.

Samuel wondered what would happen to her. Gloria Ho had no medical insurance and it was only because of her delicate circumstances that had prevented her from being shipped off to Bathville County. When she would, inevitably, be moved, Samuel didn't want to lose sight of her, she had had no visitors in the eight weeks she had been here, and he couldn't bear her being all alone in the world.

With a resolute sigh, he checked the print outs from her monitors one last time, stroked her hand to provide her with some human touch he didn't even know she could feel and left her to go and finish his rounds.

Gloria Ho slept on in her private world. She had no recollections of the man called Troy who had come to her apartment and beaten her up. She had no recollection of Troy's connection to her or to Xavier Petcelli, their mutual boss in a seedy nightclub called The Blues Haven. She had no recollections of anything.

But Troy knew she wasn't dead. He had followed her progress daily, phoning the hospital and posing as a concerned friend to get the information he needed. He hadn't always been given information, not with the strict privacy laws that didn't allow even the next of kin to receive any updates without a signed release of information, but sometimes he got lucky and was able to wheedle what he needed out of a naïve nurse or assistant. Now, eight weeks later, he was patiently waiting for the time when she would show signs of recovery, then he would go in and finish the job properly. He didn't entirely agree with having to wait for her to show some improvement but the boss had given him instructions to bide his time so that was Troy had to do.

Also, Petcelli had promised Troy a large cash sum to take care of Gloria when the time was right. Troy wasn't about to give up the money, not for anything and certainly not for a tramp like her.

Her death would be worth it.

CHAPTER SEVEN

Paul was eagerly waiting the time when he could go and pick up Krista and Cathy at their hotel and take them out for a drink. He didn't know why he was so excited about seeing them again, all he knew was that he had very much enjoyed their company over lunch and he wanted to enjoy it some more. Dave could deny himself the pleasure all he wanted, Paul wasn't prepared to deny himself anything, not when it involved two pretty ladies who spoke with strange but adorable accents, who were amusing and entertaining and who each possessed a wonderful sense of humor.

When he arrived at the hotel, it was only 7:30 and he wondered why he had come half an hour earlier than planned. He sat at the bar, sipping a Coke and, as 8:00 slowly rolled around, he found himself to be growing increasingly nervous.

For why, he had absolutely no idea.

At 7:55, he pushed himself up and went back out to the lobby where, with a flash of his badge, he found out from the front desk clerk what the girls' room number was. He stood indecisively for a moment, wondering if he should call them on the house phone first to announce his arrival or if he should just go on up. He opted for the latter and pressed the button for the elevator. He located their room on the third floor and, after checking his palms weren't sweaty, his breath wasn't about to wilt flowers and his zipper was up, he rapped sharply on the door.

Cathy answered his knock almost immediately. "Hello there, Paul," she greeted with a friendly smile. "Come on in."

He stepped inside and gave her a quizzical look when he thought she didn't appear to be dressed for going out. "Aren't you coming?"

"No, and I hope you don't mind." She blushed slightly. "I, er, I have a headache and I'm so tired, I can hardly keep my eyes open."

Indeed, she did look a little pale and he smiled his sympathy. "That's too bad. Can I get you anything from the drugstore?"

"No thanks, I have painkillers in my bag."

"Okay, good, hopefully they'll help. It sounds to me like you've maybe got jet lag, which is too bad. Has Krista got it too?"

"She had a three hour nap this afternoon," Cathy said dryly. "I think she's fine."

He dutifully chuckled and was about to say something about the weather when Krista appeared from the bathroom. All small talk flew from his mind at the sight of her and he was barely able to silence a sharp intake of breath.

Earlier, Krista had been wearing a navy blue short skirt, a simple white blouse, low heeled navy pumps and natural hose and he had very much admired the charming shape of her legs. Tonight, she had changed into deep purple dress pants, a pristine white silk blouse and black patent leather high heels. He was able to see more clearly the smooth definition of her hips, narrow waist and the generous curve of her breasts and he certainly liked what he could see.

"Hi, Krista," he said as nonchalantly as possible while all he could hope for was his voice wouldn't start to croak on him. "You look…um…very nice."

"Thank you," she answered with a shy smile. "So do you."

In fact, to her eyes, he looked very good. His hair was shining, he was cleanly shaven, and he smelled of lemons and he was dressed in black chinos, a pale blue open-necked shirt, a darker blue sweater and a pair of highly polished black shoes.

He sat down on one of the chairs, looking a bit awkward as he watched Krista standing at the mirror applying a soft pink shade of lipstick to her sensuous, full lips. He could hardly take his eyes off her and he knew he was staring and that Cathy was watching what he was doing, and he wished he could be more discreet, but, hell, the show was worth watching and he couldn't help himself.

Cathy was suddenly glad she wasn't going out with them. The electricity between the two of them had been subtle at lunchtime and was now swiftly going into overload and Cathy knew she would only have been in the way tonight.

Krista came over to her and gave her a brief hug. "Hope you feel better, chum," she said earnestly. She picked up a black clutch bag, looking expectantly at Paul, who recognized the cue and walked with her to the door. She looked back over her shoulder at Cathy. "See you later."

"You two have fun."

Krista and Paul didn't say much as they waited for the elevator, but when it seemed to be taking a long time to arrive, she moved to break the silence. "I, er, I hope I'm not overdressed, I didn't really know what to wear."

"No need to worry," he said softly. "You look great." *Sensational, in fact,* he said into himself. The elevator came, and he let her enter the carriage first. As they rode down, he said, "I'm sorry Cathy couldn't come."

She slipped him an uncomfortable glance. "Is it a problem that it's just going to be you and me tonight?"

He smiled quickly to reassure her that it was really all right, he didn't mind at all. "Of course not, as long as *you* don't mind either."

"Why should I? Do you bite or something?" She threw him a mischievous smile and stepped out of the elevator after it had ground to a halt on the first floor. When they arrived at his car, she walked around it with an appreciative expression. "I meant to tell you earlier, this is a really nice car. What is it?"

"It's a Ford Mustang, only six months old. It's fully loaded, racy, sporty and I just love it."

She hadn't failed to hear the pride in his voice and she smiled down at the pure white vehicle. "We don't have Mustangs back home, although I've certainly heard of them, but we do have Fords. Do you think I could have a drive in it sometime?"

"I, well, I don't know. Can you handle a stick shift?"

She looked at him blankly. "A what?"

"A stick shift. You know, not an automatic."

"Oh, you mean a clutch. Of course, I can drive a whatever you just called it. That's what I learned to drive in back home, the way most of us do."

"Really? Okay, I'll let you take her for a spin right now, if you like." Actually, the words had come out of his mouth before he'd had the time to think about them and he couldn't believe he had been willing to let a perfect stranger, and a woman at that, get behind the wheel of his precious baby.

But she managed to save him the bother of having a massive coronary by reluctantly shaking her head. "Maybe some other time, Paul. I'm legal to drive on my UK license until I get my American license, but I've never driven on the wrong side of the road before, and I'd be even more uncomfortable doing so in such a beautiful car. Maybe it isn't such a good idea."

"Yeah, some other time," he agreed and was surprised when he realized that he even meant it. As he held the door open for her, he caught a hint of her heavenly perfume and he briefly closed his eyes in appreciation of a good thing.

He was more and more looking forward to spending the evening with her and since he had already decided where he was going to take her, he wasted no more time and drove her to the bar he and Dave frequented often. It was called Tubbs, a lot of cops came here when they wanted to escape the regular cop hangouts, and despite its mediocre décor, it had a relaxed, cozy atmosphere that wasn't spoiled by loud nightclub music blaring in their ears, giving them the opportunity to do some decent talking.

He pulled into the parking lot and escorted her inside. There were only a few clientele in the place tonight and he picked a table in the corner of the room, away from the door and close to the bar. "What would you like to drink?" he asked Krista when a waitress came over for their order.

"White wine would be fine, thanks."

Paul ordered the wine for her and a beer for him and after the waitress left, a brief silence fell upon them. Then he smiled and said, "You nervous about tomorrow?"

"About going to the police academy? A little bit. But I'm excited too. Captain Hamilton told us all about what to expect, gave us a few pointers and such and Cathy and I are just anxious to get started."

"I'm sure you are, and you'll be fine, trust me. Dave and I, we'll come and pick you up in the morning and take you to the academy."

"Oh, we couldn't impose. We were going to get a taxi."

"All the way out to New Braintree? It's close to an hour's drive – longer if it's rush hour traffic, which it will be by the time we hit Boston's city limits. Nonsense, you'll do no such thing in getting a taxi, this is the sort of thing we're supposed to be doing for you. And besides, we want to."

Krista smiled warmly. "Only if you insist."

"I do." He paid for the drinks that arrived then and watched as she took a tentative sip from her glass. "It's okay?"

"It's fine." She traced the rim of the glass with her forefinger and, for the first time that evening, began to feel quite relaxed in Paul's company. She had been *really* nervous since waking up from her nap that afternoon and so far, she was pleased with herself that she hadn't shown it. She didn't even know why she'd been nervous. "So," she began, "how long have you been a cop?"

He gave a wry shake of his head. "Oh, about ninety-three years now, it seems." He chuckled softly. "Sometimes it just feels that way, but, in reality, it's only been a little less than seven years. I started the ball rolling when I was twenty or twenty-one, I think, did all the courses, graduated from the academy, worked in Brooklyn for three years, came up here after passing the Captain's program and here I am, just turned twenty-eight years old, and fulfilling my life long dreams to be a detective." He looked down at his beer and then back into her eyes. "I don't regret leaving New York either, the crime rate there is phenomenal, and I was desperate to get out of *that* particular jungle. And here, of course, is where I met Dave and the rest, as they say, is history."

She looked at him inquisitively. "You really like Dave a lot, don't you?"

His eyes opened wide in genuine surprise. "Of course I do. He's not only my partner, he's my best friend and closer to me than any brother could be. I would do absolutely anything for him, I would gladly lay down my own life for him and I know he would do the same for me. He's quite honestly the only real, true friend I've ever had."

Krista admired the way he spoke so openly about another man and she sensed Paul felt the same way about Dave as she did about Cathy. "Is he always so quiet?"

Paul laughed and quickly shook his head. "No way, he just has a tendency to be very…wary, I guess, around strangers, particularly women. Once he starts talking, it's usually very hard to get him to stop."

"Why is he wary around women?" she asked, then quickly shook her head in embarrassment. "I'm sorry, that was very rude and forward of me, you don't have to answer that one. Sometimes I ask questions without really thinking about them first."

"That's okay, you're going to be a detective soon, asking questions, forward ones or not, is something you'll actually get paid for." Paul hesitated, wanting to tell Krista the truth about his partner but he didn't know how she would take it, or if it would shock her, and then he figured, what the hell, it was no big secret down at the precinct – Dave himself had seen to that a couple of years ago - so she would probably be finding out soon enough anyway. "No need to be sorry, Krista, you asked a fairly legitimate question so the least I can do is try and give you a legitimate answer."

He looked at her solemnly, making her heart quicken with the intensity in his clear blue eyes and then, having chosen his words as carefully as he could, he proceeded to tell her the truth about Dave.

CHAPTER EIGHT

"Like I said earlier," he began, "Dave is from Nevada and when we both moved here, we hit it off *immediately*, as if we'd known each other for years instead of just minutes. Dave can be very withdrawn around strangers but once he gets to know you, he warms up and opens up. But with me, on our initial meeting, he was warm and open and very friendly from the get go. As I recall it, *he* was the one who started up the conversation and, after only a few minutes in his company, I heard myself telling him about my upbringing and he told me about his." Paul paused and took a sip of his beer, wondering if Krista thought he was digressing. But when he stole a quick look at her, he found her genuinely interested and eagerly waiting for him to continue.

"Go on, please," she said, just to convince him further.

"I won't go into the details of his upbringing, I think they're for him to tell, not me. Anyway, as friendly as he was that day, there was a look in his eyes I had never really seen in anyone else before. It was something raw, something…painful, something terribly wounded, and he must have known I had noticed something was amiss because he told me, quite frankly, what the trouble was. You see, Dave really is a very special person, he would quite literally give anyone the shirt right off his back but when he told me what had happened a few years before he left Nevada, I could understand why he was so hurt. Dave doesn't naturally trust a lot of people. Especially, as you've already ascertained, women."

"But why?"

"Because Dave was married and his marriage and divorce both happened within less than a year of one another."

"Dave was *married?*" Krista repeated in surprise. "Oh my

goodness, if you've been here for four years and if he'd already gotten a divorce, he must have been very young when he got married."

"He was nineteen, so yes, he was very young. From what I have gathered, although the divorce was never contested by his ex-wife, it was still a very painful thing for him to have to go through." He looked at her again, gauging her reaction and when he saw her growing upset, he felt a huge bolt of alarm. It wasn't that she was on the verge of tears or anything melodramatic like that (not that he would have minded her tears), but she did seem very distraught and agitated.

"Poor Dave," she said. "Nobody should have to go through a painful divorce, particularly when they're so very young. But why did he seek a divorce after such a short time of marriage?"

"Because he came home one day and found his ex-wife in bed with another man, in his words, very obviously enjoying herself. In *their* bed too, just to really rub salt into the wounds. You see, not only is Dave very kind, he's also very loyal. As far as he knew, up until that point when he walked in on them, he had thought his marriage was going along just fine, but when he saw what she did, something inside him just died and he simply could not understand why his loyalty couldn't have been reciprocated by his own wife. He really did love her once upon a time, even though they were both so young – high school sweethearts – and catching Terri, his ex, like that destroyed a lot of his character and self-esteem. And, naturally, it destroyed a lot, if not all, of his trust of women."

"Oh my God," Krista cried with genuine distress, "it's easy to understand why he's like that. How simply terrible it must have been for him."

Paul nodded pensively. "He was already divorced when he started studying his criminology. I'm sure he threw himself into his studies, anything to help him forget but, to be honest, I think it's only within the last couple of years or so that he finally stopped loving her. In the meantime, he seemed to keep blaming himself for the divorce – not for the cause of it but for the fact that he had failed on something as sacred to him as marriage is. When I got to know him better – which didn't take long – anytime he happened to mention her or his short-lived union with her, there was always that look in his eyes I told you about, that terrible, pain-filled look I've never seen in anyone else before."

Krista could tell by the troubled look in Paul's eyes just how worried he must have been for his friend way back then and it warmed her heart that he could care like that. "If it's been four years since he left Nevada, hasn't he had anyone else in his life since then?"

Paul smiled, but it wasn't a happy smile. "There have been other women, yes. The first couple of years that I knew him, there were a *lot* of women and, I'm sad to say, he treated them all like dirt, taking them out for one date, bedding them and then dumping them immediately afterwards. He was a Class A jerk, but I guess it was easy to understand why he was acting like he was. A woman had treated him abysmally, he wanted to treat women in the same way. And then, quite simply, he realized what he was doing, realized it was wrong and wised himself up. Only he went way overboard with the way he cleaned up his act, in my opinion anyway."

"Which was?"

"It was a couple of years ago that he started to see the light and he eventually did a complete about face from his wild and wicked ways.

Figuring women were the root of all his troubles, he decided to stop seeing them, even for a casual date. He has been with no one, and I mean *no one*, in well over a year and will barely even talk to a woman now unless he absolutely has to or if he knows that woman is married or engaged or involved with someone and therefore doesn't pose as a threat to him. I know he's doing it on purpose, to try and make up for all his bad ways, but he's bound to forgive himself sooner or later, so hopefully one of these fine days, he'll come round to the land of living and will start dating again. Properly this time, of course."

"But he's a very good-looking man so surely he must have had loads of admiring females falling at his feet half the time. Doesn't he ask *any* of them out at all?"

"Nope. Not one, he has a natural knack of making it perfectly clear to the ladies that he's just not interested. Anyway, I hope I've helped you understand him a bit better and I know that once you get to know him, you'll be able to see for yourself what a swell guy he really is."

"I hope so too and thank you for filling me in. I just hope he can forget I'm a single female and will start to look upon me as a friend."

"He might. Just let him do it in his own time. Dave's very independent and stubborn and he hates being backed into a corner or being forced to make a decision he's not ready to make. He also has a very bad temper and he loses it at least ten times a day. And, believe it or not, that's not an exaggeration. Any excuse to fly off the handle and he'll find it. But he has a great sense of humor too as I've already told you and underneath that brusque exterior of his, he's really a pussy cat." Figuring he had told Krista all she needed to know about Dave for now, he decided he wanted to hear about her and he got right to the point with a warm smile right into her eyes. "Now that I've told you all about Dave, I'd like for you to tell me about yourself, Krista."

She blushed prettily, never having been one to wax poetic about herself. "There's not much to tell, I'm afraid."

"Go on," he coaxed, "I want to hear everything about you and I don't want you holding anything back either." Unlike Dave, Paul had taken the time to read the girls' dossiers, so he already knew a bit about their working backgrounds and such, but he was anxious to find out the informal details, to see the person beneath the really very beautiful outer shell.

"Okay, but you'll be sorry you asked," she said, sighing dramatically. "I've lived a very boring, humdrum life." She sat back and crossed her legs, giving him a heart-stopping eyeful of her long, slender thigh clad in the deep purple pants. Unaware of the appraisal, she looked quite relaxed as she squinted up at the ceiling, as if she was trying to think of where to begin. "I was an only child, but I was brought up in a very loving home by the best parents in the whole wide world," she said in her soft, lilting accent. "They always wanted me to make my own decisions and whatever that decision was, they always supported me. From an early age, I had always wanted to be a doctor and when I left school, my parents supported me in my decision to follow my dream. So off I went to University."

Already, Paul was impressed. If she had wanted to be a doctor so badly and had gone to University, she must have had the smarts to get that far. "A doctor, eh? So, what happened for you to end up in the police?"

She chuckled fondly. "Cathy is what happened. I met her after I had completed my first year. She was already in the police and it was she who talked me into hanging up my stethoscope and I did, halfway through my second year. For the first time, my parents had misgivings, I mean, being in the police in Northern Ireland can be a very dangerous occupation, plus I'm a Catholic and therefore of the minority in the force, but Cathy, who was very close with my parents, convinced them I would be doing the right thing. They loved her enough to listen to her, and loved me enough to let me change my career choice so, with their continued support, I joined up. Within a very short space of time, I knew I had made the right career move, I enjoyed the work immensely, even more so than being a doctor. I was lucky enough to have been put in the same station Cathy was in and it helped a lot to have her close at hand." She paused and seemed to reminisce for a moment, then she continued, "I don't know how much you know about the goings on in my country, but, despite the so-called cease fire, there's still a lot of unrest. The bombings may not be on the scale they were back in the 70s and 80s, but they're still happening, and the shootings and the killings certainly haven't gone away either. People in my generation, and older generations, are still teaching their children and grandchildren all about bigotry and how to hate, instead of going the other way and teaching them it is okay to be friends with a Catholic, or a Protestant, whichever side you're on. It's a never-ending battle, literally and figuratively, and sometimes all that mindless bigotry and hatred and Political hypocrisy in my country got too much for us to stomach, and that's when we decided to try and do something more positive with our chosen careers. And the rest, as they say, is history."

"It must have been hard on your parents when you, as their only child, decided to emigrate. Have you spoken to them since you arrived here?"

A very strange look passed over Krista's face, dulling the sparkle in her eyes and he knew instinctively he had somehow managed to hit on a raw nerve. "Hardly," she murmured.

He shook his head in bewilderment. "I don't understand. What...?"

Krista took a long sip of her wine, her expression composed as she deliberated over her next words. Then she said, quite matter-of-factly, "My parents are both dead, Paul. I lost them both just a little over two years ago."

He hadn't been expecting to hear something as tragic as that and he hissed in a sharp breath, understanding her pain. He silently kicked himself for being so insensitive. "Oh Krista, I'm so sorry, if I'd known, I wouldn't have...I should have..."

"It's okay, really it is. How could you have known? Maybe I shouldn't have been so blunt in the way I said it."

"I was only..." He stopped, the disgust with himself evident in his eyes. "Did you... um...did you lose them in all the fighting that goes on over there?"

She emitted a short, bitter laugh. "Oh no, nothing as melodramatic as that. They were killed outright in a car accident, simple as that. One minute they were driving along without a care in the world, the next...well, they were gone. They apparently hit a patch of black ice, careened down a steep bank...and their lives ended."

The pain was obviously still too close to the surface for her, making Paul just want to pull her into his arms and hug it all away for her, but he knew he couldn't do that. "I really am very sorry, Krista. You must miss them a lot."

"I do, I won't deny it. There's not a day that goes by that I don't think about them or that I don't miss them. I'm sure you can imagine I was pretty much a basket case after I lost them, but Cathy helped me through it all, bless her. I owe her a lot for getting me through what was easily the worst time of my life, but she was only too glad to help me. She's my whole family now and I'm grateful I have her in my life."

"And *I'm* glad you had someone there to help you through your sorrow." He lifted his beer and drank some of it slowly, still berating himself for having pushed her to open up like that, but he was admiring her for her honesty too, and her directness, and he gave her a tender smile, which she accepted gratefully.

When she noticed his obvious discomfort, she immediately lightened her tone. "Right, that's all you need to know about me for tonight. Your turn."

He groaned comically. "How did I know that was coming?"

"Because turn about is fair play, Detective Cameron."

He smiled in defeat. "All right, young lady, you win." But he paused before he said anything further. He had shocked her about Dave. Now he was going to shock her again. This time, about himself.

And the strange thing was, although he didn't have a past he could exactly be proud of, he wanted to tell her about it. Gory details and all.

CHAPTER NINE

There was no preamble this time, no forewarning, he just started talking. "I was born and brought up in Brooklyn in New York, in a very tough neighborhood." Tough neighborhood was actually something of an understatement, but he deliberately downplayed it this time, he could tell her the complete truth some other time. "I have one sister, she's older than me by three years and I haven't seen her in a very long time, since long before I even became a cop down there. I haven't the faintest idea where she even is right now, nor, I'm almost sorry to say, do I even care anymore. We used to be close, then, the older we got and the more difficult our lives became, I became a thorn in her side, a kid brother, another mouth to feed and obviously a burden to her." He stopped abruptly, wondering how he could downplay the next bit when he realized it was only going to shock her. He mulled it over for a long moment and then he said as easily as he could, "I grew up in a very poor household…all my father's fault, I suppose. He flitted from one job to the next and any money he earned, he spent on booze and drugs… he was a very heavy user and an equally heavy drinker. I guess you can imagine there were never any good times when I was growing up, no gifts at Christmas time or at birthdays, that sort of thing, but I accepted that all as a fact of my life, I really was no different to any of the other kids in the rest of the neighborhood. Anytime my father got drunk – which was pretty much every night, money permitting – he would fly into a violent temper. I spent most of my younger days dodging blows from him, but I wasn't always lucky, most of the time, his fist or his shoe or his belt connected with somewhere, anywhere, on my body. He abused me a lot as a child, not sexually or anything, but physically, the sexual abuse he saved for my sister. What my mother wouldn't give him, he got from my sister and I hated him for it as soon as I was old enough to understand what was going on."

Krista shook her head, truly appalled at what she was hearing. "Paul, I'm sorry, I really am. If you'd rather not tell me about this, seeing we've only just met and everything, then you don't have to, I'll understand."

He shrugged indifferently. "I really don't mind talking about it, I came to terms with it a long time ago and since I'm away from all that now anyway, it really doesn't bother me much anymore." That much was true, he really had accepted it. It had taken some time, a *lot* of time actually and a lot of therapy and talking it out with friends and colleagues and Internal Affairs and other people who were prepared to listen and offer help, but he had made it. "Anyway, my father continued beating up on us kids and as for my mother, she turned a blind eye to it all, buried her head in the sand, so to speak."

"Your *own mother* didn't try to protect you or your sister from him? That's absolutely despicable. Couldn't you have gone to a social worker, or a teacher or *any*body who could have helped you?"

"What, and risk getting thrashed to within an inch of my life if my old man ever found out I had ratted on him? No, I really couldn't do that."

"But you could have been placed into foster care, taken away from him and he would never have seen you again."

"He would have found us. I know that for sure."

"But surely someone must have known what was happening to you. Surely there must have been someone who would have seen bruises on your body."

"There were never any bruises on parts you could see. My father had the smarts to beat me only where he knew my clothes would cover me. And as for my mother, I never really knew that woman well, she always managed to keep herself so detached from us all. It was only when I was five or six or so and starting to get very street smart that I realized she was nothing more than a junkie herself. And when I was sixteen, she committed suicide anyway, took a lethal, clearly intentional, overdose of heroin. That was her way of coping with the disaster that was her life, by buying her way out of it. No sooner was she buried than I ran away from home – without ever going back – knowing full well it was because of my father that she had killed herself."

Krista stared at him incredulously, feeling tears pricking the back of her eyes. Never in her wildest dreams could she have ever guessed he had come from such a background, he seemed so self-assured, so easygoing and even so at peace with himself. "So how did you manage to turn out so nice?" she asked, her voice husky, her eyes wide and unwavering.

He chuckled modestly. "I don't know about that, maybe I just got lucky. I had one thing they all didn't and that was a sense of humor. True, for the first few years of my life, I didn't know I had one, but I sort of adopted a family that lived in the neighborhood and I went there any opportunity I could get to escape my home life and being among boys and girls and their parents who really *knew* how to be a close knit family, I found that sense of humor and when I was at home, I soon learned that it's a lot less painful to laugh than it is to cry. I also promised myself at a very early age I would never be anything like my old man, wanting to dispel the myth like father, like son. If I thought for one moment I was even remotely like him, I think I would lock myself away somewhere for a hundred years. Anything I may have achieved in my life so far, I've achieved it all by myself, or with some help and guidance from Dave." Dave, in fact, had been more than just a help, Dave was the one who had listened the most and had always seemed to understand, despite having lived a life and lifestyle as far removed from Paul's as the sun was to the planet Saturn. "At the risk of sounding immodest, I'm damned proud of myself but I don't kid myself either. I thank God for making me the sort of person I am today, and I can truly say, hand on my heart, I never have or never wanted to hit a woman or abuse a child, flown into a violent rage after consuming enough alcohol to sink a battle ship and I have never even so much as smoked a cigarette, never mind a joint. All that's nothing but a loser's game and one thing I ain't is a loser."

"I can already see that without you having to tell me," she said earnestly.

"Thank you, that's what I like to hear, then I know I'm doing something right."

"What did you do to take your mind off your home life?"

"I discovered sports," he answered with a mischievous twinkle in his eye. "I love sports of any kind, but my favorite is easily ice hockey. I was put into my first pair of skates when I was six years old and I soon found out I could take my frustrations out in the rink. I actually play for the local team here, the Bathville Blazers, I've been playing for them for three years now and I like to get as many games a season in as I can – which isn't always possible, what with my work schedule. But the Coach is very understanding, he hasn't axed me for bad time keeping yet."

"That implies he thinks you're worth having on the team, that you're good."

"I don't know, maybe I am, but as far as I'm concerned, there's always room for improvement. I find hockey very therapeutic, either watching it or playing it, it's a good way to let off steam. And -" He paused and raised his eyebrows up and down *a la* Groucho Marx. "I'm very pleased and proud to announce all my teeth are still my own."

Krista chuckled softly. "That's certainly good to know. What else did you do to help you forget your father?"

"I found music too. I got myself a job when I was still in high school and saved real hard to get myself a guitar. It was a second hand one out of a pawnshop, but it was in excellent condition and I taught myself to play it too and, at the risk of sounding immodest again, I'm not too bad at it. Dave bought me a really beautiful *brand new* one the Christmas after we became partners – told you he was generous – and I treasure it with my life, it's my second greatest love after my car. And, to wrap it up, I joined the police academy and here I am today."

In spite of all she had just heard, Krista chuckled again and, without even giving it a second thought, she settled her hand on his and squeezed it. "Thank you for telling me about yourself like that, I know it can't have been easy to admit to me what you just did. And I really am sorry you had such a rotten childhood."

Paul shrugged and looked down at her long, slender hand, finding he liked the shape of her fingers and the warmth of her skin against his. It felt like the most natural thing in the world for her hand to be where it was, and he automatically folded his other hand over the top of hers. "You're the very first woman I've ever told this to," he admitted softly. "I don't even know what made me tell you, seeing it's not exactly a history to be proud of and seeing as how we only met this morning. But hey, I'm glad I told you, I really am."

"And I'm glad too. If it's any consolation to you, I think you're a very nice man, one of the nicest men I've ever met."

"Oh yeah?" His eyes crinkled up into a smile. "Well, don't go telling anyone, please, I've got a reputation in this town I'd like to keep."

She laughed and then, suddenly realizing their hands were still entwined, she reluctantly pulled hers away. She looked down at her wine glass. "You've certainly earned yourself a reputation with me as far as *not* being a perfect gentleman. My glass is empty."

Wishing she would just put her hand back where she'd had it for a very enjoyable long moment, he laughed in amusement and hailed the waitress over. "Same again, please."

Krista reached into her bag and took out her wallet. "This round's mine."

"No way, lady, I asked you out tonight, the least I can do is pay for the drinks." He found himself looking into her eyes longer than was necessary and he could actually feel his heart beat quicken over something he couldn't quite identify. He regretfully pulled his gaze away and they indulged in good-natured bantering about who should pay for the drinks.

The bar wasn't exactly crowded this evening and the waitress returned with the drinks quite quickly. Paul won the battle of throwing the money, including a generous tip, on her tray and Krista pouted comically.

"Oh, knickers," she said, "You beat me!"

Oh God, she looks so cute, Paul thought, *and did she* really *just say,* oh knickers? He had a sudden, crazy urge to kiss her pouted lips, making him have to literally struggle to turn his mind to other things. Because he couldn't think of one thing to say and also because Krista was searching through her purse for a Kleenex, the conversation lulled a bit.

Her expression was normal again, but she hadn't known how badly Paul had wanted to kiss her just then. She wiped off the ring of condensation where her first wine glass had rested on the table and placed the new glass in front of her. She took a few sips of her wine and then, with a swift glance at his left hand, she said, "You never told me if there was a Mrs. Paul Cameron." Just because he wasn't wearing a wedding ring didn't mean he wasn't married after all.

Paul blinked in surprise. "*That* was certainly a direct one."

"It's a trait about me," she answered unapologetically. "So…is there?"

"Well, now that you mention it, yes there is. *And* a Paul junior into the bargain."

"Oh." She looked awkwardly away. "Oh…I see…"

He couldn't bear to see her look so crestfallen and he couldn't keep his face straight any longer. "I'm kidding, honest to God, I'm only joking. I never got married, just haven't found the right woman yet, I guess."

She narrowed her eyes and studied him suspiciously, coming to the swift conclusion he really had only been teasing her. "I think I've just decided I don't like you," she announced cheerfully.

"Serves you right for being so nosy, Ms. Nolan."

"I'm not nosy, I'm just…. inquisitive," she returned primly.

He threw his head back and laughed gaily. "You mean there's a difference, you witch?" He turned to look at her again and immediately felt his laughter die in his throat at the sight of her incredible green eyes as they coolly scrutinized him. Then her eyes shifted away, a slight smile of bewilderment and underlying amusement tugging at the corners of her mouth and he wondered what had caused the bewilderment. "Krista, what's wrong?"

"I…uh…I don't know. I…you have a wonderful laugh and…and I like your eyes when you smile… or even when you don't smile and…oh Jesus, I'm sorry, I don't want to make you feel uncomfortable, please just forget I spoke."

It wasn't the compliments that set his heart racing all over again, it was the shy way she had said them that did it and, not being able to contain himself any longer, he reached out and gently touched her cheek, causing her to look at him in astonishment. "I *won't* forget," he said hoarsely. He dreamily traced the outline of her jaw and then he said softly, almost as if he was talking to himself. "You are so beautiful…so very beautiful."

Krista's breath caught in her throat when their eyes met and locked. The feel of his fingers was both soothing and sensuous and time seemed to stand still for a moment as if to let her savor his touch. "Thank you," she whispered in wide-eyed amazement.

Something was happening here, something was happening far too quickly for Paul's liking and because he still didn't know what it was, he chided her under the chin with a small smile and reluctantly pulled his hand away from her face. An awkward silence followed and then he said, "Tell me about Cathy. I think it's her turn to be examined under the microscope."

A look of pure apprehension suddenly came into her eyes,

alarming him at the same time it mystified him. She cleared her throat and looked down at the crumpled, soaked tissue and she seemed very uncomfortable and also quite anxious to find an easy way out from his innocent statement. She cleared her throat a second time, smoothed her brow and laughing awkwardly, tossed the tissue into the ashtray.

"Well, *that's* what I would call a pregnant pause. Cathy doesn't like talking about herself and she doesn't like me or anyone else talking about her either and I was just trying to think of a way to tell you that without sounding rude."

"Why doesn't she like even you talking about her?"

"Because she just doesn't. Particularly about her upbringing, or even much before just a few years ago. It's very private, personal and hellish for her, Paul, and that's all you need to know."

More than a little surprised at that comment, he nodded slowly. "Okay, sure, whatever you say."

"I *can* at least tell you she's very sweet, very honest and very loyal. She's also very generous, shy around strangers, down to earth, free-spirited, doesn't hold a grudge, quick to admit she's been wrong, loves children, is an amazing cook and can stop a man dead in his tracks with just one look from those lovely blue eyes of hers. She's very smart, but she has a lot of insecurities about herself…and I mean a *lot*. But she's a wonderful friend to me, we're as close as sisters, maybe even closer, she loves me, and I love her, and I won't let anyone say one word against her." She stole a look at him and winced sheepishly. "I've upset you, haven't I?"

He quickly shook his head. "No, of course not, you just startled me, that's all. Maybe if… no, maybe *when* I get to know her better, she'll open up a bit more to me all by herself. You think?"

"Honestly? No. I know she won't. But don't let this create a barrier between the two of you. You'll find out for yourself just what an amazing woman she is, and I guarantee it that very soon, you'll feel honored to have her in your life, no matter how small her role may be."

"Then I'll just have to wait for that to happen, won't I?" He looked at his beer bottle. He had drunk it down quickly, without even being aware of it and he contemplated a third. He remembered he was driving and forced himself to make what he had left last for the remainder of the night. "Let's get unto something more neutral then. Tell me about Ireland."

So, she did, and he was intrigued to hear her talk so passionately about the country of her birth, how green it was, how rugged and beautiful it was, about the undaunted spirit of the people who offered hospitality that was second to none to strangers, despite having seen their homeland being torn apart by bombs, religious difference, bigotry, hatred and, probably the hardest one to break, politics. He learned that Northern Ireland and Southern Ireland, although on the same land mass, are two separate countries, with different governments and even a different currency. He also learned that Northern Ireland is part of the United Kingdom and therefore classed as being under British rule. He learned that Belfast is the capital city of Northern Ireland and is home to where the Titanic was built and, much to his surprise and delight, that it even had its own ice hockey team that had played in many international games and tournaments. He was impressed to hear that, despite its diminutive size, Northern Ireland was very agricultural and could alone support her population with dairy, beef, pork, lamb, poultry, as well as any vegetable or fruit that could grow with or without aid of a greenhouse. And as he listened to her words, he could almost feel himself being transported across the Atlantic and actually seeing it for himself and he told her how he was feeling and expressed a sudden and heartfelt wish that he would love to go over some day and see what it was truly like, and maybe even take in a Belfast Giants hockey game or two while he was there. When he told her that, her eyes shone with happiness, which in turn made his heart soar, so she went on to tell him that sheep roamed freely in the fields alongside major roads, but he wasn't to assume the whole of Northern Ireland was like that, she informed him that it was a very industrial part of the United Kingdom and many International companies were still taking their businesses there despite the worldwide economic woes over the last decade. But, despite the influx of new companies, the global recession had hit Northern Ireland hard too with job losses and foreclosures, and everyone was praying the economy would turn around again, and soon.

And then, as 11:00 came and went with neither one of them being aware of the time, Krista tried, and failed to stifle a yawn that was followed seconds later by another one. "I'm sorry, Paul, but for my body it's still four in the morning. Would you mind if we called it a night?"

His soaring heart sank when he realized the evening with her was drawing to a close, but he could see for himself that she really had become very tired. "Of course I don't mind. I have an early start in the morning too unfortunately, but don't worry, Dave and I will still be there to pick you and Cathy up to take you to the academy."

He escorted her out to the car and he didn't even seem to be aware that he had placed a hand on the small of her back. Touching her just seemed to be a very natural act for him and being touched by him seemed to be just as natural for her.

It was a beautiful night, except for a cool breeze that reminded everyone that this was still officially winter. Krista could hear the rhythmic, soothing tumbling of the ocean in the distance and, turning her head up, she stared at the stars twinkling like jewels in the velvety blackness of the sky.

"Pretty, aren't they?" Paul said softly, following her gaze. "So near and yet so far."

Their eyes met and held, and they were standing very close together and he had to again fight that dangerous urge to kiss her, but she was driving him crazy just by sight alone and the added input of her perfume wasn't exactly helping matters. But he knew he didn't dare kiss her, it would probably frighten her off and he certainly didn't want to do anything that might jeopardize this new and wonderful relationship. True, they had managed to cover a lot of ground between them tonight, a lot had been said, deep secrets had been shared and he felt very close to her because of all that, but it still didn't give him a reason to kiss her.

Allowing himself only a brief squeeze of her hand, he opened her door for her and when he got in beside her, he took her back to the hotel, driving slowly just to prolong his time with her. At the hotel, he walked her inside as far as the elevator and, while waiting for it, she turned to him with a shy smile.

"I had a lovely time tonight, Paul," she said softly, earnestly. "Thank you."

"The pleasure was mine." *You'd better believe it was, beautiful lady,* he added to himself. Suddenly, he felt awkward, confused as to what his next move should be. Should he kiss her after all? Squeeze her hand again? Give her a hug? Although any or all three of those would be very nice, he didn't know what was appropriate for this moment and just as he deliberated, she sensed his confusion and made his mind up for him, just as the elevator arrived.

She tilted her face up and gently kissed his cheek, letting her lips linger for a moment. "Good night," she whispered with the merest of smiles that was still enough to make him go weak at the knees. She turned away, stepped into the elevator and gave him one last smile just as the doors closed over.

Paul touched his cheek where she had kissed him and then, with a happy sigh, he went back out to his car, grinning broadly from ear to ear and feeling very contented at the knowledge he would be seeing her again very soon.

Krista let herself into her room as quietly as she could in case Cathy was sleeping but she was still very much wide-awake and dying to hear all about her evening. Krista flopped down on Cathy's bed and kicked off her shoes. "Oh Cathy, I had the best time imaginable tonight. Paul is *so* funny and *so* sweet *and* he just oozes this incredible, wonderful sex appeal."

And, because she was still on a high, Krista proceeded to recount practically every minute of the evening to her friend, gesturing wildly and talking nonstop, at the same time undressing herself and even taking off her make-up. She seemed so energetic and keyed up, Cathy wondered if she would be able to sleep that night.

"I feel like I've made a whole new friend tonight, Cath," Krista enthused, "He and I talked about anything and everything and it truly felt as if I'd known him for years and years. I think he even felt the same way about me and I can't wait to see him again." She realized she had let that last bit slip out unintentionally and she looked sheepishly at her friend. "Oops!"

Cathy rolled her eyes. "Yes, oops indeed, young lady. For your sake, I'll pretend I didn't hear that."

"It wasn't meant as it sounded," Krista offered and then let out a deep, throaty chuckle. "Who am I trying to kid? I meant it exactly as it sounded."

With a wry shake of her head, Cathy smiled. "Time to say good night, I think."

"You're right. Good night, I think." And with that, Krista crawled in under the covers and fell asleep surprisingly quickly, leaving Cathy to ponder if there was more to this new friendship than met the eye.

Since Krista wasn't one for school girl crushes or even fickle relationships, Cathy could only assume that it was, at least for now, nothing but innocent.

CHAPTER TEN

It was the next morning, just about two hours before Cathy and Krista had to report at the police academy for the first leg of their induction into the Bathville Police Department. It was nearly 6:30, dawn was just about shaking itself free from night's dark clutches and was spreading a few tentative fingers of light out into the sky, getting ready to break on what was going to be a perfect late winter day, with temperatures in the high 40's, a mild breeze and lots of sunshine.

And in her hospital bed, Gloria Ho felt, for the first time in weeks, the carefully controlled warmth of her room and the cozy weight of the blankets lying on top of her. She could also detect clean, antiseptic smells all around her and she could hear the monotonous beep of some sort of monitor she didn't, as yet, know was hooked up to her.

It was a strange world she now lived in, everything seemed bathed in a light, ghostly gray mist, most sounds were muffled and completely foreign to her and she sometimes sensed, rather than could see, the presence of several shadowy forms whose faces were never fully revealed to her.

And yet, she wasn't scared. She didn't think she had anything to be scared of, those sounds, forms and even the mist weren't threatening in any way. If anything, they were comforting, even helpful, although she didn't know why.

She felt the need to open her eyes to check out her surroundings and ensure she really was safe, but the effort was too great and so she slept.

At a little after 7:00, Doctor Samuel Warren came in to check on her. He looked into her eyes before examining the print out from her EEG and the response he got prompted him to look at the monitor immediately.

It was really happening, her brain wave activity was increasing, her vitals were slowly but surely improving, and he was so pleased, he nearly let out a whoop of joy.

He didn't, though, he was nothing if not a responsible and professional man, ever mindful of other patients and caregivers around him and so he whooped on the inside, his sleepy eyes twinkling softly with pleasure.

He made a mental note to ask at the nurse's station if the friend who kept calling about Gloria Ho had left a return phone number yet and, stealing a quick look around and seeing no one was looking at him, he leaned over and settled a very gentle kiss on Gloria's cheek.

*

When Dave arrived at the station, it was almost 7:15 and he found Paul already at his desk, reading a day-old newspaper and whistling quite cheerfully to himself. Dave greeted his friend warmly and, seeing Paul already had one in front of him, Dave poured himself a cup of coffee and sat down facing him.

"What has you so chipper this morning?" Dave asked conversationally. "Did you get lucky last night or something?"

Paul folded up his newspaper and looked over at him with a contented smile. "Nothing like that. Contrary to popular belief, I do *not* get lucky every night of the week."

"Yeah, I suppose you have to give your right hand a rest sometimes," Dave quipped.

"Get bent, Andrews."

"Right back at you." Dave remembered then what Paul had

planned for the evening before. "Oh yeah, you took the two Irish ladies out last night, didn't you?"

"Nope, lady, Dave, just one of them."

"Which one didn't go?"

"Cathy."

"So how was Krista?"

Paul smiled slowly. "She's a major babe and a total sweetheart, if you must know."

Something in Paul's tone prompted Dave to give him a suspicious look but he chose not to pursue it further for the time being. "Do we still have to pick them up?"

Paul glanced at his watch. "Yes, in about ten minutes, soon as you finish your coffee."

Dave took a sip from his cup and instantly grimaced. "Who made this grunge this morning anyway?"

"Probably nobody, it's probably been sitting there for the last ten days and someone just decided to heat it up again."

"Well, it tastes like goat's piss to me."

"Thought so myself. Come on, let's go to Dunkin's and I'll treat you to a proper cup, then we can go on to the hotel. I've already told the Captain what we're doing this morning and he okayed it."

Dave threw his coffee cup one last look of disgust and followed Paul out to where Paul's car was parked. "So, you think Krista and you have hit it off?" he inquired casually.

Paul glanced at him briefly, then turned his full attention to the heavy stream of early morning traffic he was trying to break into. He slipped in between a red Corolla and a green Prius, checked his rear-view mirror and shot over to the far-left lane so he could make his turn one block down. Driving in Bathville, although not as bad as Boston, or New York City, could still prove harrowing, particularly in the morning and evening rush hours, but Paul was more than used to it and he answered Dave's question without even giving the traffic a second thought.

"Yeah…I hope so, anyway. I really like her, and I think she likes me too…God, I really do hope so."

Dave's suspicion instantly came back, turned almost immediately to certainty and he groaned comically. "Moving a bit fast are we not?"

"Not really, we just seem to have a lot in common, that's all I'm saying. It's not exactly *my* fault we hit it off so quickly, is it?"

"I guess not," Dave conceded. "Stop going on the defensive."

"I'm *not* on the defensive."

Dave chuckled. "See?"

Paul blew him a very loud and very perfect raspberry and swung into a Dunkin Donuts parking lot. Two minutes later, two coffees and two donuts in hand, he returned to the car and they sat in silence for a while to enjoy their usual morning treats. Fingers licked, mouths wiped, and excess sugar and crumbs swept from clothing and the car seats, Paul re-joined the traffic, keeping a careful eye on his coffee cup that it wasn't about to spill its contents all over the interior of his car.

"About the two ladies, Dave," he began, "are you going to stop acting like a jerk around them?"

"Don't know what you mean."

"Oh yes you do. You went out of your way yesterday to be rude to them and to ignore them completely and frankly, I was not impressed. Loosen up a bit, be more natural around them, let them see you for who you really are. I'm not asking you to jump into bed with either one of them or anything – chance would be a fine thing to get you to do *that* – but just try and be nice towards them. Just because they're females does *not* make them the enemy, you know."

"Really?" Dave asked in barely concealed amusement, laced heavily with sarcasm. "I'll bear that in mind, shall I?"

"Dave!"

"Oh, all right, I'll *try* and be nice. In fact, I'll go one step further and be my usual charming self with them. How's that?"

"I know you and your usual charming self and that's what I'm afraid of."

"Gee, thanks, partner. I'm warning you right now, don't you dare go making eyes at Krista all the time you're in her company. I really can't stomach it when I have to watch you doing your male mating dance ritual thing."

"I could be so lucky."

They arrived at the hotel shortly afterwards to find Krista and Cathy waiting patiently for them in the lobby. Paul immediately went to Krista's side and, although there were dozens of people milling around them, helping themselves to the free breakfast or checking out or whatever, as far as Paul and Krista were concerned, they were the only two people there.

She smiled into his eyes and lightly touched his arm. "Hi."

He returned the smile in the same way. "Hi to you too. Did you sleep okay last night?"

"Like a log."

"Good, that's what I wanted to hear." His smile deepened, and he couldn't resist looking her up and down, albeit as surreptitiously as possible and he came to a very swift (and not very difficult) conclusion that she was even a knockout in a sweat suit and sneakers and wearing no make-up at all.

Dave held himself back as he idly watched the exchange between his partner and Krista and when he happened to glance casually in Cathy's direction, he realized with a start she was observing him coolly.

Remembering his promise to Paul, he cleared his throat and said, "Good morning. How are you?"

Since it was the most he had said to her since they had met the day before, and since it was he who had opened the conversation for the first time between them, Cathy couldn't help looking at him in surprise. But Krista had told her about Dave's divorce and his shyness/wariness around women and she no longer thought him as rude as she had the previous day.

She smiled faintly. "Fine, thanks. And you?"

"Pretty good. All set for today?"

"I hope so. I'm looking forward to it and everything but now I feel a bit nervous too."

"Don't be." He smiled kindly at her. "There's really nothing for you to worry about."

Cathy found herself warming to him even more just because of his smile, she liked the way it turned his eyes up at the corners and softened the deep blue within. "Shouldn't we be going?" she asked anxiously, glancing at her watch.

Paul heard her and turned towards her. "We've got plenty of time, Cathy, don't worry. Hey, I almost forgot, I was speaking to Captain

Hamilton this morning he told me to tell you that he heard your furniture and stuff has cleared Customs and is being delivered to you tomorrow. It's as well he managed to get you that apartment for rent over in Augustus Court, you can get the keys tonight and he's also arranged for you to have tomorrow off from the academy so that you can receive your belongings. When we leave the academy this afternoon, he says I'm to take you to the Port Authority, so you can sign for your goods and show them the necessary paperwork."

Captain Hamilton had told the girls about the home he had picked out for them once he had heard their requirements, he had even driven them by it yesterday morning and they had agreed it looked fine (at least from the outside) and that it seemed like it was in a nice neighborhood.

Cathy nodded her head. "The Captain phoned us this morning and told us our stuff had arrived." She patted her gym bag on the side. "I've got the paperwork right in here and we've even called a moving company who are going to pick our boxes up at the warehouse at the Port and deliver them sometime tomorrow. The Captain also told us that first thing tomorrow morning would be time enough to pick up the keys. All we have to do is see the landlord to sign a lease and we're all set. We've been living in a hotel for nearly a month now, three and a half weeks in Belfast after they took our stuff away and the last few days here and I'm really looking forward to a home-cooked meal again. Getting catered to is fine, but the novelty soon wears off, it'll be nice to get back into the daily routine again."

"I'm sure it will be." Paul checked his watch. It was fast approaching 7:45 and to settle Cathy's nerves, he declared it was time to go.

Unaware that soon their lives were going to be linked with an ex-erotic dancer who was at this moment slowly but surely finding her first steps to recovery from a two-month long coma, Cathy and Krista followed Dave and Paul out to the car.

But although Cathy and Krista were, for the most part, looking forward to the start of their new careers, the long-anticipated day was going to end in a way neither of them could ever have expected.

And it wasn't going to be good.

CHAPTER ELEVEN

The morning was spent filling out forms for income tax purposes and security clearances and all the other humdrum but necessary forms when applying for a new job that involved precise information and complete honesty as police work did. Questions like: *Have you ever been under the influence of marijuana?* or *Have you ever tried opium based or related drugs?* were right in there with regular questions like: *Do you have epilepsy/abnormally high blood pressure/heart disease/AIDS or the HIV virus/diabetes* and so on and they were all the kinds of questions Cathy and Krista had already answered in one way or another or else they wouldn't be here.

They, along with eighteen other men and women were given a one-hour lecture on the community relations aspect of police work which was, again, just a formality. The real classroom work would be beginning in a couple of days, for Cathy and Krista anyway. The rest of the students were here for the full twenty-five-week course and Cathy and Krista would only see them when their paths happened to cross, such as at the shooting practice range or the driving course.

After a light lunch, the girls were separated from their classmates and brought into a gym that was fully equipped with exercise machines and weights and floor mats. Their instructor, a gruff but helpful and professional man by the name of Jay Ackerman, who was six foot four and two hundred and twenty pounds of steeled muscle despite being in his late fifties, wanted to check the girls' individual fitness. He put them through their paces on the treadmill and stair climber, carefully monitoring their heartbeats and respiration and, after over an hour, he pronounced them "a lot fitter than I could have hoped for".

He took them into a smaller gym room that had no exercise equipment in it, just a lot of blue mats strewn on the floor, several ropes suspended from the ceiling and a seven-foot-high climbing apparatus. These last two items weren't going to be used today but by the end of their course, Cathy and Krista would have come to know them intimately, hate them completely but would have mastered them to the point of exhaustion and obsession.

Ackerman demonstrated a few self-defense moves and, because Cathy and Krista were both of slight build, he focused on teaching them how to apprehend a would-be attacker by first overpowering him, regardless of his height or weight, second, by landing him on his front/back/bottom to render him unable to continue with his attack and third by disarming or immobilizing him completely.

"Okay, Nolan, you're first up," he said when they assured him they understood what he was talking about. Krista dutifully bounced up and placed herself on the mat where he told her to stand. "I'm going to come up to you from behind, put my arm around your throat and make as if I'm going to steal your purse. Do *not* treat this as an exercise, treat it as the real thing. You could be in a very real situation like it tomorrow when you go to the store to pick up milk. I am no longer your instructor, I'm a big, bad guy who's high on crack and desperately looking for money so I can score my next hit and when I'm desperate and possibly heading into painful, scary withdrawal, I get very dangerous. Do you understand?"

Krista nodded. "Yes, sir."

"Good. Going by what I've just shown you, you're going to do your best to stop me. Don't think you'll damage my ego if you manage to toss me on the mat, you'll only make me satisfied that I'm doing my job in teaching you properly."

Krista turned around and waited for him to make his move. He did it with surprising speed and she instantly grabbed the arm he had put around her neck, held on to it as tightly as she could, pushed herself forward, spun around and tossed him neatly on his back on the mat, using his arm as her lever. She pretended to produce handcuffs and, keeping her knee firmly planted on his chest, also pretended to snap them on his wrists within three seconds.

Telling her what she had done wrong and congratulating her on what she had done right, he got her to go over the maneuver again and this time, she kicked the feet out from under him, sent him sprawling on his stomach and, grabbing his arm again, she twisted it up his back and pretended to handcuff him again.

"Well done," he said, jumping to his feet and cracking his knuckles. "You still made a few errors, but you got the job done and in real life situations, nothing ever happens text book perfect anyway."

Krista re-tightened her ponytail and got her breath back. "I think I would have found that a lot harder to do if you had been any heavier, Jay."

"You've just brought up a good point, Nolan. What does a policewoman do if she's met with an attacker who is twice her weight and towers over her by at least a foot? She is, say, off duty and she doesn't have her gun with her because she was going shopping for new shoes and she didn't think she would need her gun in the mall. Well, the answer is simple…" Jay smiled disarmingly. "I shouldn't be telling you this at all because it really goes against my ethics but if I was a woman and in that kind of scenario I just described, I would go straight for the groin. If he is going to try and rape you, or come at you with a knife, are you really going to care if you're going to harm his family jewels or not?"

Krista chuckled. "No, I don't think so."

"Exactly. And always remember one very important thing about kicking a man in the groin. It *must* be a *direct* hit if it's going to effective. Slightly to the left of his testicles, or to the right, or above or below will only result in angering him and leaving you with an even more dangerous attacker to contend with. Okay, Nolan, you can take five. Edwards, your turn."

At that moment, Paul and Dave arrived to see how the girls were making out. They had gone upstairs, where they could watch what was happening in the gym through the viewing windows and neither Krista nor Cathy had seen them. Which was unfortunate for Cathy.

Her first attempt at flooring Jay failed dismally. So did her second. When she was pinned on the mat by him for the third time in a row, she sat up breathlessly after she was released and looked at him in confusion and annoyance.

"What am I doing wrong?"

"Only a couple of things that I can see. You're taking the time to think about it first, therefore not giving yourself time to act first and you're breaking contact with my eyes. Keep your eyes on mine. Come on, try it one more time."

Paul felt really sorry for her, he knew she wanted to do well on her first day and he didn't think she would be too impressed with herself if she couldn't get this maneuver right. Dave had watched her disastrous attempts without so much as a flicker of emotion. If anything, he looked a bit bored.

They watched her assume her position once again and this time, to her credit and immense delight, she managed to get Jay exactly where she wanted him and repeated the act two more times in succession. Paul and Dave looked at each other and even Dave, who wasn't as bored as he appeared, nodded in approval.

For the next thirty minutes, Jay put the girls through a couple more self-defense stratagems. Paul couldn't help but be proud of the fact that Krista seemed to be doing very well and making few errors. Cathy, however, was not being so fortunate but Paul could see she was clearly determined not to let her mistakes get the better of her, picking herself right up off the mat immediately, ready to start all over again. He realized that, with more adrenalin flowing through her, she was doing better, and she was obviously willing to learn from her mistakes by correcting them or asking appropriate questions to make sure she wouldn't make the same mistake again.

When it seemed Jay Ackerman had finished with the girls on the completion of their first day, Paul and Dave went back downstairs and entered the gym. Ackerman had already left by the time they arrived, and Krista and Cathy were picking up their gym bags in preparation to go to the showers, but Krista saw them first and smiled in pleasure.

"Hello there," she greeted warmly. "Have you been waiting long?"

"We came about an hour ago." Paul pointed up at the windows set high in the wall. "We were watching from up there." He returned Krista's smile, thinking to himself how gorgeous she still looked, even with her face flushed with the proof of her physical exertion.

Cathy heard what he had just said, and she flushed too, only for her it was in deep embarrassment at what had been, to her anyway, a rather poor performance. "Oh my God, you were watching us *that long*?"

Paul turned to look at her in surprise, as did Dave. They each recognized her obvious chagrin and Dave tried, unsuccessfully, to conceal an amused and almost smug grin.

"Yes, we were watching," he said softly. "Why?"

Cathy looked down at her sneakers. A ringlet of her natural curls fell over her forehead and she absently brushed it back. She looked as if she was about to burst into tears and she shuffled her feet together as she fought to get her embarrassment under control. "Oh, nothing," she murmured, her eyes still downcast.

"Hey, don't worry about it," Dave said, truly meaning it but at the same time too taking an almost snide enjoyment out of her discomfort. It wasn't like him to be like that, it really wasn't, not unless it was with the bad guys who deserved it. "You still did quite well there…."

She looked up at him suspiciously. "But…?"

"Oh…considering…"

Now her suspicion was growing to impatience. "Considering *what*?"

If Dave wasn't mistaken, Cathy seemed to be challenging him and one thing he never backed down from was a challenge. Later, when he would have had the time to think over what was about to happen, he would realize he had probably been the only one responsible for it having happened at all, but by then, it would be too late, and he would already have made his mind up to carry through with his intended course of action.

While Paul and Krista innocently watched and listened to this little exchange, Dave held Cathy's eyes for a long, hard, decisive moment and then said, in something close to contempt, "Oh, you know, considering Ackerman towers over you by at least a foot and that in the end, he probably *let* you floor him so he could end his day."

At that, Cathy's heckles instantly arose. "What's that supposed to mean?"

Dave knew he had unwittingly hit a sore spot on her and he looked her slowly up and down in anything but an appraising way. "It means…tall you ain't, lady. And maybe you're wasting your time being here."

Outraged for Cathy's sake, Paul stepped forward. "Dave, really -"

Dave silenced him with a brief glance. *Keep out of this, Paul.*

Krista didn't say a word, she had seen the hurt leap into Cathy's eyes, linger there for a mere second and then disappear to be replaced by cold anger. Krista didn't *have* to say anything, she knew Cathy could and would seek her own retribution if that anger alone was anything to go by.

Cathy raised her chin up in a gesture of defiance, her eyes boring right into Dave's. She smiled almost sweetly. "Is that what you think?" She shrugged indifferently, seemingly as if she had accepted his words and was prepared to let the matter drop and then, suddenly, with no warning whatsoever, she grabbed his arm, twisted it out towards her, flipped him over and landed him neatly on his back on the mat. She stepped back quickly out of his reach and looked down at him in triumph. "Personally, I don't care *what* you think, Detective Andrews. But *I* think I did rather well there… considering you tower over me by at least a foot." With one last, filthy look in his prone direction, she turned away, retrieved her gym bag and flounced off towards the showers, leaving Paul and Krista staring after her in astonishment.

Dave got to his feet, momentarily too stunned to do or say anything. But the last bit of warmth had been snuffed from his eyes, telling Paul he was bordering on a temper outburst.

There was a long, awkward silence and Paul was the one who broke it. "Without meaning to take sides, Dave, don't try telling me you didn't deserve that."

Dave glared at him. "I *didn't* deserve that," he snapped. *Oh yes you did,* a little inner voice told him, a voice he pushed away with great haste. "I was only teasing her, for Christ's sake. Krista, what, exactly, did I say to warrant her acting like that?"

"Well, first you insinuated she's not very tall and, although I know you don't know it about her, she has a very deep insecurity about her height, the same way some people might have a hang-up about the size of their nose or the shape of their ears. Second, she's been trying hard all afternoon to learn these maneuvers and you brought it home to her how inadequate she was sometimes. You hurt her feelings. Deeply. And she retaliated by showing you she *could* look after herself, that she *can* toss a fully-grown man on his back."

Dave wasn't appeased one little bit and it was all he could do to stop his lips from curling into a contemptuous sneer. "Yeah, well, I think she went way overboard in demonstrating her capabilities."

Krista looked at him unhappily, then excused herself to go to the showers, leaving Paul and Dave together. Paul knew how to handle Dave, and, in truth, he was starting to see the funny side of it anyway, so Paul didn't try to refrain in his laughter.

"Shame on you, buddy boy," he teased, "letting a little, biddy female get the better of you like that. Take you by surprise, did she?"

"Shut up, Paul, I'm not amused."

"Aw, somebody's pride been hurt has it, along with his tushy?"

"I said, shut up." Dave wouldn't even look at Paul, but his jaws were clenched tightly together to stop himself from saying out loud, *yes, my pride has been hurt* and *my butt, seeing you brought it up.*

"Come on, Dave," Paul said soothingly, "lighten up. At least now you know she may be small but that size is no guarantee of strength. She executed that move to perfection, give her some credit."

"At least now I know she may be small but that she's nothing but a proper little vixen."

"How can you say something like that when you only met her yesterday?"

"After what she did to me, how much more proof do I need? If she ever tries something like that on me again, she's going to be sorry about it. *Very* sorry. Now, if you'll excuse me, seeing I'm here at the academy, I'm going to go and check out when I'm scheduled next for the rookie shooting tutoring. I'll see you at the car." Dave turned on his heel and walked abruptly away, Paul's peals of laughter still reaching his ears as far down as to the end of the corridor.

Any other time, Dave would have seen the funny side of it too, but just not his time. If it had been a man, for example, who had just tossed him on the mat, he would have been able to laugh it off in no time, but he wasn't exactly accustomed to letting a goddamned *female* get the better of him and the memory of what Cathy had just done to him was going to stick in his throat sideways for a long time to come.

Women, he decided for the hundredth time in his life, were

nothing but trouble.

When Cathy came out of the showers, she was seemingly quite calm again, but that might have had something to do with the fact that Dave was nowhere in sight. She apologized to Paul for maybe having upset him, she had already apologized to Krista and he, warmly, accepted her apology and convinced her that, really, she had done nothing to be sorry for.

As soon as they met up with Dave again at Paul's car, however, her eyes grew cold again and she certainly didn't seem like she was about to apologize to him. She wouldn't even look at him, or he at her and they ignored each other completely the whole drive to the Port Authority main building and after that on the way back to the hotel. She knew he was still angry with her, but she didn't exactly care, and he knew she didn't care, which only added fuel to their already raging fire.

Dave wanted Paul to just drop the girls off at the entrance but instead, Paul suggested they all go in for a drink and Dave could have choked him there and then. Dave's own car was still at the station, his apartment was on the other side of town, getting a taxi quickly during rush hour would have been a joke and there was no bus service near the hotel so, left with no choice, Dave shot Paul a withering look and followed them all inside.

The bar was quite crowded at this time of day, with business men and women coming in for a quick one to help unwind after a hectic day, or to seal a major deal or to steal a visit with their mistress/lover before heading home. There was only one table left that could sit four and Paul grabbed it quickly before someone else could.

He looked at Dave and Cathy ignoring each other, caught Krista's eye and jerked his head in the direction of the bar. "Come up with me, Krista, the waitress will take ages to get to us with this crowd here."

Krista look at Dave and Cathy ignoring each other too, understood Paul's intentions and dutifully followed him through the laughing, talking throng to the bar.

Dave and Cathy would have had to have been stupid not to realize what Paul and Krista were up to and Cathy, who never had been one to bear a grudge for any longer than was necessary, and also figuring she had damaged Dave's pride enough for one day, made the first effort to put things right for them.

"Look, Dave, if you think I over reacted in the gym there…then I'm sorry."

"It's okay," he said tersely, ignoring her extended olive branch.

"I don't usually act like that at all, unless I really believe the person on the receiving end of my temper deserves it. But that's still no excuse for me to have done what I did."

Dave picked up a beer coaster and started shredding it to pieces, wishing she would just shut up. "Look, I said it was okay. Forget it."

Cathy instantly bridled. She wasn't expecting him to draw her into his arms for an acceptance of her apology embrace but she wasn't expecting this cold, curt indifference either. "*I* can forget it all right, but something tells me you won't. I said I was sorry and I truly meant it too, either you accept my apology, or you don't, I really don't care."

Dave shot her a brief glance and saw that she really didn't care, that she had tried and failed to make the peace and therefore wasn't going to lose any sleep over it. Begrudgingly, he said, "In that case, I, er, I'm sorry I said something that obviously offended you. I'll try not to let it happen again."

"Thank you," she said crisply, "I would appreciate it."

They lapsed into a cold silence and, feeling increasingly uncomfortable, Dave inwardly sighed and began to remember his words to Paul that morning that he would try and be nice to the girls. He thought quickly of something to say and even managed to come up with a very good idea. "About your furniture and things arriving tomorrow… would you like for Paul and me to help you move into your place? I mean, I know that moving can be a real bummer and…well…if you want another couple of pairs of hands, just say."

Cathy looked at him in puzzlement, wondering why he was suddenly being so nice compared to the monster he had been only a moment before. "Aren't you supposed to be in work tomorrow?"

"In the morning, yes, something came up and we can't get out of it. But we can make ourselves available in the afternoon no problem. The Captain has released us from any cases until you and Krista are settled, and we want to help you feel at home as quickly as we possibly can."

"It's entirely up to yourself, then. Will Paul mind?"

"No way, Paul usually doesn't mind anything. Besides, he'll look upon it as another excuse to see Krista."

A genuine smile spread over Cathy's face, chasing the shadows from her eyes and easing the tension between them. "You noticed it too, huh?"

"What, that Paul can't take his eyes off her and is practically drooling all the time in her company? No, I never noticed it at all."

She nodded, the smile still playing at the corner of her mouth. "I just hope they're not going to do anything foolish, it's way too quick…

too soon… for them to be acting like this."

"It just sometimes happens that way, I guess."

With nothing to add to that, they lapsed into another silence and Dave drifted off into his own private world and, coupled with his brooding and the noise in the bar, he didn't hear Cathy say something to him until it was too late.

He looked up at her, startled. "What…?"

She jumped to her feet and glared down at him, her eyes glinting furiously. "How dare you ignore me like that! I said something to you *four times*, I even raised my voice, there was no way you couldn't have heard me. I have never met anyone as rude and as boorish as you are and tossing you on your backside wasn't enough for you earlier, I should have tossed you on your head as well, if only to knock some manners into you."

Paul and Krista returned from the bar just then and they looked in despair from Cathy to Dave. Paul set the drinks down and looked Dave right in the eye. "Okay, pal, what did you say this time?"

Dave was still smarting from Cathy's angry words and accusations, but he was also genuinely puzzled at her reaction to his innocent wool gathering. "I didn't say anything, I swear I didn't."

"Yeah and that's just your problem, isn't it?" Cathy sniped, "you *never* say anything. You just sit there in our company with what seems to be a permanent chip on your shoulder about something and your lips shut tight and refusing to enter into any kind of conversation unless it's with or about Paul. And then you ignore me completely. I have never met anyone as rude as you. You're not just rude, you're despicable and the less I see of you, the happier I will be."

Dave rose to his feet too. "No more happier than me, lady."

Cathy had paled, and she was trembling and when she retaliated to that, her voice had dipped dangerously low. "Then I think we each know where we stand with the other."

"I think we do."

"Then if you'll excuse me…" Cathy looked at Krista and Paul. "I'm going up to my room, or as far away as I can get from *him*. I'm sorry you had to witness this."

Paul looked helplessly at Dave and then at Cathy and he quickly caught her arm as she turned away. "Cathy, wait, please. Krista and I…we were going to suggest going somewhere for dinner."

"Dinner?" She shot Dave an evil glare, which he dutifully returned. "Is *he* going to be with us?"

"I really want him to be, yes."

"Then forget it. You three go on, I'll order room service and at least be able to enjoy my food without having to eat it while looking at *his* sour face." With that, she strode angrily away.

Krista stared after her, then gestured at Dave to sit down so that he wouldn't attract any more attention from the other patrons than he already had. She sat down beside him. "You seemed really bewildered as to why she would shout at you like that, Dave."

"I am," he agreed. "I drifted off, that's all, and I truly didn't hear her say anything to me. And then she just blew up before I had the chance to explain or apologize."

She looked unhappily at Paul, who seemed to be really believing Dave's words and she rose to her feet again. "I'd better go talk to her. Maybe all four of us will be able to go for dinner after all. I'll be back as soon as I can."

Once alone, Paul handed Dave his beer, which he took a hearty swig from. Paul sipped on his own beer, testing the tension level with Dave. "You know, pal, I'm sorry this had to happen between you and Cathy."

Dave snorted in disgust. "You're not the one who has to be sorry."

"Maybe, but I still am. Before this can get too serious, if Krista can talk Cathy into coming with us for dinner, I'd really like for you to come too. It would mean a lot to me."

"I have to eat sometime," Dave stated, which wasn't really an acceptance of Paul's terms. "But I'm particular who I eat with."

"Come on, Dave. You and Cathy have just got off on the wrong footing, tonight would be the perfect opportunity to start all over again."

Dave rounded up the pile of coaster shreddings with his little finger, avoided Paul's hopeful eyes a few more seconds and then gave up with a weary sigh. "Okay, I'll go. And regardless of whether that bitch…I mean *Cathy* goes or not, I'll still go."

It still wasn't quite what Paul wanted to hear but he knew Dave well enough to know that this was as close as he would get to calling a truce. "Great, thanks, partner," he said warmly.

Fifteen minutes later, Krista came back down, with Cathy in tow. They were each casually dressed in jeans and sweaters, but Cathy had applied a light touch of make-up, signifying that she wouldn't be eating dinner from room service all alone in her room.

Paul beamed a smile at her and, although she didn't acknowledge Dave in any way, shape or form, at least she seemed relaxed enough and quite eager not to let her personality clash with him interfere in her having a good time.

They went to a steakhouse not far from the pub Paul had taken Krista to the evening before. It was a new place, but Paul and Dave had eaten there before, and they had each enjoyed the food, despite the rather natty western theme that was the restaurant's taste in décor.

During dinner, something interesting happened, for Dave anyway. He found he truly liked Krista. She was so down to earth it was hard not to like her, and she seemed every bit as sweet as Paul had said she was. Her sense of humor seemed to be almost as wicked as Paul's too, another added incentive to like her and, despite her dry wit and her tongue in cheek humor, Dave knew instinctively she could be very sincere and he managed, although hesitantly, to put aside any feelings of animosity he had intended to have towards her.

But Cathy was a different matter entirely. She didn't try to speak to him again and continued with the cold shoulder treatment all evening. Every time he said white on a subject, she said black, if he deemed to talk to her at all he was always met with a cold, disinterested stare first and then a monosyllabic answer a few seconds later.

It was obvious to anyone but themselves that they were each as stubborn as the other and each seemed to be going deliberately out of their way to provoke the other, either by snide remarks or cold silences and neither of them seemed to care that this wasn't a good start to any kind of relationship.

Dave decided she was nothing but a troublemaker, someone who possessed a barbed tongue, who was two-faced, who didn't know what it was like to have a sense of humor never mind know how to crack a smile now and again. Cathy decided he was nothing but an arrogant, belligerent, ill-tempered specimen of the human race and she couldn't wait for the evening to end just so she could get away from him.

When Cathy came off with one particularly scathing remark aimed in his direction Dave came to the very swift conclusion he actually hated her. It should have been unusual to come to such a conclusion after only knowing her such a short period of time, but he had made it willingly and with a clear conscience.

Krista he had warmed to, yes, and yes, he could even let her be his friend and he hers, but Cathy could drop off the face of the planet or drop dead any time and he wouldn't mourn her loss one bit.

And once Dave felt that way about somebody, it was impossible to get him to change his mind.

Upon arrival back at the hotel, Dave accepted Krista's good night hug. So, naturally, did Paul. Cathy thanked Paul for the lovely evening and went inside without a word or a look in Dave's direction. It seemed she had come to the same conclusion about him as he had about her.

"Thank you again," Krista said, "for taking us out and treating us to dinner. We'll return the favor sometime soon. See you tomorrow, okay?" With one last, lingering look in Paul's direction, she headed inside to catch up with Cathy.

Paul, who was still remembering the feel of her body against his when she had hugged him, reluctantly snapped himself back to attention. "Well, that was certainly an entertaining little night we had tonight," he said dryly to Dave. "Dinner and a show, with you and Cathy as the star attraction."

Dave shrugged his indifference. "So what?"

"So what? I've never seen you deliberately go out of your way to be downright mean to somebody and that's exactly what you did tonight with Cathy."

"I think she deserved it and I can't exactly help it if she brings out the worst in me, can I?"

"Now you're just being unreasonable. Even though she managed to give as good as she got tonight – and I'm even glad she did – there were a couple of times after you had said something to her that I noticed real hurt in her eyes."

"Paul, she's a tough cookie, she must be able to take what's coming to her because she's sure as hell good at dishing it out. Come on, let's go, it's getting late and I just want to hit the sack."

"Dave, please -"

"Are you going to take me for my car or do I have to find myself a cab?"

Recognizing the subject was firmly closed, Paul inwardly sighed. "No, I'll take you to the station." He knew when not to push it and the drive to the precinct was passed in relative silence.

But as Paul headed towards his own apartment, unaware of the conclusion Dave had made regarding Cathy, he vowed that he would do everything in his power to set Dave straight and stop him and Cathy from turning into bitter enemies.

CHAPTER TWELVE

Cathy and Krista were extremely pleased with what their new home had to offer when they saw the inside of it for the first time early the next morning. The landlord, Mr. DeFazio, was a kindly man in his late fifties and was only too pleased to show them their two-story apartment before they signed the lease. Their concern had been that they had relied on Captain Hamilton's judgment and taste and despite their specifications they had given him prior to landing in the States, they didn't know what his taste and judgment were like, but they quickly saw their concerns had been unfounded.

In truth, they had been expecting something small, but it was quite large with a spacious, airy living room that would catch the afternoon sun, two equally good-sized bedrooms, a huge kitchen with a separate dining area and two bathrooms that had a full-sized bath as well as a walk-in shower. There was plenty of closet space, the décor was done in muted tones of blue, gray and cream, the carpeting throughout had been freshly steam cleaned, the paintwork spruced up, the tiles in the bathrooms scrubbed of mildew and, what made it even more appealing was the cost of the rent, which was easily within their budget.

Their furniture and thirty boxes of clothes and other household items amazingly arrived at the promised time of 8:30 and the girls worked flat out to get as much set in place and washed and put away in appropriate cupboards and closets as they could. It was a minor miracle in itself that so far, of the boxes they had opened and emptied, nothing had been broken or even cracked, which made checking off the items against their insurance form very easy.

When Paul and Dave arrived just after lunchtime, they were

surprised to see how much the girls had got done by themselves. Boxes and wrapping paper and general mess aside, the living room was already taking shape, as were the two bedrooms so Paul and Dave helped where they could by hanging pictures, washing china and dishes, setting up the beds and placing the heavier items of furniture, like the bedroom dressers, exactly where the girls wanted them. By dinnertime, almost everything was in its place and as it should be.

Dave and Cathy, although having hardly spoken much to each other, had at least managed to be cordial to one another that day, which pleased Paul and Krista immensely. In fact, Dave had been privately impressed that Cathy had worked so diligently without any breaks all day and in seemingly good humor too and, knowing she must be totally exhausted, he made the effort to be nice to her and even congratulated her on her hard work.

"Thank you," she accepted in surprise, "but we couldn't have gotten even half the things done if it hadn't been for you and Paul."

"We were glad to help." It was just the two of them at the moment, Paul and Krista had gone out to get some pizza to bring it back for dinner. Feeling awkward, Dave looked slowly around the living room, looking for a CD player or MP3 player or even just a radio he could put on to provide some background noise to alleviate the silence he knew was going to happen between them. He couldn't see any such thing, nor any other electrical item for that matter, no television, DVR, no lamps, nothing. Which meant he had to make small talk with a woman he detested.

"You've got a lot of nice stuff here," he commented.

"Most of the things are Krista's but a few of them are mine. We lived together back home, in her parent's house and when they died, everything automatically became hers."

"Paul told me about her parents. Were you close to them?"

"Very, they took me under their wing…after…well, just after." She deliberately left the sentence hanging and for a moment, Dave saw real pain in her eyes. Then it was gone, and she gestured around the room. "Anyway, most of the things belong to Krista but she insists that they're as much mine as they are hers."

Dave couldn't help but wonder why she had stopped dead like that, but he didn't particularly care enough to ask her to divulge further. His eyes rested on a picture hanging on a wall, one that Paul must have hung, and he went over to it for a better look. "Where's this of?"

"It's called Cavehill, one of Belfast's many landmarks. It towers over the north of the city."

"It looks nice." And it did, all dark green and brooding and rugged, the artist had captured it well. "Is Belfast very big?"

"I have no idea how big it is in terms of area, but I think it's bigger than Bathville. In terms of population, there's about half a million people."

"Half a million? That's a lot, I didn't think Ireland had that many people, never mind that amount living in the one city."

"Belfast is in *Northern* Ireland," she quickly corrected him, but at least she didn't snap at him. "When people say 'Ireland' they're usually referring to the South and I'm under the impression from the few people we've talked to here that they don't realize the North and South are two entirely different countries, the same way, say, North and South Korea are."

Dave recognized that she was only trying to be informative and he nodded. "I see. Well, I will try and remember that for the future." He turned away and looked at a few of the other pictures and ornaments. Everything seemed expensive and well taken care of, but there was also a sense of warmth about the room, it was somewhere he felt he could come into, kick off his shoes, flop down on the sofa and relax in.

"Er, would you like a cup of coffee?" she offered, interrupting his thoughts.

"No thanks, a soda would be fine."

"Oh, I'm sorry, I haven't got anything to drink except coffee, water or milk, we haven't had the time to do much shopping yet." She suddenly slapped her hand to her forehead in vague embarrassment. "In fact, I can't even make you coffee yet, we still have to buy a teakettle. We have to buy everything electrical too, in case you hadn't noticed, lamps, iron, you name it and I'm just glad these units come equipped with a fridge and stove and that there's a separate laundry room so that we won't have to buy any of those big things."

He smiled faintly. "It doesn't matter, I'll do without until Paul and Krista get back, they should be bringing a couple of bottles of Pepsi or something with them." At the mention of Paul and Krista, he glanced underhandedly at his watch and wondered what could be keeping them. They seemed to have been gone for ages and he was anxious for them to get back, so he wouldn't have to pass the time with Cathy for much longer. He sat down on the edge of the sofa, the silence spinning out between them and he literally had to struggle to come up with something to say. When he did speak, the question sounded pointless, even to his own ears. "So, how do you like it all so far?"

"Living in Bathville? I don't know, it's a bit too soon to tell. Ask me that a year from now."

He found himself listening intently to how she pronounced each word. Her speech sounded weird to his ears, but he had to admit he liked her accent, it was a novelty to listen to. Her voice held a very slight lilt to it that he found charming and sometimes it was flat and broad, but not monotonous. If only her personality could be as nice as her method of talking, he mused…

He glanced at his watch again. "Paul must be bending somebody's ear somewhere," he said.

"Talk a lot, does he?"

"Never shuts up."

"Then he and Krista are well suited because she never shuts up either. Does Paul have a girlfriend?"

"No, he and his last girlfriend had a parting of the ways a couple of weeks ago. It wasn't very serious anyway."

"I see. Do you have one?"

"What do you want to know for?" Surprise at her question made his tone sound a bit harsh but he wasn't about to apologize for it.

"I'm just curious. Sorry."

"For your information, then, I'm between women myself." Which was, of course, something of an understatement, not that she would ever know that as far as he was concerned.

"Okay, keep your shirt on, I was only asking. No need to bite my nose off."

"I didn't mean to, I…" He stopped and shrugged nonchalantly. "I just don't like being asked questions about my personal life."

Cathy looked at him long and hard, the blue of her eyes seemingly having been dipped in ice. "I'll certainly bear that in mind for the future," she told him crisply and went into the kitchen just so she could get away from him.

She was still there when Paul and Krista returned five minutes later, and they couldn't fail to sense the hostile atmosphere as soon as they walked through the door. "I'll handle this," he said and passed her the two boxes of hot, tantalizingly aromatic pizza. "Bring these through in a couple of minutes." He strode into the living room and flopped down on the sofa beside Dave. "Nice place, don't you think?"

"Not bad. What took you so long?"

"Long line up at the pizza place, should have phoned the order through. Cathy in the kitchen is she?"

"How the hell should I know where she is? Where's the food? I'm starved."

"Krista's taking care of it. I take it you and Cathy had words again?"

"So what if we did? Seems to be pretty much par for the course."

"But it doesn't have to be that way. She seems really nice and I hate that things could get very serious between the two of you when really there's no need. Why can't you at least *try* to get along?"

Dave looked as if he wasn't going to reply but then he saw the genuine distress in Paul's eyes, so he decided to tell him the truth as he saw it. "I just don't like her, Paul, okay? It's all so difficult with her, she seems to take great delight in deliberately trying to rub me up the wrong way. And, naturally, I have to retaliate."

"But you seem to instigate it most of the time and really, I think even for you you're going way overboard."

Dave instantly bristled. "Why do I get the feeling you're taking the side of a complete stranger? Thanks for the loyalty, *pal*."

Paul rolled his eyes in exasperation. "Come on, Dave, I'm not taking anybody's side. All I want is for us all to get along, to be friends, where's the harm in that? There's enough fighting going on in the world without you and Cathy adding to it."

"Oh, stop with the Peter Pan outlook on life. I don't like her, and she doesn't like me and that's all there is to know."

"Just because you don't like one another doesn't give either of you the right to be nasty to each other."

"Okay, put like that, I've just come up with the perfect solution. She stops talking to me, I'll stop talking to her, ergo no more fighting, no more picking on each other. Sound good?"

Paul groaned. "No, it sounds like a crock."

"Too bad, that's the plan, like it or lump it, I personally don't give a shit."

"No, you never do. Come on, bro, try and end this for my sake, it would mean a lot to me. And to Krista too, I'm sure of it."

"Just go see what's keeping the pizza."

Paul gave up and went back into the kitchen. Krista, who hadn't been able to get much of an explanation out of Cathy, looked at him expectantly but he could only shrug in derision in way of an answer. "How's it going in here?" he asked as cheerfully as possible. "Everything nearly ready?"

"Seems to be," Cathy said vaguely, without even looking at the tray Krista was setting with napkins, glasses and plates. "Paul, I counted the money I have in my wallet there and I have $223. Is that enough to get some groceries in and also buy a teakettle?"

"More than enough, sweetie."

"Good. How far away's the nearest supermarket?"

"A couple of blocks, not far. If you go out to the street, turn right and you'll almost be able to see it."

"Okay." She turned to Krista. "I'm going to get the groceries in, seeing our cupboards are bare. I'll see you later."

Krista looked at her in surprise. "But what about your pizza?"

"Save me a slice, I'll heat it up in the oven when I get back." Cathy was already putting on her jacket, obviously anxious to leave as quickly as possible. She also had a determined look on her face, which meant no one could dissuade her from her intended course of action.

"You don't need to go right now," Krista said, hoping to dissuade her anyway. "Why don't you wait a while and we can go together later?"

"Because I just want to go now. I want to get some fresh air seeing I've been cooped up in here all day, so the walk will do me good. I can get a taxi back if I over buy and can't carry everything myself."

"No need to get a taxi," Paul said, "call me when you're through and I'll come and pick you up."

"I can't, I don't have a mobile phone yet and I don't know your number either. See you." With that, Cathy grabbed her bag and banged the front door shut on her way out.

Paul and Krista looked unhappily at each other and she emitted a soft, rueful sigh. "Cathy hates to go shopping, you know, for anything but particularly groceries. Seems to me she just wanted to get out of the house and was using the groceries as an excuse."

"She didn't want to get out of the house, she wanted to get away from Dave. Why do you think they can't get along?"

"I really don't know. But let's not worry about it too much for now. I think it's just because they don't know each other yet but I'm sure they'll start hitting it off eventually."

"In the way you and I have been hitting it off?" he teased lightly.

"Yes, if you like." As soon as she said that, she blushed deeply and quickly busied herself by finishing preparing the tray. "Do you want to grab the pizza and carry it through for me?" And with that, she bade a hasty retreat to the living room.

As they sat and ate their pizza, the conversation was light-hearted and jocular, even from Dave's direction. Krista found herself wondering over and over why Cathy couldn't warm to him at all because he really did seem like a really nice, enjoyable man. He was a good one for keeping the conversation going, he kept up a witty repartee with Paul that had her in stitches and when Dave tipped her a broad wink after getting a very obvious dig in at Paul about his love for women of all shapes and sizes, she could only hope that she had found another new friend, one who was as worthwhile having as Paul was already shaping up to be.

She only wished that Cathy could have been there too to join in with the camaraderie and to see this more relaxed side of Dave, but he didn't even mention that Cathy was absent.

Nor did it particularly seem to bother him that she was.

CHAPTER THIRTEEN

A week after Gloria Ho started to show signs she was coming out of her coma, she opened her eyes for the first time, looked all around her and asked a startled but nonetheless attentive nurse if she could have a glass of water. Of course, her words came out very slurred and raspy, but she was perfectly understandable and, moments after the nurse disappeared, she came back not with water but with a kindly looking young doctor who smiled directly into Gloria's eyes.

"Hey there, young lady," Dr. Samuel Warren crooned, gently taking her pulse at her wrist. "You've been under for quite a while, giving us all a scare. Welcome back."

Gloria blinked her heavy lids and felt in danger of drifting back to sleep again. It seemed to be the easiest thing in the world to do, just close her eyes and drift slowly off to a serene place called Slumberland was all it really required, but her mind was seeking information more urgently than her need for sleep and, after her pulse had been recorded, her blood pressure taken, and her monitors checked, she struggled to push aside the dreamy, ghostly mist that threatened to pull her under again and tried to remain as alert as possible.

"Doctor…?" she asked croakily and instantly winced at the harsh dryness of her throat. Swallowing felt like her throat was coated with barbed wire that had just been dipped in acid and then set alight.

"Ssh, Gloria," he advised, "don't attempt to talk just yet, just let yourself find your bearings first. Do you know where you are?"

Gloria nodded dutifully, then frowned. She knew she was in a hospital, she just didn't know which one. She assumed it was Bathville General. It could even have been Bathville County, but she really didn't think so. Despite her low income and lack of insurance, Bathville General was closer to her home and would have been the most sensible one to come to if she'd been in an accident. "B-Bathville… hosp…pital…"

"That's right. In a little while, we're going to be running some tests on you, in the meantime, I'm going to leave word at the switchboard that if that friend of yours calls again today, that he's to be put through to me immediately. At least he'll hear some good news this time, I gather he's been very worried about you."

Despite her grogginess and her overall weakened state, despite the feeling that she was sinking slowly into a great big hole padded with cotton wool, the doctor's words somehow hit through to her and she opened her eyes wide in alarm. She had no immediate family and the only two friends in the whole world she had were both female, she absolutely did not have any male friends at all. And suddenly, she knew who the doctor was talking about, it was *him*, wanting to get her, wanting to finish what he had started, wanting to end her life so she would take a secret to the grave with her. She recalled standing in front of her apartment, searching for her keys and just when she inserted the key in the lock and pushed the door open, *he* had been there, right beside her before she even stepped over the threshold into relative safety and then he had slapped her and beat her and kicked her and then…Oh God, she had been raped, by *him*…by…Troy…yes, that was his name, Troy, who had raped her and beaten her to within an inch of her life and had surely left her for dead, only somehow he had found out she wasn't dead, that she was very much still alive, still capable of disclosing the secret that remained elusively hidden from her memory but which she knew instinctively was bad. Perhaps very bad.

And now he was posing as her *friend* so he could keep track of her progress and then come back to finish the job and it was awful, it was terrible, he was going to come back and kill her, for sure this time, and in her growing distress, Gloria started to whimper and she would have screamed if she hadn't been so weak and her throat hadn't been so sandpapery dry and in her agitation, her heart beat accelerated and Dr. Warren had to inject her with a sedative to calm her.

It took a while for the sedative to take hold and for her whimpers to trail off and just as she was about to fall into Slumberland after all, a Slumberland that was no longer white and airy and serene, but which was now filled with menacing shadows and sharp corners around which any hidden danger could be lurking, she murmured a few words that Dr. Warren just about managed to hear, although they didn't make sense. "Petcelli," she whispered, "…. him… Petcelli, but *not* Petcelli." And then, at last, she succumbed to the effects of the sedative.

Samuel, who was just coming off rounds anyway, stayed with Gloria until he was sure she was deeply under. He supposed she had begun reliving the events that had brought her to the hospital in the first place, which wasn't unusual, but he knew, almost intuitively, it had something to do with that mystery friend that kept calling. He made the decision that he would definitely wait for the next call from this person, whoever he was, tell him that Gloria was becoming more and more alert but that she couldn't receive visitors yet and probably wouldn't be able to for a while. By the time it was deemed suitable for her to have visitors, she would already have been shipped over to Bathville County by which stage, Samuel would have been able to run some sort of background check on the friend, with the aid of several contacts he had in the police department. He might even be able to get a police officer outside Gloria's room, particularly if the background check revealed the friend had some sort of record.

Gloria Ho had been brought in under criminal circumstances, after all, she had been badly beaten, not to mention raped and it was only because of her coma and the lack of clues when her body had been found that the police had put her case on hold until such a time when she started to become coherent and advised the police she even wanted to press charges on whoever had done this to her.

Samuel, following his gut instinct, was feeling very apprehensive about this faceless, nameless friend, but he had put too much time and energy into saving his patient and he wasn't about to let anything happen to her now.

Later that evening, Troy called the hospital and was immediately transferred to Samuel's line. Samuel was in his office, dictating patients' notes that his secretary would transfer into the Electronic Medical Records the next day. He was exhausted and when the phone rang, he welcomed the interruption from his most hated task.

"Dr. Warren," he announced.

Taken aback, Troy quickly composed himself. This was the first time he had got to speak directly to the doctor. "Yes, Dr. Warren, I'm calling about Gloria Ho? I'm checking on her progress?"

"Yes, Gloria Ho. And who am I speaking to?"

"A friend."

"And your name?"

Silence, for a long moment and then, "I need to know how she's doing, I've been very…um…worried about her."

"I'm sure you have, if you're a friend. I didn't catch your name."

"Oh… sorry… it's…Danny, Danny Smith."

Samuel raised an inquisitive eyebrow. Somehow, he knew, just *knew* that wasn't the guy's real name but he didn't want to appear suspicious so he continued to act normally. "Well, Mr. Smith, as I'm sure you've been told each time you've called that we really shouldn't be giving out a patient's information to someone who isn't a family member, I know that you are genuinely concerned and since no one else has called about her, I can tell you this time that Gloria has definitely started pulling out of her coma."

Troy's heart skipped a beat. "Really?" Remembering he was posing as a "friend", he made himself sound relieved. "Oh, that's wonderful, just great. She…er…she had me so worried. When can I come see her?"

"Unfortunately, not for some time, Mr. Smith. Gloria is to be kept as quiet as possible, the only people allowed at her bedside are myself and other medical staff. We have a lot of tests to run, most of which are exhaustive, and we can't excite her too quickly, it will…er… it might send her back into a coma again."

"I see. I'll call back. Thank you."

And with that, the call was disconnected. Samuel replaced his receiver and looked thoughtfully at the phone. He scribbled the name Danny Smith on a scrap piece of paper, along with the time and date of the call, and, as an afterthought, he recalled the few words Gloria had said just prior to her slipping into her sedated sleep so he wrote them down too with the intentions of taking the information to one of his buddies in the police department. With an uneasy but weary sigh, he finished dictating his notes and half an hour later, left the hospital to go and get some much-earned sleep.

Less than an hour after Samuel's exit, Troy was at the hospital, carefully keeping watch outside Gloria's room. Her room was right across the corridor and, after careful observation, he discovered that she didn't have a guard posted outside her door, that a nurse went in every twenty minutes or so to check on her and in between those times, Gloria was left quite alone.

Looking all around him, Troy saw a door marked LINEN SUPPLIES. He went over to it and, after making sure no one was watching what he was doing, he opened the door (half expecting it be locked, but it wasn't) and sneaked inside.

The room was quite small, but the space had been well utilized. Three rows of shelves, each several stacks high, were laden with towels, patient gowns, bathrobes, and sheets. On a separate rack on the other side of the room and towards the back were green scrubs pants and tops. There were also boxes of paper masks, green surgical caps and sterile rubber gloves and, at seeing those latter items, a plan formed swiftly in Troy's mind.

Within three minutes, he was dressed in a green scrubs top and matching pants, a green cap and had a mask hanging around his throat, ready to pull up over the lower half of his face if anyone should be coming his way. He wasn't sure if doctors really did walk around hospitals dressed like this, but according to any medical show he'd ever watched, they did, so Troy hoped he wouldn't appear too conspicuous. In fact, Troy hoped he would blend right in, that no one would think it unusual for a young doctor to be checking in on a patient while he was dressed like this.

He stored his own clothes under a pile of freshly laundered towels, edged the door open a crack so he could peek outside to see if the coast was clear or not and when he saw it was, he left the supply room and sauntered assuredly, although hurriedly, to Gloria's room, his head bowed slightly so that no one would be able to see his eyes.

It took less time to kill her than he could ever have thought possible. She had been sleeping, still under the effects of the sedative, but she had seemed to sense his presence and her eyes shot open just in time to see him bringing the pillow down on top of her face. She had struggled, she had struggled extremely well and strongly for a girl who had lay in a coma for about two months, but in the end, her struggles had become less severe, her muffled cries for help less urgent.

She died with the pillow over her face and, as soon as her heart monitor emitted a single high-pitched tone when her cardiac rhythm stopped and she flat-lined, Troy threw the pillow to one side and bade a hasty retreat back to the supplies room and when he emerged in his own clothes again, minutes later, a team of doctors and nurses were too busy trying to bring back to life an ever more dead patient to even notice him.

Mr. Petcelli was going to be *very* pleased about this, Troy mused. And he, Troy, was going to be better off by a nice healthy $10,000 bonus. Life was good.

But Gloria's death was proved not to have been an accident and it was a disbelieving and very distraught Samuel Warren who contacted the police and told them about the mysterious friend with the name of Danny Smith, which was more than likely a bogus name. Samuel was put through to the Detective Division in the 7th precinct.

Which was how Paul and Dave initially became involved with the murder of an ex-exotic dancer.

CHAPTER FOURTEEN

Paul and Krista continued on an upward trend with one another and Dave and Cathy continued in a steady decline. It seemed to be the way things were going to be and, as far as Paul and Krista were concerned anyway, it was really quite entertaining to watch them together. They simply did not realize how like one another they really were.

Paul seemed to come up with a lot of excuses just to see Krista and be able to spend even five minutes in her company. Anytime Dave wanted him for anything, more often than not he would find him at the girls' place. Dave knew his friend wanted to pursue his relationship with Krista as far as possible and Dave was surprised Paul was taking it slowly and was being overly cautious, something he usually wasn't.

But even Dave had to admit that Paul and Krista seemed to be a perfect match and if romance was ever going to blossom between them – which really did seem inevitable – then he, as Paul's friend, could only be pleased for them.

However, from Paul and Krista's point of view, although they each wanted to jump right in, neither of them were particularly over anxious to make the first real romantic intention clear to the other. If ever they would be asked to explain their reasons for dragging their heels, they would only be able to reply that they each wanted to be one hundred per cent sure they would be doing the right thing and at the moment, they were just content enough to enjoy the anticipation.

They were already fast friends that only, luckily for them, served to add extra sizzle to their expectations. Paul knew all there was to know about Krista, how vastly intelligent she really was, how she could speak French like a Parisian and also German, Spanish and Italian fluently and how she was so easy going, she didn't even seem to know what it was like to lose her temper. She knew all about him too, how he, like Dave, knew everything there was to know about martial arts and self-defense, how much he was respected as a detective, how street smart he really was and also how kind he could be.

The two of them could talk for hours about any topic under the sun, usually sharing the same opinions too as they lost themselves in the glory of each other's company, excluding themselves from the rest of the world when all they were really doing was portraying to that world that they were a couple in everything but name only.

More and more frequently now, when Paul left Krista's company, he would have to go home and take a cold shower. He was more than just sexually attracted to her, he was physically drawn to her, she was like a sexual drug that had gotten in deep under his skin and had spread her heat through his veins until it almost became blissfully, beautifully unbearable for him. Sometimes, the cold shower wasn't enough to quench his ardor and he often went to bed sexually frustrated, only to fall asleep and dream about her. It was heaven and it was agony and he wouldn't have changed it for the world.

One of the things he loved about Krista was her enthusiasm for life. She was getting through the course at the academy extremely well and Captain Hamilton, who was keeping close tabs on the girls' accelerated journey through the academy, was extremely pleased with their progress. The Captain wasn't the sort of person who breathed down anyone's neck all the time but, since he had a lot invested in Cathy and Krista, he insisted on a report every day to see for himself how they were making out. When each report told him they were passing every test with flying colors, that was all he needed to know. He knew without any question of a doubt he had done the right thing in letting them come over to the United States to work for him and he also knew that they would be graduating from the academy at the time he had tentatively marked in for them, within a maximum of four weeks. He was even willing to bet money on the fact they could be graduating within three weeks, so confident was he.

Cathy and Krista enjoyed immensely their training, although it was hectic and time consuming for them. But it was well worth the long days and the hard work as they learned everything from every aspect of police work, like community relations, how to go through the proper channels to obtain a warrant to either arrest somebody or search their premises, how to drive a car at top speed in a potential car chase, how to deal with the guilt if they should ever have to shoot somebody, fire arms control and learning the use of, even street names for drugs and weapons, the ladies just loved learning as much as they could.

They passed their driving tests on the first attempt too, were issued with Massachusetts driving licenses and, as April progressed in a flurry of cold rain showers, warmer days, budding trees and the green returning to the snow-deadened grass, at last they were able to get their own cars.

Dave, who would probably have been a car mechanic if he hadn't become a cop, definitely qualified for knowing a thing or two about used cars and he graciously took the ladies around all the car dealers in Bathville. After careful deliberation of the vehicles, some with strange names they had never heard of before, Cathy opted for, a spotlessly clean, dark blue, six speed, Bluetooth equipped, air conditioned, four door, two-year-old Dodge Dart Aero that had space on the console to mount a police radio and mike. Krista, after equal deliberation and after receiving Dave's second seal of approval, chose an immaculate cayenne red, six speed, air-conditioned, two-year-old Nissan Sentra, also with Bluetooth.

It felt good to get their own wheels again and, naturally, the first passenger Krista had in her new vehicle was Paul, who quickly learned she wasn't stereotypical of women drivers and had therefore passed his ruthless inspection to be able to drive his beloved car.

Paul and Dave had known the ladies for exactly twenty-one days when they became fully-fledged detectives for the Bathville Police Department. The girls touched their badges proudly when they received them, pleased and more than a little awed that they had done well and come this far already.

Even Dave was genuinely pleased for them, he knew how hard they had worked to get what they so badly wanted and, to show them just how happy for them he really was, he suggested they all go out for a celebration dinner that night. What made the offer sweeter was, despite the still distinct wariness between him and Cathy, he had still made it willingly and good-naturedly.

Paul and Krista readily agreed to go but Cathy hesitated a bit at first before saying yes or no, mainly because it had been Dave's idea. Then she realized how genuine the offer had been and she decided to accept it in the well-intended way it had been extended, figuring it was time she let her hair down a bit anyway.

They went to the House of Ming, one of Bathville's finest Chinese restaurants and they enjoyed an absolutely superb dinner, which was made all the more enjoyable by the fact that Dave and Cathy seemed to have silently declared a truce for the evening. They didn't argue or bicker once, the whole evening up to a certain point was totally relaxed and, as a result, everyone had a good time.

The restaurant boasted a nightclub on the upper floor and, after their meal, they decided on a count of four to none, to check it out.

It was a Saturday night and the club was filling up nicely so at least that proved it was a popular spot. They found a table in the far corner from the exit that was near the bar and away from the loud speakers of the music equipment.

After ordering drinks, Cathy and Krista arose to go to the ladies' room to freshen up a bit and as they walked across the still deserted dance floor, Paul just simply couldn't take his eyes away from Krista. She was wearing a short, black dress tonight, one that dipped low in the back (to show, his throbbing sex drive insisted, she wasn't wearing a bra) and which also hugged her figure tightly, showing it off to perfection. Her black high heels enhanced the sway of her hips as she walked and Paul all but drooled as he watched her walk away.

"Wow!" he exclaimed in unashamed delight to Dave. "She's driving me absolutely crazy and she doesn't even know it."

Dave rolled his eyes in practiced patience. "So why don't you just hurry up and do something about it, Paul? Like, you know, take her in your arms and kiss her to death or something."

"No, I can't, I…I'm afraid to, in case…well, in case it scares her off… or something like that."

"Why? Are your kisses *that* bad?"

"Get bent, you know what I mean."

Dave watched Krista disappear into the ladies' room, then he turned back to Paul, his eyes solemn. "I somehow don't think anything you do would scare her off, pal."

"Really?"

"Really."

"But do you think she even likes me?"

"She seems to like everybody." Catching the uncustomary crestfallen expression that swept over Paul's features at that innocent – and yes, thoughtless and careless – remark, Dave quickly added, "But hey, I've seen her checking out your buns on more than one occasion. And always when she thought no one was watching. Also, I've seen that dreamy, goo-goo way she looks at you from across the room, so I really think you have nothing to worry about. She *is* mighty cute, though, someone else might snap her up while you're still dragging your heels and then you'll have lost out completely."

"That's just it, Dave, she *is* cute…no, she's gorgeous, in fact, she's easily the most beautiful woman I've ever seen. But I'm not just attracted to her face or that incredible body of hers, I'm attracted to everything else about her. And she's driving me *nuts!* When was the last time you saw me act like this over a female?

"Oh…about… never, I guess."

"Exactly."

"So, are we talking the L word here? You know, love, as opposed to mere infatuation?"

"I don't know." Paul shook his head in bewilderment, wishing he could explain to Dave how he really felt but the truth of the matter was, he couldn't even explain it to himself yet. "I'll give it a few more days," he decided, "and if she hasn't made the first move by then, I will. For sure…maybe…I hope… unless I know for sure it's not going to scare her off."

Dave smiled sympathetically. He had never seen Paul be so insecure about a woman before, which could only mean he must have very strong feelings for her. Already. But then, Dave reminded himself, wasn't that the way it sometimes happened? Hadn't he fallen for Terri, his ex-wife, in a matter of days too? "It won't, Paul, trust me."

"And since when did you become the authority on women, bro?" But Paul was only teasing, and the two friends shared a warm smile.

"Speaking of authority, aren't you glad I picked the House of Ming for somewhere to go tonight? That sure was a fine meal."

"It was excellent. And what made it even better was that you and Cathy got through it without one single cross word to one another. Congratulations. See how easy it can be when you set your mind to it?"

"She just seemed a lot friendlier tonight, a lot easier to get along with, that's all."

"So, if you can see that she's not the big bad ogress you're making her out to be all the time, could that mean you might even start liking her a teensy bit?"

"Over the last week or so, I've realized that maybe I was a bit too rash to say I couldn't stand her. Not that I'm saying I want to become bosom buddies with her, I don't, but after seeing how well she did at the academy in such a short space of time, I think we can now at least have a working relationship with one another."

"Well, at least that's a start." Paul paid for the drinks that arrived then and he took a sip of his beer to wet the back of his throat. Then, because it was just a one on one with Dave at the moment, Paul decided to put him on the spot. "Cathy looks awfully pretty tonight, did you notice?"

"Paul, I'm a detective, it's my job to notice all kinds of things." Which wasn't a yes or a no to Paul's question, but Dave didn't want him to know that yes, he *had* noticed how pretty she looked tonight and he had noticed a lot of the men in the club noticing it too when she had walked across the dance floor. She was wearing a dress in similar style to Krista's, only hers was a rich shade of royal blue that enhanced the color of her eyes beautifully. "I noticed also that she has got very stunning eyes," he continued slowly, hardly even aware he was saying it. "How blue they are and how very expressive."

"A-ha!" Paul pounced on him immediately. "Contrary to popular opinion, you're *not* dead from the brain down after all."

Realizing what he had just said out loud, Dave shifted uncomfortably. "What do you mean?"

"As I recall, you always did like a chick with stunning eyes and long lashes. It's always the first thing you notice about her."

"So what if I like a woman with nice eyes? It doesn't mean I'm attracted to her, I'm only giving a compliment where it's due, that's all." Dave took a sip of his own beer, his gaze leveled coolly at Paul. "Don't think I don't know what you're up to, partner."

"Pardon?" Paul said innocently. "I don't know what you're talking about."

"Oh, I think you do. Now that you're in love, you want me to be in love too and since you're in love with Krista, you want me to be in love with Krista's best friend, just to make a cutesy, cozy little picture. Well, forget it. I'm not in the least bit interested in Cathy, in any way, except how she's going to make out as a detective. Don't you dare try to make something out of nothing here, I'll never forgive you for it if you do."

The storm was back in Dave's eyes, but it didn't bother Paul, he was more than used to these inclement changes that happened at least ten times a day. He did, however, know enough to let the matter drop, even though it was Dave himself who had opened the discussion this time. And Dave, who knew exactly what he had done, made the silent vow to himself that he would never leave himself wide open like that again, that he would continue to remain aloof around Cathy, if only to prove to Paul he meant all that he said.

Dave's defenses securely up again, by the time Cathy and Krista returned to the table, he had succeeded in retreating safely behind the walls of his fortress where he slipped himself into his broody little shell of indifference and remained there, detaching himself from any conversation with anyone, even Paul. Cathy could sense his not too subtle personality change and, simply not understanding it, she frowned at him on more than one occasion when anything she said to him was answered in a monosyllable, if she was even lucky to get that. Paul and Krista didn't seem to notice the way Dave was behaving, they were too busy having a deep conversation about something or other and Cathy swiftly grew impatient, wishing the evening would now just come to an end.

But by the look of things, she was going to have to wait and, because she had nothing better to do now, she started looking all around her at the other patrons in the nightclub. They were a mixed bunch of people all right, male, female and who knew? Short, tall, fat, thin, over dressed, under dressed, pretty, ugly, handsome, drunk, sober, some even probably a bit stoned, all typical nightclub clientele. Cathy loved people-watching and her mind wandered off completely as she observed the shenanigans and comings and goings, and she was totally unaware that a young man, who was standing at the end of the bar near their table, hadn't been able to take his eyes off her since he had first spotted her a short while ago.

He had observed the whole group and had figured it out that, although the blond guy and the other lady seemed to be an item, this lady and the other guy definitely weren't. They were sitting as far apart as possible for starters, they didn't seem to be talking to each other much either, so they were probably either brother and sister or a blind date that hadn't worked out.

Figuring it would be safe to try and make a play for her, he lifted his drink, sauntered confidently over to her table, set his drink down uninvited and smiled directly into Cathy's eyes. She looked up at him, startled at first by his intrusion as anyone would be, then she shrank back in her seat in irritation because she had just smelled strong alcohol on his breath and seen the slightly glazed look in his brown eyes.

"Care to dance?" he enquired.

"No, I, er…no thanks." She glanced quickly at Krista for some sort of help (like a suggestion to go to the ladies' room right now would be very wonderful, please and thank you) but Krista had only just disengaged herself from her conversation with Paul and hadn't even heard the intruder's first words, so she was absolutely no help whatsoever at the moment.

The young man extended his hand towards Cathy. "Come on, one dance isn't going to hurt."

Cathy ignored the hand and glared up at him. "I know it's not, but

I said no thanks. Please leave me alone."

Instead, he grabbed her by the arm and pulled her roughly to her feet. "Be a nice little lady and have one dance with me," he cajoled.

"Be a nice little gentleman and take your paws off me," she retorted and yanked her arm free. She was positively fuming by now and she wished that the guy would just leave her alone when she had made it blatantly obvious to him that she didn't want to have a dance with him. But it was also obvious to anyone that he had had a lot to drink and wasn't going to take a simple no for an answer.

Paul summed the situation up in a second and, on seeing it was heading for disaster, he moved to bail Cathy out, but it was Dave, who by some miracle had managed to tune into the events right from the start, had seen a look beneath the annoyance in Cathy's eyes he had identified as fear, who got to his feet first and pulled the poor, unfortunate man to him.

"Leave," he advised coldly. "Like five seconds ago."

Stupidly, the man ignored the warning in Dave's voice and turned back to Cathy. "Who's this? Your boyfriend or something?"

"No, he, huh, he's my…" She had been about to say 'friend' but Dave wasn't really that and she floundered for a second. "He's just someone I know," she finished.

"If he's not your boyfriend, he won't mind you having a dance with me then, will he?"

Dave grabbed him by the lapels of his jacket and brought him right up against his face. "Listen, asshole, the lady doesn't want to dance with you, she has said no on more than one occasion. Now, take my advice and just go, right now, unless you want the imprint of my fist stamped permanently on the back of your throat."

"Jesus!" he cried indignantly and pulled himself free. "Some people can be so touchy. All I wanted was one miserable dance with a pretty lady and instead I get threatened by a raving lunatic."

Dave smirked and, reaching inside his jacket, he pulled out his badge, which he flashed directly in front of the man's nose. "And lookie here, not just any lunatic, turkey, but one who can arrest you for disturbing the peace. Just not your lucky night tonight, is it?"

At the sight of the badge, the man instantly started to fluster. "I, uh…I think…I'd better go. I, huh…no hard feelings, pal, okay? Hey, a guy can try, can't he? I mean, she's a good-looking chick after all, so no hard feelings." But Dave had clearly lost all interest and he slunk quickly away before he could talk himself into more trouble.

Cathy breathed a sigh of relief and, although she was still annoyed, she sat down and turned to Dave with a warm smile. "Thank you for coming to my rescue like that, Dave. I hate it when men try to touch for me like that, I never really know what to do about it."

"It's okay," he said indifferently. "I was…" He was what? He didn't know but he took a wild guess. "Er, I was glad to help." He made eye contact with her for the merest of moments and he was instantly sorry he had. He looked downwards to hide his irritation and suddenly felt someone clapping him on the back.

It was Paul. "Any excuse to get flashing the old badge, eh pal?"

"Yeah, something like that." He gestured vaguely at the table. "Whose round is it?"

"Yours, as if you didn't know."

Dave wanted an excuse to get away so, instead of calling a waitress over, he went up to the bar himself to get the drinks. As he stood waiting for his order, he wondered why he had come to Cathy's aid like that. He hadn't wanted anything bad to happen to her but he had always preferred to let people fight their own battles and so what if she had seemed a little bit out of her depth, it wouldn't have lasted long, the fear he was sure he had seen would have disappeared too and she would have been more than capable of tossing that guy on his rear end – Dave was still smarting from the indignity of *that* little episode in the gym at the academy – and he wouldn't have had to interfere. So, why had he?

He didn't know, and, with a shudder of dissatisfaction, he put his guard up again and by the time he returned to the table a few minutes later, he had managed to work himself into a black mood.

Paul, who could read him like a book, knew instantly something was very clearly bothering him, but he dismissed the idea when he figured it couldn't be anything too serious. Paul had his mind on other things anyway, he had been dying to ask Krista up for a dance all night and he decided that now was as good a time as any to take the plunge. She was moving in her seat anyway to the beat of the music – it was an oldie by Erasure and therefore danceable to – and he used that for an excuse.

"Do you like that song?" he asked.

"I love it," she said, bopping away, wishing he would ask her to dance.

"I like it too. Would you like to dance?" He offered up a silent prayer of thanks when she nodded enthusiastically and, excusing himself from Dave and Cathy, he led Krista up to the dance floor. However, just as they found a space, the record was faded out and a slow one started up in its wake. They stood uncertainly for a moment and then she smiled and put him at his ease.

"I promise I won't step on your toes," she teased, "that is, if you still want to dance with me, of course."

He returned the smile in way of an answer and, clasping her hand in one of his and putting his other arm around her waist, he pulled her close to him. The song that was playing, although one he had never heard before, was soft and sultry and full of sexy promises and innuendoes and, closing his eyes in pleasure at the feel of her body next to his, they swayed slowly together in time to the music. She felt warm and soft and she smelled delicious and, without even thinking about what he was doing, he laid his cheek against hers.

Krista, instead of feeling strange at being in his arms properly for the first time, felt as if she had been born simply to be held by him. He had a solid but yielding frame and his strong arms around her made her feel safe and protected.

Unfortunately, neither of them had long to enjoy this new and heady contact with one another because disaster was just around the corner and it was Krista who first realized it was about to happen.

CHAPTER FIFTEEN

Cathy was watching Paul and Krista and she couldn't help but notice how natural they looked and moved together. She turned to Dave to comment about it, but he had a faraway look in his eyes and when she tried, unsuccessfully, to get his attention, and when he was making it perfectly clear he didn't want to be with her like this, highly insulted and infuriated, she grabbed her bag in preparation to go to the bathroom.

Just as she turned away, the strap of her bag got caught around one of the glasses on the table and, before she could grab a hold of the glass, it overturned and spilled neatly down the front of Dave's dress pants. Before she could even begin to apologize for her clumsiness, he bounced up and glared at her.

"Just…just *look* what you did!" he spluttered angrily. "Just look at my pants, you stupid bitch, they're ruined."

She pulled her chin up in indignation at his name calling. And his unnecessary accusations. "It's only beer, Dave, it will wash off. Calm down, for crying out loud, it was an accident."

"Oh yeah?" He grabbed a cocktail napkin and tried blotting his soaked crotch and upper legs with it, but it was a futile operation. "Why do I not believe you that it was an accident?" Oh God, that beer was *cold,* trickling all the way down like an icy river towards where the sun doesn't shine, the shock of it hitting his skin had surely caused his heart to go into arrest and he knew he was being unreasonable and he knew he was getting angrier by the second, but he didn't exactly care because that beer was *cold,* damn it, and *wet,* and it was all her fault.

"*What?*" Cathy spat in absolute disbelief. "It *was* an accident and I really am sorry about it." She stared at him in complete surprise and bewilderment, wondering why on earth he was acting like a complete and utter hot-tempered jackass over something that anyone else with half a brain would have recognized instantly as being an accident.

Dave threw the sodden napkin to one side and, at last, looked at her. "I don't think you *are* sorry *and* I think you did it on purpose."

Her temper snapped, just like that and, her eyes boring right into his, her voice dipped dangerously low. "No, I didn't." She picked up her own drink, which was still quite full and flung it directly into his face. "*That* was on purpose. Spot the difference? Or do you want me to demonstrate again? Because I will….no problem."

Just before Cathy did that, Paul decided he was in seventh heaven as he and Krista swayed slowly to the music. Her lips were only inches away from his and he pulled his head back slightly, so he could look into her eyes. They passed a silent communication to him and she seemed to be inviting him to kiss her, he hoped, but just as he dared to, a movement caught the corner of her eye and she instinctively turned towards it. He felt her stiffen in his arms and then emit a gasp of horror.

"Oh my God!" she cried.

"What's wrong?" He followed her line of vision, just in time to see Cathy throw the drink over Dave and he groaned deeply. "Jesus and Mary, what's going on now?"

Dave brushed the ice cubes from his jacket and he glared at Cathy, his temper matching hers exactly. "What the hell did you do that for?" he demanded.

"Why the hell do you think?" she retorted, not budging an inch.

He pulled back at the venom in her eyes and all but sneered at her. "Well, for that, you can just drop dead, lady."

"After you," she invited.

Paul and Krista arrived just in time to hear Dave say what he did and also to hear Cathy's reply. Hardly able to believe his ears, Paul quickly stepped between them before anything else could happen. "Okay, what's going on here, guys?" he asked as calmly as he could.

Cathy was still completely livid, and she was positively shaking with fury too. "Ask your dickhead of a partner," she said icily and then, with one last, baleful glare in Dave's direction, she pivoted on her heel and strode quickly and proudly towards the exit.

Krista moved to go after her but when she got halfway to the door, she stopped, reminding herself that Cathy always wanted to be left alone when she was that angry and that it would be pretty pointless to try and talk to her until she had calmed down. The reluctant decision to stay made, Krista turned and went back to Paul and Dave, looking silently at the latter for an explanation.

Dave's face was still dripping wet, but he didn't even seem to be aware of it as he stared at the exit, still furious, but something else too. He was also quite taken aback. No other female in the whole wide world had ever dared face off to him like that and he had to admit he was suitably impressed. He had pushed her into it, he knew that now only too well. He had wanted to intimidate her, but it was obvious she couldn't be intimidated so easily and, for reasons he couldn't as yet understand, now he wanted to go running after her so he could tell her he was really sorry, he hadn't meant to be so churlish and so cruel, would she please forgive him.

But it was too late, there was a taxi stand just outside the restaurant, so she would probably already have managed to flag down a cab. Her celebration evening had just been officially ruined. By him. And he knew it.

He remembered that Paul and Krista were still waiting for an explanation and he forced his mind back to reality with a weary sigh.

"I…er…she was right there, I'm nothing but a dickhead. She threw that drink at me because I drove her to it. Maybe one of these fine days…" He trailed off in bewilderment, his fury deflated, his heart heavy. "Maybe one of these fine days she'll let me make it up to her." He looked down at himself and absent-mindedly wiped his face with his hand. He chuckled in vague embarrassment. "Excuse me, please, I'd better get to the men's room to dry myself off a bit."

Paul watched him walk away and was, for the moment, stunned into silence. He had heard something in Dave's voice and had seen something in Dave's eyes that for once Paul hadn't been able to understand. Before he could even begin to figure it out, he felt Krista's hand slipping through his and her special touch warmed him again.

"Are you okay?" she asked softly.

"I'm fine, I'm just terribly sorry that this had to happen. However, I'm hoping this little scenario has managed to open his eyes to see that he's not going to win on whatever it is he has made his stubborn little mind up on. I think he's just met his match as far as Cathy's concerned and, for some reason, I also think he likes that idea. A lot."

"I hope you're right, Paul, I really do. I've been so worried about them because they haven't been able to get along and, much as I hate that this has happened, I hope that this has given them the right push in the right direction towards a permanent truce." She gestured towards their seats. "Come on, let's sit down while we're waiting for Dave."

After a few moments of trying to figure out what had gone wrong, Paul wryly shook his head. "It's terrible, this evening has turned out to be a bust."

"No, it hasn't. It's not your fault and I was enjoying myself, very much, up until a couple of minutes ago."

"So was I," he quickly agreed. "Right up until we had a Clash of the Tempers."

Krista chewed pensively on her bottom lip, her fingers working nervously at the gold chain around her neck. "You know, there's one thing that really puzzles me about this latest episode. Cathy's not usually so demonstrative in a crowded room like this. She hates being the center of attention and she certainly hates making an exhibition of herself. Dave must have provoked her enough for her not to have realized that at least fifty per cent of the people in here were watching her. She's normally a very private person, she keeps everything to herself, particularly her deep, personal thoughts. You wouldn't even know she was in any kind of pain, mental *or* physical because she's so good at keeping everything inside. And yet, there she was, in full view of everyone, throwing a drink round someone. She may as well have just put up a neon sign that read 'LOOK AT ME'."

"Why is she like that? Good at keeping everything inside, I mean?"

Krista half smiled. "Her upbringing, the one I'm not at liberty to discuss with you, remember."

"Oh, I'm sorry -"

She absently waved his apology away. "Forget it. I can say this, though…it may be a bit away from the subject but it all ties in… Cathy needs people to like her, Paul."

"Excuse me? I don't think I understand."

"Cathy is convinced that…well, that I'm the only person in this whole wide world who actually likes her."

"*What*? But *I* like her. I like her a lot."

"I know you do and hopefully through time she'll see that for herself. She may act like a toughie, but she craves love and affection and it's just such a sin to watch her coming in contact with a person she wants to be friends with only she's too afraid of being turned away or shot down… or even scorned because she wasn't the one who made the first move…she *can't* make the first move, she's just too afraid of the negative responses she feels she'll get." Realizing she was beginning to digress, Krista paused and glanced at Paul, but he was listening quite intently, his eyes narrowed thoughtfully. "Anyway, what I'm trying to say is, knowing that we'll be working together as soon as tomorrow, she wants to be able to get along with Dave but the more they continue to argue and fight and snipe at one another, the more it will hurt her and the more insecure she will become about herself. Do you understand that?"

Paul nodded slowly, carefully. "I do, Krista. I guess we will just have to wait and see if they grow tired of yelling at one another and in the meantime, we can act as buffers between them until they can work out a mutual understanding of one another."

"I guess you're right."

"Here's Dave coming back, let's change the subject." Paul fixed a casual smile on his face and absently slipped his arm around the creamy smoothness of Krista's shoulders, only because it seemed the most natural thing in the world to do. When he realized what he was doing, he pulled his arm away but when he was to think about it in passing afterwards, he would recall that Krista hadn't seemed to mind one little bit.

When Dave sat down, he seemed very subdued and a lot distracted. He kept glancing at his watch, or nervously towards the door, his eyes dark and troubled. After only a few minutes, he stood up. "I think I'll call it a night, guys. I, huh, I have an early start in the morning."

"No earlier than all of us, partner," Paul said calmly.

'Yeah, well, I need my beauty sleep, you guys don't…or at least Krista doesn't. Besides, the hand dryer in the restroom wasn't working too well and I'm still soaked through in places I'm not supposed to be soaked through and all I want to do is get home, get out of these wet clothes, get showered and hit the sack. Krista, congratulations again, sweetie, on your achievement today, you sure as hell deserve your badge. I'll see you tomorrow, okay?"

Paul and Krista shared a look when Dave walked away and, understanding it, Paul quickly called him back. "Hey, Dave, wait up. It *is* getting kinda late, so we may as well all call it a night. I'll give you a ride home."

Dave glanced at Krista and actually broke into a smile. "No need, pal. I'll get a cab downstairs."

"Nonsense. Come on, let's hit the road." Because it was more practical, Paul dropped Krista off at her place first. They bade each other a fond, but unfortunately kissless, good night and, once he had watched her walk up the path that led to her front door, open it and disappear safely inside, he pulled away. "You're mighty quiet, Dave," he remarked after a few minutes.

"Yeah, I'm tired… got a few things on my mind is all."

"Cathy?"

"What about her?"

For once, there was no harshness in Dave's voice and Paul took that as a good sign. "Let me put it this way then. Are you still pissed at what happened between the two of you?"

"Yes, I'm still pissed," Dave admitted. *Just not at her anymore,* he said to himself, *I'm only pissed at myself now.*

"Then why did you let it happen?"

"How the hell should I know? It just happened. Look, I don't want to talk about it, it's over with. I'll apologize to her in the morning about it…maybe." He subsided into silence for the rest of the journey and as Paul watched him walk away into his apartment, his shoulders hunched and his head down, Paul suddenly felt very sorry for him.

Paul wanted more than anything to help him on whatever it was that was going through his mind, but he knew he couldn't, that Dave had to learn to help himself first. And stop being his own worst enemy. Krista's words about Cathy from earlier were still weighing heavily on his mind and, although normally he would have talked his concerns over with Dave, this time he obviously couldn't. Dave *was* the concern, the real reason behind Cathy's reaction tonight and any other time they'd had a clash and, although he knew Cathy wasn't entirely innocent of blame, Paul knew that Dave was the chief instigator. How many times had he realized that and how many times had he tried to get Dave to see it too? *Too* many times. And Paul no longer knew what to do about it.

When Krista let herself into the apartment, she found Cathy, already dressed for bed, curled up on the sofa in the living room. Cathy was listening to a classical music CD on their new sound system…

Beethoven, her music of choice to clear her thoughts and relax by. Her face was scrubbed clean of make-up, her hair brushed into loose curls that tumbled around her shoulders and down her back and she was nursing a cup of hot chocolate. As soon as she heard Krista, she sat up and turned the CD off using the remote control.

"Hi Kris," she greeted sheepishly, "I'm sorry I stormed off like that without giving you a proper explanation, but I was just so mad, and I couldn't abide being around that man for one second longer."

Cathy always had been good for offering her apologies quickly, but Krista saw that she had been crying and she quickly assured her she understood. "It's okay, whatever it was that made you do what you did, I'm sure it was perfectly justifiable. Have you calmed down any?"

Cathy shrugged and wiped her nose with a bunched-up tissue she took from the pocket of her bathrobe. "I'm calm with the rest of the world but I'm still furious with *him.* What is it about that man that he can rub me up completely the wrong way?"

"Why do you let him do it?" Krista countered wisely.

"I don't know and that's just it. What did I ever do on him to make him hate me so much?"

"He doesn't hate you, chum, far from it…and I'm sure of that."

"Then why does he insist on bringing out the worst in me?" Tears of utter frustration were threatening again and, setting her cup of hot chocolate carefully on a coaster on the end table, Cathy flopped back down on the sofa in a reclining position. "Everything I say, he contradicts, everything I do, he laughs at or tries to make me look stupid. *And* he seems to get a sick satisfaction out of doing it too. I can't stand him, Kris, I really can't and if he continues upsetting me like this…well… I'm just going to have to do something about it."

Krista kneeled beside her and sympathetically patted her hand. "What do you have in mind?"

"I'm going to ask Captain Hamilton if he can make sure I don't have to see much of him during working hours and that I won't have to work much with him after we finish our first case together." Cathy looked down at her tissue and started shredding it to pieces. Her lower lip was still trembling, and she seemed more than just frustrated, she seemed very vulnerable and hurt too. Then she smoothed her brow and pushed out her chin, her gesture of defiance. "I've decided I'm just going to ignore Detective Sergeant David Andrews from now on," she declared. "I've let him find my weak spots too many times and I'm sick to death of it, so, because I absolutely hate his guts and because he obviously hates mine, I'm going to keep my distance, not let myself get set up for a fall anymore at his doing…*and* I'm going to maintain nothing but a professional relationship with him – if he's going to be lucky to get even *that* from me."

And, to Krista's dismay, that seemed to be Cathy's final words on the matter.

CHAPTER SIXTEEN

It was nearly 2:00 in the morning and still Dave couldn't sleep. He tossed and turned, trying to get comfortable, but to no avail, it looked like sleep was determined to elude him for a while yet. He stared up at the ceiling, trying to clear his mind, counting sheep, but nothing worked. He was exhausted, totally drained, and the knowledge he would have to get up for work in another four hours' time wasn't helping him get over any easier.

He was no stranger to little amounts of sleep, ever since he had become a cop, his whole system had had to adapt to a totally different lifestyle, like eating breakfast when it was really supper time, going to bed at eight in the morning when he should have already been up and about, or going for his morning workout at the gym at four in the afternoon. He had trained himself to make do with a minimum amount of sleep but tonight, of all nights, he wanted the full eight hours like any other normal human being. He knew he wouldn't be worth two cents in work if the sandman didn't hurry up and do his duty and send him to sleep soon.

At last, he did drift off and eventually he started to dream and when he awoke, it was with a smile on his face and he was feeling refreshed and ready to face the day ahead. He whistled cheerfully to himself through his shower, burst into song while shaving and when he made it to the kitchen ten minutes later, he decided to treat himself to a hearty breakfast of bacon, eggs, sausages, home fries, toast, orange juice and coffee. He even did his dishes afterwards and tidied up before he left for work and when he walked into the office, Paul was already there and seemingly surprised to see him in such good spirits.

"Morning, Paulie," he greeted brightly. "What's new?"

Paul looked past him at the doorway, as if he was expecting the *real* Dave Andrews to come through it any second. This sunny disposition was in total contrast to the moody, broody man Paul had left off at his apartment the previous night. "Nothing," he said slowly. "What's with you? Why are you looking like the cat that swallowed the canary?"

Dave flopped down on his seat and grinned impishly. "Because I got myself laid last night."

Paul had just taken a sip of coffee and when he heard that, he started choking. "Excuse me?" he spluttered.

"You heard."

Paul hurriedly wiped his chin, staring incredulously at his friend. "I know what I *think* I heard. You're pulling my leg here, aren't you? I dropped you off at 12:30 last night, I saw you go straight inside your apartment. How could you have gotten laid? Did you have someone waiting for you when you got home or something?"

"Nope, nothing like that."

"Then what? How...? You didn't...you know..." Paul made a few gestures that implied a self-motivated, self-gratifying sexual act but he really didn't know what else Dave could be referring to.

"That's perverted and no I didn't."

"Then how the hell could you have gotten laid?"

Dave smirked. "I dreamt it."

"You *dreamt* it?" Paul rolled his eyes in perfectly justifiable exasperation. "Oh man, you're sick."

"No, I'm not. Don't you see what I'm trying to tell you here? I actually dreamed I was having sex."

"I know, you told me. So?"

"So, that's the first dream like that I've had in a very long time. And you know what? And this is the God's honest truth here – it's actually given me a taste for the real thing again – soon as I find the right woman of course."

Paul knew Dave could only be joking, he *had* to be… only the more Paul looked at him, the more he couldn't be so sure. "Are you serious? You actually want to prove there's still fire in the old furnace after all?"

Dave chuckled. "Put like that, then I guess so."

Paul shook his head in amazement. "Well I'll be a monkey's cojones. I try for months – no, *years* – to get you back on track with the fairer sex and just when I'm about to give up, you have one horny little dream and that's it, you wise up all by yourself. If I'd known it was going to be that simple, I would have slipped into your room each night and read extractions from *Penthouse Forum* while you slept, or something."

"Don't get so excited over this so soon, Paul. In order for me to follow through with this, I still have to find the *right* female, remember?"

"And how long is that going to take?"

"How the hell should I know?" Dave decided to toy with him a little while longer and he added in perfect innocence, "And I could change my mind again anyway."

"Don't you dare go building up my hopes, Andrews. You've been celibate for far too long, it's time it ended and with this admission, I'm going to keep on at you. So, who was she?"

"Who?"

"The woman in your dream?"

Dave suddenly frowned in genuine bewilderment. "I don't know, now that you mention it. I can't recall seeing a face, but I do remember seeing a body...a beautiful body that was filled out to mind blowing perfection in all the right places...and I think she had long hair, but I can't be sure. Other than that, apart from what she was doing to me with her mouth at one stage, the picture is blank."

"She must have been good," Paul remarked slyly.

"Very good, just like I always remembered it."

"I didn't think your memory was that good, pal."

"Aren't I just full of surprises then? But I'm going to warn you right here and right now, Paul, if you're going to insist on trying to fix me up with a female, then this conversation never happened and the deal's off. This I want to do all by myself, with no outside help whatsoever. I could very easily change my mind again, at any given moment too and if I don't feel comfortable going out into the great wide world again, so to speak, I'm not going to. One horny dream does not a sex maniac make and if I still haven't gone out on a date by this time next year, that's just the way I want it to be. Do you understand?"

"No, not really. Does this mean you're still going to be aloof around the fairer sex?"

"Only if I don't like her."

"Then why did you even bother telling me about your dream? You don't like any woman, seems to me you're really no further forward."

"I only told you because I thought you would have liked to hear it. I wasn't looking for advice or looking to join the I Just Got Laid Club or anything, I just thought I would put you out of your misery and let you know I'm not dead in the nether regions after all."

"Then go out and prove it to me."

"In my own good time." Dave lifted a folder from a pile of folders on top of his semi-jumbled desk but before he had even got it open, he realized there was something different about the office. He only hadn't noticed when he had first come in because he had been anxious to let Paul know about his dream (although why, he didn't know) but now he did notice, and he looked quizzically over at Paul. "Why have the desks been changed around?"

Paul glanced in the direction of Captain Hamilton's office, but the door was closed, and the blinds were drawn. "They, er, well, it's like this, Dave, the desks are for, um, Cathy and Krista."

"*What?*" Dave was clearly not impressed, and Paul instantly felt his heart sink.

"Yeah, the Captain wanted them in here, with us. Neat-o, huh?"

"No, it most definitely is not. Why couldn't he have put them in the main office with everyone else?" Or down the hallway, or another precinct, or the next plane back to Belfast, Dave didn't particularly care where, as long as he wouldn't be forced to look at Cathy for any more than was necessary.

"How the hell should I know? Chill, man, it's no big a deal. Mark and Jim were moved to the main office and, since they're still only going to be a few feet away they didn't seem to mind. *I* don't mind either, so why should you?"

"Because I happen to like working with Mark and Jim. And you only don't mind because it's given you the golden opportunity to drool over Krista some more."

"So, what? She's worth it." Paul stared calmly back at him. "*Both* girls are a far nicer sight to look at than Mark and Jim. And while we're on the subject, are you still mad at Cathy for what she did to you last night?"

"Maybe I am, maybe I'm not and I really don't think it's any of your business." But in fact, while unable to sleep, Dave had thought of nothing else except his confrontation with Cathy and now, in the pale light of this early spring morning, he knew he was no longer mad at her, but he *was* intrigued. *Very* intrigued. And it was going to be interesting to see what their first meeting since the incident would be like.

He didn't have long to find out because a few minutes later, Cathy and Krista walked into the office. This was their first real day on the job and they seemed excited but also anxious and apprehensive. But they were starting their new careers today and they were both alive with anticipation too.

Paul beamed warmly at them. "Top of the morning, ladies," he greeted, "and welcome officially to the 7th precinct of the Bathville Police Department." He gestured around the office with a grin. "As you can see, the puke cream décor leaves a lot to be desired and that tacky cork notice board over on that far wall there, the one with pictures of the late Bin Laden's men and other low life citizens fit to be put on America's Most Wanted list really should be taken down and retired to the garbage can, but to us poor, overworked and grossly underpaid cops, it's a home away from home so please, don't knock it. But I just want to give you one friendly piece of advice to set you merrily on your way. Steer clear of the coffee on this floor, it sucks, big time. If you really need a caffeine fix, go to the canteen on the first floor or to Dunkin' Donuts a couple of blocks away."

"Thanks, we'll certainly try to remember that," Krista answered with a chuckle, obviously delighted to be near him and in his company again. He looked so handsome this morning, dressed in a light blue sweatshirt and black jeans, his hair shining and his gorgeous eyes twinkling softly in good humor. What was it about him that set her heart racing like this every time she saw him? She never had been one to fall for a man simply because he was pretty to look at and Paul didn't have smooth, flawless, clean cut, pretty boy features anyway because there were several small scars on his forehead and cheeks she never had gotten around to asking where they had come from, but there was just something about him and she was driving herself crazy lying awake at nights trying to figure out what it was. Yes, he was incredibly handsome, yes, he had a good, solid, well-muscled body and yes, he had a wonderful personality but all those attributes aside, she knew there was something more. Despite his honey blond hair, his eyebrows and lashes were quite dark, his skin looked as if it would tan easily, rather than redden and his smile alone had surely won quite a few female hearts and yet, with all that, he was so unassuming about his looks and she wondered if that was the reason she was trying to find. Realizing she was staring as she tried to work it all out, she reluctantly tore her eyes away from his and greeted Dave with a warm, friendly smile too. "Hi Dave, how are you this morning?"

"Fine, thanks," he replied amiably and tipped her a wink. He and Cathy hadn't even given each other so much as a bare acknowledgement, which told him the episode of the night before was still very much between them. *Oh well,* he thought, *if that was the way she wanted to play it…*

Cathy was standing to the left of his desk, looking all around her and trying, no doubt, to get a feel of the place. She wondered if the two empty desks were for her and Krista and she found herself hoping they weren't.

Paul had pulled Krista over to the coffee machine to show her what he had meant about the coffee, leaving Cathy and Dave momentarily alone. She rested her gaze briefly on him, trying to assess if he was still angry with her, but he wasn't even looking at her, he seemed to be making himself look busy just so he could ignore her. Not particularly caring what he did, she moved over beside Paul and Krista.

Paul looked past her at Dave and inwardly groaned at the tight expression he saw on his partner's face. Nothing had changed, nothing at all, nor did it seem like it was going to.

Captain Hamilton breezed into the office just then and indicated with a jerk of his head that they all follow him to his office, which they did. They seated themselves in front of his large, paper-cluttered desk and waited for the big man to speak.

"Good morning, people," he greeted. "Krista, Cathy, welcome to our team and good luck on the commencement of your new jobs, you each deserve to be here, and I am extremely glad that you are. And now, ladies, tell me how good you are at dancing."

The last sentence was the last thing on earth Cathy and Krista had been expecting to hear and, completely taken aback and not yet knowing it had something to do with their first case, they looked at each other and then back at their Superior. He was waiting expectantly for their response, only neither of them knew what to say.

CHAPTER SEVENTEEN

"Dancing?" Cathy repeated dubiously.

"Dancing," the Captain confirmed.

"What kind of dancing do you mean?" Krista asked carefully.

Captain Hamilton kept his expression carefully blank. "Erotic dancing." He narrowed his eyes expectantly at his two newest detectives, calmly awaiting their reaction. It wasn't long in coming, once they properly found their tongues again.

"Are you serious?" Krista cried.

"Do we look like the type of people who do erotic dancing?" Was Cathy's indignant retort.

The Captain held up a hand to silence them. "Yes and no respectively to each question, ladies. Please just hear me through before you get all bent out of shape because this involves your first case. As you have been told, I wanted to throw you in at the deep end for your first case and put you undercover right away."

"So, you decided to find the sleaziest case you could for us?" Cathy asked coolly.

"Not by choice," he admitted, "but this is the one that came along. Paul and Dave here have already started the ball rolling and, in order for you to become involved, I need to know if you can dance or not."

"And what if we can?" Cathy snapped, clearly unimpressed with what he was asking of them. Going undercover was one thing, having to be a dancer, wearing next to nothing on stage or on a stranger's lap, was another matter entirely. "I think there's a limit to what you can expect from us and I even think it's fair to say that."

"You're quite right," he agreed, "it is fair. But if I didn't think you were capable of doing this, I wouldn't be asking. I would be putting two other female cops on it."

"Great, exploit two *different* females."

Dave couldn't contain his amusement at Cathy's obvious chagrin and, before he could stop himself, he said, "Don't worry, Cathy, you won't have to take your clothes off in front of strangers if you don't want to…but then again, maybe you *like* doing that sort of thing for all those hot-blooded males out there."

She slowly turned to face him and the look she gave him was enough to stop him short. "I happen to find that remark really offensive and sexist," she told him icily, "but at least that confirms my suspicions that you really are nothing but a sexist pig. Don't *ever* say something of that nature to me ever again, is that clear?"

He gave her the palms up, back off gesture, but he was still finding her reaction very amusing. "Hey, steady on there," he drawled, "keep your panties on…if you're wearing panties, of course…I was only kidding."

Paul had known he was joking, the Captain had known he was joking, even Krista had known he was joking and, although Cathy had known it too, she couldn't let him off so easily and she haughtily raised her chin up.

"Well, I don't exactly appreciate your sense of humor, it certainly leaves a lot to be desired. In fact, I would even say your sense of humor is practically non-existent so please don't try to "kid" around me anymore."

"Yes, *Ma'am*," he mocked, even giving her a mock salute.

"Thank you." With the small victory of getting the last word in, she shot him one last particularly contemptuous look and turned her attention back to the Captain.

He was watching this little exchange with seemingly a lot of interest and it had just been brought to his attention for the first time that there was some – no, make that a lot – of animosity between Dave and Cathy. He wondered if it had anything to do with the way Dave always was around women, but he really didn't think that had anything to do with it, he had seen Dave act amicably enough with Krista. However, he didn't have time to dwell on it, he just made a mental note that he would observe from a distance and draw his own conclusions when he needed to. "That's quite enough, the both of you," he chastised softly. "Let's get back to the matter on hand. *Can* you ladies dance? You have yet to answer."

"We may not be auditioning for a starring role in *Dirty Dancing II*," Krista informed him, "but we can hold our own on the dance floor."

"Good, that's what I want to hear. Okay, here's what's going down and first I'll fill you ladies in with what Paul and Dave already know. Back in January, a young Asian woman was brought into Bathville General, suffering from multiple wounds all over her body, rape and a severe blow to her head that left her in a coma for over two months. Upon admittance to the hospital, it was determined she had indeed been raped, but whoever had done it had used a condom, there was no semen extracted from her vagina and not even any other pubic hairs mixed with her own. Because we are certain there was no chance for her to fight off her attacker, we didn't get any skin samples from beneath her fingernails, so with that and the lack of sexual fluids, we had nothing to do a DNA test on to run through the computers to give us a perp. About ten days ago, she started to come round and on the day she finally opened her eyes and spoke for the first time, she didn't get a chance to say who had attacked and raped her because she seemed to remember something terrible – the doctor working on her case, Dr. Samuel Warren, believes it was the attack itself that she remembered – and immediately had to be sedated. Before she went under the sedation, Dr. Warren said she murmured a few words, which were, "Petcelli… not Petcelli" which didn't make sense to the doctor and really don't make sense to us either. However, Xavier Petcelli is the owner of a nightclub called the Blues Haven, over on the west side. It's a lovely neighborhood, ladies, full of crack heads, street gangs and all other lowly forms of life…and it's the same nightclub that Ms. Ho used to work at as a dancer and the same club that now has four dead members of staff on its hands. All female workers, three of them dancers and the other victim a waitress, and all of whom have died under mysterious circumstances."

"This Petcelli chap must be the prime suspect, I assume?" Cathy remarked.

"He *was*, but the alibis he gave us for his whereabouts when each murder was apparently executed all checked out perfectly."

"The way you're talking," Krista interrupted, "Gloria Ho is now the fourth victim?"

"Exactly. Before she even awakened from the sedation Dr. Warren gave her, someone went into her hospital room and smothered her with a pillow. We have every reason to believe it was a male and it could well have been the man who attacked and raped her, we certainly cannot rule out the possibility he went back to finish the job, once he heard Ms. Ho was coming out of her coma. Apparently, a man who just called himself a "friend" had been calling the hospital practically on a daily basis since Ho's admittance and on the day she died, the same man called and was put through to Dr. Warren's line, at Dr. Warren's request. Without trying to scare the man away, Dr. Warren asked for his name and was told it was Danny Smith. There are several Dan, Danny and Daniel Smiths listed in Bathville and surrounding areas, but we now know none of them is the man who called all those times and we are to assume that he gave Dr. Warren a bogus name. So, ladies, any ideas as to why Ms. Ho's killer would risk his neck in a busy hospital for, to finish off his job?"

"Probably because the woman knew something she shouldn't," Cathy said. "Something major and possibly incriminating, towards either her attacker or whoever her attacker is working for. Which could mean he works for this Petcelli guy."

"Correct, Cathy, well done. Which brings us to the reason why I asked if you could dance. We'll need you to go to the club, keep it under surveillance. Paul and Dave haven't been to the club yet simply because I need them to go undercover too and I don't want anyone recognizing them as the cops who've been there asking questions. Detectives Turner and Chipman, who you ladies have yet to meet, have been doing the surveillance work so far and they have every reason to believe by listening to conversations of the bar staff alone that the club has a lot of illegal activities going on. Selling stolen goods is one possible by-line and what the merchandise is, we have no idea as yet. The club is due to be hit with a hefty fine too for allowing staff and clientele to smoke on the premises during normal opening hours. Smoking in public restaurants and bars, ladies, became illegal in Massachusetts in 2004. We also suspect some drug trafficking and, of all things, a gambling racket."

"But as far as I can remember reading, gambling is no longer illegal in the state of Massachusetts." Krista remarked.

"That's completely correct," the Captain agreed, "but in an establishment like the Blues Haven, to run a private gambling party, you need to apply for a license and no such license has ever been applied for by Petcelli or anyone else working for him. Turner and Chips also noticed something else, something really rather unusual and that is that the club has a rather extraordinary turnover of staff. The murder victims, for example, all females as I mentioned earlier, would all have to be replaced once they had been eliminated, for whatever reason. And this is where you all come in. Paul, Dave, you both know I've been waiting to get you into this place, well, now the opportunity has arisen because the word is, they're looking for four new members of staff. *Four* new members, people, at the one time, so what does that tell you? Although we really don't think those four positions have come about because of foul play this time, it's still rather strange that four places come up at the same time, so either the club isn't a good place to work or Petcelli isn't a good boss to work for. Turner and Chips couldn't find out what the positions were, hopefully they'll be for bar staff or bouncers for Paul and Dave's benefit and waitresses or dancers for you ladies. Hopefully you can all start as early as tonight, if not tomorrow, which means you're going to have to go for your interviews this afternoon."

"Is the club open on a Sunday?" Cathy asked.

"Seven days a week, Edwards, from twelve noon until five in the afternoon and from nine in the evening until two in the morning. Don't all of you arrive at the same time…" The Captain trailed off, contemplating, then he added, "Paul, why don't you and Krista pose as boyfriend and girlfriend? Might as well try to give some sort of realistic background. Krista, with your looks, you should be snapped up as a dancer in no time."

"Thanks…I think," she said dryly.

"You're welcome. Cathy, you go in about half an hour later, ditto you, Andrews. I don't think it's the type of place that will ask for references, but I can get you all fake ones run up in no time just in case. Any questions?"

"Yes, I do," Krista said. "What should Cathy and I wear for our so-called interviews?"

"Something that will show a bit of cleavage and a lot of leg, but you don't have to go overboard if you're not comfortable with that. Gentlemen, jeans and t-shirts should suffice, I somehow don't think it's the type of place where you would have to wear a shirt and tie to make an impression."

A thought suddenly occurred to Cathy. "What about Krista's and my accents, Captain? Wouldn't the manager think it unusual two apparent strangers who talk the same turning up on the same day asking for a job?"

"Mm, good point, let me see." The Captain pondered for a mere moment. "Okay, I really want to keep Paul and Krista as a couple romantically involved so the only way to beat this is for you, Cathy, to go in with them. You girls could make up some story about having been in the States for the last few months or so and you might want to make it obvious that you're desperate to get a job. Hopefully Petcelli, if he's there to do your interviews, won't think to ask about your green cards or if you can legally work in the States. If he does, we'll get something organized for that too to prove that you can. Which reminds me of something else. Use aliases for your last names. While you're down there this afternoon, you should be able to get a feel of the place, check out the best vantage points, that sort of thing. Just keep your eyes and ears open for anything suspicious. Unfortunately, Turner and Chips weren't able to uncover anything concrete, nothing that would stand up in court anyway, which is why you all have to do this but, with a bit of luck, it won't take too long to get it wrapped. All clear?"

"Just one thing, Cap," Paul said. "What if we don't get the jobs you want us to, or say only two or three of us get hired, that the other positions have already been filled?"

"Take any job that's offered to you, just as long as you all get in there. And I just got the word before I left home there that, up until closing time at two this morning, all four positions were still available. Since the club opens at noon, that's the time I want you three to be there and for you, Dave, no later than five minutes after you see them leave." The Captain stood up to conclude the meeting. "Okay, people, that's it for now. I want you to spend the rest of the morning in each other's company and, after the interviews at the club, I want you to spend the rest of the day in each other's company too. I want you to get the feel of working together." He paused and looked directly at Dave, having not forgotten Dave's intentions of being distant to the two girls. "No exceptions," he stated meaningfully.

Dave stared calmly back at this Superior. Actually, he was secretly pleased that the Captain hadn't dictated that he, Dave, should become Cathy's "boyfriend" that would have been just too much and would, in turn, have given Paul something to latch on to for the rest of his life. He beamed his most disarming smile at the Captain. "Yes, sir."

"I don't care what you do with your time, you're not needed here so you can leave the station if you so desire but as long as you two men give our two newest recruitments as many pointers as you possibly can. Just remember, take great care if and when you start working in that place – and don't forget to let me know how your interviews turned out. Cathy, Krista, the two vacant desks out in the other office are yours. Dave, Paul, you're to remain where you've been for the last four years."

Dave's smile had already disappeared, and he barely masked a sneer as he jumped up, obviously anxious to get away for a while, but he knew that wouldn't be fair to Paul to leave him to do all the work, so he reluctantly sat down at his desk and, having some paperwork to finish off anyway, he became engrossed in that.

Seeing the keep-your-distance look on Dave's face, Paul took it upon himself to start showing the girls the ropes and he was pleased to see that they seemed to be fast learners. Even Dave, as he listened to some of the questions the girls asked, had to admit they both seemed bright because their questions and remarks were intelligent and well-constructed. Almost without realizing he was doing it, he found himself joining in, telling Cathy and Krista some things Paul had overlooked or clarifying points Paul hadn't been able to.

As Cathy and Krista watched, listened and learned, they were each under the impression that the two men handled their business by not quite keeping within the rules, not quite going by the book. It was something they would come to realize as true more and more as the weeks and months ahead passed by. Today, though, they weren't told or shown anything completely off the wall or bad, they just knew it was *different* to the way they had already been taught.

At 9:00, Paul threw down his pen and announced cheerfully, "Let's go to Dunkin Donuts for a coffee. Dave can buy."

"Maybe in your dreams," Dave stated. "My money is my own."

He had only been teasing, of course, and Cathy, who had yet to find out how generous Dave really was – that he would happily have bought the whole Department a coffee and a donut for instance – immediately felt herself bristling again at his remark.

She turned to face him with a very sweet smile. "Don't worry, Dave, if I was ever that hard up that I needed someone to buy me one cup of coffee, you would be the last person on this planet I would ask." She looked back at Paul. "I'd be more than happy to buy whatever *you* want, Paul, in fact, it would be my absolute pleasure. If Dave decides he wants something, he can either buy his own, or die of thirst, or not even go with us, I don't particularly care."

Dave shrugged he didn't really care either. "You needn't think you can try and plan my day for me, lady. And for your information, I'm going to go with you anyway, for two reasons. One, the good Captain has dictated that we spend as much time together today as possible and two, I know you don't want me to go at all, which is *really* why I'm going. Thank God they put lids on the coffee cups, though, I might end up getting my face washed again."

"The lids can easily be removed," she smoothly reminded him. "And this time, the drink would be piping hot. Paul, I'm going to take my own car and I'll see you at the coffee place. It's out of here, turn right, then first left, isn't it?"

"Right, Cathy." Paul watched her leave and he turned to Dave with an exasperated look. "Ten out of ten, Big D, you did it again. *I* know when you're only kidding around but Cathy doesn't so *please* stop acting like an antagonistic jerk around her."

"Just can't seem to help myself," Dave said sarcastically and started to walk away. "See you at the car."

Over coffee and donuts, Dave decided, again, to see just how far he could push Cathy. He seemed to be taking a sick satisfaction in doing his utmost to get any sort of a negative or angry reaction from her and, although she really did know better than to rise to his challenges, she did just that. The more aggravated she became at his terse remarks, the more amused and entertained he became and, apprehensive enough about the commencement of her first case, by as early as 10:00, her nerves were all but shot.

Paul was furious and, when Dave rose to go to the bathroom, Paul followed him and, after Dave had done his business, Paul pulled him over to one side to give him a good talking to.

"Just stop it!" he hissed. "For the last time, just stop it. You're being totally unreasonable and grossly unfair to her. Just leave her alone before you make yourself one bitter enemy out of her. I can't believe the way you're treating her, you're way out of line, even you must surely know it, and it's going to stop right now. What do you wish to gain from all this anyway?"

"Sick satisfaction," Dave retorted carelessly.

"Well, you've gone far enough, *too* far. Remember how it was last night between the two of you before that interesting little episode in the nightclub? During the meal, you got on really well with her and she with you, you even confessed to liking her, so why don't you bear that in mind? She looks like she's going to burst into tears, is that any way to be putting her at her ease?"

Dave was a very proud and stubborn man but when it was Paul

who pointed out his misbehavior, Dave listened, simply because he trusted Paul's judgment. "No, I guess not," he admitted reluctantly.

"Exactly, so let it drop. Please. And now I'm going to suggest a little walk in the park to help the girls relax – and while we're enjoying the stroll through the park, you're going to be nice to Cathy. Got that?" Paul didn't give Dave time to answer and left him standing there.

And, as Dave stood at the basin washing his hands, he began to feel suitably chastised and even a little bit guilty. But the truth of the matter was, he genuinely didn't know why he was being so nasty to Cathy. If he had accepted Krista, why couldn't he accept Cathy too? The two girls were, for the most part, pretty similar in personalities after all, especially when it came to interacting with friends and acquaintances.

Because soon Krista's going to be involved with Paul, the little voice of reason said inside his head, *which means she's no longer a threat to you, if she ever really was one. And you know fine well she never really was. Except in your sorry little head. Cathy, on the other hand, is one very interesting woman* and *she's incredibly gorgeous too, have you noticed that? Have you noticed too she's hot-tempered, not afraid of speaking her mind and she can't be intimidated by you, which means* SHE *can be a threat,* SHE *has so far shown you a lot of the qualities you admire the most in a woman and have you noticed the way her eyes look when she's angry, how blue and stormy and icy they can get? And have you noticed the way the sun catches auburn highlights in that amazing hair of hers? Have you noticed...? God, have you noticed...?*

Dave slowly and methodically dried his hands off on paper towels, his head tilted in bewilderment as he realized something else, probably what the voice of reason had been trying to tell him all along.

Cathy was the very first woman in a very long, lonely time who had the power to intrigue him like this. She was also the very first woman in a very long, lonely time he had actually noticed was drop dead gorgeous.

Could it be, he wondered, *that I'm actually…God forbid…*attracted *to her? That this is what all this nastiness and backstabbing has been about?*

And, to add to his pains, the little voice of reason chose that time to have an attack of silence.

CHAPTER EIGHTEEN

It was to be a quick walk through the park, but Cathy and Krista appreciated Paul's suggestion anyway. It was such a heavenly spring day, even the breeze coming in off the Atlantic was mild and a stroll through the pretty park, where birds were chirping gaily overhead, squirrels were hopping playfully around, the trees were bursting forth with buds and spring flowers such as crocuses and daffodils were profuse with color, seemed like a perfect interlude before they had to go to the club.

As they walked along the path, Dave, much to Paul's surprise and pleasure, was the one who started first to put the girls' minds at ease. Having at last sensed their trepidation about the case, Dave did his best to reassure them that they had nothing to worry about and he even managed to be civil to Cathy when he had to talk directly to her. When Paul took over the talking, Dave felt he had contributed enough for now and retreated into his shell for a while and when he snapped out of it, he realized it was just him and Cathy strolling along together, and he had no idea how they had become separated from Paul and Krista.

In truth, he and Cathy weren't exactly *together*, she was a few feet ahead of him, but she was walking slowly enough in a subconscious effort to remain within his immediate vicinity and, for once, he didn't really mind it was just the two of them. He increased his speed just a little bit and, catching up with her, fell in step beside her.

There was the usual awkward silence between them and Cathy, who was grateful to him for having tried to relax her regarding the case, suddenly felt fed up with their constant needling and wanted to try to make the peace.

They were approaching a children's boating pond but just before she could say anything, she saw Dave stop and then frown at whatever it was that had caught his attention. She followed his line of vision and understood instantly why he looked so annoyed.

A little boy of no more than four years of age was standing by the edge of the pond, his fists scrunched into his eyes as he sobbed his little heart out. He was only a few yards away and Dave, with a swift glance all around him, approached the little boy and carefully kneeled down beside him.

"What's the matter, tiger?" Cathy heard him ask gently.

The little boy, surprised for the moment by the intrusion of this strange person, bobbed his blond, curly head up to look at him, stopped crying and pouted miserably. "Please go away, mister. My mommy told me not to talk to strangers. And please don't try to offer me candy either, she's says I'm not supposed to take anything from anybody I don't know."

Dave smiled kindly. "Your mommy told you the right thing to do. But don't worry, I'm not going to hurt you and I don't have any candy on me, I just want to know why you're standing here all alone and crying. Do you want to tell me your name? Can you at least do that for me?"

He slowly shook his head, then he said warily, "P-Peter."

"Peter? That's a good name, Peter. My name's Dave. Want to tell me what's wrong?"

Peter looked woefully all around him and immediately burst into tears again. "I can't find my mommy," he wailed, "I've lost my mommy."

"You've lost your mommy?" Dave had already guessed that much but he'd had to make quite sure before proceeding any further. "I'm a cop, Peter and I'm very good at finding people. Do you know what a cop is?" At Peter's nod, Dave smiled. "Do you want me to show you my badge like the cops on TV do and then let me help you to find your mommy?"

Peter nodded slowly and turned watery, soulful brown eyes up to him. "Yes, please," he murmured.

"Okay, you got it, tiger." Dave stood up straight and, after showing his badge to the little boy, which he studied carefully, even though he probably didn't really know what he was looking at, Dave folded the boy's hand into his. "Come on, let's go. Can you remember where you last saw her?"

"Over there." Peter pointed towards a common, where there were a lot of other children playing, with adults carefully in attendance.

Cathy had never seen this tender side to Dave before and as she watched the two of them walk off, her heart suddenly gave a lurch. Dave had won that little boy's trust quickly and easily with a gentleness she would never have thought possible of him. He had even brought himself more or less down to the boy's height level by going down on his knees and therefore seeming less intimidating, he had introduced himself by using his first name and saying he was a cop and he had done it all with patience and as if it was as natural to him as breathing. Cathy suspected that, in a way, it all *had* been natural to him. She didn't even know why she felt like that, but it just felt... right.

What an enigma you are, Detective Dave Andrews, she said to herself, *you can be so cold and callous one minute, so warm and caring the next. Now, which one is the* real *you?*

Dave came back a few minutes later, minus the little boy. "I found his mom, thank God. The poor woman was tearing her hair out, looking everywhere for him."

"That was very nice what you did there. He seemed to trust you straight away."

"I just like kids, that's all."

She eyed him closely, perhaps to see if he was being sarcastic or not, but he seemed sincere enough and she smiled tentatively. "So do I. I love them, in fact."

"Yeah?" Something flickered across the deep blue of his eyes, something that was, perhaps, delight at her saying that, but it was only a flicker and she wasn't really sure if she had even seen it at all. He gestured up the path for them to start walking again. "Shall we?"

She solemnly shook her head. "No, Dave, not yet, I want to talk to you."

He narrowed his eyes suspiciously. "Oh? What about?"

"About last night. I'm really very sorry that I threw that drink at you. Although the first one that spilled on you really was an accident, the second one obviously wasn't, and I just want you to know that I've never done anything like that to anyone in my life before and when I woke up this morning and remembered what I had done, I nearly died with shame. Please let me at least pay for the dry cleaning on your trousers, if not buy you a new pair."

Startled by her obvious heartfelt apology, he quickly looked away and let his gaze rest on the playing children in the distance. That was another thing he had noticed about her, that she was quick to apologize when she thought it was due. "No need for you to do either of those things, the pants will wash." He looked back at her, figuring that if she could be nice, so could he. "And I'm sorry too, I guess. You had every right to be as pissed at me as you so clearly were. I ruined your celebration night and whatever you did to me, I deserved it."

Cathy smiled faintly, making a tiny dimple appear in the corner of her mouth. "I promise I'll never do anything like that again."

"Just forget it."

"Thank you." She remained silent for a moment, relishing the fact they were making some sort of headway, but there was still more she wanted to say to really get the air cleared between them. "Look, I suppose you could say you and I haven't exactly gotten off to a good start with one another, have we?" she said carefully. "So, if it's all right with you, I'd like for us to start all over again, on the right footing this time."

His eyes searched hers, wondering if she really meant it and, realizing she did, he dipped his head in a brief nod. "That would be fine by me," he murmured.

"I just want you to know that I *can* be a nice person, once you get to know me. I'm not usually such a bitch, Krista can attest to that." She was hoping to raise a smile from him but all she could sense from his direction was a lot of negativity and even more hostility. Her feelings hurt, again, she did as she always did with him and let herself grow increasingly more annoyed with him. "Just what is it with you, Dave?" she demanded. "From day one, you've been nothing but nasty towards me and okay, so I haven't exactly been an angel with you, but quite frankly, I don't think I did anything to you to deserve some of the rotten treatment you've been dishing out to me. Paul has assured me time and time again that you are a really nice person but I'm beginning to believe that he's looking at you through rose-colored glasses. I want to believe him, I want to see you in the way he does, and in the way Krista does, but you're not exactly giving me the opportunity to do that. You seem to get on fine with Krista and I always thought she and I were pretty much the same, so what is it about me that you don't like?"

Dave would have to have been a real cold-hearted person not to have heard the genuine distress in her voice and since he was many things but not that, he began to feel ashamed, again, for all the cruel things he had said to her earlier that morning, and the night before and any other time before that too. But he still wasn't ready to admit to her that he liked her, that he found her very interesting, so he by-passed her question.

"Look, you're right," he admitted earnestly. "We haven't exactly been hitting it off. I know it's largely been my fault too and I really don't know why I've been acting the way I have towards you, I've never given anyone just cause to accuse me of being nasty before. But believe it or not, I *am* sorry, I really am, it's just…well…" He trailed off, suddenly struggling to come up with the appropriate words, but he couldn't seem to find them, and he gave up with an exasperated shrug.

Cathy seemed to guess what was on his mind and she filled in the blanks for him. "You just didn't want to have to work with two females, right? And not just any females, but foreigners to boot?"

"Yeah, something like that," he agreed, surprised that she had managed to hit the nail right on the head. The funny thing was, he no longer minded the idea of having to work with her and Krista, he just minded the fact that Cathy was so goddamned gorgeous and each time he was with her, he was finding it more and more difficult to keep his barrier up around her. If he wanted to be completely honest with himself – and God knew he was due to do just that – he knew he wanted to find out more about her, in fact, he wanted to find out everything about her. But he was just too afraid too, in case he might end up putting down his guard completely and let her get inside his mind. And his lonely heart. Which she might hurt on him.

"Well, if it's any consolation, I can understand why you feel like that," she continued, blissfully unaware of what was going through his head. "I can safely speak for Krista as well when I say this, but we're not out to try and cramp your style or anything. We're new to this job…and this country too, after all, and we would appreciate any advice you or Paul may want to give us. Captain Hamilton put us together for reasons probably only known to him. He has also given Krista and me a job to do and we want to do it to the best of our abilities because this first case of ours is very important to us. I think we should at least try and get along for the duration of the assignment, if not for the Captain's sake, then at least for our own. But if you don't like that idea, why don't you just apply for a transfer off the case?"

Dave had to turn away. He couldn't bear looking into her eyes for much longer. They were so blue and breathtaking and so full of sincerity, his stomach insisted on turning somersaults every time he saw them. And right now, in their cool, direct gaze, he felt very small. What she had just said had made perfect sense, but he had seen enough of her by now to realize that she was more than capable of reading a situation exactly as it should be.

More than mollified by now, he turned towards her again and suddenly extended his hand towards her. "What you said is sadly all true. I *was* pretty pissed at the Captain for forcing Paul and me to work with two women. I just couldn't understand why he picked us out of a whole department full of people, for one thing. But I truly am sorry for my behavior, it was highly uncalled for and totally unprofessional."

Startled, Cathy took his outstretched hand and firmly shook it. "Apology accepted, but really not necessary. I suppose my nose would have been put out of joint too if my working habits were about to be disrupted."

"There's more to it than that, I'm afraid. I just felt really dumped on when we were assigned to look after you and Krista. I really didn't think it was fair. After all, I see myself as a detective, not as a chaperone, which is maybe why I've been giving you such a hard time since we met. Not only that, but to have to work side by side with you too? That was another thing that really burned me because for the longest time, it's just been Paul and me working together, nobody else. True, if there's something big going down, we work with the other officers, but at the end of the day, it's just him and me because that's the way we prefer to do things. He can adapt far quicker than me, though, as I'm sure you've seen, he's just so easy to get along with, nothing ever bothers him. But me, I'm not like him."

"Then what are you like?" she asked softly.

"I don't think you really want to know," he answered with a faint smile, "but if you insist, I can tell you a little. I know I'm a very direct person, Cathy, I always have been and always will be. I like speaking my mind and, although I do try to be tactful, if you don't like what I say or how I say it, or even how I do things, then I really don't see that as being my problem. Got that?"

"Yes *Sir,* she said sternly, then chuckled impishly.

He heard himself return her chuckle. "And I'll also have you know that I'm not usually such a jerk either. Promise."

She comically rolled her eyes. "*That's* certainly a relief to hear," she teased. "Not that I'm entirely sure yet what a jerk really is but I can guess it's something similar to a twit."

"*I* know what *that* is, and you've guessed correctly." He was still smiling, and he acknowledged the fact that this was the most they had ever said to one another without any nasty jibes from either party. And it felt good. He was admiring her more and more, not just her looks, or the way she spoke, but her style, her spirit, her direct ways and, probably most of all, her incredible honesty. He knew instinctively that, in different times under different circumstances, he would have been quite content to let himself fall for her, fall big for her, start a proper relationship with her but, despite his raunchy dream of the night before and what he had said to Paul earlier about changing his mind regarding the opposite sex, the promise he had made himself a long time ago still stood. But at least now he assumed…no, at least now he *knew* he could have Cathy as a friend, even though he was still determined to play it cool with her, not in a wary, I hate you way anymore, just in a keep-a-safe-distance-until-I'm-sure-I-can-trust-you way.

Feeling her spirits uplifting for the first time in weeks, Cathy smiled her first, real, warm smile at him. "I'm glad we've had this chance to talk, Dave. I feel loads better already."

"Me too," he said, sounding a bit surprised because he actually meant it. "I reckon Paul and Krista will be glad to hear we've managed to bury the hatchet."

"And not in each other's back this time."

"How true."

She paused for a moment as she watched his smile, thinking it made such a total contrast to the usual mean and moody expression she was accustomed to seeing on him. He had a very nice smile, it softened his whole face and he had a lot of laughter lines around his eyes so maybe he wasn't such a bad person after all. But she felt the conversation was getting a bit too deep and she wanted to change the subject. "Look, speaking of Paul and Krista, how do you feel about their interest in one another?"

"How do *you* feel?" he countered.

"Personally, I think everything's happening just a wee bit too soon for them but I'm certainly not going to stand in their way or anything. They're both consenting adults, after all, they're both old enough to make their own decisions."

"Does that mean you approve?"

"I neither approve nor disapprove. It's been building between them for three weeks now, so I've had time to adjust to it. Krista has really surprised me, though, I know she didn't want to get romantically involved with anyone for a while, until she had at least got settled, but sometimes these things happen, don't they? You meet someone when you least expect it and that's it, nothing more you can do about it."

"Sounds like the voice of experience talking," he said softly.

"No, not really," she said awkwardly. "I usually don't hurry into anything." She glanced at her watch and was saved further explanation when she saw what time it was. "I'd better go in search for Krista, we should be going home to get ready. See you later, Dave… and thanks."

He watched her trot off, feeling as if a huge weight had just been lifted from his shoulders. "No," he murmured, "thank *you,* Cathy."

He started to walk slowly back in the direction they had come.

Cathy found Paul and Krista just as it seemed they were about to share their first kiss. Cathy clapped her hand over her mouth and stared at them in pained contrition. "I, well, huh…sorry to interrupt your fun," she said at last.

Krista chewed on her lip and looked at her friend in only faint embarrassment. And there was a very distinct twinkle in her eye too. What had been about to happen was something she had been *dying* to have happen – Paul had instigated it too, which made it all the better – but because Cathy had inadvertently thwarted it told Krista it just wasn't meant to have been. This time. Paul was still standing beside her, a great deal more than faintly embarrassed and she thought that was awfully sweet.

"Hi, Cathy," Krista purred nonchalantly. "Er, what you just saw…or at least what you *nearly* saw…it was just Paul and I practicing at being boyfriend and girlfriend… um, just like the Captain wanted us to."

Cathy rolled her eyes in obvious disbelief of that explanation. "Sure, Kris, whatever you say." She looked calmly at Paul and she had to try very hard not to laugh at his obvious mortification. "I just came to say that it's time Krista and I got home so we can get changed. It's after eleven and we have to sort out a suitable wardrobe."

"Oh." Paul nodded and tried to still his beating heart. *So close,* he thought, *so very, very close.* Then he realized the slight urgency in Cathy's voice and he came back to planet Earth with an undignified bump. "Oh, right. I tell you what, you two go on home in Cathy's car, I'll wait here for Dave to take him back to the station so he can get his own car and then, since we all have to arrive at the club together, I'll swing by your place and pick you up at about quarter to twelve. Think you can be ready by then?"

"We'll have to be, won't we?" Krista stated.

"True. Hey, where *is* Dave?" He caught a hint of a blush on Cathy's cheeks and he inwardly groaned. "Don't tell me you two had another fight?"

"No, nothing like that. Truthfully. He's coming along the path right now, I can see him. Come on, Kris, we'd better move it."

Paul couldn't tear his eyes away from Krista as he watched her walk away. His heart was refusing to settle after their near kiss and, despite his excitement, he felt strangely disquieted too. That made it twice his attempt to kiss her had been foiled and he could only hope that this wasn't going to be an omen for the way it was going to be for them.

Dave came and stood beside him just then and he couldn't fail to notice the wistful expression that clouded Paul's face when Krista disappeared out of view. "Done anything with her yet?" he asked softly.

"No, and more's the pity. Not through lack of trying, mind you."

"All in good time, pal of mine, if she's worth waiting for."

"She is, Dave, for sure. Only trouble is, I don't know how much longer I *can* wait for. She's sending me out all kinds of signals, each one of them driving me totally crazy."

"It's been over three weeks since you had any sex, no much wonder you're going crazy."

"It's not just the sex part, Dave. I just can't stop thinking about her and yes, I want to have sex with her, but I also want to make love with her. For the first time in my life, I can actually understand the difference between those two. And it's a *vast* difference."

Dave's eyes shot open wide when he heard that. "You really are smitten by her."

"Oh yeah. I won't even try to deny it anymore. I'll be seeing her again in about half an hour and I already can't wait."

"You taking her to the club?"

"Have to, for the reason the Captain told us and also because neither Cathy nor Krista know where the club is or even how to get to it. Come on, partner, I'll take you back to the station for your car."

On the ten-minute drive, Paul heard, with a lot of relief, that Dave and Cathy had managed to talk things over and had even reached a hopefully permanent truce. When he pulled into the underground garage at the station, where Dave's car was parked, an idea so heartwarming, naughty and delicious struck Paul that he felt he had to share it with Dave.

"Hey, after that dream you had last night, maybe it was Cathy whom you took to your bed. Maybe you've been attracted to her all along, so she's been in your sub-conscious."

Dave rolled his eyes. "Oh, Jesus Christ, where *do* you get them from?"

"Well, you said she had long hair and Cathy has long hair. You said she had a beautiful body and Cathy has that too."

"Yeah. So?"

"So, I think I'm actually right here. You want to bang Cathy and it took a dream for you to realize that."

Dave wearily shook his head. "You really do talk the biggest load of crap at times."

"Maybe, but at least it's intelligent crap."

"That, my friend, is entirely a matter of opinion. I may have told you this morning I was ready to start going out with women again, but I can't recall ever mentioning Cathy's name – whether she's been in my sub-conscious or not. I also told you I could change my mind again, very easily, and if you think you're going to push Cathy and me together, I'm going to do just that."

Paul carefully suppressed a grin and patiently listened to Dave rant on for two more minutes about the same subject. Then, figuring he would much rather be over at Krista's place than right here, Paul quickly ushered him out of the car. "See you at the girls' house later. Take care. And stop off at a drugstore on your way over."

"What for?"

"A condom…or twelve. Just in case."

Dave flipped him the finger, but Paul didn't see it, he had already taken off with a loud squeal of tires.

CHAPTER NINETEEN

Paul pulled up outside the girls' apartment right on schedule and, just as he was about to get out of the car, he found them to be right on schedule too because they appeared at their front door, saw him, and started walking down the path towards him. His jaw dropped when he saw what they were wearing.

Krista had on a short, black, leather mini skirt, with sheer black pantyhose and three-inch high-heeled black shoes. Her blouse was a rich shade of red of an almost see through material. She had unbuttoned it all the way to about mid-way down her cleavage and had tied it in a knot just above the waist of her skirt, giving an onlooker a generous amount of smooth, creamy skin to ogle at. Her long dark hair had been swept up to one side on top of her head and was held in place with a barrette and the nearer she approached him, he could see her make-up had been applied perfectly for the task on hand – just slightly on the whoreish side to complete the ensemble of a woman of slightly loose repute. Even though this obviously wasn't her normal style of dress, she still managed to pull it off with the greatest of ease and confidence, which he admired her all the more for.

Paul switched his attention to Cathy next. Her garb was something similar, complete with a heart stopping short, black leather mini skirt, black hose and black high heels but her blouse was a deep, electric blue that she had pulled down to expose one shapely shoulder (and hint at the fact she might not be wearing a bra). It was a short, buttonless top that didn't meet the top of her skirt and every time she lifted her arms even slightly, she flashed a bare midriff. Her naturally curly hair had been piled high on her head in a ponytail and he saw her make-up had been applied as perfectly as Krista's. She seemed a bit more self-conscious of her appearance than Krista did of hers, but he couldn't fault either one of them on their choice of wardrobe, in the short time they had had to get ready, they had both done rather well.

"Humm… you ladies look… great," he said, having to clear his throat in mid-sentence. "Did you actually have clothes like that right on hand?"

Krista saw him unashamedly and openly stare at her legs and she grinned impishly. "We sure did," she told him. "Cathy and I like to party, and we *love* to dress up to do just that."

He thought she had to be joking, only the more he looked at her, the more he couldn't be so sure. "I see," he said slowly.

Cathy rolled her eyes. "Kris, don't lie to the man, that's not nice." She looked down at herself and then at Paul in sudden panic. "You don't think we went overboard, do you?"

Paul held the door open for her and she slid into the back seat and when Krista got into the front, he stole another furtive glance at Krista's legs, a sight he obviously enjoyed looking at. "No, Cathy," he replied momentarily, "not at all, you both look just the way the Captain wanted you to, I promise."

Krista caught the way his gaze kept slipping between her legs, her cleavage and the road and she desperately wanted to tease him about his subtle approach, but she didn't think it would be fair to him with Cathy in the back seat. She had already found out that day that he could get very easily embarrassed, after all.

On the drive over to the Blues Haven, they concocted new surnames and Krista and Cathy rehearsed a story about their being in the

United States. Paul gave them the best advice he could for the moment and that was that they relax, don't overact or over-*re*act and simply let themselves go with the flow.

The club was, indeed, in a very dangerous, sleazy area of the city and, when Paul parked his car in the adjacent parking lot, he hoped the car would still be there and in one piece when he came back outside. He made a mental note that he would request a department vehicle for his journeys to the club for the duration of the case and silently kicked himself that he hadn't already done so.

With no time to dwell on it, he glanced at his watch. It was 12:05 and, after a few moments of just watching and waiting and seeing nothing untoward, they got out of the car, and sauntered slowly over to the building they had yet to see anyone go in or come out of.

It was a low, sprawling, red bricked structure, with numerous windows that were either filthy or had been shaded over with thick mesh. An unlit neon sign that showed a couple of palm trees on a small sandy beach, and the club's name, hung above the main door. Paul hadn't seen any side doors, so he guessed there had to be at least one fire exit door to the back of the building that probably led directly into an alleyway.

Halfway across the parking lot, Paul muttered reassurances to the ladies. "Okay, just remember to play it cool. Krista, put an arm around me, boyfriend, girlfriend, don't forget, so we must make this look as authentic as possible just in case somebody might be watching us from the inside. Turner and Chips assured us they couldn't see any outside surveillance equipment like cameras, but I really don't want to take any chances until I find out for myself. Let me do most of the talking at first and just follow my lead as soon as you're comfortable. When the manager talks to you, don't give too much of yourselves away unless he specifically asks for clarification or something. If he asks you about your background, ad-lib or stick to the story you've thought up, whichever seems the most appropriate, but remember *every*thing you tell him. One slip and it's all over. And acting natural is the name of the game. Happy enough?"

The two girls nodded in somewhat trepidation as they suddenly realized this was it. Krista put her arm around Paul's waist, found that she liked the feeling and just having him so close to her like this helped dispel all her nerves.

Once inside, and after not having to fight to get a table in the dim room, they each looked around as casually as possible at their surroundings. The table and chairs had all been situated around the focal point of the room, a large, raised stage that had a backdrop of a shimmering, sequined red curtain and which had spotlights strategically placed above and in front of it. A well-stocked bar took up most of one side of the room to the left of the stage and between the bar and the stage there ran a passageway towards the back of the building, with two doors leading off it. To the right of the stage there was another passageway, which led to changing rooms and restrooms. The décor was dingy and dirty, the floors were all dulled hardwood that might have been handsome once upon a time, but which were now scuff marked and covered in cigarette burns that looked like bullet holes from a small caliber gun. And that was basically the club called The Blues Haven.

Stale sweat, cheap perfume and cologne, cigar and cigarette smoke and booze permeated the air and seemed to cling to their clothes, making Cathy and Krista automatically wrinkle their noses in disgust.

Only two other tables were being used by the shady looking clientele, all men, who momentarily stopped what they were doing to stare with great interest at the newcomers, particularly Cathy and Krista. The girls managed to ignore the appraising glances.

A waitress with blonde hair the color of brass, came over to them with her tray and a sullen expression. "Order?" she asked with little interest.

"We'd like to see the manager if he's around," Paul requested.

The girl looked up, startled, revealing heavily made up blue eyes. She had obviously been expecting a drink order, certainly not a request for the manager and she wondered if she had served this guy some time and now he had come back to complain about her. She slapped her notebook back down on the tray and scowled. "I'll just go get him," she snapped unpleasantly.

Two minutes later, a small, very bald and very fat man waddled over to their table. He was wearing an extremely sour expression that instantly dissolved as soon as he saw Cathy and Krista. "Yeah?" he asked.

"If you're the manager," Paul said, "we're just wondering if you're doing any hiring, Mr....er...?"

"Petcelli. Xavier Petcelli. You're lucky you caught me, I'm not usually here this early on any given day but I had to do an inventory. What makes you think I'm looking for new staff?"

"A buddy of mine comes in here from time to time, Floyd King, he told me there might be some openings."

"Floyd King? Never heard of no Floyd King."

"Well, doesn't surprise me about old Floyd, he likes to keep a low profile, if you know what I mean? He's a short guy, red hair, built like a brick shithouse. He drinks draft beer all the time."

"So do a lot of my customers." Petcelli drummed his fat fingers on the table, trying to remain professional when he was actually trying hard not to stare at the two ladies before him. "What kind of work are you looking for?"

"Anything that's available. Bar work, whatever."

Petcelli looked more closely and appreciatively at Krista and Cathy and they simultaneously felt their skin crawl. He rested his gaze on Krista. "Can you dance, cookie?" he asked, staring right down her cleavage and this time not even being discreet about it.

"I can indeed," she said, pouring as much seduction as she could into her voice. "I dance for my man here every night…" She pouted sexily at Paul, "…don't I, darling'?" Then, for Petcelli's benefit, she crossed and uncrossed her legs as slowly and as provocatively as possible.

"Okay, let's see what you're made of then. Get up on the stage and work that body of yours." Petcelli averted his gaze from her legs back up to her cleavage again. "And, if I think you're any good, you've got yourself a job."

Krista looked swiftly at Paul who, on seeing she was nearing panic, nodded coolly at her. "Go ahead, sugar, just show the man what you can do. Show him what it is that turns me on every night."

She ambled slowly over to the stage, inwardly cringing at the thought of having to dance in front of the crude looking characters, but she kept a faint smile on her face and let her hips sa-shay beautifully as she walked across the floor. Paul saw beads of perspiration appear on Petcelli's face as he watched her, and it seemed to Paul that Petcelli's eyes never left the vicinity of Krista's bottom.

So far, so good, Paul thought.

Krista went to the CD player sitting on the stage, selected a CD and, picking up the rhythm, she started to sway slowly to the music. She danced as wantonly as she could, shutting her mind to the fact that she was in a sleazy club, being ogled by the equally sleazy manager. The music she had picked didn't exactly help make her feel any better either, it gave her the impression she should be in an Arabian harem or somewhere.

She continued for a few minutes until Petcelli, mercifully, barked, "Enough!" He was perspiring heavily now, and he absent-mindedly wiped his forehead with the sleeve of his jacket.

Krista bent and turned the music off, giving him one last glimpse of her backside and the inviting rim of lacy black panties hiding beneath her skirt and then she sa-shayed back to the table. Before she sat down, Paul, who really couldn't help himself and had been unashamedly enjoying her moves just as much as anybody else in the club who had a penis and a pulse, simply couldn't resist the temptation for any longer and he gently patted her bottom, even letting his fingers linger for a moment.

"Well done, sugar," he congratulated, then turned to Petcelli. "Well?"

"Uh, she…she's good," the fat, sweaty little man enthused. "Very good. I, er, don't usually come in at this time of day, as I said earlier but I had to today… paperwork, inventory, you know how it is…and I'm glad I did for that little show."

"So, does that mean I got the job?" Krista asked, catching her breath, although she already knew the answer.

"Yeah…yeah…. yes, sure, honey, the job's yours." Petcelli stole one last glance down her blouse and turned to Cathy. He dutifully started ogling her cleavage and her creamy, bare shoulder. "Now then, little lady, I'm afraid I only had the one vacancy for a dancer."

Cathy pouted unhappily, her eyes suitably downcast and woeful. "Oh no."

"Don't fret, my dear," Petcelli said in his best fatherly voice. "Can you wait tables?"

"I have waitressing experience," she said, brightening quickly. Paul was proud of her, she was doing everything right so far, particularly when he knew she was extremely uncomfortable under Petcelli's lewd gaze and was doing an excellent job of not showing it.

"Good, that's what I like to hear…experience counts, you know. Stand up, give me a look at yourself. My, er…clientele like their waitresses pretty."

Feeling like a prize show mare, Cathy stood up and spun slowly around, wiggling her hips and letting her top slip down a little more off her shoulder. When she flashed Petcelli a sexy smile, he all but drooled and she arched a well-defined eyebrow at him. "Well? Do I make the grade?"

"Oh yes, you certainly do." He watched her sit down and cross her legs and, when he realized he wasn't going to see up her skirt, he reluctantly shifted his gaze to Paul. He appraised him for a long, silent moment and decided he would certainly keep his female customers happy. "Can you work the bar?"

"Sure can, bar work is second nature to me." Paul sat back in his chair, all calm and deliberately self-assured.

Petcelli nodded in satisfaction. "Okay, that's it then, I don't need to see or ask any more because you're all hired. Can you start as soon as tonight? You'd really be doing me a favor if you could."

"Yeah we can start tonight," Paul said, "but what about our pay?"

"You get paid cash…minimum wage all round, I'm afraid, it's the best I can do. But I can guarantee you'll make it up in a lot of tips."

Here's a tip for you, you fat little worm, Krista thought to herself, *eye my cleavage one more time and you'll be spitting teeth for a week.* She smiled sweetly. "A job at last," she gushed, looking gratefully at Petcelli as if he had just given her the world on a plate. "Thank you so much, Mr. Petcelli, this is just wonderful news."

"My pleasure, cookie."

"What do I have to wear on stage?"

"Well, to be honest, as little as possible. I don't do nude here, but I like to leave little to the imagination, if you know what I mean. There are costumes backstage you can take your pick from." He jerked a podgy thumb in the direction right of the stage, presumably to let her know where the changing rooms were located. "By the way, I didn't get your names for my, uh, books."

"Paul Hutchison."

"Cathy Tanner."

"Kris Riley."

"Okay, good. Cathy, I have a uniform I like my evening girls to wear. What size are you? I'm guessing a six."

"Six or eight, depending on the style. Is that a problem?"

"Not at all, there are several sixes and eights to choose from. Paul, wear whatever you're comfortable in, but no blue jeans." Petcelli paused and looked at Krista again, thoughtfully this time. "You have a remarkable accent, cookie. Mind telling me where it's from?"

"Ireland," she said calmly, deliberately not differentiating between the North and South of Ireland.

"Really? I have cousins on my mother's side from there.... Cork, I think. Been here long?"

"A few months."

"And I take it you've been finding it hard to find a job, huh?"

"Very much so. You're the first person who has been willing to even give Cathy and me a chance and I really do want to thank you."

"No problem." He shrugged in a way that must have been his idea of modesty and then, with a swift glance at his watch, he closed the meeting. "I'm a busy man so I'll see you all later at around 8:30. The hours of the night bar are from 9:00 until 2:00 but one thing I do insist from my staff is punctuality." With one last leer at Krista's cleavage, he heaved himself off the chair and this time, behind his back, she was able to give way to a shudder of revulsion.

"Yeah, I know what you mean," Cathy agreed. "Come on, let's get out of here."

Happy to get back out into the fresh air again, Paul breathed a sigh of relief when he saw his car was still intact. "No sign of Dave," he remarked and looked at his watch. It was only 12:25, which surprised him because he felt as if they had been inside the club a lot longer than twenty minutes. He quickly texted Dave to let him know to get to the club within five minutes.

"Do we wait for him?" Cathy asked.

"Better not, we're not supposed to know who he is. Come on, I'll take you ladies home. I told him to come there after he was through here."

He got into the car and pulled out into the steady Sunday afternoon stream of traffic. "By the way, you both did exceptionally well in there, considering how nervous you were. You had that toad eating out of the palm of your hand."

Krista shuddered again at the image of Xavier Petcelli, this time eating out of her hand. "Ugh! Imagine waking up in the morning and finding someone like *that* lying beside you. If he calls me "cookie" one more time, I think I'll vomit." And her look of disgust said it all.

By 1:15, Dave had arrived at the girl's home. He hadn't been fortunate at getting a bouncer's job, but he had been offered a position as a barman or, if it was exceptionally busy (and to keep the female clientele happy, he had been told, not knowing it was one of the same reasons Paul had been hired for), a relief waiter. He too was starting that night and they had already informed a jubilant Captain Hamilton.

"What did you tell Petcelli your last name was?" Paul asked him.

"Dave Mitchell."

"Charming character Mr. Petcelli, isn't he?" Cathy remarked dryly.

Paul told Dave how Petcelli had unabashedly leered at Cathy and Krista and how repulsed they were by him. Dave had missed seeing the girls in their slutty gear too, by the time he had arrived at their place, they had changed back into more normal clothes and had taken off their goopy make-up.

Krista stood up and stretched lazily. "It's been a long day already and it's only 1:30. Still, I'm absolutely starved, and you two gentlemen are welcome to stay for lunch."

"I'm certainly game," Paul said. "Dave?"

"Sure, as long as it's free, I'll eat anywhere."

"Okay good, four for lunch it is then." Krista looked over at Cathy. "Want to give me a hand, Cath?"

Before Cathy could respond, Paul jumped up. "I'll help instead," he offered eagerly and followed Krista into the kitchen.

"Mushroom soup and ham and cheese sandwiches?" she suggested. "Or would you prefer something different?"

"I'll eat anything. So will Dave. When you live on your own you learn to come up with good, nutritional meals or snacks and I'll have you know I make very good sandwiches."

"Fine, then you're on sandwich duty, I'll make the soup." She lifted a couple of cans of Campbell's mushroom soup from the cupboard and as she began to open the first one, she shot him a sideways glance. "Did you *ever* live with a woman?"

His hands froze in the plastic bread bag and he stared at her in surprise. "You certainly do know how to be direct, young lady."

She shrugged indifferently. "Yeah, I know, you've told me that already. So, did you?"

He looked into her eyes. *Oh God, those eyes,* he thought, *the kind of green you only read about but rarely see in real life…and those beautiful flecks of gold through them…* Realizing she was waiting for an answer, he solemnly shook his head. "No. Never."

She smiled slowly and in slight puzzlement, wondering what was going through his mind at the strange look that had moved over his face. Then their eyes locked and all notions of making something to eat were quickly forgotten about as they stared at one another and, in less than an instant, they were on the same wavelength and thinking of exactly the same thing.

But Krista wanted to place the ball firmly into Paul's court and force him to make the first move, just to be entirely sure that what she wanted, he definitely wanted too. She waited, but not for long.

Paul felt his heartbeat quicken as he picked up on her signals and he knew that this was it, this was going to be the moment when his dream would finally be realized. Twice, he reminded himself, twice he had nearly had the opportunity to kiss her and he only knew he wasn't going to let the opportunity pass him by again. He took a few steps closer to her and hesitantly reached out with trembling fingers to touch her burning cheek.

A soft sigh of pleasure escaped his throat at the mere feel of her. "You are so…so beautiful," he whispered hoarsely and then, tentatively, he bent his head towards hers, his eyes closing as his lips sought out hers.

A first kiss is always the most special kiss of all because it can happen only once in a lifetime between the same two people and Krista responded to this first kiss with this man whom she knew was already very important in her life, shyly at first and then, the more eager he became, so did she. He didn't try to force his tongue in, not until she opened her mouth to grant him entrance and neither of them seemed to want the kiss to end and he had already pulled her into a tight embrace against him, letting the very feel of her body against his cause delicious shivers up and down his spine.

This was probably the most perfect moment of Paul's life as he tasted her and savored her and ran his fingers through the silky strands of her hair and when at last they broke apart, it was obvious they hadn't wanted to, and they couldn't stop staring at one another in nothing short of sweet, beautiful awe.

He shook his head in sudden bewilderment. "Wh-What just happened here?"

She could have come up with a smartass response to that but that would have killed the moment and she only shook her head in the way he had. She was trying to force her legs to stop from buckling at the knees and she realized, with a start, that this was the affect one of his kisses could do to her, that he kissed *amazingly* and every nerve ending in her body was responding as if they had been hit with electric shocks to prove it.

"Whatever it was," she said huskily, "it was beautiful."

"For me too," he said in dazed wonder. "I think you've had me under a spell since the very first day I met you because I've only wanted to do that since that first time I took you out to the bar."

"So, what stopped you?"

"You did," he admitted softly. "I thought that if I had kissed you then you would have rejected me or something and quite frankly, my dear, I couldn't bear the thought of that." He gently cupped her face in his hands and looked deeply into her eyes again. "I really mean it, you know, you've had me under some kind of spell."

"You found me out," she teased. "But it's good to see I still have the ability to cast spells when I want. I was in a witch in a previous life, you know, but I was a good witch."

"Is that so?" He chuckled softly. "Cast me under your spell any time, lady."

She smiled gently. "I will, as long as you keep kissing me like that."

"Can be arranged." He dreamily traced the outline of her jaw and then his fingers hovered over her lips. "You know, Krista, this…umm…well, this isn't the way I usually do things. If I want to go out with a woman, I'll go out with her, but you… you've done something to me and I'll be darned if I can figure out what it is. I only knew I had to take it slowly with you, I wanted to get to know you completely and I'm sort of glad I dragged my heels a bit because, after only three short weeks, I already feel that you're very important to me." He hoped he wasn't scaring her off, but she didn't even flinch at his softly spoken words.

"Then that makes it unanimous because I happen to feel the same way about you."

"You do?" He pulled her back into his arms. "Come here, you." He started kissing her again and this kiss was as perfect as the first one and he wanted more and more from all the riches her warm, soft mouth had to offer so he didn't stop, nor would he until she pulled away first.

But Krista didn't, so it was in this passionate state that Cathy found them when she walked into the kitchen to get herself and Dave a drink. "Oops, oops," she said, feeling like an intruder on them for the second time that day. "Well, I seem to be making a habit out of this, don't I?" she said cheerily. "Don't mind me, you children just carry on, pretend I'm not even here and I'll be out of your way in no time."

"Don't worry, Cathy," Krista said with a deep, throaty chuckle. "I needed an intrusion before I was tempted to do something terribly naughty."

Paul instantly groaned. "Don't say that, woman," he begged, "don't put an idea like that into my head, *please*, I'm only desperately trying to be a gentleman here."

Cathy comically rolled her eyes. "Now you're just making me sick," she said in dry amusement. "Good thing for you two my stomach's too empty to throw up on. You came in here to make something to eat, remember? Dave tells me he's starved and so am I so, if you can stay apart for long enough, start making." But Cathy was clearly delighted for Krista, the inevitable had, at last, happened for her.

Krista turned back to one of the cans of soup and showed that she had at least started to pop up the pull ring. "Look," she announced, "I've already made a start. *Now* will you leave us in peace?"

Cathy grinned impishly. "Of course." She tipped Krista a wink, quickly lifted two sodas from the fridge and hurried back to the living room. "Seems like lunch is going to be a little later than planned," she stated happily to Dave.

"Oh? And why's that?"

"Because Paul and Krista are busy at other things."

He looked at her coolly. "Now why doesn't that surprise me?"

Something in his tone made Cathy narrow her eyes quizzically as she tried to assess his feelings on the matter. Although he seemed neither angry nor annoyed, or even pleased, she could see a definite hint of something lurking in his eyes and she tried to guess what it was.

Maybe he *had set his sights on Krista,* she thought, *maybe he thought that Paul wasn't going to make a move on her, so he decided that he would, if the coast was definitely clear.*

But she couldn't have been more wrong in what she was thinking.

CHAPTER TWENTY

Dave arrived at the club first and he had just been given a guided tour by a doorman called Brad when Paul, Krista and Cathy appeared. Dave did a double take when he saw the girls in their gear, but he composed himself quickly when he reminded himself he wasn't even supposed to know them.

They all stood uncertainly for a few moments until they spotted Petcelli waddling towards them.

"Ah, you've arrived," Petcelli said, stating the obvious and, right on cue, he sneaked a peek down the front of Krista's blouse. Paul pretended not to notice and kept a well-practiced smile on his face. "Good to see you're on time, like I said earlier, I like my staff to be punctual." Remembering his manners, he introduced Dave to the rest of them, they shook hands all round and then Petcelli turned all professional. "Girls, there's a changing room just through that door to the right of the stage. You'll find everything you need in there, including your – ah – uniforms. Cathy, soon as you're ready, I want you on the floor and Kris, you'll be starting your first dance on stage at 9:30. You dance by yourself, for thirty minutes and then you're entitled to a thirty-minute break. That's the way you'll go until closing time. All clear?"

The girls nodded and went in search of the changing room, which turned out to be every bit as shabby as the rest of the building. At the back of the small room, there was another door and, thinking it might lead to a bathroom, Krista went over to it but found the door locked.

"Maybe it's just a stock room," Cathy suggested.

"Maybe. Let's see what the toad has picked out for us to wear." Krista went over to a rack of clothes and started rifling through them. "Oh my God!" she exclaimed, holding up an extremely skimpy gold lamé thong bikini that had her name on a piece of paper pinned to it. In fact, the piece of paper was almost as big as the two items of material. "He can't be serious! He expects me to wear something like this?"

Cathy's eyes opened wide in astonishment. "Doesn't leave much to the imagination, that's for sure. You poor thing! I hope you've waxed your bikini line recently."

"Sure… a full Brazilian, remember?" Krista said impishly, then looked at the costume in complete disdain and wryly shook her head. "Captain Hamilton obviously hasn't realized just how sleazy this club really is. But he's definitely off my Christmas card list."

"Mine too." Cathy suddenly grinned. "Hey, just remember not to sneeze out there, the customers might get more than they bargained for."

"Ha, ha, funny you're not," Krista said, clearly unamused.

As they were changing, another girl came into the room and she stopped short as soon as she saw Cathy and Krista. "Oh…I'm sorry," she said timidly, "excuse me, I wasn't expecting anyone to be here."

"That's okay," Krista said amiably. "We're new here. You?"

"Er, no, I've been here for nearly two months. I'm a dancer."

"So am I. My name is Kris Riley and this is my friend, Cathy Tanner. She's a waitress."

"That's nice. I'm Ruth O'Brien." She was a very pretty girl, with long auburn hair and startling gray eyes. She was probably in her early twenties and her figure was slim and curvy but her whole manner told Cathy and Krista she was very uncomfortable being in their company so they tried to put her at ease.

"That's a great Irish name, Ruth," Cathy said with a warm smile.

"And that's where we're from, Ireland."

"Oh, I see. *That's* why you talk funny." But Ruth didn't even make an attempt to return the smile.

"So, seeing it's our first night here," Krista said, determined to draw some conversation out of the poor girl who seemed as timid as a mouse, "what's it like working in a club like this?"

"It's okay, except for…" Ruth trailed off and her eyes darted nervously towards the door Krista had just tried to open. "Never mind," she finished lamely.

"Except for what?" Krista probed gently.

"Nothing, I didn't say nothing so please don't ask."

Behind Ruth's back, Cathy raised an enquiring eyebrow at Krista, who gave her the merest of shrugs in return that she didn't know what was wrong with Ruth either.

"Okay, I'm sorry if I made you uncomfortable." Krista decided to quickly change the subject and she held up the bikini. "Does Mr. Petcelli seriously expect us to wear this sort of thing?"

At that easy question, Ruth visibly started to relax. "Yeah, I'm afraid so." She emitted a short, bitter laugh. "Sort of makes you wonder if there's not an easier way to make a living, doesn't it?"

Krista gave her a warm smile. "This is our first job since we arrived in the United States so we really can't complain…not that I'm saying we'll be here forever, in the club I mean, but for us it's a start. You know, you're a very pretty girl, haven't you ever considered taking up modeling or something?"

Ruth rolled her eyes in consternation. "Ran away from home when I was fifteen to do just that and look how I've ended up." She gave another bitter laugh and then her expression hardened. "Still, beats being on the streets. I've done that too, you know and that was a real barrel of laughs, all those men paying you for favors that they couldn't get their wives to do for them at home. Man, I'm glad I'm out of *that* lifestyle, what with STDs and God knows what else going around." She looked down at a spot on the floor, obviously realizing she had said far too much about herself and she clamped her lips together in annoyance.

Krista looked at her sympathetically. "It's never too late to get out of a rut, you know. How old are you anyway, twenty-one, twenty-two?"

"I'll be twenty-two next month."

"Did you ever graduate?"

"Who are you, my mother?"

"Of course not and I didn't mean to pry but, if you want, I can be a friend, if ever you need one. I'm an awfully good listener."

"Well thanks, but no thanks. I've made my own bed so I'm going to just have to lie in it."

Krista bit her tongue to stop from saying anything further and she glanced over at Cathy, who by now had changed into her uniform and was staring down at herself in poorly concealed disgust.

"I may as well have nothing on," she lamented. The black skirt she had on barely covered her panties, and her top, which was a hideous shade of orange, wasn't much bigger than a bra and she was sure the outline of her nipples was painfully apparent for all to see. She wanted to die with embarrassment.

Krista looked her critically up and down. "At least it just about covers the essentials – and you're still going to have on more than me, so consider yourself lucky."

Cathy nodded unhappily. "Oh well, better get out there, I suppose. What time does it usually start to get busy, Ruth?"

"On a Sunday night, same as every other night. Round about now."

"Great. Good luck, Kris, talk to you later." Cathy went out to the bar, trying not to look as self-conscious as she felt. She walked straight over to Dave, who had his back to her and didn't see her approach. "Someone owes me big for this one," she told him through gritted teeth.

He swung round at the sound of her voice and as soon as he saw her and what she was wearing, or, more to the point, *not* wearing, his eyes nearly popped out of his head. He quickly masked his surprise (and an uncommon and sudden interest) and turned to Paul. "Hey, Paul, look at what Cathy has to wear," he whispered.

Paul looked up from the lemons he was slicing and stared at her, clearly quite stunned. "Holy shit! That's practically obscene. Is Krista wearing something like that too?"

"No." Cathy picked up a tray and smiled sweetly. "*She's* having to wear even less. Remind me to shoot our good Captain for this one."

"I'm really sorry, Cathy," Paul said in genuine distress. "If I'd known it was going to be like this for you and Krista, I would have persuaded the Cap to give us another case. One that involved you keeping your clothes on."

She was touched by his concern and she offered him a smile. "You weren't to know, so no reason for you to feel bad. I just never pictured that I would have to serve drinks to people while looking like I should be in the centerfold of *Playboy*, know what I mean?" With that, she turned and walked away.

Dave watched her go over to the nearest table and, before he could stop himself, he said in an undertone to Paul. "She sure is one hot looking momma all right."

Paul looked at him in surprise. "Did I just hear that right?"

Dave's eyes were fixed firmly on Cathy's legs and the barely hidden, appealing curve of her buttocks. He caught a glimpse of lacy black panties and suddenly, his motor was running in top speed. "I don't know, what do you think you heard?" he asked absently.

"That you actually paid Cathy a well-deserved compliment?"

"So, what if I did?" Finally realizing what he was saying, Dave quickly turned away to make himself busy, but Paul, naturally, wasn't going to let him off so easily.

"I think this means that Mr. Celibacy of the Year might actually be willing to let his guard down around a female – who just happens to be absolutely gorgeous – sooner than he thinks."

For Paul's troubles, Dave awarded him with a filthy look. "Where did you get such a crazy idea from? And why do you always insist in reading something into something that's never there?" But even as he spoke, he couldn't resist the temptation to look in Cathy's direction again and when he did, his expression visibly softened. He quickly composed himself again. "So, what if she has incredible legs, a cute ass and an adorable pair of…eyes? So have a lot of other women out there but that doesn't necessarily mean I'm interested in her just because I notice these things, does it?"

Paul raised a skeptical eyebrow in Dave's direction but before he could say anything in way of a retort, he was called over for an order by one of the other waitresses.

The club was indeed getting quite busy even though it was a Sunday night and the start of a new work week loomed ahead. Half of the rather weird looking clientele had come into the club already well intoxicated it seemed and, fueled with a lot of alcohol, their conversations were being carried out in anything but hushed tones. Coupled with the loud music that was playing, it was nigh impossible for any decent talking to be done behind the bar and Paul and Dave literally had to strain to hear above the din just so they could fulfill a waitress's order.

Cathy seemed to be holding her own as she whizzed from table to table, clearing dirty glasses and empty bottles away and emptying ashtrays as if she had been born to it and when one order earned her a five dollar tip, (*Just for you, sweet tits,* the horrible looking customer had told her when he stuffed the bill into the waist band of her skirt), she smiled her sweetest smile at him, went up to the bar and gave the bill to Dave to look after with the rest of her tips.

"This is terrible," she told him in a harsh stage whisper. "Five dollars or no five dollars, the idiot who gave it to me just happened to remark on a certain part of my anatomy before he insisted on putting it into the top of my skirt. He wanted to put it down my top instead. Can you believe that?"

Dave shot a glance at her cleavage, saw why anyone with hot blood running through his veins would want to go mining in that area and innocently shook his head. "Some people, Cathy," he commiserated dutifully. "Apart from that, how are you making out?"

"Apart from people like him, it's not too bad."

He smiled faintly. "Tell me that at around midnight when your feet are probably killing you."

"Too late, they already are. I'm not used to running around in high heels, I'd trade them for a pair of flat shoes anytime. It's all a case of mind over matter." She was about to say something else when she caught a signal from a table and, with a roll of her eyes, she walked briskly away.

Promptly at 9:30, Krista came out to the stage and Paul did a double take as soon as he saw her. All he could do was stare at her body in total amazement and he knew he was staring but he simply couldn't help it.

Krista caught his look and smiled ruefully as she indicated to herself and her costume with a subtle sweep of her hand, shaking her head in half-disgust and half-embarrassment. "Help me!" Her expression begged him quite clearly.

Wishing he could do just that, he tore his eyes away from her and tapped Dave on the shoulder. "You want to see hot stuff, look over there," he stated and nodded towards Krista.

Dave glanced over at her, certainly saw what Paul meant and smiled at his friend. "Put your eyes back in your head and take your mind out of the sewer, you disgusting, horny devil."

"But look at that body, Dave, look at those legs… and oh baby, look at those -"

"Paul! Enough already, I get the point. Shut up and keep working."

With one last, appreciative glance in Krista's direction, Paul tore his eyes away again and got down to the task at hand.

Despite the introduction from Petcelli, it seemed to take a few minutes for it to clue into the crowd that there was a new dancer tonight. But as soon as it did register, the customers went wild and Paul felt his heckles rise on hearing some of the very rude, very suggestive remarks they called out to her. Krista, although she could hear them just as well, took everything in her stride, losing herself in the music and totally ignoring the ribald and very blue comments that were thrown her way as she concentrated instead on her dancing and on maintaining a slight, sexy smile on her face throughout her number. Because she came across as being aloof and cool, the crowd loved her all the more.

By midnight, Paul and Dave were stacking up drink after drink in a never-ending stream and Cathy herself barely had time to catch her breath. During her breaks, Krista was the only one who had the opportunity to watch for anything suspicious but nothing seemed out of the ordinary, making her realize that she was going to be subjected to more jeers and cat-calls for at least one more night.

At last, 2:00 rolled around and the bar closed. By the time it took for the last of the customers to be escorted from the premises by the impatient bouncer, Cathy felt dead on her feet and the only thing she was looking forward to was her bed. Even when Dave told her how much she had accumulated in tips - $93, not bad for a first night on the job – it did nothing to cheer her up. He watched her come out of the changing rooms, struggling to get into her jacket and he suddenly felt sorry for her.

"Tired, Cathy?" he asked softly.

"Yeah, can't wait to get home." She smiled slightly and remembered how busy he had been too. "You must be tired as well."

"A bit, not much. Paul taking you home?"

"I think so…I *hope* so." She had changed back into her mini skirt and a somewhat sensible top but he could still see her legs, a sight he decided he definitely liked looking at. She caught him looking at her in a way she couldn't quite interpret but she was too tired to even want to.

He looked so terribly handsome tonight, she couldn't help but notice, and ever since their talk that morning in the park, he seemed to have lost the hardness around his mouth and the iciness in his eyes. She barely suppressed a sudden shiver of delight and prayed he hadn't noticed but if he had she was saved any explanations because Paul appeared from the bathroom just then and, seconds later, Krista came out of the changing room.

Petcelli waddled over to them to let them know they had done well for their first night and to give them their schedules for the rest of the week. They were all working through until Tuesday night, Paul and Krista were in on Wednesday night, Dave and Cathy Thursday night and all in together again on Friday night. They accepted the schedule with as much enthusiasm as they could, each secretly hoping they wouldn't have to be around to work it.

Paul took the girls home and when he pulled up outside their place, Cathy was nearly asleep in the back seat but she had the sense to know when she wasn't wanted. "Good night, Paul," she said with a yawn. "Thanks for the lift. Krissie, I'll see you in the morning because I'll be asleep before you come up, I can assure you."

"Okay, love, sleep tight." Krista waited for her friend to get out of the car and when they were alone, she turned to Paul. "Tired?"

"A little, but I'm a bit too wound up yet to want to sleep." He had been strangely quiet, almost distant even, in the car on the way back from the club. He seemed troubled too and, as another silence spun out between them, he suddenly lifted her hand off her lap and folded it into his. He looked down at her fingers, drew in a deep breath, let it out slowly and said, "Krista, we need to talk."

She looked at him in growing bewilderment and then, at the tone of his voice alone, she felt her spirits slowly start to sink. "Okay, if you like," she said as calmly as she could.

She didn't know what he wanted to talk about but she could certainly guess it was about the two of them and she had a very sneaky suspicion that she wasn't going to like what he had to say.

CHAPTER TWENTY-ONE

For a long, heavy, silent moment, Paul stared out into the darkness through the car window then at last, he turned to her again. "It's about this afternoon."

Krista nodded hesitantly. "I thought you were going to say that."

"I don't quite know how to say this, so please, just be patient with me." He paused, seemingly at a loss for words, then he said, "I've only known you for such a short time but already I know you've very special… very *important* to me. When I kissed… when *we* kissed this afternoon, it was as if nobody had ever kissed me like that before and it was as if something came alive in me for the very first time in my life." He paused again, suddenly realizing that if Dave had heard him saying that, Dave would go all out to give him the biggest ribbing of his life, only Dave would make sure to turn the remark into something crude. That thought, however, did nothing to cheer him up.

Krista studied his face, searching for a clue as to what he was getting at. "I really don't know what it is you're trying to tell me, Paul," she admitted at last. "Are you saying you're sorry now that we kissed?"

"No way!" He returned sharply. "Never in a million years am I sorry, don't ever think that. What I'm trying to say is this, or at least *one* of the things I'm trying to say is…well…I'm not usually a possessive person, I firmly believe that everyone is entitled to their space, but tonight, when you were up dancing – hey, cute costume, by the way – and when I heard all those sleaze buckets calling out what they would like to do to you, I got really angry and…" He paused yet again and swallowed hard, "…and really very jealous."

"But why? I wasn't even listening to them. To me, I was only up on that stage doing a pretend job."

"I know that and that's the right attitude to have, especially in a place like that but the jealousy took me completely by surprise because I've never felt anything as strong as that before…and it sort of scared me."

"Scared you? Why would it scare you?"

"I don't know, but it did… and it still does. And I know something else too, I know that even if we hadn't kissed, I would *still* have gotten jealous."

Krista shook her head in bewilderment and even in the dim light thrown in from the overhead street light, she could see he was terribly perplexed. "Does that mean you can't…or maybe don't want to, have those sorts of feelings? That you just can't handle them?"

"No, that's not what I'm trying to say at all. Look, all I know is, I've come to realize that I have feelings for you, Krista, feelings that are deep and strong…and very very real. To be honest, I think I've had them since the very first moment I ever set eyes on you, only I was afraid to push it in case what I was feeling wasn't real at all but was only wishful thinking on my part." He turned to stare through the window again and a few moments later, he surprised her completely when he suddenly started to chuckle. "You should see the bruises on my body from pinching myself to see if this is all just a crazy dream or not." But when he turned to look at her again, his expression was very serious, as if his warm chuckle had never happened. "And if it is a dream, then I think I don't ever want to wake up from it as long as you continue to be in it."

Krista felt her heart lurch up to her mouth at his softly spoken words, knowing instinctively that he meant them. They had had many in depth conversations before this, but only on general topics, like world famine, or police work, or save the whale campaigns, but certainly never one like this, where they seemed to be getting into uncharted territory. True, they had been flirting with each other from day one, but that had only been to test the waters and now she wondered if he was maybe starting to flounder, that he had found he was in way too deep and didn't like it anymore. Or maybe he had received a cautioning from Captain Hamilton to stop fraternizing, or maybe he really hadn't liked their kiss earlier on at all and he was just trying to let her down gently, or…

She snapped herself back to reality, trying to quell a feeling of rising panic and when she spoke, her voice was hoarse. "If that's what you want, you've got it."

Paul quickly shook his head. "No, Kris," he started, and her spirits sank even lower. "I'm not the only one whose feelings count here, this has to be what we *both* want, please understand that. If you don't want it to happen, then fine, I'll go home right now, drink a bottle or ten of beer and then shoot my foot or something off for making a big time fool out of myself for talking to you like this. Or, if you *do* want it to happen but would rather take it slowly, or if you think I'm coming on too strong, just tell me and we can play it cool for a while. We can get to know each other better and then we can simply start all over again if and when you feel the time is right."

She quite literally couldn't believe her ears at what she had just heard. Paul was actually taking the time to consider her feelings, something no other previous man in her life had ever done for her before and she knew now she no longer had to be afraid, that Paul cared for her as much as she cared for him. In a flash, her apprehension vanished and she smiled into his eyes. "There'll always be a right time for you and me, Paul," she said softly. "We don't have to 'play it cool' for a number of reasons but mainly because I want you to know that every time we're apart, I'm quite literally counting the seconds until I know we'll be together again. We don't have to get to know each other any better because we've been doing that ever since we met and anything else we may have to discover about each other from now on in will only be an added bonus. And I'm glad we know each other so well already, I'm glad I know I can be myself with you because I've never felt anything like this before with anyone." She stopped to take in a breath in preparation to carry on and in that instant, she caught him clenching his jaw and setting his lips in a firm line, as if he was irritated at what she was saying. She had been about to lay her hand on his again but, on seeing his expression, she faltered and let her hand rest on her knee instead. "Oh boy…Paul…I think *I'm* the one who has just managed to make a fool of myself here. I think I've read everything totally the wrong way, that instead of me thinking you wanted this as much as I did, what you really want is to make our relationship platonic, that you don't want to get romantically involved with me at all. You were only trying to let me down gently, weren't you? You're sorry now, that you've let yourself get so close to me after such a relatively short space of time…aren't you?"

Paul had no idea that she had managed to read something like that into what he had thought had been a blank expression on his face and he was shocked that she had managed to take his words and twist them around into an entirely different meaning. In truth, the first part of her speech had touched him deeply and he had only been trying not to appear too eager when all he had really wanted to do was pull her into his arms and hold her for a very long time. It was the first time since they had met that they had not been on the same wavelength and as he slowly turned to her and saw the hurt and the panic etched clearly on her beautiful face and in her eyes, he only knew he would never hurt her like that again. "Is that what you think?" he whispered hoarsely. "That I'm sorry I've finally met the woman of my dreams? No way, *no way* am I sorry! I was only thinking of you, I didn't want you feeling that I was coming on too strong, that's all, and I was afraid I would only end up losing you if I continued to come after you in the way I've been doing, that I would stifle you or smother you and turn you off me completely. Please believe me, there's nothing I want more than to start a proper relationship with you. In fact, I've hardly been able to think of anything else. I'm sorry I so obviously upset you there, that was definitely not my intentions when I started this conversation but if I have to spend the rest of my days making it up to you, I'll be only too glad to do just that."

For the moment shocked into silence, Krista stared at him and her heart started pounding madly in her chest. "I've already told you I never thought you were coming on too strong…quite the opposite, in fact. I was beginning to think we would still be flirting with one another by the time I turned 78. And as long as you don't think that *I* was coming on too strong to *you*, then I'm only glad we've reached some sort of agreement at long last."

"Is that so? Then I'll say amen to that." He blew a sigh of relief that everything was more or less settled between them now and he couldn't be happier about it.

Tilting her head slightly, she looked at him shyly. "So…does this all mean you now…um…want me…as your girlfriend?"

He rolled his eyes in amusement at her question. "No, it means I've been trying to find out if you will do my laundry for me." He quickly caught her arm before she could whack him one for that and he chuckled softly. "Of *course* it means I want you as my lady. Isn't that what you want too?"

"I don't think there's anything I want more."

He leaned over and gently caressed her cheek. Even at nearly 3:00 in the morning and taking into consideration that she had been up for what was probably closing in on nearly twenty-four hours, she still looked beautiful. "Me neither," he murmured. "And I promise you, you'll never be sorry."

She smiled slowly. "Neither will you." She moved closer to him and wrapped her arms around his neck. "Do you want to continue from where we left off?" she asked lightly.

"Where and when?"

"In the kitchen this afternoon, before Cathy interrupted us. Do you remember?"

He pretended to carefully consider for a moment. "Nope, can't say that I do," he teased. "Care to help me out here? What were we doing? Something naughty…I hope?"

"As if you didn't know," she scolded and moved to get out of the car. "Oh well, seeing you've got a very bad memory…for a detective…I may as well leave now. See you around."

He chuckled again and grabbed her quickly. "You little witch, stop playing hard to get."

"Just shut up and kiss me," she urged, melting back into his arms.

And of course, he was only too happy to oblige. As their lips met, he heard her emit a soft sigh of pleasure and when he kissed her more deeply, she only knew she didn't want this moment to end, that she wanted him to kiss her like this forever. It was quite some time before he reluctantly tore his mouth away from hers and when their eyes met, he couldn't suppress a groan of sheer bliss.

"I think you'd better get out of this car right now before I end up taking advantage of you, woman."

"Any more kisses like that and I'll gladly let you," she purred happily. She planted a little trail of kisses from his lips, down to his neck and then around to his ear and when she started nibbling softly on his earlobe, she immediately heard his sharp intake of breath.

"Krista…I…huh, I'm warning you…oh boy…Krista…" He rolled his eyes. "How did you manage to find my weak points so soon?"

"Lucky guess, I think," she murmured and moved her lips back down to his neck, where he smelled clean and faintly of lemons.

Paul felt a delicious, hardening throb way down there and he desperately wanted her to touch him, to release him from the restraints of his clothing, but it was too soon to expect that sort of thing from her, for all he knew, she was too shy to make the first move and besides, he knew that it would only take one gentle caress and he would more than likely explode. Literally. A first-time impression he certainly didn't want to make.

"Krista," he whispered breathlessly, "please, no more, okay? You, um…look, you've managed to steam up the car windows already."

She laughed gently and then, with a regretful smile, she pulled away. "All right, Sergeant Cameron, I can take a hint. Good night."

As he watched her start to get out of the car, he knew he definitely didn't want her to leave just yet and he quickly pulled her back towards him. "Don't go," he requested huskily, "not yet. Just one more kiss and then you can go, okay?"

Of course, there's no such thing as just one more kiss and half an hour later, they still hadn't parted company. By this stage, Paul was genuinely amazed at himself that he had managed, apart from a few heart stopping moments when his hand had roamed up the length of her thigh and his thumb had brushed the hot, moist vee of her panties – panties he had just wanted to push roughly aside and explore more deeply - to practice such great self-control in not taking it any further, despite her encouraging deep sighs of pleasure. It was plainly obvious all he wanted to do was take her into the back seat of the car (or pull her on top of him in the front seat, he wasn't particularly bothered) and make love to her, and his incessant and obvious arousal was living proof of him wanting to do just that. But he knew without any question of a doubt that he would have to be patient, that there was going to be a first time with her and he wanted it to be special and romantic, certainly not performed in the back seat (or the front seat) of his car.

Krista seemed to know what was going through his mind and she smiled. "Okay, I'm really going this time, it's getting awfully late. Do you want to take me to the precinct later on?"

"Um… no, I don't want to do that."

"Why not?" she asked in surprised

"Because the Captain isn't expecting to see us until around two or three o'clock and that's too long from now to wait until I see you again. I have a better idea instead. Why don't I pick you up around noon, take you for a bite to eat and then we can go down to the station later together?" A slight frown suddenly creased his brow as a thought occurred to him. "That is, of course, if Cathy won't mind being left on her own for a while?"

"I really don't think she'll mind, she's pretty easy going about a lot of things and I'm sure this will be one of them."

"Okay, if you're sure, seems like we have ourselves a date then." He leaned over and, not being able to resist, gave her one more kiss. "Good night…sweetheart."

"Good night, love," she murmured tenderly.

Paul watched in contentment as she walked up the path towards her home and then, with one last wave, he pulled away, a huge, happy grin on his face and a wildly beating heart that was full of awe and wonder in his chest.

CHAPTER TWENTY-TWO

As he had promised, Paul came round to pick up Krista at around noon. However, she was running a bit late and had only just stepped into the shower about a minute before he knocked on the door, so it was Cathy who answered him and led him into the living room.

"You may as well have a coffee or something, Krista might be a while. She's not exactly renowned for her speed first thing in the morning."

"A coffee would be great, thanks." Paul sat down and waited for her to come back in from the kitchen and when she did, he saw she had a cup of coffee for herself too. He took his from her, waited for her to make herself comfortable on an armchair by curling her legs up underneath her and he looked at her warmly. "Did you sleep well?"

"Eventually. You look as if you've been awake for hours."

"I'm used to little amounts of sleep." He sipped on his coffee and he suddenly looked very shy when he glanced over at her again. "Do you know…? Did Krista happen to mention about…?"

"About you and her?" Cathy finished easily for him. "Oh yes, Krista and I have no secrets. She and I talked about her and you just a little while ago. I think it's so nice, I really do and I couldn't be happier for you. A little surprised, maybe, but only a little, I've seen this coming practically from day one."

"You did? And I thought I…I thought *we* were being totally cool about the whole thing. I told Dave this morning and he took it typically Dave like, which means he didn't say too much about it except for his congratulations." Paul took another sip of his coffee and then carefully set the cup down on a coaster on the table in front of him. He smiled ruefully.

"Was it really that obvious?"

Cathy chuckled. "Oh yes, you weren't exactly subtle, but then again, neither was she. For what it's worth, though, you two seem to belong together."

"Thanks, Cathy, I appreciate you saying that. I wasn't exactly sure how your feelings on the matter were going to be when you found out."

"Why?"

"In case you thought I would be taking Krista away from you or something. I know she's all you have over here at the moment and I didn't want you to feel left out in the cold or anything like that."

Krista had voiced more or less the same concerns and Cathy felt as touched by Paul's genuine sincerity for her wellbeing as she had when Krista had brought it up. She gave him a soft look of gratitude. "No need for you to feel like that. Krista means the whole world to me and her happiness is what comes first. Besides, she's not the type of person who would leave her best friend without company all the time, she's far too caring and classy for that. I already told you I was happy for you both and I truly mean it from the bottom of my heart."

He looked at her warmly, feeling totally relaxed and comfortable in her company. They were only a very short span of time away from becoming firm, fast friends and this conversation would mark the laying of the foundation stones for their future relationship. "You're a very nice person, Cathy. Now I know why Krista talks about you with nothing but the deepest respect."

"It cuts both ways, Paul. I wouldn't let anyone say a bad word against her." With a twinkle in her eye, she pointed a stern finger at him. "So, if you ever do anything to her, it's me you'll answer to. Got that?"

"Yes, ma'am," he dutifully agreed. "I consider myself duly warned. I'm awful glad she has someone like you to look out for her all the time."

"She looks out for me too. For the longest time, it's just been her and me against the world and we're each as protective as hell of one another. We've known each other for four years and in that time we've never even had one cross word between us. We're very compatible, even despite our different religious backgrounds – and don't forget, where we come from, it's unusual for people of opposing religions to get along without some underlying animosity, especially in our profession. She and I clicked on the very first night we met, it was as if we were meant to come together as friends…soul-sisters, even, if I may be a wee bit dramatic here. Krista's an absolute peach, she's so very sweet and, because of her looks and her easy-going nature, people have tended to take advantage of her in the past. I hate seeing the hurt in her eyes when she realizes she's been taken for a ride, when something hurts her, it ends up hurting me too. I lash out at the people responsible with my tongue because I don't like her being hurt. I can't help being protective of her and it's never going to change."

"Don't worry, Cathy, I'm not out to hurt her in any way, please believe me. Already, she's very important to me."

"Then that's all I need to hear." She drank her coffee for a few moments, her brow knit in concentration as her mind went off on a completely different tangent. "It would be nice if all four of us could get along," she said softly. "I want you to know that I'm trying very hard to like Dave, but he just doesn't always make it easy."

"That's just Dave being…Dave, I guess. He's a multi-faceted, very complex kind of guy, but don't ever forget he's also a very desolate, lonely and afraid one too. I'm not making excuses for him, that's just the way my partner is. Please just bear with him, Cathy, I want you to see what a truly great guy he is. Dave means the world to me, the way Krista means to you, he's closer to me than any blood brother could ever be and therefore he's the only family I have that I actually give a damn about."

Cathy knew Paul wasn't giving such a report about Dave just for the hell of it and she admired him a lot for being able to speak so openly and honestly about another man. But Dave was still too much a thorn in her side, despite their mutual truce from the day before and despite her recalling of him helping that little boy Peter in the park the way he had. Just because she had seen him in a different light for a few minutes didn't yet make up for all the harsh words and bitterness that had gone on before.

And then, unbidden, came the memory of the way Dave had looked at her just before they had left the club earlier. He'd had a real softness in his eyes…hadn't she felt her insides flutter in anticipation?

Pushing the memory to one side as hastily as she could, Cathy casually moved the conversation unto a more neutral topic. They were discussing, of all things, the invasion of Irish music, such as U2 and Chris DeBurgh into North American in the early 80's, the Cranberries in the early 90's, and Snow Patrol in the 00's, when Krista could be heard running down the stairs and seconds later, she bounced into the room and immediately planted a kiss on Paul's cheek.

"Hello there," she greeted cheerily. "I thought I heard voices. Sorry if I kept you waiting."

"That's okay." Paul was clearly delighted at seeing her again if his smile was anything to go by. "Cathy and I were just shooting the breeze. She's very knowledgeable about a certain band called U2 and for that, she has just shot way up in my estimation." He tipped Cathy a wink, glad they had been able to talk freely with one another. He stood up and encircled Krista's waist with his arm. "Shall we go eat, my lady?"

"Certainly, I'm starved!"

"Hey, Paul," Cathy interrupted, "what she just said there, get used to it. You'll hear it at least ten times a day from her."

"Thanks for the warning, Cathy."

"And thanks for talking about me as if I'm not here," Krista said. She chuckled then, blowing Cathy a kiss, she dragged Paul to the door. "See you later, Cath," she called on their way out and banged the door after them.

Cathy carried the coffee cups through to the kitchen, rinsed them out and left them to dry on the drainer and she was just about to return to the book she had been reading in the living room before Paul's interruption, when the phone rang. It was Dave, much to her surprise.

"Cathy or Krista?" he asked.

"Cathy."

"Sorry, I still can't distinguish your voices yet. How are your feet after last night? Still sore?"

"I took a nice long soak in the bath this morning so they're not too bad."

"Glad to hear it. Look, what I'm calling for, is Paul there?"

"He's just gone through the door this minute, give me a sec and I'll see if I can catch him." She rushed outside just in time to see Paul pull out on to the road and she returned to the phone. "Sorry, Dave, you've just missed him and I'm not expecting him back. Is there anything I can do for you instead?"

There was a brief silence and as it spun out, for some reason, she began to regret asking the question. Then, at last, it was answered. Very tersely.

"No, you can't…er, thanks all the same. When I was speaking to him earlier, I forgot to ask him what time he was going to the station at, that's all. The Captain phoned me a little while ago breathing down my neck for a report on last night."

"I didn't hear him mention what time he was going to the precinct at but he and Krista have gone out for lunch, it's 12:30 now, so I would reckon he'll be going there between two and three. Why don't you try his cell phone?"

"I did, it's not on. Besides, it's not that important. I'll see him when I see him."

"Then why don't you and I just go down to the station for 2:00, rather than wait for what could be ages for Paul and Krista? We can give our reports over to the Captain and that will at least keep him off our back until Paul and Krista join us."

There was another silence, this one heavier and longer and once again, she felt herself regretting this question too.

"Haven't you anything better to do?" he asked in a way that implied he did.

"No, as a matter of fact I don't. Look, it was only a suggestion, you don't have to take me up on it if -"

"No, it's okay," he interrupted impatiently. "I guess, seeing we're all working on the same case, we may as well meet up at the station. I need your input anyway, same as you might need mine. There were too many times last night when I was preoccupied and because you were free to move around on the floor, maybe you might remember seeing something I didn't. Okay, I'll meet you at the station between 2:00 and 2:30."

"Fine by me, Dave," she said crisply and hung up before he could.

She chewed thoughtfully on her bottom lip for a moment, suddenly feeling annoyed at herself for having regretted her perfectly innocent questions. She hadn't meant any harm by them and after all, she had as much right to suggest to do whatever she wanted as she had the right to be on the same case as him. If he wanted to be his usual aloof self, she wasn't going to upset herself by dwelling on his ever-changeable moods any more than she had to.

A little while later, when she was getting changed, she knew, just *knew* that Paul really was seeing Dave through rose colored glasses. Paul *had* to be because no one who could be as rude and curt as Dave so constantly was could possibly be even remotely nice.

Try as she could, she could not get herself round to Paul's way of thinking and, once again, she asked herself the all-important question:

What is it about Dave Andres that he continuously rubs me up the wrong way?

And, as usual, she had no answer.

CHAPTER TWENTY-THREE

Seated in Captain Hamilton's office, alone, Cathy had arrived there before Dave and when he came through the door and saw her there, he barely masked a brief frown of annoyance. He was hoping he would have gotten there first, he had also hoped Captain Hamilton would have been present, but the big man had obviously gone out to do an errand or something and it *was* just after lunchtime too after all and now Dave would have to make small talk again and why had he bothered agreeing to seeing her like this anyway?

A semblance of a polite smile flickered over his face and he sat down beside her without making eye contact. She had given him only a cool nod before he had turned to sit but he had noticed…hadn't been able to *help* notice…that her cheeks were blooming with a very faint rose blush that seemed to reflect in her eyes and make them sparkle becomingly.

Before he could start with the dreaded small talk, Cathy reached into her bag and took out a spiral notebook, which she started leafing through with noticeable concentration. Dave figured she had done that on purpose, perhaps because she didn't want to make small talk either…or…or maybe she was as uncomfortable as he was. He truly hadn't stopped to think before that she could maybe be feeling the same way in his company that he felt in hers and it helped put things into perspective for him.

He cleared his throat and decided he *would* talk to her anyway. He didn't think the world was going to come to an end just because they were conversing like two normal people. "You, um…did you get a chance to eat lunch yet?"

She glanced up at him in vague annoyance. "Yes, thanks." She eyed him warily. After all, she was more than accustomed to his mood changes by now and just because he had opened a conversation didn't mean he was in a *good* mood. Then she saw the lack of ice in his deep blue eyes and the softness around his mouth and she came to the conclusion that his attitude on the phone earlier had been misinterpreted. Maybe. She set her notebook back into her bag. "Did you sleep okay? You seemed tired when we left the club."

"I slept pretty good. I usually do. It was quite an experience that club, wasn't it?"

Cathy rolled her eyes and bemusedly shook her head. "I wasn't too impressed by it, that's for sure. Even the tips I made did nothing to cheer me up." She smiled suddenly, a warm smile that lit up her whole face and made her eyes dance, quite startling him with the unexpected, but very beautiful, transformation. "As far as anyone in authority knows, I only made about $20 in tips last night, okay?"

Dave grinned. "I thought it was more like *$15.*"

She chuckled lazily. "You think the way *I* do. I'll buy you a drink for that."

He wanted to keep the sparkle in her eyes and he started to say something else but Captain Hamilton chose that moment to return and Cathy immediately put up her professional façade. Dave didn't mind, in fact, he even understood. Cathy was the new kid on the block, out to make an impression and, being a female in a typically male environment, she had to work twice as hard to show she was as worthy of being here as anyone else.

The Captain settled his not inconsiderable weight on his chair, which immediately groaned and creaked in protest. He looked at Dave first, then at Cathy, then towards the door as if he was expecting someone. "Where are Paul and Krista?"

"They'll be along very soon," Dave said smoothly. "You wanted to see us?"

"Yeah, I want to know what went down last night."

"Nothing, really. Paul and I, from behind the bar, scoped the room, looking for security cameras and such but there weren't any. Not even any out in the parking lot. Paul checked out back, where there's an alleyway, but it was clean too. Pity there weren't any cameras, we might have been able to find even one important clue by viewing the footage. But, last night anyway, the club, its owner and the staff were acting as normal as you or me. We didn't even overhear any strange conversations."

"Krista and I did, sort of," Cathy relayed. "We didn't know quite what to make of it." She told Dave and the Captain about the brief and awkward conversation with the dancer, Ruth O'Brien and they listened with great interest until she had finished. "I was thinking about her on the drive over here just now and I came to the conclusion, I don't know why, that she has seen or heard something she shouldn't have and that she's frightened by it. In the changing rooms, there's a door at the back wall but it was locked and where it leads to, I just don't know. But she kept looking at it and every time she did, she grew troubled and very uncomfortable."

"It might be an idea to get the blueprints or floor plans of the joint," the Captain mused. "Or you or Krista could ask around, casually, of course, without making it seem terribly important."

"Should we try to get Ruth to open out a bit more? Maybe she might tell us all we need to know."

"Let Krista handle her. As a fellow dancer, they already have something in common and Krista can use that to her advantage."

Cathy quickly jotted that instruction down, in order to remember to tell Krista later. "Ruth is as timid as a mouse, we'll have to handle her with kid gloves."

"See that you do, then."

"What's our next move?" Dave asked.

"You know I can't answer that, Andrews. This is one of those cases where you'll just have to play everything by ear and don't go rushing into anything. You might hear or see what you need to tonight, then again, you might not hear anything until next week."

Cathy immediately groaned. "That's not very reassuring to hear, Captain. Have you any idea what Krista and I have to wear in that damned place? Particularly for Krista, it's next to pornographic and we are not one bit amused."

"I'm sorry for that, Edwards, I really am but unfortunately you'll just have to smile your best smile and get on with it. Any other business to discuss?"

"Not from me," Cathy said.

"Nor from me," Dave remarked.

"Then you may as well go on home seeing you had a long day yesterday. But I want to see you tomorrow again, around 4:00 for a more thorough recap. And this time, Cameron and Nolan had better be here too. They shouldn't be MIA right now, they're your partners and should be here. Where did you say they are, Andrews?"

"I didn't, I -"

Dave was saved further explanation when the prodigals came in right at that moment. Paul and Krista strolled into the Captain's office as if they hadn't a care in the world. Paul had a very relaxed smile on his face and Krista's eyes were shining with delight, a fact about each of them that the Captain noticed straight away. He viewed the happy couple a second longer and inwardly groaned.

He had sensed their attraction to one another almost from day one and he had tried to turn a blind eye to it, only hoping they wouldn't have started anything between them, or at least done it so soon. But they had and the adoration they had for each other would have been obvious to a blind man.

"Cameron, Nolan, so nice of you to drop by," he said with just the right amount of sarcasm in his tone.

"Glad to be here, Cap," Paul returned cheerily. "You wanted to see us?"

"Yeah, sorry to interrupt your…um…schedule and all that. Don't mind me, I just wanted to know if you have anything to report on last night."

"Did Cathy tell you about Ruth O'Brien?" Krista asked.

"Yes, and I'm leaving it up to you to get as much out of her as you can. Just befriend her and gain her trust, we don't want to scare her off with too many questions. Cathy said she is under the impression O'Brien has seen or heard something that she shouldn't have, therefore she is our only hope in finding a lead so far."

"Then I will do what I can to draw her out," Krista stated.

"See that you do." The Captain glanced at his watch. "Okay,

people, go home and get some rest. You all had a long day yesterday and you're going to have more late nights ahead of you for God knows how long. Come in around 4:00 tomorrow, we'll have another briefing."

They said their farewells and once out in the parking lot, it was obvious Paul and Krista didn't want to part company just yet. Dave shook his head in amusement at the sight of the two of them making puppy dog eyes at one another, but he was glad to see them this way too, Paul needed a good, strong woman in his life and Krista seemed to fit that description perfectly.

Cathy was standing at her car, waiting to see if Krista was coming with her or not. Cathy was intending to go home to take a nap but she patiently waited to see what the two lovebirds were going to do.

"Do you want to go for a coffee?" Paul suggested.

Krista glanced over at Cathy and sadly shook her head. "I wish I could but I have to get home, it's my turn to do the housework and it really needs done."

Cathy overheard that remark and she quickly stepped in. "It's okay, Krissie, away you go. There's not that much to do and I can do it…if not, it can wait until tomorrow, no problem."

"But Cathy, it doesn't seem fair, I can -"

"Forget it, chum. Just go. Have fun."

"Thanks, Cath, you're a gem. Tell you what, though, I'll bring you something back for dinner, how does that sound?" Krista turned to Dave, who was standing closer to Cathy than he was to anyone else and had therefore obviously heard the conversation. "Dave, would you like to join us back at our place later on? You'd be very welcome."

Dave shot Cathy a sideways glance. She was looking at him

solemnly and he wished he could read what was going on behind her eyes. If he saw something in them that would prompt him to accept the offer, he would, but he didn't see anything and he turned back to Krista. "Thanks for asking but I've a few things to take care of before I go to the club." He looked back at Cathy again, thought he read disappointment in her eyes (but he was probably mistaken) and his own eyes immediately softened. "Maybe some other time."

Paul, surprised by the look Dave had just given Cathy, quickly changed his plans. "Oh damn, I'm sorry, Krista, I've just remembered something I have to take care of too. Can I pick you up within the hour sometime instead?"

"Sure, no problem." Oblivious to anyone, she gave him a lingering, soft kiss on his lips, which he gladly returned, then she waved good bye to Dave and got into Cathy's car.

Paul watched them drive away and when they were out of sight, he tapped Dave on the shoulder. "Come on, pal, let me buy you a beer."

"Thought you had something to do?"

"I have, I can do it over a beer."

Warning bells sounded inside Dave's head. "Is this leading into another pep talk?" he asked warily. "Because if it is, I'm not interested."

"Nope, no pep talk. Just a talk. If you don't want to go for a beer, I can talk to you right here, don't matter to me."

Dave sighed dramatically. "Then hurry up. Out with it."

Paul was as direct as Dave, which meant he got right to the point. "You and Cathy seem to be getting along better these last couple of days."

"Yeah, so? You were told yesterday we had managed to declare a truce and we're doing our best to maintain it."

"I can see how well you're both trying and I just wanted you to know that I'm really glad for you…for her too."

Dave eyed him suspiciously. "Marvelous. I'm glad too."

"Good. And I'm glad that you're glad. So glad am I, in fact, I have come up with a perfect idea for the both of you."

"Idea?" Dave instantly groaned. "Oh no, why do I get the feeling I'm about to be set up here? Okay, whatever, let's hear it."

Paul kept his expression as carefully blank as he could. "Why don't you ask her out on a date?"

"A d- a…excuse me?" Dave suddenly began to chuckle, then he started to laugh, obviously finding the so-called idea very amusing, but his laughter slowly diminished when he realized Paul was being deadly serious. "Oh Jesus, you really want me to do this, don't you?"

Paul stared quite calmly back at him. "Uh huh."

"I see." Dave nodded as if he understood perfectly but he didn't, not really. He frowned deeply. "Why do you want me to do something as ridiculous as ask Cathy, of all people, out on a date for?"

"Because I happen to think she's a perfect match for you. *And* I saw those looks you were giving her last night when you thought no one was looking so don't try telling me they weren't for real because I know they were. Also, Cathy is the first female in a long time you've actually shown even a remote bit of interest in so why don't you do something constructive with it? It could mean you coming out of this celibacy rap thing of yours for starters, *plus* it could mean the start of something big and wonderful and fully rewarding."

"You're just not prepared to give it a rest, are you?" Dave cried in ever growing irritation. "Every time we're alone now, you bring this "end the celibacy thing" up and, sorry about it, pal, but you're really getting on my nerves now. You're beginning to sound like a broken record."

"Whatever. Well?"

"Well, what?"

"Will you do it?"

"Nope."

"Dave, come on -"

"Paul, no, forget it, eighty-six the idea, okay? I make it a rule not to date anyone I'll be working with for the simple reason it will save any embarrassment between us further down the road if it doesn't work out. And as for those looks I was giving her last night? Big deal, okay? They didn't mean anything, all it proved was that I'm not blind. And I'm also *not* interested, in her or anyone else but mainly her." Under his breath, Dave nearly added, *but I could be persuaded now that you've put the idea into my head,* but he was afraid Paul would hear him and he carefully clamped his lips together.

Paul eyed him for a long, assessing moment and then gave up with a shrug of his shoulders. Just for once, he wasn't quite sure if Dave was telling him the complete truth or not. "Okay, Big D, whatever you say."

Dave's brows shot up in surprise. "What happened to the broken record? You're actually going to let it go without a fight this time? I'm impressed."

"Shut up or I'll bring the subject up again. Now, are we going for a beer or not?"

"It's okay, you were going to meet Krista so we can take a rain check. Besides, I've things to see, people to do, so I'll see you later, at the club"

"Yeah, later, pal." Paul watched his friend walk away and narrowed his eyes in suspicion. "You're hiding something from me, Andrews," he murmured, "you definitely are. And I'm going to find out what it is." He got into his car and as he drove away, it didn't take long for his mind to return to Krista.

Even the very thought of her was enough to make his heart run a marathon in his chest and, with a soft sigh, he began to wonder if maybe, just maybe, he was falling in love with her.

But so soon? Could it *really* happen so soon? And while he was on the subject, what was love anyway? Something he had never been in before…so how would he know the real thing if it came along? But then again…he had never felt this way about a woman before so if this was what love was all about, then he had nothing to doubt, nothing to analyze and he could readily accept then that he *was* in love.

So, he did.

At this admission, a slow, self-satisfied, I've got it all smile appeared on his face and it was still there one mile further along the road when he stopped at a set of traffic lights. The lights seemed to be taking forever to change and he suddenly had the strange sensation that he was being watched. Turning to his left, he saw a car had pulled up alongside him and the driver, an elderly woman with a little wizened up face and a purple rinse in her hair, was staring at him in bewilderment (and a little bit of disgust), wondering, no doubt, what he could be smiling about as he sat all alone in his car. He didn't care one little bit if he looked foolish, he was *in love* after all – couldn't she tell? – and, as soon as the green light appeared, he tipped the old lady a wink and a salute and carried cheerfully on his way.

CHAPTER TWENTY-FOUR

Around the same time Paul was admitting his love for Krista to himself, Ruth O'Brien was waking up for the start of her day. She always slept late, she had become a night owl since she had been on her own, she preferred seeing the world and living her life from late afternoon onwards into the wee small hours of the morning. It was at these times that she truly felt alive and even confident, if she dared admit that to herself...But alive and confident as she thought she was, she also knew she was just not happy. She had not been happy in years, a fact she would not admit to herself.

She arose, finger swept the tangles out of her mane of auburn hair and padded, naked and beautiful into the tiny bathroom of her small, back street, scrupulously clean apartment. Fifteen minutes later, she was showered, dressed and nibbling on a toasted English muffin, spread thick with honey.

Sipping on her coffee, she leafed through a magazine and smoked a cigarette. Her hand was shaking slightly as it passed the cigarette from her lips to the ashtray and the nails of both hands had been chewed right down to the quick. She was living totally on her nerves and had been for a while now and it was Xavier Petcelli and the Blues Haven's fault.

She wished, not for the first time, she hadn't seen what she had seen that awful night a little over two weeks ago. It had been a classic case of being in the wrong place at the wrong time but that theory didn't make it any easier for her to bear. She was still in trouble, treading on very thin ice, and she knew it.

But she didn't know what to do about it. Petcelli had seen her watching the activities of his illegal gambling party and he had made his intentions perfectly clear what he would do to her if she ever told anyone, particularly the cops, of what she had witnessed.

Ruth suspected that Petcelli was also somehow responsible for the deaths of four girls who had used to work in the club. She hadn't known the girls personally but she had certainly heard of them through the media and, although every instinct had told her not to work for someone like Petcelli in a place like the Blues Haven, particularly after the stories she had heard or read about, she had been in desperate need of money at the time. She had gone for her interview and when she learned she was hired, she went each night to the club with the determination that she was just there to do a job and to get paid for it and to not let anyone from the club or any activity, illegal or otherwise, about the club, interfere with her personal life.

Everything had worked out fine until that night she had seen all the illegal gambling going on. Her first instinct had been to go and place an anonymous phone call to the police but Petcelli had caught her first and had implied what could and would happen if she were ever to do something foolish.

She still wanted to do the right thing, she wanted to go to the police… but she was just too scared of Petcelli and his threats.

If only she could leave Petcelli, the Blues Haven and even Bathville, far behind, then her troubles would be over. But where could she go? She would have to go through the motions of finding another job…she would *not* sell her body on the streets again, that was one thing she was adamant about…but with no job and zero prospects, how could she support herself in the meantime? Go crawling back to her parents? Have them tell her for the rest of their lives what a mess she had made of her own life? Have them throw it up in her face at any given opportunity that she was a loser and a waster? No, she would not and *could* not put herself through that. Anything, even being homeless and jobless was better than that.

Maybe she could get herself a man who would support her…there was Rick, a barman at the club, whom she knew had an interest in her. She had always politely, if not with a little amusement, turned down his offers of a date, but she had to admit she liked him, he was different from the other staff, not as rough, not as vulgar and seemingly a real nice, sweet guy.

But Rick worked for Petcelli too, therefore she would still have a connection to the Blues Haven and that was what she was trying to get away from.

Of course, there were plenty more fish in the sea, Ruth knew she was attractive enough to grab any male's attention but she was a loner too, afraid to open up to anyone, so that concept didn't appeal to her at all.

She felt she could trust Rick, so maybe she could get him to leave the club too, to get a better job, either as a barman in a more prosperous and less seedy place, or at a regular nine to five type of job. He had always said he was good at car mechanics….

Sighing deeply, Ruth refreshed her coffee and lit another cigarette straight from the butt of the first one. Her hand was still shaking but she didn't even notice it anymore. She went over to the window in the shabby but tidy living room and looked out into the alleyway four floors beneath her, her brow puckered in a frown of worry, her startling gray eyes as stormy and troubled as the Atlantic Ocean that flowed and ebbed endlessly three miles away from her apartment.

The phone rang, making her jump and causing a drop of coffee to splash out unto her hand and burn her slightly. She didn't feel it as she stared at the phone in surprise and with a sudden, sinking sense of doom. Nobody called her during the day, ever… so who could it be?

There was only one way she was going to find out so, shaking more than ever, she grabbed up the receiver. "Hello?" she asked as strongly and as clearly as she could.

For a long moment there was nothing but silence and then she heard, "Hi there, Ruthie, how are you today, darlin'?"

Ruth's heart sank. It was Petcelli. She would know his oily, condescending voice anywhere. "Fine, Mr. Petcelli."

"Good, my dear…so glad to hear that. Don't want my favorite dancer getting sick on me. Need you to be in top form for my customers tonight."

"I've never called in sick, Mr. Petcelli, you know that."

"Yeah, you're a good girl, Ruthie…aren't you?"

There was a double meaning in his question all right and Ruth would have been stupid to try and ignore it. She dragged deeply on her cigarette and squinted through the swirl of blue gray smoke. "Yes," she said softly, "I'm a good girl." Gaining some courage from a source she often forgot she had, she added, "For what am I owed the pleasure of this call, Mr. Petcelli? And how did you get my number? You never asked me for my number when I went to see you for my interview, you never asked me for it since and my number is unlisted."

"Oh now, Ruthie, don't be silly. Of *course* you gave me your number, surely you remember? You know I don't record much information about my employees in the books, just in case I was ever robbed. I look upon it as a safety feature for my employees, that some whacko who decides to break into my personnel files isn't going to note addresses and telephone numbers and start harassing you, so I recorded your number in my little black book, the one I keep in my pocket at all times. You *saw* me write the number down, you gave me the number and then stood beside me as I recorded it. Don't you remember?"

Ruth hesitated, suddenly unsure. She truly *couldn't* remember giving him the number…but how else could he have gotten it? Reluctantly, she chose to believe him. "Sure," she admitted, "Sure, I remember. At least tell me why you called?"

"Oh…no reason…just wondered how you were doing. You don't hang around much after hours anymore, we haven't had the chance to…talk. About…things."

At that precise moment, Ruth realized one thing. She hated Xavier Petcelli, totally despised him. She *had* to get away from him, she just *had* to. "What did you want to talk to me about?"

"Just checking that you're not about to do anything…um…stupid. About that little matter of a couple of weeks ago."

"I already told you I wouldn't tell anyone. I gave you my word."

"Yes, your word. Hope you know how to keep it."

"I do. I…well, I…value my life, Mr. Petcelli." After saying that, Ruth instantly cringed in remorse. *Don't get him angry, you stupid bitch,* she told herself. *Let him condescend and come off with hidden, double meanings all he wants, just don't get him angry.*

Surprisingly, Petcelli laughed. "*I* value your life too, darlin'," he said smoothly. "I wouldn't want to hurt you, not at all…not unless I had to."

Right then and there was when Ruth should have dropped the façade, disconnected the call and contacted the police. She had just received a warning, a very clear warning...but she was still too afraid to act on it and, instead, chose not to. "Yes, Mr. Petcelli, I understand, Mr. Petcelli."

He laughed in her ear again, the same oily, stomach turning laugh of a moment before. "Good, Ruthie, my girl. I'm so glad we...*understand* each other. Makes my life... and yours...a lot easier, don't you think?"

Ruth closed her eyes tightly, fighting a wave of nausea. Why hadn't she just unplugged the phone when she got home, or before going to bed, and kept it off? "Yes," she agreed hoarsely. "Yes."

"Fine. I'll see you at the club tonight. Maybe, after hours, you'll stick around this time, have a drink or two...on me, of course."

"Thank you, yes, I'll see."

"Great, will look forward to it. You have a fun day, Ruthie girl and I'll see you later."

She hung up without saying good bye and instead of just shaking, she began to tremble. She clutched her upper arms in an effort to control herself but she was even more scared now...until something suddenly occurred to her, something that absolutely terrified her.

Nobody from the club knew where she lived and Petcelli had just more or less said there that he didn't record addresses or numbers in his employees' personnel files. So, if no one from the club knew where she lived, or knew that Petcelli had her telephone number recorded in his own little black book, if something happened to her... how would anyone know where to start looking for her?

The only thing Petcelli had ever asked of her was her Social Security number and, although she was always paid her wage in cash, she knew for a fact that was the only piece of information he had on her that would be traceable.

For a brief moment, Ruth thought about that new dancer from the night before. What about been her name? Kris something? Yeah, Kris Riley, that was it. Kris really had seemed very nice, very friendly and also seemed to have a genuine wish to help Ruth, even if it was just to lend her an ear when she needed to verbally offload. Maybe if she opened out a little to Kris, by the end of the week if she felt comfortable enough, she could give Kris her phone number *and* address, she could pretend she wanted to do the "girlie" thing, like have Kris over to join her in a bottle or two of wine, watch a chick flick on the DVD player, maybe even ditz boys, if they wanted. And at least then, if something ever *did* happen to Ruth, then someone would know where to start looking for her.

Another thing she could do was sit down and write a note and leave it in a prominent place, like pinned to the mirror she had hanging on the living room wall. The note wouldn't have to be very long, just a few lines saying that if anything suspicious should ever happen to her that the first person to look at for the responsibility was none other than Xavier Petcelli, owner of the sleazy club The Blues Haven.

If she didn't feel comfortable enough giving Kris her number and address by the end of the week, she would definitely sit down and write that letter. Maybe she would even take it to a photocopier place and have it Xeroxed and she could leave the copy in her car somewhere, like behind the sun visor or in

the glove department.

Yes, she decided… these were two options, two options she hadn't had only ten minutes ago.

Feeling only marginally more confident, she reached for her pack of cigarettes again and shakily lit one up.

It was her third cigarette in less than half an hour.

CHAPTER TWENTY-FIVE

Dave decided to treat himself to a nice, relaxing hot shower before he went to the club that night. He was feeling a bit tense and a lot tired and he wasn't really looking forward to the long night ahead, but a job was a job was a job and so far this case had been nothing but a breeze so he knew he shouldn't really complain.

"Another day, another dollar," he reminded himself as he stepped under the steaming hot water. Summer or winter, he loved his shower to be as hot as was humanly acceptable. "Must remember to ask the Cap if I'm getting paid double overtime for this gig."

He started shampooing his hair and out of nowhere, he found himself thinking about Cathy. Every time he was with her now he discovered something new about her. Today, sitting beside her in the Captain's office, it had been her scent, which had been faint and musky. As he had sat really only half listening (and yet still being able to take it all in) to her recount of the events of the previous night, he had had to fight the temptation to move closer to her just so he could breathe in her perfume. He had always loved the smell of musk on a woman, he found the scent to be provocative and alluring and such a turn-on.

As he bent his head to rinse his hair, he suddenly envisaged Cathy standing naked, bathed in a pool of light coming in through her bedroom window, liberally spraying her whole body with his favorite scent. The light brought the auburn hints in her dark hair alive like flames of a fire and she had a secret smile playing at the corner of her mouth, as if she knew that he was covertly watching the show she was giving him, only he didn't know that she knew.

With this tantalizing picture in his mind, he hissed in a sharp breath and opened his eyes in astonishment, only to close them again with a grunt and a profanity when shampoo dripped into them, momentarily blinding him. He splashed water on his face to rinse out his stinging eyes, cursing even more and wondering why in the hell he had been thinking about Cathy in what could only be described as a purely lustful way.

"Grab a hold of yourself, Andrews," he scolded, "you're acting like a teenager in junior high who's just discovered the fine art of fantasizing. So, she wears musk, big whoopee deal, no need to have *those* sorts of thoughts about her. Okay?" He muttered away to himself as he finished his shower, giving himself a good talking to and telling himself repeatedly to wise up and stop being so foolish over a mere scent…And the woman who wore it too.

By the time he was dressed, he was totally annoyed at himself and when he arrived at the club half an hour later, he was in rare form. He glowered at anybody who came near him, offered absolutely nothing in way of conversation to anyone and completely surprised himself when he felt his dark mood evaporate as soon as he saw Cathy coming through the door. His expression visibly softened when he noticed she was looking all around her, still obviously feeling uncomfortable in a place like this but still doing her best to appear quite at home. He walked out from behind the bar, greeted Paul and Krista like the mere strangers he had only met the night before and turned his full attention to Cathy.

"Hi. Did you remember your flat shoes for tonight?"

At his question, she immediately pulled a face of annoyance. "No, I'd forget my head sometimes if it wasn't screwed on. I can remember phone numbers I haven't used since five years ago, what my Great Aunt Sally got me for Christmas ten years ago and the birth dates of every member of the Royal Family…but something as important as comfortable shoes to save my feet… forget it."

Dave clucked softly in sympathy. "If it's any consolation, Petcelli has just told me that if it's not busy tonight, the bar staff can take a break any time it's quiet."

Cathy immediately brightened. "Good, you've just cheered me up no end." She caught Krista's attention, indicated they should go and get changed and then, with a shy smile at him, she said, "See you in a wee minute," and left him.

He watched the two girls walk away, unaware that Paul was observing him with great interest and it was only when Dave turned to go back behind the bar that he noticed Paul's very expectant expression. "What?" he asked warily.

Paul grinned. "That's about the closest I've seen you to drooling over a female yet, Dave," he stated cheerily.

"Drooling? Who was drooling? Certainly not I. I think you've got far too much testosterone running through your veins at the moment, time to do something to get it released."

"I'm working on it. What were you thinking about just now?"

"Really don't think that's any of your beeswax, Paul."

"Yes it is. Come on, you don't usually keep anything from me, just tell me what it is you're thinking of. If it's something juicy, then I definitely want to hear it, if it's not, then you've got nothing to hide."

Dave rolled his eyes in exasperation. "Oh Jesus, what did I ever do wrong to deserve a partner who doesn't know how to take no for an answer?" He threw his hands up in surrender. "Okay, I'll tell you, seeing you're so obviously dying to know, but I'm warning you now, you might be disappointed. I was thinking of what Cathy just said to me there. She told me she'll see me in a "wee" minute and I was just wondering what on earth a "wee" minute is. Aren't all minutes the same length of time anymore?"

Paul instantly knew Dave was only teasing and he groaned in defeat. "You jerk, that's not what you were thinking about at all, but now that you mention it, everything Cathy or Krista talks about happens to be "wee". A wee cup of coffee, a wee bite to eat, a wee man who is probably well over six foot tall, a wee anything. And I think it sounds kinda cute, the way they use the word in such quantity."

"Yeah, well, you would." But despite the slight teasing in his tone, Dave didn't want to admit that he too had found himself noticing more and more the girls' vocabulary and the way they put their sentences together. Half the time, it took him a moment or two to clue in to what they were really talking about and sometimes he even had to give up, but more often than not, he at least could get the gist of it and could then mentally turn their sentences into the more familiar American way. To change the subject, he fixed a lazy smile on his face and said, "Come on, let's get moving. Petcelli wants us to check we've got a full stock behind the bar tonight, seeing we were so busy last night."

And off he went, leaving Paul staring after him with a long suffering but fond shaking of his head.

When Cathy and Krista walked into the changing room, they noticed right away that there was something different about the room compared to the way it had been the night before. It took Cathy only a moment to figure out what the change was.

"It's the costume rack," she stated, looking at the heavy steel frame on which the dozens of skimpy bikinis and quite indecent skirts and tops were hanging. She looked at it more critically and noticed that someone had, for some unbeknownst reason, taken the castor wheels off the bottom, as if to prevent it from being easily moved out of the way. "It wasn't in front of that door before, it was over behind the chairs. *And* I remember being able to roll it across the floor quite easily last night." She looked behind the rack, then tried to open the door it was blocking, but the door was locked. She stepped back again and raised an inquisitive eyebrow at Krista. "If that door is always locked, why try to barricade it off with a clothes rack too? Maybe I'm reading too much into this but I think someone is going to great lengths to keep people out of this room."

"You could be right," Krista added. "Let's move the rack away from the door and see if it gets put back sometime during the night."

The clothes rack really was heavy but between the two of them, they managed to shift it against the wall to the left of the door.

"Maybe no one will even notice," Cathy remarked, "but if they do, and they're suspicious, just say that you dropped an earring and it rolled behind the rack. Moving it was the only way you could get it."

"Okay." Krista glanced at her watch. "You'd better get a move on and get changed. I wish Ruth would hurry up and get here, I want to have the chance to open up some sort of a conversation with her, see if she can tell me anything of what's going on around here."

"If anybody can do that, you can." When Cathy was dressed a few minutes later in her skimpy, utterly deplorable uniform, she looked down at herself, tried in vain to make herself look a bit more presentable and clicked her tongue in poorly concealed disgust. "I'm definitely not one bit amused at having to wear this, you know," she grumbled. She tossed her curls over her shoulder and strode indignantly to the door. "See you outside, Krissie." Not looking where she was going, she collided with Ruth and nearly sent her flying. She quickly caught a hold of Ruth's arm to steady her. "Oh, I'm so sorry, Ruth. Did I hurt you?"

Ruth immediately pulled her arm back from Cathy's grasp, her face flushing with red. She shook her head, her eyes downcast. "No," she murmured timidly, "it's all right."

"Well, if you're sure," Cathy said, feeling awkward for the poor girl. "Clumsy's my middle name. Sorry, anyway…and I'll see you later."

Ruth mumbled something unintelligible in return and came on into the room. She threw her purse on one of the overstuffed easy chairs and took off her coat without even looking in Krista's direction, never mind giving her a greeting.

So, Krista did it for her. "Hi there, Ruth, how's things?"

Ruth awarded her with a brief, uncomfortable glance. "Er, fine…thanks…er, Kris, isn't it?"

"That's me." Krista closely scrutinized her for a long moment and saw that, if it was even possible, Ruth looked even more scared than she had the night before. "You okay, Ruth?"

"Sure," Ruth answered, a little sharply. Then, remembering what she had thought up that afternoon after Petcelli's phone call, about maybe befriending Krista, she forced a cheery smile on her face. "Sorry, nothing's wrong. Why did you ask?"

"Well, you look a bit pale."

"Oh…well, I got cramps that hurt like a bitch."

"I see." Krista knew she was being lied to but chose not to pursue it. She found her usual gift of the gab had dried up on her too and she had to struggle to come up with something to say. She decided to set the ball rolling in the way she wanted right away and gestured towards the locked door. "Oh, I meant to ask you last night, what's behind this door here?"

Ruth's eyes darted nervously towards the entrance door and finally came to rest at a spot somewhere just below Krista's left ear. "No-Nothing," she stammered, "nothing that I know of, that is. I've never been through it so I don't know."

Once again, Krista knew she was being lied to and she knew to tread carefully. "There must be *some* sort of room behind the door," she persisted lightly. "Is it a stock room or something?"

"Yes…yes, that's what I think it could be," Ruth was quick to agree… too quick, Krista thought. "I think now I can remember someone telling me it's a stock room."

"Wonder what's stocked in there? Can I look inside to see?"

Ruth's gaze went back to the entrance way again but when she looked back at Krista again, this time she suddenly seemed agitated. "What are you so interested in a stupid old stock room for?"

"Oh, no reason, just being nosy." Krista shrugged nonchalantly and decided that now would be the best time to let the matter drop. But her curiosity had definitely been aroused and she made a mental note to tell Cathy and Captain Hamilton of the conversation. She glanced casually at her watch. "I suppose I should get changed and get out there to the oh so adoring public. The sooner I get tonight over with, the sooner my feet are going to thank me."

For the next fifteen minutes or so that Krista remained in the changing room, the more Ruth seemed to clam up. Any even innocent questions were answered with a monosyllable so that Krista was almost glad to escape from her when the time finally came.

She ambled out to the stage, half hoping the bar would be dead tonight but, although not as busy as the night before, it was still at least half full with the expected rough looking characters.

She immediately sought out Paul and when their eyes met, her surroundings seemed to fade away until they no longer seemed there. He was smiling gently at her and she slowly returned the smile, feeling her heart uplift and cheering her spirits just by his mere presence.

With a soft sigh, she reluctantly turned away, took off her robe, hung it on the hook behind the stage and when the music started, she picked up the beat and decided she would dance solely for his pleasure tonight. She had to block from her mind all the rude jeers and cat calls that tonight's charming clientele were throwing her way to do just that, but she succeeded.

Krista had been dancing for about five minutes when Cathy spied Xavier Petcelli standing a few feet away from her along the bar, talking heatedly with another man. Petcelli's companion was small and weasely looking, with shifty brown eyes and greasy, slicked back reddish-brown hair. They looked as if they were in a conspiracy with one another and, curious, Cathy took a few barely noticeable steps closer to them to try and hear what they were saying above the din of the music. She engrossed herself in her notebook as if she was reading an order but it wouldn't have mattered if she had stood on her head because neither man even noticed her.

Petcelli was the first one she heard talking and his words sent her pulse racing in sudden anticipation.

CHAPTER TWENTY-SIX

"I told you, Herb, Friday night, we'll be having our fun this Friday night."

Cathy heard the man referred to as Herb clear his throat and then he said, "Yeah, and big stakes too, Petcelli – and no fixing the cards this time either."

"Herb, my man, I'm hurt at such an accusation. I've never let you down before and I've never fixed the cards before either, have I?"

Herb didn't answer that one. "What about that crazy guy who showed up last time?"

"Crazy guy?" Petcelli's voice was dripping with ice. "Who do you mean? There was no crazy guy."

Cathy could see that Herb was suddenly scared by Petcelli's tone and maybe something in his eyes too. She couldn't see Petcelli face on from her angle but she could definitely read Herb's and in those few brief moments, she could see he had become genuinely scared. Then he quickly adapted a cool expression. "Yeah, whatever. What about that dancer girl who walked in on us last time? Have you taken care of her like you said you were going to?"

Cathy saw Petcelli glance towards the stage to see who was dancing and he seemed mighty relieved that it was Krista. "Who, Ruthie? No, she's still with us but only because she swore to me she would never tell anyone of what she saw or heard. I have the poor little bitch so shit scared she'll keep her trap shut and I've made it quite clear that if she even thinks about squealing to the pigs, she'll be gotten rid of. Permanently. She won't cause…" At that, Petcelli and Herb walked away out of earshot.

Knowing she had just heard a very clear threat and also a reference to a possible gambling event coming up on Friday, Cathy immediately caught Dave's attention. With a quick look around her to check no one was watching them as they talked, she moved in closer to him. "There's something going on this Friday," she said breathlessly, "but more importantly, we need to take care of something else."

"Really?" Dave picked up her excitement but kept his expression carefully blank. "Look, we'll have to wait until a more quiet moment to talk about it Cathy, okay? We definitely will talk about it, just not here. I don't know what you've heard or where you heard it but just continue to keep your eyes and ears open. In the meantime, I need you to do me a favor. Don't turn around just yet but there are two guys sitting at the table third left from the stage. I've had my eye on them ever since they came in here about twenty minutes ago. They haven't ordered anything to drink yet and they're not even watching Krista dance so I think they could be in here for other reasons than refreshment and some entertainment. Don't ask me why I think that, just a gut feeling. I saw one of them stuff something under the table so why don't you go see if they want anything and while you're at it, try and find out what they're up to too. I'll signal Krista and get her to watch them when you have to come back to the bar."

"Okay, I'll see what I can do." Cathy had no problem whatsoever picking out the two men Dave had just referred to. They were two surly looking characters all right, whose faces didn't even fit in with the rest of the rather dubious looking patrons who were in the club. She walked over to them. "Good evening, gentlemen," she greeted brightly and teased them with one of her sexiest smiles, which managed to grab their attention at least. "My name's Cathy and I'm going to be your waitress for the evening. Would you care to order anything from the bar?"

"Nope," the one on her right barked unpleasantly.

"Not so fast, Jerry, I think I've just been put in the mood for a beer," said the other as he eyed Cathy appreciatively up and down.

"Certainly," she purred. "Will that be draft or bottle?"

"Draft."

"Coming right up." Cathy returned to the bar and Dave came over to her as soon as he could.

"Well?" he enquired.

"That's only a jacket he has under the table. But there are several pieces of paper on the table with what looks like telephone numbers on them so when I take the order down, I'll try and get a closer look. Why are you so interested in them anyway?"

"I told you, I've just got a gut feeling about them. But not only that, I saw Petcelli over talking to them earlier and the conversation seemed to be getting rather hot and heavy. Petcelli kept pointing the finger a lot, like he was ordering them to do something that they didn't seem to want to do, which started a heavy debate between all three of them. Or maybe negotiations were being made, I don't know, but whatever it was, I just want to find out. Krista's keeping an eye on them too but don't even look at her when you walk by the stage, she's going to let Paul or myself know as soon as possible if she sees anything amiss."

"Okay, I'll let you know how I get on." When Cathy got back to the table, she put down a coaster, then a napkin and then the beer. Neither of the men were watching what she was doing, they were too busy eyeing her bottom and her legs so she had ample opportunity to read the pieces of paper. The light was dim and she could only make out one number in full, but she memorized it swiftly. After the man paid for his beer, she emptied the ashtray, set down a clean one, smiled sexily again and returned to the bar.

Dave and Paul deliberately ignored her for a few moments then, as it was quiet enough anyway, they thought it would be safe to look as if they were just having a casual conversation with one another to pass the time.

"Able to get anything?" Dave asked her.

"Just this." She scribbled down the telephone number on her pad and passed it over to him. "Is it a Bathville number?"

He looked at it and nodded. "Yes it is, somewhere down around the docks, I think. I'll check it out first thing in the morning. You did good there, Cathy." With that, he looked straight into her eyes and with that one look, she suddenly felt herself go unexplainably weak at the knees.

It was the first time since they had met that he had actually praised her and it was also the first time he had looked at her in such a way while there had been a witness in the form of Paul around and, realizing too late what he had done, he looked quickly away, tight-lipped. He didn't want to make it obvious to anyone, particularly Cathy herself, that he was becoming more and more attracted her with each passing hour and when another waitress came over to get served, he went over to her immediately.

Cathy watched him walk to the other side of the bar and from what she could see of his profile, he seemed pretty annoyed at himself. But the way he had looked at her with those powerful blue eyes of his still had her heart racing in her chest and his obvious annoyance at leaving himself wide open to her like that filled her with hurt and dismay.

Paul hadn't failed to notice the little exchange between them and, at her crestfallen expression, his heart immediately went out to her. But he knew when not to say anything so he reluctantly kept his mouth shut.

While all this was going on, Krista was just finishing her first stint. It was barely 10:00 and already she was feeling tired and the only thing that was keeping her going was the break she had to look forward to every half hour. As she turned to go to the changing room, she caught Cathy's downcast expression and she looked enquiringly at Paul for some sort of explanation, who could only shrug helplessly at her in reply. Krista glanced at Dave, saw the tight look he had on his face and quickly put two and two together. She immediately beckoned Cathy over. "What just happened between you and Dave? Don't tell me it was another fight."

Cathy shook her head and rolled her eyes in growing aggravation. "No, we didn't fight, not this time."

"Then what is it? Why does he seem so annoyed? Was it something to do with those two guys he wanted us to watch?"

Cathy glanced back at Dave, still trying to assess his sudden turn around. He had seemed genuinely pleased to be in her company tonight after all, he had even greeted her with a warm smile when she had first come in, so why was he back to the cold shoulder treatment? "No, it's got nothing to do with those two guys," she murmured. "I really don't know what his problem is."

"Cathy? You're not holding anything back from me now, are you, chum?"

She gave a non-committal shrug. "Not on purpose. It's just I think…" She paused and laughed tersely. "Well, I know it may sound stupid and I'm probably only reading something into something that isn't there, but I think that for a moment there… well, it seemed almost like he looked at me as if he could be sort of interested in me. But now, of course, as usual, it's back to as if I don't even exist."

"You actually got the impression he could be interested in you?"

"Yes. Told you it was stupid."

"No, it's not! It's terrific if he feels that way. So, what are you going to do about it?"

"What am *I* going to do about it? *I'm* not going to do anything. If *he* wants to, then he can, but I'm not."

Krista narrowed her eyes thoughtfully. "Does that mean you want him to do something about it?"

Realizing she had said more than she should have, Cathy started to clam up but then she reminded herself that this was Krista she was talking to and she never kept anything from Krista. "I'm not sure," she admitted. "Maybe. I just don't know. Even if I wanted to do something about it – and I'm not saying that I do – he doesn't get interested in women, remember? It was one of the first things we learned about him so that part I would have to respect, no matter what."

"So maybe he's ready to change his mind. Do you feel any differently towards him because of that talk you had with him yesterday in the park?"

"I'm trying my hardest to like him more, if that's what you mean and up until now, it was getting easier. I saw the effort he was making too to be nice to me, therefore I do see him in an entirely different light. And I have to confess, he *is* gorgeous. Those eyes of his, his smile – when he remembers he has one, that is – even the shape of his hands… and what a body…" Cathy stopped and frowned in irritation. "But all that aside, and even if I was deeply attracted to him, all his good qualities are spoiled by his mood swings and the way he's just acted is living proof he's determined to keep his distance from me." Her frown deepened. "Oh well, if that's what he wants, he's got it."

Krista squeezed her friend's arm in comfort. "Don't worry, love, the way I see it, he desperately wants to let himself be attracted to you but he just wants to be cautious until he gets to know you better. If it's going to happen, it's going to happen so I can guarantee he'll come around eventually. Get back to work and don't let this bother you this time. I want to go and rest my feet, so I'll see you later, okay?"

"Yeah, okay, go rest your feet, you lucky devil. But spare a thought for poor me who has to keep going."

When Krista returned to the dressing room, Ruth was still there, dressed in her stage clothes, sitting reading a magazine and smoking a cigarette. She glanced up when Krista came in and groaned. "That time already?"

"Afraid so."

"Great, just great." Ruth extinguished her cigarette and stood up. "What are the animals like tonight?"

"Quiet, compared to last night."

"That's unusual for that crowd. See you in half an hour."

Krista waited for her to leave and then turned to slowly survey the room. Nothing seemed to have been moved while she had been gone, the clothes rack was still where she and Cathy had placed it. She wrapped a robe around herself and went to the bathroom on down the hall but when she returned a few minutes later, the rack was back in front of the door again. She waited five minutes and went out to the bar so she could tell Cathy but she was busy so Krista approached Paul instead, who was delighted at her appearance.

"Hey, pretty lady," he greeted, "what can I do for you?"

"Nothing this time, thanks. I came out to speak to Cathy so she can fill you in later if she gets the chance. Look, there's a waitress wanting to be served." She saw Cathy was now free and she beckoned her over. "Guess what, Cathy? The clothes rack has just been moved back in front of that door. It hadn't been when I went to tell Ruth it was her turn to go on but I went to the bathroom and while I was there, someone came in and moved it. Did you see Petcelli or any other member of staff head that way?"

"No, it was busy there for a while. Maybe Paul or Dave did, they have a better view of that side of the room than I would have. You go back and rest those feet of yours and I'll ask them."

"Okay, I'll talk to you later."

Cathy took the time to clear a few tables before she returned to the bar. Paul was still tied up with the waitress and, left with little choice, she reluctantly approached Dave. When he saw she evidently wanted to talk to him, he fixed a cool expression on his face and went over to her.

"What is it?" he asked indifferently. "Do you have an order?"

"No, I just wanted to tell you something." She wanted him to at least look at her while she filled him in on what had just happened so she put a warm smile on her face and briefly laid her hand on top of his, which certainly did the trick of grabbing his attention when he looked startled into her eyes. She took her hand away, leaned over closer to him and told him as quickly as she could about the incident with the clothes rack, starting from when she and Krista had first arrived that evening and finishing with what Krista had just told her. She kept the smile on her face and her voice low and even touched him now and then in a way that any observer might think she was just flirting with him.

He picked up instantly on what she was trying to do and, even though he was surprised by what he knew instinctively was uncharacteristic brazenness for her, he decided to flirt right back with her. Because she was only a few inches away from him, he picked up her musky scent again and thanks to that, he was beginning to find it hard to concentrate on what she was saying, finding himself looking instead at her bare shoulders and her very inviting cleavage. He tried to force himself to listen to her but instead he started staring at her lips as she talked. Each time she touched his arm, he felt his skin tingle beneath her fingertips, which wasn't exactly helping matters either.

She paused for a moment when she thought he was only pretending to flirt with her too but she couldn't deny she didn't feel a sudden atmosphere between them now, one that was charged with an underlying current of mystery and even anticipation.

At last, he had the nerve to look into her eyes and when he saw her slight look of confusion, he had a sudden, crazy and very beautiful urge to take her into his arms and kiss her. And the more he thought about it, the more he wanted to do it too and he barely concealed a shiver of pure pleasure that had just traveled up and down his spine. He struggled with these old, almost forgotten, feelings of sexual attraction and finally, after a huge battle, he managed to get a grip on himself. He shook his head when she asked him – for the third time – if he had seen anyone going towards the changing room.

"No, I didn't, but don't forget the rest rooms are through that way too," he stated and was extremely pleased with himself when his words came out sounding quite normal to his ears. "Any number of people could have gone through there in the last ten minutes."

"Yeah, true, I suppose. Do you think it's worth following up on?"

"Couldn't hurt."

Cathy nodded then, looking around her to make sure there was still no one within earshot, she proceeded to tell him what she had heard earlier between Petcelli and the man called Herb. Dave listened as best as he could but his mind was wandering about her again and the strange light in his eyes made her trail off uncertainly. "Dave, are you all right?" she asked in genuine concern.

"Mmm?" he said vaguely then, knowing it was getting a bit ridiculous now, him standing there and gawking like a fool, he gave himself a mental slap on the face to bring himself back to reality. "Yes, yes, I'm fine. Sorry, the music in here's just starting to get to me, that's all. What was that about Ruth?"

"She has apparently seen something she shouldn't and Petcelli more than just implied that she will be taken care of if there's a repeat performance or if she goes to the police. Should we get her some sort of protection just in case?"

Dave finally managed to clue in all the way to the matter on hand and he nodded. "Yeah, for sure, sounds serious. I'll certainly look into it tomorrow. I don't get it about the crazy guy, though. Who on earth is that in reference to?"

"Your guess is as good as mine. But Petcelli's whole attitude changed soon as Herb asked about him…and Herb certainly looked as scared as hell at Petcelli's denial of any crazy guy."

"We'll just have to question Petcelli when we finally get to run his ass in. And if something's going down on Friday night, we'll have to let Captain Hamilton know as soon as possible too."

Before she could say anything else to him, she was called over for an order and he felt his legs go weak at the sight of her swaying hips as she walked away. Paul, who had finished with the waitress ages before and had been watching their little tête-à-tête, grinned at the pure lust that had appeared on Dave's face.

"Go for it, buddy," he urged gently, "she's not going to bite."

For once no longer trying to keep his feelings a secret, Dave looked over at his friend and shrugged helplessly. "Have I suddenly gone nuts, Paul?" he asked in bewilderment. "Or have I just been mad all along? I mean, I'm looking at this chick like I've never seen one before and suddenly... suddenly I'm liking what I'm seeing now. Liking it a lot." He groaned in despair. "I've tried my damnedest to ignore her, I've even tried to pretend like she doesn't exist, I've tried to remind myself over and over she's nothing but a fellow cop...but nothing's working anymore. She is absolutely drop dead gorgeous, she looks so incredibly sexy – and it's got nothing to do with that stupid uniform she's nearly not wearing either." He stole another furtive glance in Cathy's direction and groaned again. "I mean, just look at her, Paul, she just oozes sex appeal and she's not even aware of it. Please, tell me I'm not going crazy."

"You're not going crazy, you're just opening your eyes. At long last! And now's the time to do something about it."

"Like what?"

"Like not going and shutting yourself up like a monk anymore for starters. All you have to do is take it nice and easy and the rest will follow naturally. Just go with the flow and see what happens. The worst she can do is reject you but the best she can do is accept your advances. If it were me, I know what chance *I'd* rather take."

Dave looked at his friend for a very long moment, then sighed deeply. "Easy for you to say, you always were a love-sick fool." He felt his defenses go up again, purely by automatic reflex, but even he had to admit to himself they didn't feel as strong or as secure as before. "I'll see what I can do," he said quietly. "No promises, though, I'm not about to make any promises on what could easily turn out to be the second worst mistake of my life."

"Don't you dare go backing out already on this one, Andrews," Paul hissed sharply and looked him square in the eye. "For once in your life, just go with what your heart is telling you to do instead of analyzing everything to death first in that stupid head of yours. You never know, you just might end up finding yourself being pleasantly surprised."

"You really think so?" Dave asked warily.

"Yes, damn it! Cathy's a great girl, she's sweet and she's beautiful and she's honest and you're right, she's so sexy…" Paul paused, hoping he was getting through to him. "And she desperately wants you to at least *show* her you like her because I know she likes *you*. A lot."

By now, Dave's defenses had fallen by the wayside but he was still cautious, still afraid and he knew he couldn't even begin to explain how he was feeling to Paul, or to anyone, when he knew he couldn't even explain it to himself. He and Paul had always shared an easy going, open and direct friendship, one that they could talk about anything under the sun with each other. But this was different, this was something Dave would have to work out all by himself, only he wasn't sure if he even knew where to begin. With one last covetous glance in Cathy's direction, he decided to turn the conversation around to business again but he had one more thing he wanted to add, seeing he knew Paul was genuinely concerned for him and wanted only what was best for him.

"I just don't want to make any promises I might not be able to keep, Paul, okay? I want to be one hundred per cent certain before I open my heart to any female again."

"Okay, partner," Paul said softly, "I understand, I truly do."

"Thank you. Now, I don't want to sound as if I'm deliberately trying to change the subject or anything -"

"No, you'd never do anything like that, would you?" Paul teased, recognizing that Dave needed a time out.

"Up yours. Just shut up and listen, will you? I have to tell you what it was Cathy and I have just been talking about."

Paul listened intently and with a lot of interest to what Dave had to say and when he had heard everything, he mulled the information over for a few minutes. "Okay, Ruth's obviously in danger. Make sure you remember to get her some protection, starting tomorrow."

"Don't worry, I will, but it isn't going to be easy to put into action since we don't know her address or anything. We can't bring anyone else in here to keep an eye on her either because the Captain doesn't want anyone else to get involved."

"Getting her address will not be a problem, I'll get her license plate number tonight and run it through the DMV tomorrow. So, Friday night's the night, by the sound of things. All four of us are working then are we not?"

"Yup and that should give us plenty of time to prepare for what might be going down. It's just a pity we have to continue working here in the meantime but I suppose this might be the only way to find out what the stolen merchandise rap is too. In the morning, I'll phone that number Cathy got and follow up on *that* lead too – if it *is* a lead, of course. Those two guys were probably just born looking suspicious, they know Petcelli quite innocently and they're as squeaky clean as you or me. That number could belong to one of their grandmothers for all we know."

Paul nodded in agreement then glanced swiftly all around him. "It's definitely quieted down, I'm going to go see if Krista's all right or if she wants anything to drink. Be right back."

He left the bar, threaded his way through the tables and when he entered the girls' dressing room, he found Krista sitting reading a magazine. She was idly twirling a strand of her silky dark hair around one finger, she seemed totally engrossed in what she was reading and, after he had admired her beauty for a long moment, he had to clear his throat to announce his arrival.

She immediately whirled round and her face broke into a smile. "Paul!" she cried happily, bouncing up and flinging herself into his open arms. "Oh, I missed you," she bubbled and kissed him lingeringly on the lips.

"Mmm, miss me all you want as long as you keep kissing me like that." She dutifully obliged for a few moments and he had to remind himself that she was practically naked underneath the robe, making him want her all over again. He was sorely tempted to just rip the robe right off her and devour her entire body, but, with no other choice, he had to refrain. Instead, he had to content himself by pulling her into his arms and just holding her closely against him. "Don't be saying anything about the case," he murmured, "walls have ears, know what I'm saying?"

She looked up at him and nodded. "So," she began casually, "have you been very busy tonight?"

"Not really. Started out that way then it tapered off." He looked her slowly up and down, then gazed deeply into her eyes. "I just wish the night would pass more quickly because I sure as hell can't wait to get you out of here."

Suddenly unsure of what he really meant, she smiled faintly in amusement and decided to play him at his own game. "Why's that, Paul?" she purred. "You want to do something that might just make it worth my while to leave?"

He tried to look sternly at her for putting him on the spot like that but it didn't quite work. "I can certainly think of one or two things I'd like to do…with you."

"Is that a fact? Like what?" she asked, immediately putting him on the spot again.

"You're nothing but a witch, young lady."

"So you keep telling me." She decided to take pity on him and let him off the hook so she reluctantly extracted herself from his arms and sat down on her chair again. "I've something interesting to tell you, about Cathy."

"No, please, let me go first because I have something interesting to tell you too, about Dave. Seems he's coming back to the land of the living again, at least as far as starting to admit that women are NOT his natural enemy."

"Hey, that's good!"

"Uh-huh, but that's not all. Tonight, of all nights, he even actually started seeing Cathy as a potential romantic interest and, even though he's still afraid of letting his guard down all the way, he's getting there, he really is. That was the reason why he was acting like a jerk with her again earlier on. Seems like your best friend and my best friend could become an item after all."

"Oh, I'm so happy to hear that!"

He held up a hand to silence her enthusiasm. "Not so fast, honey, it could still take Dave a while to come fully around and Cathy strikes me as being the sort of person who won't make the first move, so don't go getting too excited just yet."

"Okay, I'll try not to."

"Something tells me you will anyway. What was your news on Cathy?"

"Actually, something pretty similar to what you've just told me. She actually admitted to me she finds Dave very attractive, which, in her language, translates to she could let herself become interested in him. Not that I mean on his looks alone, but for her to say that at all, I read between the lines and got what she really meant. But she doesn't like his mood swings one little bit, although I think that's just because she doesn't really understand them yet."

"She'll get used to them. I did and it didn't even take long. I love Dave, you know that and I only want what's best for him. I think Cathy *is* that best, even if he doesn't quite realize it yet."

Krista bounced up again and flung her arms around his neck. "That was a really nice thing to say about her, particularly as how you hardly know her."

"If she's anything like you, then I think I'm safe." Paul glanced at his watch and gave her a swift kiss. "I'd better get back in case it's gotten busy again out there."

"What a pity," she said, pulling an unhappy face. "Here, though, here's something to remember me by while you're behind that bar, setting up drink after drink." Pressing her body against his, she kissed him deeply for a long, lingering moment, her tongue playfully searching his mouth and her lips fully on his.

The sensation of her against him like that, and the kiss, caused his body to react immediately and with a soft groan, he quickly pulled away before she could feel him. "I... huh, I'll see you later," he said hoarsely and hastily cleared his throat, which made her laugh. "And oh yes, you've certainly given me plenty to remember you by."

"Then I'll refresh your memory like that any time you want," she teased.

"Good...you witch." He blew her a kiss from the doorway and he could have stood there for ages, just looking at her, a sight definitely worth the watching but he reluctantly reminded himself that he had to go. "See you," he said softly and returned to the bar.

Dave wasn't busy at all and as soon as Paul appeared, he looked at him expectantly. "So, did Krista want anything to drink?"

Paul slapped a hand to his forehead. "Man, I sort of forgot to ask."

Dave chuckled. "Otherwise engaged, were we?"

"You could say that."

Which gave Dave the perfect opportunity to rib Paul as much as he could for the rest of the night and which in turn gave Cathy the first chance to see some of Dave's sense of humor. Paul hadn't been lying,

Dave really could be very funny and quick-witted and she felt herself warming to him again as she listened to him laugh and kid around, just like any other normal human being would.

Whatever it had been that had bothered him earlier on didn't seem to be bothering him anymore, she decided. He was even back to being nice to her again, making her laugh, bringing her into conversations too and generally treating her like an equal individual instead of a third-class citizen. For the first time since they had met, she found herself actually starting to like him, *really* like him, even though she still couldn't fathom his mood swings.

But it didn't matter anymore, she liked this other side to him and she even began to suspect that *this* was the real Dave, not the cool, aggressive and terribly rude person she had mainly seen thus far and she was glad she had been given this chance to see him in his true colors.

Sadly, the rest of the evening passed uneventfully in regards to the case, except that Cathy was able to get the license plate number of the car driven by the two men she had gotten the telephone number from. She obtained it purely by chance too, she had just gone outside for a few minutes to get some fresh air. When the two men had come out of the club, they hadn't even noticed her standing in the shadows when they passed her by.

She gave the number over to Dave and he promised he would follow up on it the next day, when he would be following up on Ruth O'Brien's license plate too.

CHAPTER TWENTY-SEVEN

Although the Captain had requested they meet at the precinct for 4:00 the next day, they decided to all meet instead at around 2:00 so that Dave could get to work quickly on checking out the license plates and telephone numbers. The first license plate belonged to a Ray Carter and, after further investigations, it was revealed that Carter was a small-time crook, who liked to dabble in all kinds of shady dealings, his favorite by-line being acting as go between for people who were trying to get rid of stolen or illegal goods. He had been out of jail on parole for five months.

The telephone number belonged to a frozen food company's warehouse in, as Dave had already guessed, the city's docks area. Dave rang the company to get the full address and also to see if by chance Carter could maybe be employed there, but the person he spoke to quite bluntly told him no and to mind his own business.

"Charming, some people," Dave said in amusement when he hung up. "Paul, can you read me out Ruth's license plate number again?"

"Don't worry, while you were busy there, I followed up on it. She lives in Atlantic Drive, number 20380, apartment 14, and I've already sent a squad car down there right now to check it out. I told them to go right up to her front door and check she still lives there and I also told them to create some sort of story that they've come to the wrong address, many apologies and all that so she won't get suspicious. Once they establish her identity, between tonight and Friday night, she'll have protection right under her very nose and she won't even know it."

"Good, that's everything covered, let's go tell the Cap."

Captain Hamilton listened with great intent on what they all had to say, particularly about what might be happening on Friday night. He also had no idea who the crazy guy that Herb had referred to could be. Detectives Turner and Chipman had never heard of any reference to a so-called "crazy guy", never mind seen one for themselves. "I only wish we had more solid evidence to close the place up now but since we don't, you people will just have to stick it out, sorry about it. Dave, I want you to take Cathy down to the docks now to check out that frozen food place. I want to see if there's any sort of a connection to there and the club."

Dave sat up stiffly in his seat, his brow creasing in annoyance. "Why can't Cam and I go instead?"

"Because I want you to take Cathy. This is her first chance to stake out suspect premises and – "

"Well why can't all four of us go then?" Dave interrupted. "Krista needs the experience too."

"Yes, she does, and she will get the chance another time. Right now, I want you to take Cathy. Krista and Paul can follow up on Ruth, maybe relieve the officers watching her for a little while. Besides, I don't want four of you in the one place at the one time – having you all at the club at the same time is quite enough for me - so just do as I ask and take Cathy down there."

Paul threw Dave a sympathetic look, knowing full well his partner wasn't ready to be alone with Cathy right now. "Well, why don't you and I go to the docks, Dave, and Cathy and Krista can go to Ruth's? We can keep in contact by radio or cell and -"

The Captain quickly intervened before Dave could agree to Paul's suggestion. "I see you two gentlemen are suddenly deaf. Dave, you're taking Cathy down, end of discussion. Cam, Krista, go about your duties elsewhere."

Dave snapped his gaze to Cathy and she tried her best not to glare back at him. She couldn't believe his sudden turn around, again, but the last thing she wanted was another confrontation between the two of them. She stood up.

"I'll be out at my desk for when you're ready to take me to the docks," she said quietly before quickly striding away.

Before Paul left too, he shot Dave a pacifying smile. "It'll be okay. She won't bite, remember? I'll see you later, partner, at the girls' place."

"Yeah, whatever," Dave almost growled. "Bye."

After saying a few words to Cathy on her way out, Krista followed Paul down to the parking lot. "Did we only imagine last night?" she asked unhappily. "Is Dave always going to be like this around Cathy?"

"Nope, I think it's his last pitch at being a jerk. He can just be too stubborn for his own good at times..." Paul trailed off with a chuckle. "As you have no doubt noticed. He can say one thing and go ahead and do the total opposite and just getting him to make the first move is the whole problem. He'll come around eventually, I'm sure of it... I hope..."

"Then I can only add my hopes to yours. Come on, I have something new to learn now too, and I'm glad you're the one who's teaching me. Let's go."

Dave stood for a few moments at the door to the Captain's office, watching Cathy as she sat at her desk. She was half turned towards him, her hair tumbling over one shoulder, and he came to the swift conclusion he liked it better down like that, flowing free in a thick mass of soft, dark curls. A ray of sunlight came in through the window and shone right on her, setting her hair ablaze with her natural highlights of auburn, red and gold. He saw her squint slightly from the glare of the sun, then tilt her head away from the sun's path, deadening the fire in her hair, but not dulling the impression it had burned in his brain.

She seemed to sense she was being observed and she whirled round towards him, a faint look of surprise on her face until she realized who it was. "Are we ready to go?" she asked, her gaze completely unwavering.

"Yeah, I guess. Captain's orders are Captain's orders. Your car or mine?"

"Yours. You know the way, I don't."

"Whatever you say." Dave pushed on past her, clearly in a hurry to get this chore over and done with as quickly as possible and, with an inward sigh, Cathy grabbed her bag and hurried out after him.

Because of Bathville's proximity to the Atlantic Ocean, it was an ideal tourist spot for people who liked beautiful sandy beaches, or who liked deep-sea fishing or other water sports. On the industrial point of view, it made a good port of call for vessels bringing in oil or timber or whatever, instead of having to go further up the coast to Boston.

The shores of Bathville were patrolled night and day by the Coast Guard and Harbor Police because Bathville was also a well-used drop off point for drug smugglers, who brought their dangerous cargo in on all types of ships and small craft.

In 2013, the Coast Guard and Police had managed to foil an operation in which a tanker coming up from Columbia en-route, supposedly, to Newfoundland, Canada, had stopped off in Bathville for refueling and, thanks to an anonymous tip, a cool 22 million American dollars' worth - an amount not to be sniffed at - of prime cocaine had been seized by the authorities before it could have made its way to the streets to the dealers and the pushers and the users.

For about eighteen months afterwards, things had been relatively quiet around the shores of Bathville's fair city, but, inevitably, the operations had soon resumed and by now it was a never-ending struggle to keep the shores and the streets as drug free as was humanly possible, or as much as wishful thinking would allow.

The docks covered a large area in the east of the city and were also a good distance away from the 7th precinct. During the entire journey there, neither Dave nor Cathy spoke one word to the other. It was the first time she had been in his car, a sleek, black Chevy Camero, and she was about to tell him she really liked his vehicle when one glance at his tight expression told her not to bother wasting her breath on what would only be small talk anyway.

The awkward silence between them was more than she could bear but she didn't want to be the one who was going to break the silence first. She was totally confused by now anyway by the way he had acted towards her so far that day, compared to the friendly way he had ended up being the evening before. She didn't know what his problem was, but whatever it was, she didn't dare confront him about it in case it only succeeded in opening the rift between them again.

The warehouse was situated right on the water's edge and luckily was just opposite a public parking lot where Dave could park quite easily without drawing any attention. The warehouse wasn't very big but there was plenty of activity going on in and around it. Through the doors, they could see about fifteen employees running around doing their designated duties and two fork lift trucks were on the go, piling high crates and moving heavy bins.

"Looks like an order has just been delivered," Dave said, making Cathy jump because he had broken the silence.

After ten minutes of watching and waiting and really seeing nothing untoward, they heard a car approach and Cathy sat forward in her seat a little to read the license plate. She nodded.

"Uh-huh. That's the car from last night."

"Okay, let's just watch and see what, if anything, happens."

The car, a blue Ford Taurus, parked directly in front of the hangar-type doors and moments later, two men stepped out. One of them they both recognized from the night before so they assumed he was Ray Carter, but the other man's appearance surprised them because it was Xavier Petcelli himself.

"You were right after all, Dave," Cathy acknowledged. "There is a connection between them."

"Thought so. Let's see what's going down."

Carter and Petcelli disappeared inside the warehouse and a few minutes later, Carter came back out, carrying a box about the size and shape of a large suitcase. He stored it carefully in the trunk of his car, went back inside, and returned a short while later with another, similar sized box. This was placed beside the first one and minutes later, a third one joined them.

Petcelli reappeared and Dave and Cathy saw him glance at his watch and then exchange a few heated words with Carter. Carter acted anything like he had just been chastised because he started yelling right back at Petcelli and for a moment, it looked like a fight was going to break out between the two of them.

But then Carter seemed to say something that placated the fat little man, then they got back into the car and Carter took off with a loud squeal of burning tires.

"Wonder what that was all about?" Cathy enquired.

"Who cares? I'm more interested in what was in those boxes. Looks like whatever is in the trunk of Carter's car could be on the way to the club so we'll have to keep an extra careful eye open tonight."

"And what do we do now?"

"Go over and try to find the manager to see what he has to say. I'm just dying to find out what's in those boxes, aren't you?"

They hurried over to the warehouse and within seconds, a suspicious looking South American type came over to them. "'elp you?" he demanded unpleasantly.

"Sure, buddy, we'd like to speak to the manager," Dave said.

"'e no talk to no one without an appointment."

"Oh yeah?" Looking quite unperturbed, Dave pulled out his badge and flashed it front of the man's nose. "See this? This is the only appointment I'm going to need, pal, so do yourself a favor and go get him. Now."

The man gave him a sullen look, then left to go in search of the manager. He didn't exactly hurry himself either because nearly ten minutes passed before he returned with a middle-aged man, who was already starting to look very uncomfortable.

"I'm the manager," he said, without offering his name. "Enrico here says you want to talk to me, so let's make this fast because I am a very busy man." He was neither polite nor impolite, just seemingly anxious to get back to his work.

"Two, er, gentlemen, just left a little while ago with some boxes they carried out from this warehouse," Dave said, "and we were just curious to know what was in them."

"Um... Fish, I believe."

"Excuse me?"

"Frozen fish. This is a frozen food company."

"Oh. I see. Well, Mr..... er...."

"Harris."

"Well, Mr. Harris, we've been watching this place for some time now and the two guys I'm referring to seem to be buying a *lot* of frozen fish." It was a long shot on Dave's part but it paid off because Harris started to fluster a bit. "Do they own a restaurant or something and cut out the middle man by coming directly to you for their frozen goods?"

"No, I... well, it's...I really don't know anything."

"I think that means we can safely assume you know a lot," Cathy said. She gestured around the cluttered warehouse. "Do all these crates and boxes contain frozen food?"

"Um... yeah... that's right."

"So, you wouldn't mind if we take a look in some of them, would you?"

Harris quickly shook his head, his brown eyes bulging out a little. "No, you can't do that, I, huh, well, you'll need a search warrant if you want to do that."

Dave and Cathy looked at each other in feigned surprise. "Did he say 'warrant'?" he asked mildly.

"I think he sure did," she dutifully replied.

"Oh...well... don't they always demand a search warrant when they're only trying to hide something?"

"Yup, so I believe," she said innocently.

"Okay, in that case, do you think you could rush over and obtain one? I can phone the Captain from here, have him set it up with the Judge and he can have it all ready and drawn up for you by the time you get there. Shouldn't take that long if I tell the Cap it's urgent."

"Sure, I can be there and back in less than an hour."

"Good. Soon as I phone the Cap, I might start looking through the crates anyway so I can save a little bit more time." Dave fished out his car keys and cell phone and passed the keys over to her. "Here you go, you head back to the precinct and get Mr. Harris his... huh... warrant."

Cathy had only gotten as far as a few yards when Harris suddenly moved to grab at her. "Stop!" he shouted, desperately, "please, just... stop."

She turned and looked back at him expectantly. "Yes?" she asked in wide-eyed innocence, and behind Harris' back, Dave carefully concealed a smirk.

Harris flopped down on the nearest crate, looking anything but happy. "I don't want any more trouble," he said, "I'm just sick of it, so I'll tell you what you want to know. Those two punks came down here about a couple of months ago and asked if they could use my building every so often as a pick-up point."

"Pick-up point for what?" Dave asked.

"I don't know."

Dave instantly raised a cynical eyebrow. "Oh yeah?"

"I swear to you I don't know. I was advised way back in the beginning to keep my mouth shut so I wouldn't have to suffer any consequences. Petcelli, he's the fat one, he pays me big bucks just for the use of my place and part of the deal is I ask no questions as long as he keeps paying the dough."

"If you were advised to keep your mouth shut, "Cathy said, "why didn't you figure something illegal was going on and come to the police?"

"Because money talks. My business was going under a few months ago and Mr. Petcelli's money has helped stop it from sinking completely. And with today's economy being what it is, every little helps, ya know?"

"And why were you so reluctant to let us look in the crates?" Dave asked.

"Because I wasn't sure if Petcelli had got all that belonged to him. I didn't see how many boxes he left with and if he had left something behind and he found out that someone had been tampering with his property, my life wouldn't be worth living."

"He left with three boxes. Is that the norm?"

"Yes, never any more than three."

"And how often do they use this place?"

"Twice a month. There's always the same guy with Mr. Petcelli too, Chappell, or Cartwright or something, I think his name is.... and sometimes Cartwright -"

"Carter," Dave said, "his name's Carter."

"Right, Carter, sometimes he's with another guy, I think his first name's Jerry but usually he's with Petcelli."

"Do his goods come in on a separate consignment to yours?" Cathy asked.

"Yes, and he always times it that they come in same time as I'm expecting a huge delivery."

"And what brings his goods in. Van, boat?"

"They always arrive by van but it's a different van every time, with a different driver too. All I have to do is call Petcelli when I know I'm getting a delivery and he arranges for the van to deliver his stuff." Harris paused for a moment, then shrugged bemusedly. "That's it, that's all I can tell you, I swear."

With a quick glance at Cathy, Dave nodded. The man's body language was telling Dave he was telling the truth and he reckoned they had found out everything they needed to know. "Okay, from now on, Mr. Harris, you refuse to do business with these men, especially Petcelli. We'll continue to keep an eye on this place to make sure you do as I say. First sign of you stepping out of line, we'll close this place down so fast, your head will spin. Got that?"

Obviously anxious to keep his business going for as long as possible, Harris nodded miserably. "Yes, Sergeant, I've got that." He smiled sadly and for just an instant, Cathy almost felt sorry for him. He was, after all, simply an innocent pawn, one who had let money sway his better judgment. He caught her looking at him and he quickly masked his face again. "Anyone ever tell you that you speak strange?" he asked her, saying just about anything to change the subject. "Where's that accent from?"

She grinned. "South Africa, where else? Good day, Mr. Harris."

Harris watched her and Dave leave then, with a weary sigh, he returned to his small, cluttered office. He sat at his desk in silence for a few moments, his fingers massaging his temples as he felt the beginnings of a tension headache behind his eyes and he tried not to look at the large stack of unpaid bills sitting askew in the In-Tray. Every day, it seemed to grow that little bit higher and he stifled a long moan of despair.

He had owned his business for close to twenty-three years and now it looked like he was going to lose it after all his hard work if he was going to have to stop the connections with Petcelli. Better to lose the business on the right side of the law than on the wrong side, he mused.... but hell, he had sixteen employees to think of too, most of whom had families to support.... Although there wasn't much good he could do for them if he found himself behind prison bars....

He glanced at his watch, figured Petcelli would be back at the club by now, and quickly called him. He was relieved when Petcelli himself answered. "Petcelli, this is Harris. You may as well know, the deal's off, I can't let you use my place anymore."

"What do you mean I can't use your place anymore?" Petcelli barked. "Is this a ruse for more money, Harris? Because if it is -"

"No, it's got nothing to do with the money. I've just had two cops down here sniffing around and they know all about our little comings and goings. Appears they've been watching this place for some time now."

"Two cops? What did they look like?"

"Why's that important?"

"Because a little while ago, I had two cops in here, asking my staff all kinds of questions. They came in here every night for about two weeks and I'm just wondering if it's them because they haven't been around in a few days."

"Well, okay, the guy was tall, mid to late twenties, I'd say, dark, pretty boy features, but he had a real mean look too. The lady cop was short, very attractive, had long dark hair... and oh yes, she spoke with an accent."

"An accent?" Petcelli pounced on that immediately, his mind suddenly starting to work overtime. "She didn't happen to say where she was from, by any chance?"

"As a matter of fact, she did. South Africa, of all places."

"South Africa? Hmmm.... what a pity." Petcelli quickly dismissed the idea that had been forming in his mind and turned his attention back to the more pressing issue on hand. "I hope you didn't happen to let it slip where I can be found."

"Of course not, I'm not stupid. All I'm telling you is you'll have to get some other place for your pick-up point, that's all."

"If I didn't know any better, Harris, I'd say you were just taking the money and running. Tsk tsk, that's no way to do business, you know, it's highly unprofessional and, if I choose, very dangerous."

"Dangerous? You implying some sort of threat, Petcelli?"

"Take it whatever way you please."

"Look, it's not that I want you to stop using my warehouse, okay? I just want to keep the cops off my back, they've threatened me with a shutdown if I continue to do business with you. Surely even you can understand where I'm coming from?"

Petcelli listened to Harris' tone very carefully, deliberated for a few moments if he was being told the truth then, with practiced ease, he put understanding into his voice. "Of course, I can understand, Mr. Harris. No hard feelings, okay? As long as you didn't tell them what it is we pick up, then I'm prepared to let the matter drop."

"How could I have told them what you pick up when *I* don't even know what it is?"

"True. And that's the way it's going to stay. Good day, Harris." Petcelli hung up and cursed loudly. He sat back and wondered how he was going to get his goods from now on. He had plenty of other contacts he could use, if he wanted to, but he didn't exactly trust either one of them. Harris had been a simpleton, a desperate man desperately trying to save a business that was on its last legs anyway and Petcelli had swayed him easily with the money he had offered. And now he was back to square one. No pick-up place and no one he could trust.

At least he had what he needed for this coming Friday night... but for the next social event he had planned, he was screwed. He had three weeks to find someone and to get everything back on track.

Dave and Cathy had returned to the precinct under a cloud of silence again. He was dying to tell her she had handled herself rather well at the warehouse, playing it cool, following his lead, asking all the right questions, and the touch about saying she was from South Africa proved to him she could at least think on her feet. But every time he opened his mouth to tell her she had done well, he felt his words becoming jumbled in his brain and he couldn't trust himself to speak, so he let the silence continue. As did she.

When they sat in the Captain's office, telling him of what had happened at the warehouse, Dave, of course, had no trouble talking then and Cathy couldn't stop herself from glaring at him in scorn. "See you didn't swallow your tongue after all, Dave," she remarked dryly.

"And what, pray tell, do you mean by that?" he asked innocently, knowing full well what she meant.

"Oh, you're suddenly talking a mile a minute. Get your batteries recharged or something?"

He merely smirked indifferently in way of a response and turned back to the Captain. "Anyway, Bob, that's what happened."

"Good work...now we have something to act on. Keep your eyes peeled tonight, if there's going to be a switch, I want at least one of you to see it happening. And even if nothing happens tonight, as long as nobody's cover gets blown until Friday night, that's all that matters." The Captain glanced at his watch. "It's gone 4:00, you people can call it a day if you want. I'll see you tomorrow some time."

Cathy arose immediately on hearing that and she hurried out to her car without even bidding Dave a farewell. She was too tired to leave herself wide open to get into any more mental battles with him, he seemed to be in one of those moods today that he didn't give a damn about anyone or anything and she just wanted to get away from him. Just as she was about to get into her car, she heard her name being called and she turned to see who was trying to get her attention. It was Dave himself and she inwardly sighed in impatience.

"Hey Cathy, wait up."

She looked at him expectantly and tried to ignore how blue and powerful his eyes were, how shiny his hair was in the sunlight, how good he smelled, how... She threw her bag on the front seat of her car and turned back to him, trying to hide a look of annoyance, which, she hated to admit, was really annoyance at herself. "What is it, Andrews?" she asked warily.

He stood as close to her as he dared and smiled faintly. "I, huh, just wanted you to know that... well... that you did good at the warehouse. You played it cool and still managed to act professionally." There, he had said it, he had paid her the well-deserved compliment and it really hadn't been so difficult after all.

She stared at him in surprise. "I, well...thank you."

"No problem. Where are you going now?"

"Home. Why?"

"Because I thought we should see if Paul and Krista are there, tell them what happened today and what might be happening tonight."

She considered for a moment, and then shrugged indifferently. "Okay, if you like. If they have finished checking out Ruth's apartment, Paul's probably at our place anyway."

"Yeah, that's where he said for me to see him."

"So, I'll see you there, then."

His smile became warmer. "Sure. I'll follow you."

On the drive back to her apartment, Cathy couldn't stop thinking about Dave and his down one minute, up the next, behavior. She decided he was definitely an enigma and she surprised herself totally when she realized he was an enigma she desperately wanted to unravel now and find out more about. She even shivered in anticipation the more she thought about him and she even began to dare believe she could become very attracted to him, if she let herself...

But as soon as she pulled up outside her apartment, she dismissed those thoughts as being nothing but a waste of time and completely foolhardy.

As expected, she saw Paul's car and, hoping she wasn't going to be making yet another intrusion on them, she banged the front door loudly on her way in and called out, "I'm home!" to announce her arrival.

"In here, Cath," came Krista's voice from the kitchen.

Cathy shrugged out of her jacket, hung it up and when she went into the kitchen, she found Paul sitting on top of one of the counters, with Krista standing between his legs, hugging his waist and sharing a can of Pepsi with him.

"Hello you two," she greeted. "How'd it go?"

"Nothing to report, she wasn't even there, so we left the uniforms to do their duty," Paul said.

"Dave should be here any minute too because we want to tell you what happened at the warehouse."

Right on cue, the doorbell rang and Dave called out, "It's me."

Cathy went to let him in and all four of them retired to the living room. Paul flopped down on the sofa and Krista instantly curled up beside him, Dave sat on one chair and Cathy sat on the other, a sub-conscious effort on her part for her to get as far away from Dave as she possibly could.

Dave proceeded to tell Paul and Krista what they had learned and Cathy listened carefully while he talked. By the time he was finished, Paul and Krista were more than clear with what might be ahead of them that night. Cathy realized Dave had related everything in the exact order it had happened, and he had done it straight from memory too, without having to consult a notebook. As she thought about it as he spoke, she didn't think he had missed anything.

"And that, as they say, is that, people," Dave concluded.

"So, the Captain was right after all," Paul said, "the Blues Haven is harboring some sort of goods after all. Wonder what they are?"

"They definitely weren't appliances, like microwaves or DVD players or anything big like that," Dave stated. "The boxes were of an average size, he managed to get three quite comfortably into the trunk of his car, but they seemed heavy, the way he was carrying them. I could venture a guess that they're jewelry, or diamonds. Or drugs. I wonder if Petcelli will try and unload them in the club or could he only be acting as the middle man, that he passes them out to someone else and only uses the club as a storage place?"

"We'll see what we can find out tonight," Krista said.

"I wonder if what Petcelli picked up today has anything to do with what's happening on Friday night." Cathy mused.

"We certainly can't rule that possibility out," Paul concurred. "For all we know, gambling chips could have been in those boxes. Didn't that Herb guy demand big stakes this time around?"

"He did. I suppose we'll just have to wait and see. Kris, do you know if Ruth is working on Friday night?"

"Yeah, she mentioned it."

"Don't forget to keep an eye on her until we get her some protection. If she catches wind of something happening on Friday night, she might get caught again and we all already know Petcelli won't hesitate to get rid of her. We don't want her to be the next name on the murder list."

"I'll certainly do my part in looking out for her, but it's hard when we have to swap over almost immediately after each other's shift. Other than at the beginning of the night when we're getting changed, there's never much time to do any talking."

And as Krista would find out later, she would find herself wishing she'd taken more time to do more than just talk.

CHAPTER TWENTY-EIGHT

On that Tuesday night, their last night working together at the club for a couple of nights, the night they had been hoping would produce some action, turned out to be a complete and utter waste of time.

Throughout the entire evening, maybe as many as twenty patrons came and went. There was no sign of Ray Carter and even Petcelli himself didn't put in an appearance until just before closing time.

For most of their shifts, they stood around doing nothing except passing idle chitchat. Those of the staff who smoked, took extra smoke breaks. Krista and Ruth didn't even have to dance their full half hour stint each time and were told by the head bouncer on more than one occasion that, if there were less than half a dozen people in the club, they wouldn't have to dance at all.

They were all glad when the night came to an end, but disappointed that it had turned out to be a bust.

The next night, Wednesday, Paul and Krista were in without the back up of their respective partners. And when Krista walked into the dressing room, Ruth was already there and Krista stopped dead in her tracks as soon as she realized Ruth was crying, very heavily too.

"Ruth, what's wrong?" Krista asked, and the genuine concern in her voice only made Ruth's eyes fill up with even more tears.

She tried to answer Krista's question but she could only shake her head in desperation, choked sobs escaping her throat. She reached for her cigarettes, lit one up, inhaled deeply and raggedly blew the smoke out. She squinted through the blue gray smoke at Krista, looking like she wanted to confide something to her, but instead, she shook her head again.

"I really wish I could tell you," she murmured at last.

"Just do," Krista urged gently and knelt beside her. "Come on, no need to be afraid, not of me. If I can help you in any way, I will."

Ruth swiped defiantly at her tears and emitted a sharp, bitter laugh. "Why should you, a perfect stranger, want to help *me*?"

"Because I know there's something very clearly wrong and I really do want to help. Are you in some kind of trouble?"

"I ain't pregnant, if *that's* the sort of trouble you mean. Jesus, I almost wish I was, at least I know how to deal with a problem like that." Ruth took another long draw of her cigarette and her hand was shaking so badly, she could hardly hold it still.

"What has you so obviously scared, then?" Krista persisted. "Is it a guy? Is some guy after you?"

Ruth rolled her eyes and quickly shook her head. "Don't I wish?"

A whole bunch of reasons flitted through Krista's mind, then she decided on a long shot. "Did you see something you shouldn't have, maybe?"

"Where?" Ruth asked warily.

"Oh, I don't know... around here, maybe?"

"I... look, I just can't tell you, I'm sorry." Ruth's whole attitude suddenly changed as she went on the defensive and even her face visibly hardened. "I always believe that things have a way of working themselves out, see, so just leave me alone, Kris. I've been in situations like this before - *tougher* situations too - loads of times, and I know how to handle them so do us both a favor and back off."

Krista found herself wondering who Ruth was maybe trying to convince the most, but she knew she couldn't force the issue and she reluctantly decided to let the matter drop. "If you ever think about changing your mind about telling me, I just want you to know, I'm right here for you. Anytime, Ruth, just remember that." With that, she patted Ruth's arm and quietly arose to get changed.

The club was filling up quite considerably, in such sharp contrast to the previous night, Krista discovered when she went out to the stage. She and Paul had already prearranged that if she saw anything even remotely suspicious, she would let him know with a simple gesture and he could take it from there. However, when she finished her shift thirty minutes later, nothing untoward had happened.

When she returned to the dressing room, Ruth was nowhere in sight and figuring she had just gone to the bathroom, Krista sat down and massaged her feet. Five minutes later, Carlos, one of the bouncers, knocked on the door.

"Where the hell's Ruth?" he demanded. "The customers are screaming for their dancer."

"Isn't she already out there?" Krista asked, startled.

Carlos looked at her as if she was stupid. "Do you think the boss would have sent me looking for her if she was? If I can't find her, you're going to have to fill in for her."

"But I've just fin -" But Carlos had already disappeared and Krista sighed heavily in exasperation. Another few minutes later, she was instructed to get back to the stage. Paul looked at her in astonishment when he saw she was about to start dancing again.

"Where's Ruth?" he mouthed to her.

She could only shrug she didn't know and he looked around him in bewilderment. He knew that Ruth had been there earlier because he had seen her beat up little Civic outside in the parking lot when he had arrived, and he knew it was still there because he had just come in after getting a breath of fresh air. With a quick gesture to Krista that he was going to go use the telephone, he went out to the foyer and used his cell phone to dial Dave's number.

"Yo, Dave, it's me," he announced in an undertone when Dave answered.

"Hey, Cam, what's up?"

"I'm not sure, but Ruth seems to have gone missing. She was here earlier but Krista has just had to go back on stage to do Ruth's stint for her. I know it may be a bit soon to tell, but I've got a feeling there's something not quite right here. Her car's still out in the parking lot but she's simply nowhere to be seen."

"Okay, leave this with me. I can't go down there because my face is now too well known so I'll have to see who's available at the station, get them to come up and act like they're going to have a drink in that place. If anything happens, I'll keep myself awake, so call me if you need me."

"Yeah, later, Dave." Paul hung up and took a quick look outside. A steady drizzle was falling and a fog was rolling in, making the lights over the parking lot cast a ghostly shadow over everything. The night air was still and quiet, not even a hint of a breeze was blowing anywhere.

And Ruth's car was no longer parked in its spot.

With a soft curse, Paul went back inside and called Dave again. "You phoned anyone yet?"

"I have Rooney on the other line. What's up?"

"Don't send anyone over. Have Rooney put out an APB on Ruth's car instead, it's just disappeared from the parking lot. Also, make sure there is a guard down at her apartment."

"Will do. Keep in touch, if you can."

"Okay, partner." Paul hung up and went back to the bar, a bad feeling in his gut that told him Ruth was in some kind of trouble. Of course, he didn't yet know of the conversation Krista had had with Ruth, therefore he had no solid evidence yet to back up the bad feeling so as far as he was concerned right now, he had absolutely nothing to work with.

He tried to figure it out in a plausible way. Ruth could have been feeling unwell, had gone outside for some fresh air through the back exit, making Krista miss her and then, while Krista could have been preoccupied, Ruth could simply have told Petcelli she was feeling ill and was going on home. But although a credible enough explanation, Paul remained unconvinced it was the right one.

The more Krista continued dancing, the more tired she became but no more people had infiltrated the club tonight, it was only half full thus far, giving her a better chance to watch for anything suspicious. She wasn't just becoming increasingly weary with her non-stop dancing, the stifling heat in the club wasn't exactly helping matters either.

Perspiration was rolling off her like, she felt, a river, and she began to fantasize about a nice warm bath that was perfumed with heavenly smelling oils, or taking a dip in a nice cool pool, or standing naked behind a roaring waterfall, or...She pulled her mind away from these tantalizing thoughts back to reality and let her gaze fall on Paul. He seemed vaguely annoyed about something and he didn't even seem to be aware that he was being observed, which was maybe just as well, she thought, she didn't want him to see her blatant love for him just yet. A love that she had been feeling for quite a few days now.

She reluctantly tore her eyes away from him and a movement to the right of the stage caught her attention. She saw Petcelli standing talking heatedly with another man whose face remained in the shadows and it suddenly struck her that this was the first time all night she had seen Petcelli.

She continued observing the two men and she saw Petcelli repeatedly reach inside his jacket as if he was going to bring out something to show the other man, but the man kept shaking his head, so whatever was in the jacket remained there. Some sort of a deal was obviously being struck and Krista quickly caught Paul's attention. He followed her gaze to the two men and saw what she didn't - a small package exchange hands.

Paul gestured to Krista to stay where she was and then, after a quick word to the other bartender, he went back out to the foyer to use his cell phone to call the precinct to request a back-up. He waited for the dispatch clerk to find out where the nearest squad car was and was pleased to hear there was one only a couple of blocks away. He left instructions for what the patrolmen had to do upon arrival at the club, gave over a brief description of the suspect and hung up.

From where he was standing in the foyer, he had a good view of Petcelli and the other man and he discreetly observed them for a few more moments. When the man started walking towards the exit, Paul ran outside, just in time to see the squad car pull up.

"Hey, Cameron," one of the officers greeted him. "What's up?"

"Kill the lights on the car, Harv, he's on his way out. Approach him with caution, I don't know if he's armed or not. I'm going to make myself scarce but I'll be able to hear everything that's going on. Goes without saying that you can't let on I'm around."

Paul just about managed to slip to the far side of the dumpster at the side of the building when the man came out. He had only gotten a few yards across the parking lot when the two officers stopped him.

"Excuse me, sir," Harv said, "we have just received a tip that you could be in the possession of some illegal goods. Please turn around, place your hands on the wall and spread your legs."

The man seemed totally startled.... too startled to do what the officer had just requested of him. "Wh-What the hell's going on here?" he spluttered. "I don't know what you're talking about."

"Just make this easy on yourself, sir," Harv advised and steered him not too gently towards the wall.

Because the man had no other choice but to assume the position, he did. "What's this all about? I was just on my way home after a quick beer, don't tell me there's a law against having one drink now as well!" He grumbled and complained the whole time he was being frisked but was otherwise compliant. But when Harv reached his jacket at the breast pocket, without warning, he kicked out and tried to make a run for it. He didn't get far.

Harv caught him and pushed him back against the wall to continue the search. Seconds later, he extracted the small package from the man's jacket pocket and when the package was opened, it was found to contain several pouches of white powder, presumably cocaine.

"Well, well," Harv said amiably. "What have we got here? Mind telling us who you got this from, sir?"

"Can't remember," came the sullen reply.

"Hmm... well, either you tell us or we find out our own way, don't matter to us. But you'll only be doing yourself a huge favor if you tell us now."

"You can't pin anything on me. For all you know, I could have picked up someone else's jacket by mistake."

Harv shook his head in vague amusement and glanced over at this partner. "Cuff him and read him his rights, Len. I'm going to go have a quick word with Cam." He disappeared into the shadows behind the dumpster and, for added coverage, stood between Paul and the man he had just had his partner place under arrest. "Looks like cocaine, Sarge."

Paul clicked his tongue behind his teeth. "Great, we were hoping it was something else he was dealing in, not drugs. Take the turkey down to the station, book him and try and get as much info out of him as you can - just remember not to let on you know where he got the stuff or who he got it from. If it's obvious he's not going to talk, throw him in the slammer until someone pays his bail. If he does talk, it will be enough for us to close this joint down, if he doesn't talk, we'll have to wait until Friday night when there's supposedly a gambling gig going down."

"We'll do our best to get him to talk, count on it. Our report will be on your desk by tomorrow morning."

"Good, thanks. And let Captain Hamilton know too."

"Will do. Catch you later, Sarge." Harv went back to the squad car, helped Len get the man into the car and seconds later, pulled away.

Paul knew the whole operation hadn't taken any longer than a few minutes, but he forced himself to wait a few minutes more before returning to the bar. He ran his fingers through his hair, slick now with rain, and shivered. Typical New England Spring weather, he mused.

When he went back inside, it was apparent no one had even noticed his absence, but Krista certainly had known he was away and she breathed a silent sigh of relief that he was back and seemed to be all right. She was due a well-earned break in a few minutes and she was anxious to hear what had just happened. As soon as she finished dancing, she ran into the dressing room for her robe and hurried back out to the bar again.

Paul motioned to her to sit down and, after he had finished washing a few glasses, he ambled over to her. Rick, the other bartender, had gone on a break, the two waitresses working the floor tonight were standing sharing a cigarette behind the stage, there was no one else around and it was safe to talk.

"What was in the package?" Krista asked. "Did you find out?"

"Yeah. Cocaine. Two officers have taken the guy down to the precinct for questioning and here's hoping he spills his guts about Petcelli. If he doesn't, we'll still be here until Friday."

"Drugs after all, then. Terrific."

"Yeah, tell me about it. Practically every case Dave and I touch these days is somehow drug related and it just keeps getting worse out on the streets because drugs are just too readily available."

"I remember Captain Hamilton telling Cathy and me that the first day we arrived here," Krista mused.

"And the big guy wasn't far wrong. At least the evidence is starting to pile up against Petcelli. I can't wait to get this den of sin closed down and throw his sorry, fat ass into jail."

"Me neither. Hey, you still haven't seen Ruth around anywhere, have you?"

"Nope, and I hate to tell you this, but I'm a bit worried about her now. Her car's gone from the parking lot."

"Oh Paul!" she cried in growing dismay. "Now you've got me worried too. When I saw her earlier, she seemed so upset, crying and everything, now she's gone missing?"

"Relax, baby, maybe it's nothing, she could have been feeling ill and has gone on home, it's too soon to jump to what could be the wrong conclusion. But, well, I do have to admit I have a bad feeling here and Rooney down at the precinct is putting an APB out on her car just in case."

Krista chewed pensively on her bottom lip, going over in her head the conversation she'd had with Ruth earlier. "She didn't seem ill, she seemed upset. *Very* upset. And I couldn't get her to open out to me at all. She was definitely hiding something, something that is scaring the life out of her."

"You think so? Maybe there's been a death in her family.... who knows? We'll find out more tomorrow and *if* something has happened to her - and I pray to God nothing has - then all the more reason to get this place closed down. Providing it's connected with Petcelli, of course."

"I know that the sooner we close this place, on whatever charge, the happier I will be. I don't think my body - or my feet - can take much more of the abuse this dancing is giving them."

"Anytime you need your feet or your body - that very *beaut*iful body, I may add, massaged to ease away your aches and pains, just let me know. I have magic fingers, you know."

"You do?" She smiled slowly, sensuously. "I'll bear that in mind." She laced her fingers through his, the smile still playing at the corners of her mouth. "So, you mean it that I have a beautiful body?"

"Oh *yes*, most definitely," he stated and very deliberately leered down the front of her robe. "One of these fine days I might be obliged to...." He trailed off before he could say too much but she immediately picked up on his implication.

Their surroundings were no longer apparent to either of them, the music and conversation around them became muted and as Krista looked him square in the eye, his stomach flipped over.

"Better watch what you say, Paul, because one of these fine days I might just be obliged to let you." With that, she blew him a kiss, slid gracefully off the bar stool and retreated to the dressing room, leaving him staring after her in astonishment.

The remainder of their shifts blew by with no more incidents and Krista was so totally exhausted by closing time, she could hardly keep her eyes open. She actually fell asleep in Paul's car on the drive home and only managed to give him one good night kiss before bidding him a drowsy farewell.

"I'm sorry," she said sheepishly, stifling a yawn. "Not the best of company, huh?"

He gently caressed her cheek and shook his head. "Don't worry, you worked hard tonight, it's no wonder you're so tired. Go on, go get your sleep and I'll see you tomorrow evening." He paused as an idea came into his head and he looked at her thoughtfully. "Why don't you come over to my place tomorrow instead? You haven't seen it yet so tomorrow would be as good a time as any to remedy that."

"I'd like that but I don't know where you live."

"Not to worry, I'll call you and give you the directions. Plus, I do believe your car has GPS, not to mention your cell phone has too." He beamed an innocent smile at her and she chuckled softly in submission. "Anyway, it's only about ten minutes from here so you can't get lost."

"Okay, good night, love. Drive carefully."

He watched her walk up the path to her apartment and waited until she had disappeared safely inside before he drove away.

And all that he knew was, he could hardly wait to see her again.

CHAPTER TWENTY-NINE

Krista made it round to Paul's the next evening at a little after seven. His directions had been very precise because she had managed to find his place quite easily without having to use the GPS. A cool breeze was blowing tonight, but the first stars were peeking through the break ups in the rain clouds that had been hovering over the area for a couple of days. Sunny skies were forecast for the next few days and, despite the coolness right now, Krista felt happy and relaxed and quite glad not to be anywhere near The Blues Haven and its sleazy clientele tonight.

Paul answered her ringing of the doorbell almost immediately. "Hi!" he greeted cheerfully. "Welcome to my humble abode." He stepped back to let her in and ushered her into the living room. "Didn't get lost, I see?"

She smiled and stood uncertainly for a moment, remembering her manners as she tried not to stare at her surroundings. Paul's apartment was certainly nothing like she had imagined it would be. She had expected a typical bachelor type place, with lots of chrome and glass and cheesy furniture and with books and newspapers and clothes probably lying all over the place, as well as it being in dire need of a vacuuming too. But as she surreptitiously looked all around her, she knew she had been too quick to jump to conclusions.

The living room was decorated in soft beiges, creams and white and on the dark beige sofa and chairs, dark green cushions had been added for a bit of color. There was an antique coffee table, polished to perfection, in the middle of the floor, a small table at the end of the sofa on which was placed the telephone, a lamp and a framed picture of Paul with Dave taken, she guessed, a couple of years ago. A large flat-screened television, DVR and DVD player were situated to the far left of the window and in the right-hand corner, a state of the art sound system had been strategically placed. A shelf neatly stacked with CDs and DVDs ran along most of the wall above the sound system and the room just felt so comfortable and inviting, Krista instantly felt quite at home.

"This is really lovely, Paul," she said warmly, "it looks like it costs a fortune in -" She stopped abruptly and covered her mouth in embarrassment. "Oops, I'm sorry, that was terribly rude."

He chuckled softly at the faint bloom that had arisen on her cheeks. "No need to apologize. It doesn't cost too much or else I wouldn't be here. I like my landlord, he's pretty cool about letting his tenants decorate their apartment any way they please, as long as it's not too outlandish. I'll let you see the rest of the place afterwards and I'm glad you like what you see so far." He suddenly realized she was still standing and, quickly plumping up a cushion, he invited her to sit down. "Make yourself at home, Kris. If you want to put your feet up, go right ahead, won't bother me none. Dave does it all the time and so do I. Can I get you anything? Coffee, soda, something a little stronger?"

"A soft drink would be nice, thanks."

"Coming right up." When he returned a few moments later, he found her over at the CDs, lifting them out one by one, reading the title, then placing it carefully back where it belonged. "See anything you like?"

"I never realized you had such a varied taste in music," she stated. "Clapton, Simon and Garfunkel, Cat Stevens, U2, Adele, BareNaked Ladies, Matchbox 20, Dave Matthews Band, *all* of which I like."

"I told you, I just love music. Come on, sit down, you've been on your feet enough these last few days."

She sat back down on the sofa and when she was settled, he sat beside her. "I really do like it here, Paul," she said softly. "You keep the place really nice."

"For a guy, you mean?" he teased. "Maybe I do, I just hate mess, that's all. I love the space here and I love the apartment having two levels.... that way everything's not crammed into the one area." He paused to take a sip of his drink, and then he shifted around so he would be facing her more. "So, young lady, tell me what you did all day. I missed you."

She smiled and rolled her eyes. "I missed you too. And I'm ashamed to say I slept for most of the day. I must have slept the clock around I was just so tired. Was the Captain expecting to see me?"

"Not really, not after I told him how you'd had to dance practically all night last night. I went to see him after lunch and told him all that happened."

"Sorry I left you to do all the work. I set my alarm to get up but I must have slept right through it and Cathy was apparently out for most of the day so she wasn't even around to get me up. What about that guy you got arrested last night? Has he talked yet?"

"Nope, he's keeping pretty tight-lipped, the jerk."

"And any news on Ruth?"

"Nothing on her either, I'm afraid. Dave kept the APB out on her car all day but no one has seen it. And after you saying how upset and frightened she was when you were talking to her last night, now I'm *really* worried."

"Yeah, we were talking without her telling me anything. She just refused point blank to tell me what was wrong."

"Here's hoping it's nothing serious and she just decided to take herself off for the night. Maybe she's even gone out of state on vacation, for all we know."

"Yeah.... maybe."

Paul could see she was growing distressed talking about Ruth so he set down his drink and pulled her into his arms. "Hmm... Enough shop talk for tonight, I think. Cathy and Dave are on the job tonight, maybe they'll uncover something. But right now, it's just you and me and.... say.... have we kissed yet?"

Krista smiled. "Now that you mention it, no, we haven't."

"Then I think it's high time we remedied that, don't you?" He leaned over and softly brushed her lips with his and when he pulled away, he saw she was looking back at him, clearly unimpressed. "What's wrong?"

"Is that it?" she inquired dryly. "One tiny little peck?"

"Consider yourself lucky, my lady. Many a female would kill to get even that from me," he teased.

"So I've heard," she flashed right back at him.

"Touché, Sergeant Nolan. Deserved that one, didn't I?"

"I think I let you off too easy, Sergeant Cameron. I've only been to the station a few times and already I've heard a lot of gossip about you. From what I can gather, you're quite the ladies man."

For once, he couldn't read anything into her tone of voice and he looked at her in surprise. Her expression was completely blank but just for an instant, he caught a hint of insecurity or uncertainty in her eyes. Or maybe he was reading her entirely the wrong way, maybe she was resentful of his rather checkered past and definitely did not approve.

He knew all about the gossip she was referring to, it was no big secret and it was actually more like a running joke down at the precinct. His fellow officers liked to pick on him, tease him as much as they could about his love life because that was just the type of people they were, eager to laugh at someone else's expense, but never in a malicious, vindictive way. It was one way they all had of relieving their tensions because they were all in one of the most thankless, dangerous professions in a world that was going crazy and laughing helped ease the pain of a drug bust that had gone wrong and had resulted in the death of one or more officers, or the news that an undercover cop had walked straight into a trap and had paid with his or her life. It was just the way things were done where he worked, to an outsider it might have appeared a bit sick or even cruel, but Paul didn't care what other people thought, he worked with a bunch of people who he knew would quite gladly lay down their lives to save his, as he would for them.

But it was true, though, he couldn't deny he had been with a lot of females in the past. He was a regular, healthy guy with a regular, healthy sexual appetite, but he had never willingly hurt any of his past conquests, he had never cheated on any one of them and he certainly didn't plan on doing something like that now.

However, right now, Krista had just opened up a whole new chapter previously undiscussed between them and he knew he would have to set the record straight. He cared too deeply for her to let her get hurt over idle gossip and a cop's warped sense of humor and he wanted to chase away any doubts she may be having.

He folded her hand into his and took a few moments to carefully choose his words. "You're quite right, Kris," he began earnestly, "I *have* earned myself a bit of a reputation with the guys at the station and it's something I don't want to lie to you about or try and cover up. I have lost count of the number of girlfriends and one night stands I have had over the years and, although I'm not exactly proud of having such a large number of past relationships, particularly in this day and age with AIDS and Lord knows what else running rife, I don't want to have to feel that I have to justify them either."

"So why are you telling me about them now?"

"Because I just want to."

"You really don't have to tell me anything, Paul. What you did with your life before you met me is entirely your own business, not mine."

"But I've chosen to make it your business because I want you to know all there is to know about me before you hear the wrong thing from someone and get the wrong idea about me. Contrary to popular belief, I'm not a ladies man, I don't try and juggle two or three relationships at the one time because that is simply not my style. I am strictly a one-woman man, always have been, always will be. The most serious relationship I've ever had lasted ten months and I even thought I was in love... but I know now I wasn't. She was an office girl, with a regular nine to five job and she just couldn't cope with my hectic schedule. Towards the end, she got pretty pissed at the many dates I stood her up on if I was up to my eyeballs on a case or something and one day, I did it to her once too often. She called it quits and that was that. But what I'm trying to say is, the whole time I was with her, I never did the dirty on her and I never even looked at another woman when I wasn't with her. Can you trust me enough that that's the way I am?"

Krista nodded slowly, but at least without hesitation. "Yes, I can trust you."

"Thank you, because this isn't some line of supreme bullshit I'm feeding you just to make an impression, this is the absolute truth. What the other officers may say to you, they'll only be kidding around and besides, if they see that you and I are serious about one another, they'll back off anyway and start picking on someone else. And that's basically all I have to say, except for one more thing." He stopped and smiled faintly. "I don't intend to change my habits and turn into a womanizer just to live up to some bogus reputation, particularly now that I have you in my life. You are the most special woman in the world to me and I wouldn't give you up for anybody, or hurt you in any way with a casual fling now and again because to do that to you would kill me. Do you trust me enough on that score too?"

She nodded again as her eyes searched his. "I already trust you with my life, Paul, so I can sure as hell trust you with anything else. I'm sorry if I put you on the spot, I didn't mean to and I'm sorry too if I made you feel uncomfortable."

"Strangely, you didn't. I'm glad I told you this, I truly am and now I can safely say there are no more secrets between us and I couldn't be happier about it."

"Good!" she announced gleefully, her eyes twinkling again. "Does that mean we can seal it all with a kiss? A *proper* kiss this time?"

"You mean you made me admit all this to you just so you could get a kiss from me?" he pretended to scold. "Of all the mean, low down, nasty, vindictive tricks, lady, you've just surpassed them all."

"Just shut up and kiss me," she demanded. "Unless, of course, my kisses don't measure up to your standards seeing it seems I've had a lot of competition in the past."

"I should paddle your backside for that one," he said as sternly as he could manage.

"Watch out, I might just like that. But you'll never know until you try it."

Paul chuckled softly, enjoying the way she had managed to turn a serious moment into a light hearted one. She was something pretty special and he was falling more and more in love with her every time he was in her company. "I think we should *both* wait to find that out, don't you?"

"Spoilsport," she said with a sensuous pout.

"Stop pouting like that," he pleaded, "it makes you look so incredibly...."

"So incredibly, what?" she prompted.

"Never mind. Come here you, I reckon I've stalled for enough time and now I think I'd like to kiss you. And yes, properly this time." Which he did, slowly, drawing as much pleasure as he always did and only succeeding in wanting her all the more. He kissed her for as long as he dared without getting too carried away and only when he knew he could trust himself no more, did he pull away.

"What's wrong, Paul?" she asked in bewilderment. "Why did you stop?"

"I... uh...I... nothing...no reason. You want a...um...refill on your drink?"

"No thanks, I haven't even touched this one. Just tell me what's wrong."

Without answering her, he suddenly bounced up and strode over to the stereo. "I should put some music on. Would you like to hear some music? Your choice, what would you like? A blast from the 80's perhaps? How about Genesis? Or Bon Jovi? Or Queen. The Queen CD is actually Dave's but I think he's forgotten I have it so I know he won't mind. Or I could put the MP3 player on, just put it on shuffle and hope for the best. Or...?"

"Paul," she said quite calmly. "I don't want to hear any music. Come back over here, sit down and talk to me. Please." She waited patiently for him to come over to her and she was surprised to see him sit down again, rather stiffly this time, on the very edge of the sofa. "Okay, what's up? Your whole mood changed so rapidly there."

"Nothing's up.... really.... it's just..." He shrugged helplessly and looked down at his hands for a long moment. "I, well, I've just realized that this is the first time we've been alone together, I mean properly alone, with no fear of interruptions or intrusions and I don't want you thinking that this is the reason why I asked you over here tonight, that I was hoping to make you the next notch on my belt...in a manner of speaking. I hate that terminology, don't you?"

"It's only an old cliché, Paul and I wasn't thinking that at all. Do you want to tell me what's *really* wrong? Because so far, I can't see it."

He couldn't answer her right away but instead sat back beside her again. He pulled her close and let his lips rest on her forehead. "From the very first time I kissed you, I have wanted you, Krista, only I've wanted to wait until the right moment. Since nobody really knows when the right moment is until it happens, and since you insist on continuing to kiss me in the way that you do, I only know I can no longer trust myself around you in case...well, just in case."

"In case what?" she challenged.

"Don't Kris...please," he whispered desperately. "Have you any idea what you do to me just by being this close to me?"

She raised her eyes to his and slowly shook her head. "No," she said softly. "But I'd like to find out."

She had opened the door to him and he barely managed to suppress a groan of pleasure. He kissed the palm of her hand and was surprised to see her shiver in delight at that one simple gesture. He only knew he wouldn't be able to hold back for much longer and he brought his mouth to hers again and kissed her with as much intensity as he knew how.

The longer they kissed, the more his eagerness for her grew and he pleaded silently with his body to take some sort of mercy on him but, of course, his body seemed to be ignoring him completely. At last, he managed to tear himself away and, breathing harshly, he struggled to get a hold on himself. "We shouldn't be doing this," he cried. "*I* shouldn't be, anyway. The longer I'm with you, the more I just want to tear all your clothes off and make love to you. And here I am, desperately trying to be as noble as I can possibly be...and you kiss me like that." He paused and looked into her eyes. "I only know I can't be noble for much longer."

Krista smiled slowly, deeply touched by his concern for her feelings. She traced the outline of his lips with her forefinger, then whispered, "Who's asking you to be noble?"

His eyes searched hers and he realized she meant every softly spoken word. With a ragged moan, he pulled her to her feet and started kissing her hungrily and this time, he couldn't, and didn't, keep his hands off her as he roamed them possessively over her body, feeling her, touching her, wanting her. He felt her trembling with sheer longing for him too when he smoothed his hands down her back and pressed her even closer to him.

After what could only have been a moment, or several minutes, or a lifetime, he reluctantly pulled away and glanced swiftly around the room. "Not here," he whispered hoarsely. "Come on, baby, follow me." He led her upstairs, pausing every now and again to kiss her and they very nearly didn't make it as far as the bedroom, so eager for one another were they, but they did make it and just at his bedroom door, their eyes locked in a gesture of mutual consent for what was about to take place.

Inside, they collapsed on the bed and he started to slowly undress her. For three nights in a row, she had been unwittingly giving him heart palpitations at the sight of her in that stupid costume she had to wear at the club, but at least her body had been covered to some extent. And now, as he peeled away the lilac lace bra and the matching lace panties she was wearing, he realized she might as well have been wearing a nun's habit on stage because nothing, absolutely nothing, could have prepared him for the sheer vision that lay before him.

"Wh-what's wrong?" she asked uncertainly when she heard his sharp intake of breath.

He couldn't answer her straight away as he looked at her in nothing short of awe. "Oh my God," he murmured, "You are so...*so* beautiful." Her creamy skin held neither a mark nor a scar nor a blemish and she was soft and firm in all the right places, a portrait of perfection from the top of her head right down to the polished pink tips of her toes.

She smiled shyly and reached out to unbutton his shirt. She shrugged it back over his shoulders and kissed his chest as her fingers worked at the belt and zipper on his jeans, wanting to release him from the uncomfortable restraints of his clothing. He gasped in pleasure when she started caressing him and he helped her along the way by impatiently tearing off the remainder of his clothes. He flung them carelessly on the floor and, both of them completely naked now, they delighted in exploring each other's bodies. His fingers and hands and tongue and mouth moved expertly over her, bringing her to heights of passion she had never known even existed until she had to beg for him to take her.

"Please, Paul," she murmured urgently, "Please... make love to me...."

He savored every moment of entering her for the very first time and he heard her sigh in pleasure at the feel of him inside her. He thrust his hips slowly against her, not wanting to hurry her along when he wanted it to last forever for the both of them, but within only a few short moments, she felt the familiar pressure in her groin, a pressure that was beautiful and mystical and intense and which would only be released when she gave herself up to it and let its warmth and sweet energy flood over and through her whole body.

He knew by her breathing first what was happening and when she cried out, he raised her hips towards him to meet his quickening pace and to heighten her pleasure. "That's it, baby," he encouraged softly, "go for it.... come for me...let me hear you...."

She bit into his shoulder as each jolt after pleasurable jolt swept through her and only when he was satisfied that she was completely satisfied was he prepared to let his moans mingle with hers and share his seed with her hot, sweet product of their love making. He cursed softly and shuddered as he emptied into her, and even after he slowed the movement of his hips to a stop he knew he couldn't leave her yet and he gently nestled against her.

For a few moments, neither of them could speak and neither of them even wanted to be in a hurry to break the exquisite silence. Paul had promised himself that their first time together was going to be something like this, only even he could never have imagined it was going to be as perfect as it had been. He knew now it wouldn't have mattered if he had taken her in a king size bed in a five-star hotel, or in a single bed in some sleazy, two-bit motel room, anywhere with her would have been perfect.

"I love you, Krista," he said huskily, "I love you...so very much." He had told her, at long last, he had said the words he had wanted to say and, as if to seal them, he gently kissed her lips.

She hugged him fiercely on hearing those words, hoping them to be true and not just said in the heat of the moment. But she couldn't deny that she did feel special and cherished. And loved. "Thank you for that," she murmured.

With a soft sigh of reluctance, he pulled out of her and settled down beside her. "You are something else, sweetheart, never ever forget that. And as for that body of yours, you should carry a triple X rating with it.

"What, this old thing?" she teased as she looked down at herself in a somewhat critical fashion. "I don't know about a triple X rating... maybe just a double?"

"Trust me on this one, a triple it is."

"If you say so. And now can we get under the covers, please? This triple X body is now getting goose bumps."

He hastily turned down the bedclothes and they slid underneath them together. She rested her head on his chest and after a few minutes of a contented silence, he sensed she was thinking about something. "What's on your mind?" he asked, gently kissing the silky crown of her hair.

Krista glanced awkwardly up at him and he thought she seemed troubled. "I was just thinking about the way I sort of threw myself at you there and I don't want you thinking I'm always that easy to get into bed because I'm not. It takes me to have very deep feelings for someone before I would even consider doing something like this. Please believe me."

"Of course, I believe you, I already know the sort of person you are without you having to tell me. From the very first moment I ever set eyes on you, I knew we were meant to be together and even if we had made love on the very first night, I would still have known you're not that easy to talk into bed. You're a lady through and through and now you're *my* lady, utterly and completely, and anyone who tries to take you away from me is going to wish they'd never been born." He had never said any words like that to any other woman before but he had clearly meant them or else, she knew, he wouldn't have said them.

She reached out and caressed his cheek. "You are such an incredible man, Paul. After just a month or so of knowing you, you have become the singular most important person in my life." She looked at him steadily, then started chewing on her bottom lip, a trait he was beginning to recognize in her she used when she was pensive or upset. "But if I share something with you, will you promise not to laugh? Or think any less of me?"

He tilted his head in bewilderment. "Are you going to tell me that you've never... that this is the first time you've ever...?" He had wondered about that long before this night, but she had seemed quite adept during their lovemaking and he had taken her with wonderful ease too, without her grimacing in pain or seeming hesitant at his penetration.

She swiftly shook her head and she looked like she was going to cry, making him suddenly become alarmed. "No, you're not my first, although now that you mention it, I wish you *had* been." She laughed briefly in embarrassment and she gave her lip another good chewing before she continued any further. "It's just that.... oh hell, I may as well tell you now that I've opened up the conversation. I just want you to know that you are only the second man I have ever gone to bed with." She looked quickly away and laughed in embarrassment again. "There, I said it, laugh if you want."

But he could only shake his head in ever growing confusion. "Why would I laugh at something like that?"

"Because, after our conversation downstairs earlier, you're obviously a man of the world and I -"

"And you have nothing to be ashamed of or embarrassed about. I wouldn't laugh at something like that, in fact, I'm deeply touched you confided something like that to me." He pulled her closer beside him again and traced the curve of her breast with one finger. "And I love you." And the more he touched her, the more he wanted her all over again and it took her only a second to pick up what was on his mind. She started returning his urgent caresses, thrilling him as much as he was thrilling her and showing him just how adept she could be when she took control of the pace this time by rolling over on top of him and guiding him into her.

And when her orgasm this time triggered his own, all he knew now was she was like a drug to him, one that he would never be able to get enough of. He had fallen under her spell, hook, line and sinker and he couldn't be happier about it.

They rested contentedly in each other's arms afterwards and she suddenly began to chuckle.

"What's so funny?" he murmured sleepily.

"You are. You never cease to amaze me."

"I never cease to amaze myself," he replied and lunged for her again.

"That's not what I meant, silly. I was referring to your bedroom, it's nice and neat too."

"So? Why should that amaze you?"

"Because I've seen your desk in work and it always seems to be a mess, so I automatically assumed your house would be like that too."

"My desk is like that so I know where everything is. Anyone who tries to rearrange it for me doesn't usually live to see the light of day. But I must say, you're very observant, young lady, you should be a detective."

"I'm working on it and when I become one, I'll let you know what it's like."

"Cute, babe, real cute." He smiled slowly. "Actually, it's time to let the cat out of the bag. I have a cleaning lady who comes in once or twice a week. She does everything for me, cleans, does my laundry, tidies up, picks up my clothes...all for a very reasonable payment too."

His face was so completely dead pan, she couldn't tell if he was being serious or not. "What do you pay her?"

"Oh, not with money. She has this fetish about being banged over the kitchen sink, she seems to really get off on the smell of Lysol and bleach. I figure it's a small price to pay as long as my house stays nice and clean, don't you?"

She sat up straight and glared at him, not failing to notice his face was still completely deadpan. And the way he had told it too, he had made it sound so convincing... "No, it is *not!*" she cried, "that's easily the most despicable thing I've ever -" And then she saw him arch an eyebrow, his eyes twinkling mischievously, and she whacked him on the arm. "You horror, you made that up."

"I did," he agreed. He rubbed his arm. "Jesus, some people can be *so* touchy."

"Well I'm not about to apologize for it, if only to teach you a lesson."

He chuckled in amusement. "Lesson well learned then, satisfied? I clean my own house, honest to God I do. Where do you think a cop would get the money to pay for a housekeeper? Certainly not on my salary." He reached out to pull her back into his arms but she surprised him when she suddenly jumped out of bed. "Where are you going?"

She stretched lazily, practically making him drool at the sight of her naked body so taut before him. "To find out if this nice neat apartment of yours has a nice neat bathroom too."

"Of course it has, you'll find it through the door and to the left of the stairs."

"And does it have a bath?"

"One big enough for a Sumo wrestler. Why?"

"Good. Care to join me?"

The idea seemed to totally appeal to him because he was out of bed in a flash. He took her by the hand and led her towards the bathroom, but in the hallway, he felt her stiffen and stop in her tracks. He followed her gaze and instantly knew what had caught her attention. "Yes, that's another bedroom through that door, and the door to the left of it is another bathroom," he informed her. "And since you must be wondering why a single guy like myself has a two-bedroom apartment, I'll tell you." He felt like teasing her, telling her that he kept all his ex-girlfriends in there to use as his love slaves, but changed his mind. "This apartment complex has one-bedroom units too and when I first moved in here, it was under the understanding that I would only be staying for a month or so until the next one-bedroom unit became available. As it turned out, I liked living here and I decided I didn't want to move, particularly when I found the extra bedroom can be very useful. If I ever have a few friends over, and if someone has had too much to drink, there's always somewhere for him to crash. Dave has been known to use it on occasion too. He lives clear across town and if he's been on the go for a couple of days, without sleep, he's usually too tired to drive the distance to his own place, so he uses mine because it's more convenient and practical for him. He even keeps a few items of clothing here too and in the bathroom he keeps a spare toothbrush and some shaving stuff too. He gives me so much, I feel it's the least I can do to let him stay here and he even has his own key for when I'm not around. The arrangement works out well for both of us."

Krista nodded appreciatively. "Yet another reminder of how good you are to each other – I love seeing such a great friendship at work."

At her words and the soft light in her eyes, his answer to that was to pull her into his arms for a hug. "Thank you, baby." He suddenly groaned comically. "And stop pressing yourself into me like that, it's not fair and I cannot be responsible for my actions."

She looked down at him and then up into his eyes with a grin. "I think you're insatiable," she scolded happily. "I thought we were taking a bath together? Something tells me it should be a cold shower instead - for you anyway."

"Something tells me a cold shower would be a waste of time because I don't think it would work."

He ended up making love to her in the tub after all, just as they both knew he would and they each came down with a helpless fit of laughter when the water kept slopping out over the edge every time one of them moved. At last, he had the sense to drain the water off a bit and they were able to carry on without further ado.

When they finally got around to using the bath for what it is supposed to be used for, that is, taking a bath, the tone had been set and they kept each other in stitches by trying to outdo the other in telling the most amusing, outrageous tales they could think of.

Krista had a hundred and one of them and so, it seemed, had Paul and, as they kept up their witty, often lewd repartee, she found herself wondering how on earth she had ever lived before without this man.

She was totally and helplessly in love with him, for now and for always.

CHAPTER THIRTY

Just as Cathy had finished getting dressed for the club, the telephone rang. She peered critically at herself in the mirror, figured she had gotten the sleazy look just right, again, and picked up the phone on the third ring. "Hello?"

"It's me, Cathy," Dave announced.

"Dave? Hi, er, if you're looking for Paul, he's not here, Krista's gone round to his place tonight."

"Yeah, I know, he told me she was going over there tonight. Actually, I'm just calling to see if you're all right and to remind you to bring your flat shoes."

"I have them sitting beside the door so I won't forget them but thanks for the reminder. And I'm fine, just a wee bit apprehensive about going to the club tonight in case there's going to be some action and I don't handle it accordingly."

"Oh, I'm sure you will, don't worry about it. Just follow my lead if you have to, or if you're not too sure about something." He paused, wanting to tell her the real reason why he had called her, only he was unsure of what her reaction was going to be. He didn't want to appear presumptuous but he knew he couldn't waste much more time. "I was, er, I was also wondering if you would like me to swing by your place to pick you up."

"I, well... why?" she asked in bewilderment.

"Because it occurred to me you've never driven to that side of the city by yourself before, that Paul has always taken you to the club and I was worried in case you weren't quite sure how to get there."

Worried? She thought, *Dave had actually been worried about me?*

She mulled that over for a moment then suddenly felt quite touched and decided to take him up on his offer. "Thank you, that would be very nice of you. Paul's taken three different routes to the club and I can't remember any of them. But are you sure it wouldn't be out of your way? I can get a taxi there and back if you would prefer…or wait, I've got a sat. nav…umm… I mean, a GPS, in the car, I could use that to get me there."

"Nonsense, you'll do no such thing. And no, it's not out of my way." Well, actually it was, about ten miles out of his way but he didn't want to tell her that, especially not since she had accepted his invitation for a lift. He had been thinking about her all day, in fact, he hadn't been able to get her out of his mind at all and he had even come to the tentative conclusion that he no longer minded her being so constantly in his thoughts. He had been hoping to see her at the precinct but when he had got there, he had found out he had just missed her and his disappointment - which had been great - upon hearing that had somehow only marginally surprised him. He only knew he wanted to see her soon, spend a little bit of time on his own with her before going to the club and the offer of the lift had seemed the perfect solution. "So, I can be there within about twenty minutes, is that okay?"

"Sure, I think I can be ready by then."

"No rush, we have plenty of time. See you then, Cathy."

"Oh, wait, might it seem suspicious you and I arriving together, when we're supposed to be strangers who just met the other night?"

Dave inwardly groaned. She was right, he hadn't remembered that not so minor detail. He struggled to come up with a suitable alternative, then, because he couldn't, he clicked his tongue in derision. "Well, I'm willing to take the risk if you are," he said slowly. "If Petcelli, or anyone else for that matter, notices us arriving together, we can…I know, we can just say we were talking last night and it was discovered we lived close to one another, so I offered you a lift. How does that sound?"

Cathy mulled it over for a few seconds. "Can't see anything wrong with that at all."

Dave allowed himself a smile. "Great. See you in about twenty minutes, then, ok?"

"Thank you." Cathy hung up and looked thoughtfully at the phone. She couldn't help but wonder why he was being so uncharacteristically nice to her but she didn't take the time to dwell on the matter because if there was one thing she had already learned about him, he was always punctual and twenty minutes wasn't such a long time to finish getting ready.

She was standing in the hall at the mirror, brushing her hair, when right on time, Dave arrived. She opened the door to him and he smiled a welcome.

"Okay if I come in?" he asked.

"Of course. I'm running a little behind, though, I couldn't find my bright red lipstick and I had to go hunting for Krista's. We're not late, are we?"

"Plenty of time, don't worry." He closed the door behind him and watched, a little awkwardly, as she finished brushing her hair. When he saw her frown in slight irritation, he moved a couple of steps closer to her. "Anything wrong?"

"Oh, nothing, really, I just meant to get Krista to braid my hair for me before she left but I forgot all about it and now I'm trying to decide whether to wear it up in a ponytail or just keep it down."

"Keep it down, for sure, I like.... er, that is, it looks good on you that way."

She turned to look at him in surprise. He had just paid her another compliment. "Okay, then," she said slowly, "I'll keep it down." Their eyes met and held for a very long moment before they both looked awkwardly away and then Cathy looked brightly in the direction of the kitchen. A thought had just occurred to her, one that would ease the situation a little between them right now. "There's a pot of coffee in the kitchen, if you want a cup, go right ahead. I think there might even be some chocolate cake left too, if Krista hasn't gotten her greedy teeth into it by now. Anything you want, just help yourself, I'm going upstairs for a few minutes." She didn't really need to go upstairs but she did anyway and when she looked at herself in the bathroom mirror, she wasn't a bit surprised to find her cheeks were more than a little flushed after his compliment.

When she came downstairs again, she found Dave in the kitchen, drinking a cup of coffee after all and just finishing off a slice of the chocolate cake. He looked up at her when she entered and grinned widely. "Soon as I saw the cake, I couldn't resist it, I have a mighty sweet tooth and this cake is *good*. Where did you get it?"

"I made it, actually, I have a sweet tooth too."

"You *made* this?" he asked in amazement. "Right from scratch?"

"Yes, and don't sound so surprised," she teased. "I can do a lot of things not many people know about."

"I'll bear that in mind." Dave drank back the rest of his coffee and stood up. Cathy watched in surprise as he washed up his dishes and even carefully wiped up the cake crumbs he had left on the table.

"Domesticated too, I see?" she said dryly.

He was about to say no, that he was only trying to make an impression but he changed his mind. "Yeah, living on my own does that to me. Are you ready?"

"Yes, sorry I kept you waiting." She gestured towards the door. "Shall we?"

"After you." He escorted her out to his car and even gallantly held the door open for her. After only about a quarter of a mile of a not too uncomfortable silence, he opened the conversation again. "How are you liking your first case so far?"

"It's interesting, I suppose, but would be more enjoyable if I didn't have to wear this stupid uniform. I feel like a trollop, or a hooker." She turned to study his profile and she suddenly chuckled. "I bet you're getting quite a kick out of this, after me calling you a male chauvinist pig that time."

"Actually, no, I'm not... not in the least," he replied honestly. "It takes a lot of guts to wear something like that when it isn't your normal style. I don't know if I could do it or not."

Once again, he had surprised her into silence but this time she was able to quickly compose herself. "Don't worry, I don't think you'll ever have to wear something like this, I don't think they make one in your size. And even if they did, you'd have to shave your legs."

"No thanks, shaving my face is quite enough for me." He slipped a glance at her legs, though, not to see if they were shaved or not but because he liked looking at them. He also liked being so close to her like this, it gave him ample opportunity to open out to her more. He was even seriously thinking about plucking up the courage to ask her out for a drink sometime over the weekend, just the two of them, no Paul and no Krista. The very thought of asking her something like that still filled him with dread but even he had to admit, it was getting easier for him to overcome his fears and he had, after all, taken the first step in even thinking about her as much as he had been doing.

He had taken Paul's words from the other night to heart, when Paul had tried to convince him to let his guard down as far as Cathy was concerned and he planned to show his friend that he was at least willing to try. He trusted Paul's judgment implicitly and he knew that Paul only wanted what was best for him. If Paul felt Cathy was that best, then Dave was no longer going to argue the issue with him.

"Oh *Christ*, I forgot my shoes after all," Cathy suddenly remarked, her irritation breaking into his thoughts.

"Do you want me to turn back and get them?" he offered.

"No, we'll only be late, but thanks. I think I'd forget my head if it wasn't screwed on tight." She really did sound annoyed with herself and Dave wished he could go back for her shoes for her, but she had been right, if he did that, they would be late. She didn't let her forgetfulness bother her too much, however, because she turned to him again and, even by just the dim light thrown off from the dashboard, he could see her eyes were twinkling in mischief. "By the way, I meant to ask you, do you feel any better yet about having had to work with a foreign female?"

He smiled sheepishly, not quite sure if she was setting him up this time or not. "I'm getting there," he admitted. "But one thing's for sure, you and Krista are a lot prettier to look at than Paul is. A *lot* prettier."

Cathy emitted a deep, throaty laugh at that. "Pay me twenty dollars and I promise I won't tell Paul you said that."

"He's used to remarks like that, believe me."

"If you say so. You still haven't answered my question."

"Yes, I did, you just weren't listening." He tipped her a wink then, on seeing she obviously hadn't heard his answer, he told her again. "It's not so bad, I guess. We're all in this together and I don't mean just the case, but we're here to protect and to serve and all that shit so you're no longer the enemy to me."

"Thank you, kind sir," she teased. "Now I can sleep easier in my bed at nights knowing that you've moved into the 21st century at long last and no longer look upon women as second-class citizens."

Any other time he would have felt his heckles rise at a remark like that, but he had the sense to know he had deserved it so he smiled again. "Where did you learn to be so outspoken?"

"The Catherine Edwards School of Charm," she answered innocently. "It's a private school back home in Belfast. Only the very elite get into it and only if I approve of them."

"And where did you learn to have an answer for everything?"

"Same place."

"That figures," he said in exaggerated defeat.

"But sometimes my verbal retaliations are the only weapon I have left," she suddenly announced and he was about to come up with a suitable retort to that one when he happened to glance her way and saw immediately that her good humor had momentarily vanished and had been replaced instead by a definite sadness.

"Why did you say that?" he asked softly.

"Because it's true," she said uncomfortably. "If I had never talked back, certain people would have taken advantage of me."

"In what way? And what people?"

She turned and looked out through the window and he could sense she was getting upset... or maybe angry. "It doesn't matter, Dave," she said eventually. "I didn't mean to say that, it doesn't even make any sense to me. You know, you're going a completely different way again than Paul ever did. I don't recognize any of these buildings at all. Are we nearly there yet?"

He tried to hide his shock at the way she had just changed the subject like that and he nodded quickly. "Not far." Something in her voice had alarmed him and he sensed she had opened up a subject that she would sooner rather die than talk about so, wanting her to relax again, he changed the conversation. "I'd like to tell you something, if you don't mind."

"No, go right ahead."

"Please don't get the wrong idea here, but I just want you to know that I'm glad we've started to become friends. You're a really nice person, Cathy... and, oh, you make great chocolate cake too."

"Thank you," she said with an awkward smile. "I'll make you one for your birthday."

"You'd better hurry up, my birthday's tomorrow."

"It is?" she cried, then reached over to whack him playfully on the arm. "It is *not*!"

"You got me, it's not. I'll try anything for a free chocolate cake."

"So I see. But thank you for saying I'm a nice person. You are too." She smiled shyly at him and as if on cue, he felt his heart start to race.

"No, no, you are *too*," he returned in a good imitation of her accent.

"What was *that* supposed to be?" she asked, laughing.

"Your accent."

"I don't have an accent."

"Oh no, I'm not the one with an accent in this car, lady - *you* are."

"But I sound quite normal to my ears. You, on the other hand, you sound American."

"I do?"

"Uh huh, that's how I know you've got an accent. All Americans do."

"You think you're so smart, don't you?" he remarked dryly, just as he pulled into the parking lot of the club.

"Lose the accent, talk in a way I can understand you and I'll tell you," she said sweetly and, before he could say anything else, she jumped out of the car.

He remained where he was for a few moments, smiling to himself as he turned off the ignition, turned on the car alarm and securely locked the wheel, her teasing words still ringing in his ears. But then he recalled what she had said earlier and how she had gotten annoyed with herself for something he couldn't understand and he frowned deeply. Yes, she had sounded upset...but something else too. Vulnerable, maybe? That was it, he acknowledged swiftly, he had just witnessed a very vulnerable side to her and realization of that made him just want to protect her and keep her safe from whatever it was that had bothered her enough to show this as yet unseen before vulnerability to him.

Unaware Dave was thinking about her in that light, Cathy entered the club and strode quickly to the dressing room. She stopped in the doorway as soon as she saw a newcomer. "Hello there," she greeted as brightly as she could.

The newcomer bounced out of her seat and grinned broadly. "Hi! I'm Candy," she bubbled, "I'm a dancer and I just started tonight."

"Then welcome, Candy, and I'm Cathy." Cathy kept a smile on her face while trying to hide her ever-growing puzzlement. Hadn't Petcelli said he didn't have any more vacancies for dancers? If he had started Candy, then that could only mean that Trixie had gotten fired...or, heaven forbid, something had happened to Ruth after all. Cathy quickly hung up her coat, excused herself and went out to tell Dave.

"Son of a *bitch*!" he exclaimed. "It's all too coincidental that Ruth has suddenly disappeared and there's already a new dancer. I'll have to see what I can find out here. I know Rick, the barman, has the hots for Ruth and I heard him say the other night he was going to ask her out. Go about your work, Cathy and I'll let you know how I get on." He watched her walk over to a table that four men had just sat down at and, on seeing them give her some very appreciative looks, he quickly turned away. He went over to where Rick was standing. "Hey there, Rick," he said casually, "how's it hanging?"

"Not vertical enough for my liking," Rick replied with a comical groan. He was only about in his early twenties, of average height, average build and average blond hair, blue eye features, a real all-round average guy, but he had a good sense of humor and he seemed nice enough.

"Does that mean you haven't gotten anywhere with Ruth yet?"

"I *thought* I had," he said forlornly. "She gave me her phone number the other night - at long last - and she seemed pretty keen that I should call her but I haven't been able to get through to her. Every time I call, there's no reply and she has no answering machine. I was hoping to talk to her here last night but she was here one minute, gone the next and I didn't even get the chance to say hi."

"Did you try her again today?"

"Yes sir, only I still couldn't get through. I asked Mr. Petcelli if he had given her some time off or if he knew if she was ill or something but he just told me to mind my own business."

"Really?" Dave shoved his hands in his pockets and tried to remain as blasé as possible when all the time, his mind was going into overdrive at the information he was receiving. "Do you think there might just be something wrong with her phone? I have a cousin who works for the phone company, if you like, I could get him to check it out for you." Any white lie would do just to obtain a phone number, but this one didn't pay off.

"It doesn't matter, Dave, but thanks anyway for the offer."

"No problem. Why don't you just call round to see her? Surprise her with some flowers or something. Chicks really go for that, ya know."

"I would, if I knew where she lived."

Dave did know where Ruth lived, but the frequent reports back from the unmarked patrol car he had posted outside her apartment had been all the same... still no sign of her. And that, of course, was something he couldn't tell Rick. "Maybe Petcelli could tell you where she lives, why don't you just ask him?"

"No, I'll just wait and see if she comes in on Saturday night - that's when I'm working again next." Rick suddenly gestured behind Dave's shoulder. "That new chick, Cathy, she looks like she has an order, want me to get it?"

"It's okay, I'll get it." Dave moved to turn away, but stopped himself. "Say, what do you think my chances with Cathy would be? Do you think I should try and make a play for her?" He didn't really care about the young man's opinion, he was just trying to keep the conversation as light hearted as possible.

Rick chuckled and stole a glance in Cathy's direction. "Since I don't really know her, I can't really say but one thing's for sure, she's a hot looking babe. Talks funny, mind you, but that's not her fault, it just makes her all the cuter. Go ahead, man, see how far she'll let you get."

"I might just do that." Dave went over to Cathy and grinned. "Rick thinks you talk funny too so I think that makes it unanimous now."

"I can't sound any funnier to him than he does to me," Cathy flashed back with a sweet smile. She looked swiftly over her shoulder, there was no one even close to her but she was feeling a little paranoid and she just wanted to check. "I didn't mean to come back to you just so soon but I really do have an order. We can talk later if you want."

"No problem, I've nothing much to report anyway, other than Rick hasn't been able to get a hold of Ruth despite his constant calling. Something is definitely up and I think it's about time we found out what. Okay, what's your order?"

"Scotch rocks, two draft and a rum and Coke."

Dave started setting up the drinks and told her exactly what Rick had just told him. "Every day, something new seems to arise in this case and I don't like that at all."

"Right now, all I can think of is Ruth. We don't even know for sure if she's missing or if Petcelli has just fired her. I wish we could come back here tonight after everyone leaves and see if Petcelli keeps any employee records in his office."

Dave looked at her in approval. "That's actually not a bad idea, Cathy."

"But wouldn't that be breaking and entering?"

He couldn't help but chuckle. "Sweetie, we're cops and sometimes us cops have to do these sorts of things." He adapted a purely innocent tone. "But if it bothers you, I won't tell anyone if you won't."

Cathy thought about it some more and a brand-new idea flashed into her head. "I know what we can do instead. Petcelli doesn't seem to spend a lot of time in his office during club opening hours, I've noticed. He's always somewhere out here, drinking with his cronies, or is in the pool room, trying to shoot some pool – and I do mean *trying*. If we take a break, one of us can go into his office while the other keeps watch. I'll take these drinks over and you can think about it."

He watched her walk away, feeling pleased with her that she had come up with an idea like that so swiftly. It was a simple enough idea, granted, any amateur could have thought of it, but he had admired her more for the fact she hadn't shown any fear or hesitance in wanting to do it.

The opportunity to get into Petcelli's office arose just shortly before midnight. Two men had just come into the club and Petcelli had gone right over to their table to join them. Within no time, they were all engrossed in deep conversation and Dave quickly signaled to Cathy that the time was right to make their move.

Petcelli's office was situated behind the stage down a short corridor and, after doubly checking the coast was clear, Cathy moved towards it. Dave watched her enter the office and after a few moments, he went over and stood just a few feet away from the door. As had been prearranged, if anyone should come along, he would knock sharply twice on the door to tell her not to come out until he had gotten rid of the possible threat.

Cathy looked swiftly around the office and saw that her task was going to be a relatively easy one. Boxes of liquor piled four and five high took up most of the floor space, leaving not much room for the one desk, three chairs and a filing cabinet. The desk was bare except for a blotter, a telephone, a directory, a pen set and envelope opener and an appointments book. There was no sign of a computer tower, never mind a monitor, no laptop and, with a swift glance around, she couldn't even see a box that might indicate a Wi-Fi connection. It didn't surprise her that Petcelli probably didn't keep anything at all to do with the running of his business on computer. She went over to the filing cabinet first and opened the top drawer. There was nothing in it except for a box of condoms and three or four skin magazines, the titles of which Cathy had never heard of. The condoms and the thought of somebody like Petcelli using them disgusted her more than the magazines did.

She moved down to the next drawer and found the necessary files anyone would use for the overall running of a nightclub, like order and waybill forms for the breweries, accounting ledgers and old receipts and invoices. She glanced quickly through one of the ledgers but she didn't really know what she was supposed to be looking at so she assumed the neatly written figures were balancing accordingly and she returned the ledger back to move down to the bottom drawer.

There was only one file in it, titled EMPLOYEES and all that was in it was a list of employees dating back to six months ago. Only a few of the names had telephone numbers and or addresses beside them and quite a few names had been crossed out. Ruth O'Brien's name was still there though but then Cathy noticed that neither Krista's name, nor Paul's, nor Dave's nor her own had been added, proving that Petcelli was a little lax in the upkeep of his employee records.

With a soft, irritated click of her tongue, she replaced the file, closed the drawer, and then after quickly scanning the appointments book on the desk, but seeing nothing written on any day to the end of the month, she looked carefully around her to ensure that she hadn't disturbed anything and went back out to Dave.

"Anything?" he inquired.

She shook her head. "Not a thing we don't already know. He clearly doesn't believe in keeping proper records on his employees. There were no relative employment forms or anything, no payroll book, hardly any addresses or even telephone numbers, absolutely nothing like there should be. There's not even a computer or a laptop – unless he keeps proper records on a computer at home, of course. And unless he keeps the payroll book elsewhere, or has an accountant who does the payroll, I can bet he pays the employees under the table."

"Wouldn't surprise me if he did and if he does indeed do that, he has a lot of explaining to do to the IRS.... just one more nail in his coffin. And there was nothing to indicate about Ruth maybe even going on vacation?"

"Nothing at all." Cathy sounded despondent and, without thinking, Dave reached out and laid a hand on her bare shoulder.

"At least you tried," he said softly and then, realizing her skin felt warm and soft and smooth beneath his touch, he quickly pulled his hand away. "Come on, we'd better get back to the bar before Petcelli figures we're missing."

Cathy had thought nothing of his gesture and walked on ahead of him, unaware that he was observing the subtle sway of her hips, the swing of her hair that just about covered the bare space between her top and her skirt and the tantalizing shape of her thighs as she walked. He groaned to himself in appreciation of a sight worth watching and he made the swift decision that he was definitely going to ask her out for a drink.

When he got behind the bar again, he could hardly keep his eyes off her anymore, watching her as she moved from table to table, taking orders, smiling, sometimes flipping back her hair if it fell over her shoulder, doing nothing short of driving him crazy and not even being aware of it. Oh yes, he was going to ask her out for a drink. No more stalling, not when it felt so right.

The club was anything but busy tonight, giving Cathy ample opportunity to keep an eye on Petcelli. He was still sitting with the two men and had been for over an hour now and from what she could gather, heavy negotiations about something or other were under way. The table next to where they were seated needed clearing and Cathy moved over to do it. She took her time stacking the dirty glasses on her tray, all the while keeping a careful eye on what the three men were doing. Just as she was about to turn away, she saw Petcelli pass over a small package and the man he passed it to handed over a wad of money in return. Almost immediately after the exchange, the two men arose and headed towards the door.

Cathy darted a glance at Dave to see if he had been watching too but he was tied up with the other waitress so, after only a moment's deliberation, she decided on what course of action to take. Leaving her tray on the table, she ran outside, in the hope of at least getting a license plate number but what she didn't know was one of the men had been watching her as she had covertly observed the operation take place, hadn't liked it one little bit and had seen her following them out.

As she stepped outside and took a cautious look around her, she caught a movement to her left side but even as she turned towards it, the next thing she knew, she felt a hand being clamped over her mouth.

"What was so interesting about our table, little lady?" A voice hissed in her ear. "Did you see something amiss, huh? See something you shouldn't have, maybe?"

Cathy started to frantically shake her head no but she could barely move, the man was tall and well-built and was holding her too tightly. It was the first time in her life she had been attacked and all the training at the police academy hadn't prepared her for the sickening fear that was pumping through her veins. She had to literally force herself to keep calm and not panic and she tried desperately to remember the self-defense maneuvers she had been taught.

But she got nowhere fast because all of a sudden, she felt herself being lifted up off her feet. She was pushed brutally against the wall and as soon as her head connected with the brick, she blacked out and slid to the ground.

CHAPTER THIRTY-ONE

Dave had just finished with the waitress and he turned round to see what Cathy was doing. When he couldn't see her anywhere, he figured she had maybe gone to the bathroom so he waited for her to appear. A few minutes later, he was still waiting and he frowned slightly.

Looking more carefully around the smoke-hazed room, he realized Petcelli had moved away from the table, the two men he had been with were gone and Cathy's tray was still sitting where she had left it. Knowing she wouldn't have just left her tray lying around like that, especially laden with dirty glasses and empty beer bottles, his frown deepened and he turned to Rick.

"Hey, you didn't happen to see where Cathy went, did you?"

"Yeah, she seemed in an awful hurry to get some fresh air a few minutes ago. It must be too hot in here for her tonight."

Dave cursed into himself. "Hmm, better go and see if she's all right," he said matter-of-factly. "Who knows, maybe she just wants to do a bit of star-gazing and if that's the case, I'll see if I can help her pick out the Big Dipper or something."

Rick grinned. "Go for it, Dave, hope you get lucky. I can hold the fort down, seeing as how we're not exactly rushed off our feet tonight."

"Thanks, Rick, owe you one." Dave kept a smile on his face and headed towards the door, taking care not to hurry in a way that would bring attention to himself. He didn't know what was ahead of him but as soon as he stepped outside, the casual smile disappeared.

Cathy was still lying on the ground, not moving, and his heart all but stopped as soon as he saw her.

"Oh Jesus!" he exclaimed and quickly kneeled beside her.

"Cathy? Can you hear me?" He gently but firmly shook her shoulders and his heart began beating again when she stirred, then moaned softly. "That-ta girl, come on, Cathy, open your eyes for me."

Cathy moaned again and a few seconds later, her eyes flickered open. She stared around her in confusion, clearly not sure of where she was, then her gaze settled on him. "Hi Dave," she murmured, "goodness, you never told me you had six identical twin brothers." She grimaced in pain but she was clearly determined to sit up and when she slowly managed to do just that, she put a hand to the back of her head. Her hair felt matted and sticky, but at least not too much and, bringing her hand round to her face again, she looked at the blood on her fingertips in a mild state of curiosity. "Hmm, seems I lost *that* particular fight, eh?"

"Are you okay?" Dave asked anxiously. He was getting more and more concerned about her now, especially after seeing the blood, and the remark about the identical twin brothers hadn't exactly helped either. "Tell me who you are, who I am and where we are right now."

She seemed to concentrate for only a second, then she said, "I'm Cathy Edwards, you're Dave Andrews and we are right outside the Blues Haven."

Dave started to relax a little. "Good, that's what I wanted to hear."

"I'll be fine, Dave, really, please just help me up." When he got her to her feet, she swayed precariously and he had to grab a hold of her before she could fall over again. "Oops!" she said with a vague, embarrassed chuckle. Everything in her line of vision was dancing and swimming and floating sickeningly and she had to literally struggle to get her off-kilter world back into focus again.

"This is not good," Dave declared. "You could have a concussion and you really should be taken to the hospital for a checkup. How many fingers have I got up?"

"Three," she teased and when she saw he was anything but amused, she canceled the light-hearted approach. "It's two, I'm sorry, I was only kidding. Honest to God, I know you are holding up two fingers." The real reason why she had come outside in the first place suddenly returned to her and, forgetting her injury, she looked all around her in alarm. "Where did they go?" she cried.

"Who?"

"The two guys! The ones Petcelli has just spent the last hour with."

Dave glared at her in very justifiable irritation. "Is that why you came out here? To go after those two men all by yourself?"

"Yes, that's exactly why I came out here. Why?"

"*Why?* You ask me *WHY*? What were you trying to prove doing something like that on your own? Did you think you would have been able to toss *them* on their backsides as well?"

"Of course not!" she cried indignantly. "I only came out to try and get a license plate number, like I was able to do with that Carter guy. I was also hoping to ask them what was in the package I saw Petcelli hand over to them just before they got up to leave. Really, I didn't think it was any big deal, I thought I had it under control."

"No big deal?" he roared, knowing he sounded furious but also knowing that it was largely due to relief that she was all right that was making him furious.

"Stop shouting, will you?" she begged, holding her head and grimacing again. "You were busy and I came out here, only they must have seen me following them because the next thing I knew, my head was making contact with this wall here." She looked petulantly at the wall, then back at him. "And that wall packs a mighty punch if you must know."

On hearing what she had tried to do, all by herself, Dave's fury continued to build steadily until he was completely livid. "You stupid girl!" he spat. "This is the real world you're in now, this isn't all taking place in a training room in the academy. Didn't you learn anything at all there? You don't go after the bad guys yourself unless you have some sort of back up. Don't you know you could have gotten very seriously hurt with your heroine routine? Or even killed?"

At his cold words, her own temper flared and she raised her chin in defiance. "Well, sorry to disappoint you, Sergeant Andrews," she said, her voice dripping heavily with sarcasm, "but it seems like I'm going to live to fight another day with you after all. Better luck next time, maybe." She turned to walk away from him only she didn't get far because he grabbed her arm to stop her. She glowered at him. "Take your hand off me, Dave," she snapped. "And stop giving me the third degree over something I did that I only thought was right at the time."

"Thought wrong then, didn't you?" He was still very angry with her and he wasn't about to let her off the hook so easily, not until he had at least had his say. In truth, he was actually admiring her for her guts and he knew she hadn't done anything he himself wouldn't have done in the exact same situation. But that still didn't excuse her behavior and he wanted her to see how unprofessional she had been. Also, he wanted to make sure she was really all right, that she didn't have to be taken to the hospital. But he had made her angry now too and every time she became angry with him, all he wanted to do was keep looking into those astonishing blue eyes of hers. "Don't you *ever* pull a stunt like that again without telling me first what you intend to do," he ordered. "How could I have explained this one to the Captain if something *had* happened to you?"

"Nothing did, so just relax, you're behaving like nothing but a pompous ass."

"Sorry about it, lady, but really, you should have known better. You acted irresponsibly and if you think you're going to get off so easily, you're sorely mistaken." He was speaking harshly, his eyes drilling right into hers and just for an instant, he saw a flicker of real hurt in her eyes, hurt that was caused, no doubt, by the way he was talking to her. But then it was gone and she was staring stonily back at him again.

"And what, pray tell, can you possibly do to me, Dave?" she asked, her voice dangerously low. "What can a big, hot-shot, experienced Detective like yourself possibly do to *me*? Throw the book at me? Get me suspended or even fired? Or demoted? Oh no, forget those, you'd like to just exile me back to Belfast instead, right?" She threw him a look of the utmost contempt and, not particularly wanting any answers to her questions, she started to turn away. "Do whatever the hell you want, Dave, I really don't care. You don't intimidate or scare me one little bit." Praying she would be able to walk away without staggering or falling flat on her face, she forced stability into her shaking legs and took a few faltering steps forward, but she didn't get far because he grabbed her again and spun her round to face him.

"Oh no you don't, you're staying right here because I'm not through with you yet, not by a long shot."

"Oh yes you are." She tried to yank her arm free but he was holding her too tightly so she twisted her head around and sank her teeth into his hand, nearly drawing blood too, but she didn't care, she just wanted to get away from him and was ready to do whatever it took.

More startled than anything at what she had just done, he pulled his hand away. "What did you do that for?" he cried.

"Because I despise you and what you're trying to do to me here. Don't worry, I don't have AIDS or anything. I trust you don't either." She had been expecting a torrent of more of his fury, certainly not his surprise and just like that, her temper evaporated when her rationality told her what she had done. "I-I'm sorry, Dave," she said meekly, "I don't know why -"

"Forget it," he said tersely.

She stood uncertainly, then pointed sheepishly at his hand. "Did I hurt you?"

"Not much. Forget it happened, okay?" He knew he was acting like nothing but a sore loser now and because he couldn't accept her apology in the good faith it had been offered, he caught a glimpse of her vulnerable side again.

Cathy nodded uncertainly. "Well, I, uh, I am sorry, okay? See you inside."

Dave wanted to tell her it was all right and he reached out to caress her cheek but his hand stopped in midair and he dropped it quickly to his side again. She looked at him in growing bewilderment, wanting to question the mixed signals she was now receiving but instead turned away from him again.

He stopped her, verbally this time. "I'm sorry too, Cathy," he said softly, "It was... I was just really worried about you there."

She raised a cynical eyebrow. "Worried about me? Or worried about how this little episode will look on your report, you mean?"

Dave's temper started simmering again, she definitely knew all the right buttons to push. "Damn it, Cathy! I don't care about some stupid report, I care about..." He stopped abruptly, angry with her, angry at the world but even angrier with himself now.

She was looking at him expectantly then, on seeing his hesitancy and his discomfort, she smiled faintly. "See you inside, Dave," she murmured, just to let him off the hook.

"You know what, Edwards? You really are nothing but an incorrigible, arrogant, supercilious specimen of the human race," he said as sternly as he could, "and you're also nothing but a stupid..." His voice suddenly cracked at the hurt that had sprang instantly into her eyes at his most uncalled-for words and this time, he did reach out to caress her cheek. Her skin felt slightly heated to his touch. "You're nothing but a stupid... beautiful, beautiful woman," he finished and, no longer being able to stop himself, he pulled her into his arms and hugged her fiercely. "I'm sorry, Cathy," he whispered, "I'm really sorry, I was just so frightened when I came out there and saw you lying unconscious on the ground. I was really frightened something terrible had happened to you."

More than a little taken aback by the fact he had called her beautiful and was now hugging her as tightly as he could, she looked up at him in confusion. "So why...?"

"Something really *could* have happened to you," he said hoarsely, "we both know that. And I couldn't bear the thought of you getting seriously hurt because...because..." He gave up with a groan and then, with the tension of the moment mounting, he couldn't stop himself, nor did he even want to any longer and, leaning down, he started kissing her, tentatively at first, then more strongly, quite literally taking her breath away.

CHAPTER THIRTY-TWO

At first too surprised to do anything but let him kiss her, she came to her senses and eagerly began to respond, but as soon as she let her tongue caress and taste his, he suddenly pulled away and she stared up at him in astonishment. A silence, cold and unnerving, spun out between them, until Cathy had to break it.

"Dave, what...?"

He looked helplessly at her and abruptly turned away. "I'm sorry," he murmured, "I'm really sorry. Maybe I shouldn't have done that." But it had been every bit as beautiful as he had imagined it could be and he carefully suppressed a shiver of pleasure.

Her growing headache all but forgotten, Cathy ran a trembling hand through her hair and stared at his back, noting the slump in his shoulders and the decline of his head. But she couldn't help but remember only the thrilling sensations that his kiss had caused. Her body was still tingling all over because of it. "Tell me why you shouldn't have done that," she whispered.

He uttered a loud curse and stared stonily down at the ground. He was supposed to have taken her out for a drink first, get to know her a bit better on a one on one basis, then let it build up to a kiss naturally. It wasn't supposed to have happened like this... and yet, it had...which, he supposed reluctantly, didn't make it wrong.

"Because it was very... forward of me," he said lamely and inwardly cringed. *Jesus, Andrews,* he said to himself, *grow UP!!!*

"Oh... well.... no need to be sorry, Dave, all you did was kiss me."

"But I *shouldn't* have," he insisted, "It ... it was wrong."

"Was it really? Okay, what was so wrong about it?"

"Nothing," he said. "Everything."

"I see," she said slowly.

"Do you?"

"Not really, I lied." She looked thoughtfully at him, chewing on her bottom lip as she tried to assess what the real problem was, but since she couldn't, she gave up with a wry shake of her head. "Is it me?" she offered eventually. "Is this what all this is about? Are you.... I don't know, afraid of me, or something?"

"Well, no, I -"

"Because, really, what could you be afraid of me for? I don't bite, you know."

"Oh yes you do," he reminded her and absently touched his hand. "I'm not really afraid of anything, Cathy, least of all you." But there was little conviction behind his words, something they both heard.

She hated not being able to see his face so she moved slightly to one side so she could at least study his profile. She immediately saw the clenching and unclenching of his jaw, telling her he was just as perplexed as she was. "Then what is it?" she persisted.

"Nothing, it's nothing. Really. Just accept my apology, okay?"

"Sure, okay, if that's what you want, apology accepted." Figuring it would be best to just leave him alone, Cathy turned to go back to the club but as soon as he heard her move, he at last looked briefly her way and in that instant, she caught a glimpse of real pain in his eyes. *Oh God,* she thought, *this really is torturing him.*

But she knew instinctively he wasn't afraid of the fact that he had kissed her, that maybe he was more afraid of the consequences, that he maybe thought she was going to reject him, or never speak to him again, or.... well, she could only really speculate what was going through his mind and her heart swiftly went out to him. She began to recall Paul's words of only a few days ago, how he had told her just how lonely Dave really was and how he was always afraid of letting down his guard even a little bit in case he left himself wide open to get hurt again.

She reached out and tentatively placed a hand on his shoulder. "For what it's worth, Dave, *I'm* not sorry you kissed me. I'm surprised, yes, but certainly not sorry. It was a lovely kiss... very lovely." She paused, trying to think of what to say that could help him feel a whole lot better about the situation he had inadvertently started. "I've been told you were very hurt in the past, by a woman, your ex-wife and I'm sorry about that more than I could possibly ever tell you, I really truly am. But surely you should know by now that not every woman is like her and whatever it was she did to you, you must also surely know that she's the one who should be paying for it, certainly not you. I know I sure as hell couldn't hurt anyone intentionally and I don't know for why I'm about to say this but I just wish you would give me the chance to prove that to you. If you want to take this further than just a kiss, that's fine, I'm right here for you, but if you don't want to pursue it, then that's fine too, there are no hard feelings." Cathy stopped and waited for some sort of reaction from him but when it was apparent none was forthcoming, and because she had taken the initiative and had gotten nowhere, she sighed heavily. "Sometimes I wonder why I even bother to try to work things out with you!" she cried in defeat and irritation and with that, she quietly turned away again to go back inside.

As Dave heard her walk away, he vied with his emotions to hurry up and reach some sort of a decision, one he could no longer fight or postpone as he had been doing all along. He could finally admit it to himself, Cathy had won, she had opened up his eyes and opened up his heart and he knew now he no longer had anything to be afraid of. Not if it felt as right, as perfect, as it did.

He whirled round and saw she had nearly reached the doorway and he knew it was now or never. "Cathy, wait!" he called desperately before she could disappear inside. "Please... just wait up a second... please."

She eyed him warily. "What is it now?"

He approached her slowly and when he was beside her, he gently caressed her cheek with his fingertips. "I already know without you having to tell me you could never hurt anyone," he said softly. "And in light of what you just said, I only know I can't, or shouldn't, deny my feelings for you any longer. You mean so much to me, lady, which may sound a bit hard to believe after the way I've been treating you recently, but it's true nonetheless. What I've been fighting for days now is finally over because somewhere along the line, I've let you get in under my skin and I'm finding I'm enjoying you being there. I'm enjoying it a *lot*." He paused and earnestly searched her incredible eyes, waiting for ridicule or some other form of negativity, but he got neither and, gathering encouragement, he pressed on, he had a lot more he wanted to say. "When I saw you lying on the ground there, not moving, I thought I was going to die, I really did. And what I was trying to say to you afterwards, it's *you* I care about, not me, and certainly not some dumb, stupid report that probably isn't going to get written up until at least Thanksgiving, if I can help it." He slowly pulled her into his embrace and all he knew now was a body had never felt so good against his before. Everything just felt so *right,* as if it was meant to be. "I really am so sorry I've been acting like an asshole since we met, I've been nothing but nasty to you -"

Cathy started to protest and she shook her head. "No, you have -" But he silenced her by putting his finger over her lips.

"Yes, I have and we both know it. Please believe me when I say I never meant to hurt you, it really isn't in my nature to intentionally hurt anyone either - except the bad guys, of course, I take great pleasure in hurting them as much as I possibly can. But I never want to hurt you again and all I want to do is make it up to you. If you will let me."

Cathy looked deeply into his eyes and she saw immediately a completely different side to him, one that was a caring side, with a genuine desire to show her he truly meant what he had said and just like that, she felt a rush of very strong feelings for him. A faint smile played around the corner of her mouth. "I'll be more than happy to forgive you but I must be fair, I need forgiving too." She groaned in embarrassment and lifted his hand. "I can't believe I actually bit you like that. You must think I'm a right vicious little bitch, huh?"

"I'll live, I'm sure of it. And no, you're really not. But if it will make you feel any better about yourself, you can try and kiss it better for me...if you like."

She smiled slowly, then planted a very delicate kiss on the back of his hand. "There, all better," she declared softly.

"Thank you, but while we're on the subject of kissing things better, I feel I must share with you that I have developed a terrible, excruciating pain elsewhere." He touched his lips and looked at her mournfully. "Right here, as a matter of fact. And it's a real real bad pain too."

She shook her head in amusement. "Then it's not a kiss you need, it's a doctor." But she stood on tiptoe anyway and gave his lips a swift kiss. "Any better yet?"

He grabbed her and pulled her to him. "No way, I said it was a *terrible* pain. An excruciating one, to be exact, so I think you'd better kiss me again."

They indulged in a very deep, searching kiss this time, one that they *both* wanted and were expecting and when they finally parted, she had to put her hands against his chest to steady herself. "I... think we'd definitely better go back inside before you have to pick me up off the ground again," she said hoarsely.

"But the pain's still there," he teased. The club and the job they were supposed to be doing were all but forgotten about, he was quite content to just stand out here for the rest of his life and kiss her like this. With one kiss, he had felt old, familiar and almost forgotten sensations deep in his groin and if that was what one kiss from her could do...

Cathy chuckled softly. "Okay, but just one more." She kissed him again, even more lingeringly this time and she only stopped when she heard him groan in defeat.

"I think you're right," he said weakly, "we'd better get back inside. I'm not sure my poor, sex-starved body is ready for this yet."

"Just remember, Detective Andrews, you're the one who asked for it." It was almost as if the anger between them only a few minutes before had never taken place and she couldn't help smiling up at him in a state of wonder. He seemed to know what she was thinking about because he returned the smile. "Come on, we've still got work to do." She led the way, but once inside, they snapped back to reality as soon as they saw

Petcelli come waddling towards them, his face like thunder.

"Where the hell were you two?" he snapped.

Dave pulled himself up to his full height, making him tower over the fat little man by a good ten inches. Cathy watched in barely concealed amusement when Dave fixed him with a very cold stare. "Cathy just went out for a breath of fresh air and when she seemed to have been gone for quite a long time, I went outside to see if she was all right. But she was anything but. She was lying on the ground, knocked out cold, and when she was finally able to tell me what had happened, she said that two men jumped her, for no apparent reason. She recognized them as being two men with whom you spent a lot of time with earlier. Interesting clientele you have here, Mr. Petcelli, who like to jump an innocent waitress when all she wants is some fresh air."

Petcelli visibly began to fluster but he composed himself again very quickly. "What my clientele do once they step foot outside of my establishment is entirely none of my business."

"Maybe, but they were still technically on your premises, in the parking lot. If they come back again, I would like for you to bar them or else I might be inclined to call the cops."

Dave had just said the magic word because Petcelli instantly paled. "Cops? No, that won't be necessary, I'll see to it personally they'll never be back in here again. You have my word." He adapted a concerned air and laid a sweaty hand on Cathy's arm, dangerously close to the top of her bosom. "Are you going to be okay, cookie?"

She looked icily at his hand, then at him and at least he had the good sense to take his hand away. "I'll be fine. And the name's Cathy."

"I, um, I... well, anytime you need to take a break, you just go right ahead.... Cathy." With that, Petcelli bade a hasty retreat to his office and as soon as he disappeared from view, she shuddered.

"What an absolute worm!" she said in disgust.

"Couldn't agree more, but hey, how come you didn't bite *his* hand?" Dave teased.

"What, put something like that in my mouth? Are you serious?" She wriggled in revulsion then, without warning, she began to feel very light-headed. She felt the floor rising up to meet her and she would have fallen flat on her face if Dave hadn't been there to catch her.

CHAPTER THIRTY-THREE

It took a few seconds, with Dave's support, for Cathy to gain her equilibrium again. The room had been spinning sickeningly for her and Dave's alarmed face in her vision had doubled, tripled and quadrupled before finally settling down to normal. The pounding pain in her head made her want to throw up and it was only through sheer will power alone that she didn't. The loud music from the stage area jarred and jangled and sliced into her brain and, closing her eyes as if to block it out, she winced and covered her face with her hands.

Still with an arm securely around her waist, Dave steered her towards the nearest chair and sat her down. He kneeled in front of her, his eyes anxious. "Your head really bothering you, sweetie?"

"Just a bit," she admitted with a faint smile. "No big deal, if it gets any worse, I've got painkillers in my bag to take if needed." But Dave didn't seem convinced she was all right and she quickly widened the smile. "Thanks for worrying, though."

"Of course I worry. A head injury, no matter how minor, is always cause for concern and I think I'd like to take you to the hospital for a check-up."

"Nonsense, Dave, I have a headache, that's all, it will go away very soon, I'm sure of it."

"But it could be a concussion." He reached up and tenderly touched her head at where she had indicated earlier. His gentle, searching fingers located a good-sized bump and he hissed a sharp breath in through his teeth. "Jesus, Cathy, that bump's about the size of a golf ball, it more than likely *is* a concussion and -"

"And, nothing. I am fine, really." Sitting for a few moments had helped calm things down for her considerably and she looked earnestly into his eyes. "Really."

Clearly unconvinced, but not wanting to upset her by arguing the point, Dave slowly nodded. "Okay, if you say so. But you take it easy for the rest of the night - and that's an order."

"Yeah, and I listen to orders too." Her smile became innocent and at least it produced a reluctant smile from him in return. Not wishing to discuss her headache any further, she glanced at her watch. "I think Paul and Krista should know about what happened tonight. Why don't you go call him and tell him we'll call round to see him after we finish here? I'm sure she's still with him, even though it's late."

"I'll go do just that. Why should we be the only ones who get to stay up to an ungodly hour? But, first, are you *sure* you're going to be okay?"

"I'll answer that one better tomorrow." But she was touched by his concern for her well-being and, not being able to resist, she gave his lips a soft kiss. "And now, thanks to you, I have to go re-apply some more lipstick."

"With or without it, you still taste good enough to eat. And particularly in that uniform too." The day before, he would sooner have died first than say something like that to her but tonight, his tongue seemed to have been magically loosened, he could say all these crazy things to her, as if it was the most natural thing in the world. And he loved it.

This time, her smile became impudent. "You should see what I look like out of it," she teased and, with that, arose and walked off to go in search of her tray, leaving him staring after her in astonishment.

The rest of the night passed uneventfully and Dave and Cathy arrived at Paul's at around 2:30. By mutual agreement, neither of them had wanted to tell their friends right away that something romantic had been started between them, they wanted Paul and Krista to work it all out for themselves. On the drive over to Paul's apartment, Cathy even came up with the wicked idea of playing a naughty trick on them and Dave, delighted on hearing how it was to be executed, backed her the whole way.

As soon as Paul opened the door to them, he knew immediately something was wrong. "Hi, guys," he greeted carefully, "what's up?"

"Don't ask me, ask *him*," Cathy snapped and threw Dave a venomous glare. She marched on into what she assumed was the living room, leaving the two men at the doorway.

Paul quickly closed the door and looked towards Dave for an explanation. "Okay, partner, what have you done now?"

"I'm just so sick to death of being around that woman. She's absolutely impossible."

"What, exactly, did you do?" Paul asked, as calmly as possible.

"She's only so upset because I happened to tell her she fitted right into the role of playing a slutty waitress, as if it was all second nature to her."

"That will certainly do it."

"Yeah, well, I meant it as a compliment, that she was doing well at her first undercover job, only she jumped right down my throat before I had the chance to properly explain to her what I meant. Man, I think she has serious PMS problems, either that or else she's just a born, natural, supreme bitch." Dave pushed past Paul and went into the living room where, for Krista's benefit, he glowered immediately at Cathy and deliberately sat down as far away from her as was possible.

Krista looked uncertainly from one to the other, then forced a smile on her face. "Hello there, Dave. Busy night tonight?"

"No, not really. And before I forget, please tell your friend I would be mighty obliged if she would find her own way home after we're through talking here."

Krista turned back to Cathy. "Where's your own car?"

"*He* came to pick me up," she said icily. "Course, wish now he hadn't bothered because that's probably another thing he won't let me forget."

Paul, who was standing in the doorway between the living room and the hall, couldn't listen to anymore and he hastily cleared his throat. "Kris, can you come into the kitchen a second, please? There's something I need to discuss with you."

She caught the look in his eye and quickly stood up. "Sure."

Before Paul turned away, he looked meaningfully at Dave. "We won't be long. And yes, we'll be talking about you, just in case you're wondering. You two kiss and make up, right now."

"Please just keep out of it, Paul," Cathy requested, hoping she wasn't sounding too rude. "This is between Dave and me." As soon as Paul closed the door, she clamped her hand over her mouth and giggled mischievously, then, bouncing up, she went over to where Dave was sitting and sat down on the arm of his chair. "Very well done, Mr. De Niro."

"Right back at you, Ms. Streep," he said happily. "We really got them going." In one swift movement, he pulled her unto his knee and started nuzzling her neck. "They didn't even suspect a thing." He planted a trail of kisses from her throat up to her lips and began kissing her hungrily. Each kiss with her only made him want for more and more and she, of course, was only too happy to give him what he wanted.

They were still kissing when Paul and Krista came back in five minutes later and they nearly fell over one another as soon as they saw what their friends were doing.

"Wh-what's going on?" Paul demanded in amazement.

Dave flashed him an innocent smile. "Kissing and making up, just like you ordered us to do."

Krista, who for once seemed to have lost her power of speech, could only stare at them in astonishment and Paul, without skipping a beat, patted her chin. "Close your mouth, honey, you might drool." And then he turned his full attention back to Dave and Cathy. "Okay, guys, joke's over. Tell us what the hell this is all about or else go piss up a tree - preferably somewhere in the Arctic Circle."

Dave chuckled and pulled Cathy close again. "I thought you'd be pleased for us, pal."

"Well, I *am*, but five minutes ago, you both came in here, spitting bullets at one another - as usual - and now look at you, doing the tonsil tango with one another." The penny suddenly dropped and Paul nodded knowingly. "Ah yes, I get it now. This isn't the first time this has happened between you two tonight and you both staged that little argument just to throw Krista and me off the scent and try and give us heart failure at the same time. Am I right, or am I right?"

"What can we tell you, Paul?" Cathy said sweetly. "Seems like you're right."

"Then it looks like I owe you an apology after all these years, Dave, you're *not* the craziest fool alive, you've just managed to find yourself a perfect match. And so, to put us all out of our misery, I think I'd like to kill you both. Krista, sweetheart, will you kindly give me your gun, please? I think mine is upstairs and I'd like to get this over and done with as quickly as possible. No, wait, on second thoughts, I've got a better idea. Dave, give me your gun instead, I can make it look like a murder suicide."

"Up yours, partner. It's been ages since I've had the chance to play a little trick on you and this one was just so good, I can't wait to tell the boys down in the station all about it."

"Get that idea out of your head double quick, Big D. They know only too well about your tendency to stay away from women, so it will be a case of your word against mine. And you know how convincing I can be."

"Still nowhere near as convincing as I can be, Paulie, particularly when *I'll* be the one telling the truth."

Krista, who for some reason didn't seem to be quite clueing in to what was really happening, looked at them all in bewilderment. "Paul and I have just spent five minutes agonizing over what to do with you two and now I'm hearing about tonsil tangos and you two men trying to convince one another who's going to do the best convincing." Thinking she would get a better explanation from Cathy, she turned to her. "Are you angry with Dave, really, or are you on *very* friendly terms with him, really?"

Cathy smiled. "The latter, chum. Really."

With a cry of delight, Krista bounded over and gave Cathy, then Dave a big hug. "Congratulations!" she bubbled happily. "What started it all?"

"Never mind, Krissie," Cathy said with a wink at Dave. "I'll tell you about it some other time."

Paul expressed his joy for the two of them too, but particularly for Dave. It was finally over for his friend, Dave's long, lonesome journey was over and Paul had a premonition that Dave would never have to go through something as serious as a self-imposed life of celibacy ever again. This news was the perfect ending to what had been a perfect night for Paul and he settled contentedly on the couch, pulling Krista down beside him to snuggle in closely with him.

A little bit of banter ensued, but it was very late and, catching Cathy trying to stifle a yawn, Dave steered the conversation smoothly towards business. He proceeded to fill Paul and Krista in on what had transpired at the club and as soon as Krista heard Cathy had gotten hurt, she bounded over to her to examine her injury.

"That's too nasty a bump, Cathy," she declared, "you ought to go to the hospital for a checkup."

Cathy impatiently rolled her eyes. "Oh my, another one who's more concerned about my head than I am. I'm fine, if I wasn't I would tell you."

"Oh no you wouldn't. Are you in a lot of pain?"

"Some, not much, I plan on sleeping it off tonight."

"I hope for your sake you do because I'm not going to envy you your headache in the morning." Krista knew there was no point in arguing with her, Cathy was clearly determined not to let it bother her, but Krista made a mental note to keep an eye on her during the night. She sat down beside Paul again to get the rest of the news and on hearing there had been a new dancer at the club, she visibly paled. "Now I have a *very* bad feeling about this. Ruth disappeared last night, Rick hasn't been able to reach her and now there's a new dancer when Petcelli said he didn't need any new dancers after he hired me. If he has done something to her, I swear, I'll personally throw him in jail and destroy the key."

Paul put a comforting arm around her shoulders. "Don't worry, Kris, there's a nice warm cell with his name on it, you'll get your wish."

As they discussed the potential danger Ruth now seemed to be in, as well as the case so far, and the hope it might be wrapping the next night, Cathy felt her mind wandering off about something else. With Dave's arm snugly around her, she came to realize just how close they seemed to have become in such a short space of time. Despite her tense episodes with Dave, at least they had always managed to work comfortably and easily together and now she had no more reason to be uncomfortable in his company when they were outside working hours.

For Paul and Krista, of course, it had been easy for them since day one, but now they were *all* relaxed at being together like this and the added bonus of working as a team so well made her very happy.

After all was said and done, the time came to say good night. Dave stood up, pulled Cathy to her feet and, not even thinking about being shy about it, he pulled her close for an embrace. "Want a ride home, baby?" he asked softly.

She regretfully shook her head. "Thanks, but I'll keep Krista company. I *would* like to say a private good night to you, though." She led him out to the hall after he had bid Paul and Krista a farewell and this time, she was the one who hugged him close to her. His body just felt so good against hers, she really didn't want him to leave her at all, but another yawn crept up on her and she quickly apologized.

"It's okay, it's late and we're both tired," he said. "How's your head feeling now?"

"It's felt better, but I'm just trying to ignore it."

"I hope you'll be okay tomorrow." He kissed both her cheeks, then, not being able to resist, his lips sought out hers and he kissed her, more fervently than he already had. He just couldn't get enough of her, nor, it seemed, could she get enough of him as she matched him kiss for kiss until, at last, they had to break away before it could get too dangerous. He looked at her in a mild state of bewilderment, then he smiled ruefully. "I gotta go," he said softly, the remorse evident in his voice as well as in his eyes. "But I will see you tomorrow sometime, during the day?"

She nodded shyly and gave him one last, swift kiss. "Come over anytime you want, I'll be waiting for you."

He kissed the tip of her nose and stepped outside. The night was still and quiet, the gentle breeze on his face only slightly cool but refreshing and he smiled happily. "Good night," he said tenderly, "take care." He turned away, the smile still firmly in place. He suddenly felt like a whole new person, somebody who actually had something to look forward to now and he knew it was all thanks to this warm, wonderful, fiery, beautiful woman that God had chosen to send over from the tiny country of Northern Ireland, to come into his life at what he now knew had just been at just the right moment.

Cathy closed the door after him, smiling gently to herself and was just about to return to the living room when Paul and Krista appeared at the doorway. They had just shared a very passionate good night and

Krista had almost been tempted to ask him if she could stay with him, but, not knowing that he had been almost tempted to ask her to do just that, she decided not to be presumptuous and sadly bade him adieu.

Cathy received, and returned, a good night hug from Paul, then she took the car keys from Krista and went to her car to give the two of them a last minute or two together.

The two girls were quiet on the drive home, until Cathy suddenly said, "You don't have to tell me, you know, it's written all over your face."

"What is?" Krista asked carefully, even though she already knew what Cathy was going to say.

"It was your first time with him tonight, wasn't it?"

"Is it that obvious?"

"Krissie, it's *me* you're talking to here, I can read you like a book. I picked up on your signals practically as soon as I walked through the door tonight, not to mention Paul seemed extremely pleased with himself."

Krista chuckled softly. "I suppose. Oh Cathy, it was everything I had imagined it would be with him, only more. He gave me thrills I've never experienced with anyone before and I can't wait to be with him again."

"Spare me the details, please," Cathy teased. She caught the sparkle in Krista's eyes, even from just the dim light from the dashboard and her expression grew serious. "Are we talking love here?"

Krista looked like she was going to burst unless she shared her news and she threw Cathy a knowing smile. "Most definitely. He actually told me he loves me. That was the first time he has ever admitted it to me."

"That's great!" Cathy enthused, genuinely delighted for her friend. "Did you tell him too?"

"No... no, I didn't," Krista said with a sudden frown of irritation. "And I don't know why I didn't. But I will soon, for sure."

"Then there might be a wedding soon after all."

"Maybe, but I wouldn't go holding my breath on it just yet," Krista said lightly.

But there was a very distinct awareness in her eyes, as if she had just been given the most precious gift in the world, one to treasure always and one that she would sooner rather die than ever relinquish.

And no prize for guessing that gift was Paul.

CHAPTER THIRTY-FOUR

Friday started out as a bright and beautiful mid Spring day, but as the morning wore on, some rain clouds moved in from the west and by noon, Bathville was awash with intermittent showers. Temperatures hovered in the high 50's and, because the weathermen had promised a sunny weekend ahead, with the mercury to climb to the mid 60's, nobody really complained about the rain.

It was the sound of the rain pattering on the windowpane that had awoken Cathy. She lay for a little while listening to it and wished it would lull her back to sleep, the way it normally would have when she had nothing better to do but lie in bed. She had spent a very restless night, every time she had moved, her head had started pounding alarmingly and right now, it was throbbing wildly, despite the several pain killers she had arisen to swallow a couple of times during the night.

Knowing she wasn't going to get back to sleep, she arose and had just tied the belt of her robe around her waist when she heard the front doorbell. She listened first to see if Krista was going to answer it, but the house was still and quiet, telling her Krista was not yet up and about.

Each step she took sent fresh pain slicing into her head and she carefully padded down the stairs. When she opened the door, she managed a wan smile when she saw it was Dave, who looked at her in surprise when he saw she wasn't dressed yet.

"I'm sorry, Cathy, I *knew* I should have called first. Have I come at a bad time?"

"Of course not, come on in. Krista and I just haven't been able to make it out of bed before this so please just excuse us." She beckoned him into the kitchen and started to make a pot of coffee. Aware that he was following her every move, she suddenly felt very self-conscious about the way she must be looking and she hurriedly ran her fingers through her hair in an attempt to tidy it up a bit, but she really needn't have bothered, he was thinking she looked very appealing in her just out of bed state. Since she didn't know what was going through his mind, she turned to him and smiled awkwardly. "Sorry, Dave, I'm usually more together in the morning...." She paused and glanced at the kitchen clock, "or in this case, the afternoon, I must look an absolute fright."

He stole a not too discreet look at her legs and smiled appreciatively. "You seem mighty fine to me," he said and pulled her into his arms. He bent to kiss her but he saw her flinch and barely conceal a look of pain and it was then he noticed she was very pale. "Are you okay?" he asked, knowing she was anything but.

She clicked her tongue in irritation and slowly shook her head. "No, not really. I think I'm just tired, I hardly slept a wink all night."

"And your head?"

Feeling uncommon tears threaten at his concern for her well-being, she chewed nervously on her bottom lip, but she couldn't lie to him. "It really hurts," she admitted.

He held her at arm's length and tried not to chuckle at her woebegone expression that was greatly intermingled with embarrassment. "Okay, young lady, enough is enough, I'm taking you to the hospital."

"There's really no need, Dave. The bump has gone down a good bit already so I'm not going to any hospital. And that's final."

Dave mentally gritted his teeth, he had forgotten how stubborn she could be, but he knew instinctively he was not going to win this particular argument. "Well, do you at least have any ice?"

"Yes, in the freezer."

"Good. Take a couple of painkillers, go lie down on the couch and I'll prepare some ice for you to hold on your head. Trust me, it works."

She nodded miserably. "I'm sorry, you must be thinking I'm a real wimp if I can let a silly wee headache get me down."

"Some "wee" headache, you can hardly move your head and I just wish now I had insisted last night that I take you to the hospital. Into the living room with you right now and lie down."

Cathy was in no mood to protest so she swallowed two tablets and went to lie down on the couch. She was already beginning to drift off when Dave came in with some ice wrapped in a cloth for her and she was barely able to murmur her thanks when he placed it gently on the back of her head. She somehow managed to remember her manners and mumbled something to him about helping himself to coffee or whatever else in the kitchen he wanted, then she just let herself float off to Slumberland.

Dave watched over her until she had fully fallen asleep, then he picked up a newspaper from the day before to catch up on what had been happening in the outside world. He was totally engrossed in doing the crossword when Krista joined him a half hour later.

"Why is Cathy asleep on the sofa?" Krista asked in surprise.

"She's sleeping off the effects of having the fight with that wall last night," he whispered. "She told me she hardly slept during the night and she actually admitted to me earlier that she has a really bad headache."

Krista looked at her sleeping friend in concern. "I looked in on her a couple of times during the night and she was pretty restless. She's awfully pale on it too so if she's not better by dinner time, you and I will join together and we'll get her to the hospital for a checkup yet." She suddenly noticed what Dave was doing and she grinned. "When she wakes up, she's going to kill you for doing that crossword. That's her property and she hates it when someone else does it for her."

"I'll take my chances. There are a few clues I can't get anyway, so maybe she'll forgive me enough to help me with it later."

"Okay, but don't say I didn't warn you." Krista glanced at her watch. "Paul should be here soon, you sticking around?"

"Sure, if that's okay?"

"Of course, it is, you're welcome to stay here as long as you want, when you want. I'm just going to make myself something to eat, can I make you something too?"

"Cathy made coffee earlier, that's all I need, thanks." He took one last look at Cathy to check she was still sleeping peacefully, then he quietly arose to follow Krista into the kitchen.

As she started to prepare her breakfast, he carefully studied her profile and now he could understand why Paul had fallen so hard for her so quickly. Her finely sculpted nose, her well defined lips, high cheekbones, long-lashed, perfect green eyes that not even make-up could enhance any better, her long, shiny, almost black hair, her perfect body, poured right now into a jade green knit top and a pair of black jeans, everything about her just oozed allure.

Dave had already witnessed a large number of men who, once they had set eyes on her, couldn't look long enough at her and had made fools of themselves by almost breaking their necks just so they could get a better look at her. But although he found her amazingly attractive too, he knew he could never be attracted to her, not just because of Paul, and now

Cathy, but because he already valued their friendship and working relationship.

He waited until her scrambled eggs were well under way before opening a conversation. He needed to ask about something and he knew Krista would be the perfect one to tell him.

"Do you mind if ask you something personal, Krista?"

She shrugged indifferently. "Not at all."

"It's about Cathy."

"That's okay, go ahead."

"Well, it's just about something she said last night, on the drive over to the club, that really baffled me. We were talking small talk, even teasing one another a little bit and then, right out of the blue, she said that her verbal retaliations are the only weapon she has left and if she had never talked back, certain people would have taken advantage of her. What did she mean by that?"

Krista's eyes shot open wide in alarm but, composing herself quickly, she turned away and busied herself by buttering her toast. "Did she sound angry when she said that?" she asked carefully.

"No, not angry, she sounded - and looked, too - very sad, even a bit upset. And after she said it, she changed the subject abruptly."

Krista started chewing on her bottom lip, wondering what she could say that would explain a very delicate situation to him. "Look, Dave, I can't answer you directly because it's about something very personal and very painful in Cathy's life. I know what it is, of course, Cathy and I have no secrets between us, but I can't tell you or anyone else about it because she has sworn me to absolute secrecy and I would sooner rather die than betray her trust."

"Can't you even give me a clue?" he asked in bewilderment.

She deliberated for a long moment, her eyes locked on his, as if assessing him, or as if she was trying to look deep into his soul to see if she could confide in him without him throwing it all back in her face. She seemed to appreciate what she saw in the clarity of his deep blue eyes because her expression visibly softened in acceptance. "Okay, but as long as this goes no further than between the two of us. Cathy mustn't even know we've been talking about her like this because she'll only get upset and this *is* still all her own business anyway."

"I won't tell anyone," he said earnestly, "I promise you I won't."

"Then your word's going to have to be good enough." She slowly stirred her eggs for a moment, giving herself time to gather her thoughts and put them into appropriate words for him. "Cathy had a lot of problems, *major* problems when she was growing up and it's that part that I can't tell you about, but I can at least say her problems were caused by her family. She was put through a lot by them but she's over it all now, thank God. However, because of what she did go through, she has been left with a lot of insecurities about herself, and I do mean a *lot*. Do you think she's pretty?"

"Of course I do. Who wouldn't?"

"I happen to think she's *very* pretty, very attractive, a real stunner, only because she's so insecure, she has a hard time believing anyone who tells her, even me, just how beautiful a person she is."

"I see," he said and he couldn't keep the concern from his voice.

Krista laid a hand on his arm to console him. "I'm sorry, I didn't mean to alarm you in any way. Cathy is a very sensible person and after going through what she did, it's to her credit that she's the sort of person she is today. If I had been in her shoes, I don't know if I could have survived even half as well as she did. What she said last night is all true, her sharp tongue sometimes *is* the only weapon she has left, but she's molded that trait to her own advantage because she is very honest and direct and she will let you know exactly where you stand with her, always. Please don't tell her I told you a little bit about her past - even though I really didn't divulge too much and I'm sure you're none the wiser - but I think I only told you because you seemed so worried and I want you to be able to understand her constant urge to put herself down."

"But why should she do that to herself?" he cried in alarm. "Cathy's a great person."

"I know she is, but just try telling her that. I love her to pieces, Dave, she's the only family I have left since I lost my parents and what hurts her tends to hurt me too. We look out for each other a lot and woe betide anybody who tries to belittle her in front of me."

Dave nodded grimly, more concerned than ever now, but before he could ask anything else, the doorbell rang and, because he was closest, he went to answer it. It was Paul and as soon as she saw him, Krista brightened immediately and abandoned her eggs to go greet him with a big hug.

"Morning, darling," he greeted cheerfully. "Still as beautiful as ever, I see."

"Afternoon, love, and thank you for the compliment. Want some eggs?"

"No thanks, I've just eaten. Where's Cathy?"

"She's asleep on the couch in the living room," Dave explained. "Her head really is bothering her after last night. I think I'll go check on her, leave you two lovebirds alone."

Krista had just sat down to eat her breakfast and Paul sat down beside her to drink a cup of coffee he had just poured himself. He let her eat in peace for a few moments but there was something he was just dying to discuss with her and he couldn't wait any longer.

"We need to talk," he began slowly.

She looked up at him in alarm. "Uh oh, this sounds serious."

He quickly shook his head. "I don't mean it to be. At least, I *do* mean it to be, but it's not anything bad...or at least I hope you won't think so. I want to talk to you about last night."

"Oh." She set down her fork, her eyes troubled. He was going to tell her that everything had been a mistake, that she was nothing more than a tramp going to bed with someone she barely knew, she was...

Paul had no idea what was going through her head at that precise moment of time, if he had, he certainly wouldn't have sounded so ominous. "I just want you to know, my lady love, that I meant every word I said last night. You're truly beautiful, in every way and, most importantly, I love you, deeply. I am so in love with you and I can't get enough of you."

At his softly spoken words, her eyes started to glow and she felt herself relax. "I'm so happy to hear you say that. Particularly since there's something I've been meaning to tell you too."

"Don't tell me, let me guess. I'm the best you've ever been with, right? And because of that, you want to become my love slave?" His blue eyes twinkled softly as he teased her but for once, she didn't give back as good as she was getting.

"Not even close."

"Okay, what is it you want to tell me then?"

"Oh.... just that...." Krista caught his eyes and held them for a long, heart stopping moment, and then she smiled slowly, "Just that, I love you too. So much...so very very much."

Paul's whole face lit up and he pulled her immediately into his arms for a huge hug. "Wow, thank you for that," he murmured.

"I'm sorry I didn't tell you last night, I don't even know why I didn't because I've known it for quite a while now, but better late than never, huh?"

"Most definitely. You've just about managed to make my entire year for me... my entire *life*, I should say, with news like that, it's so incredible. And so are you."

"Thank you, but you bring out the best in me."

He held her close, smelling her fresh, clean scent and feeling as if his heart would burst with all his love for her. It hadn't even crossed his mind that she hadn't told him until now how she felt about him, but it didn't matter anymore, he loved her and she loved him. How much more perfect could his life get now?

They looked up when Dave and Cathy came into the kitchen just then and, reluctantly extracting herself from Paul's arms, Krista looked at her friend in concern. "How are you feeling now, Cath?"

"Amazingly, a whole lot better, thanks. That extra snooze, along with the ice, really did help because the headache, although still there, has greatly subsided."

Krista gave her a critical once over, searching for signs that Cathy was just saying what everyone wanted to hear, but indeed, she wasn't as pale as she had been, even her eyes were sparkling softly again and Krista relaxed.

"Good, glad to hear it. How about I fix you something to eat?"

"No thanks, chum, coffee will do."

Krista poured Cathy a cup of coffee and topped up her own cup. The four of them sat around the kitchen table and Krista realized with a start, just as Cathy had the night before, that it seemed like the most natural thing in the world for them all to be together like this, talking and carrying on as if they had known each other for years.

"Hey!" Paul said suddenly and looked at Cathy with a mischievous gleam in his eye. "Now that you're going out with my buddy, and since I have a whole plethora of them for him, I'll have to come up with a suitable nickname for you too."

Cathy groaned comically and looked at him in amusement. "Oh God, let's hear it."

He considered carefully for a few moments, then clicked his fingers. "Got it! Little dude. How does that sound?"

Dave chuckled. "Like a crock, but coming from you, I expect it."

"I think that name suits Cathy perfectly, even if I say so myself."

Cathy rolled her eyes. "If that's what you want to call me, go right ahead, I'm not going to stop you. But less of the little, please."

Paul immediately feigned surprise. "Little? Did I say little? Okay, that's it definitely settled then, *little* dude it is."

Krista giggled at Cathy's bemused expression and arose to place her dirty plate in the sink. En route back to the table, the telephone rang so she answered it. It was Captain Hamilton.

"Hello, Captain, what can I do for you? We'll be down at the station in a little while if that's why you're calling."

"No hurry. I'm just calling to let you know we've found Ruth O'Brien."

"Really? Well that's great, I was beginning to get really worried about her. Where has she been?" Because the Captain didn't answer right away, and because she could sense his irritation and anger, realization dawned on her and she sighed heavily. "Oh no, Captain, don't tell me..."

"Yeah, I'm afraid so. I'm really sorry, I know the effort you all were putting into it to try and get her protection."

"We obviously didn't try hard enough, Captain."

"You did what you could, sometimes these things happen as a sad and very unfortunate fact of a police officer's life."

Krista glanced at Cathy to see if she was listening, but Cathy seemed totally engrossed in something Dave was saying to her. "Small comfort, sir. Where was she found?"

"She and her car were found at a construction site about ten blocks east of her apartment. One of the workers saw her car parked at the far end of the site and because the vehicle was in an unauthorized area, he approached it to ask the driver to move. He found her inside, naked, and quite dead."

"Naked too? Oh Captain, how terrible. What was the cause of death?"

"Broken neck by strangulation, but there were also blows to the chest and head with a blunt weapon, like a fist or the butt of a gun. There were severe lacerations to her genital area too, which means we can't rule out sexual contact either. The coroner has swabbed her for semen and I've put a rush on it. If we get a DNA match through our computers, we've found our killer. But whoever did this to her certainly did a number on her, he was no amateur either, he knew exactly what he was doing to ensure that he killed her outright and left no trace.... other than the semen."

Krista shuddered and clasped the phone tighter, clamping down a moan of disgust. "This is just so awful. Why would someone do this to her?"

"Don't know, that's what we have to find out. You're the one who had the most contact with her so anything you can tell us about her background would be greatly appreciated."

"I really know very little about her, except that she was scared of something - or of someone - at the club. I don't know if she had a boyfriend, although I do know she gave her telephone number over to Rick, one of the barmen, but he hasn't been able to get a hold of her. But I don't know where she's from, who her family is, nothing. What about time of death?"

"Judging by body temperature, the food content in her stomach and the digestion in her small intestine, the coroner said about 36 hours."

"Is there any evidence we can tie this in with Petcelli?"

"None found so far, but we're still looking, I want every charge I can get on the son of a whore. That turkey Paul got arrested the other night still isn't talking, there's not enough evidence on the package Cathy saw being exchanged last night, so any charge I can get on him will please me immensely. Play it cool with him tonight, don't let him know you know Ruth's been murdered. When you bring him in for questioning, we'll get it out of him that way. Talk to you later, Krista."

"Yeah, later." Krista hung up, feeling saddened and sickened by this latest piece of information. She sat down beside Paul again and looked over at Cathy. "I take it you didn't hear any of that conversation?"

"No, these two men wouldn't shut up. Who was it?"

"Captain Hamilton. We don't have to look for Ruth anymore, she's just been found. Murdered."

"Oh, dear Lord." Cathy clamped a hand over her mouth and stared at Krista in disbelief. "That's awful, that's just terrible. How did it happen?"

Krista filled them all in with what the Captain had just told her and a somber silence descended over them when she had finished. "Anyway, Captain Hamilton wants to pin the murder on Petcelli, here's hoping we can."

"Damn it!" Dave exclaimed and angrily thumped his fist on the table. "This was supposed to have been an easy case. Soon as we got enough evidence on the gambling racket, that was supposed to be it and now look what we've gotten ourselves into. Gambling, drug dealing and now murder. Petcelli's going to fry for this - and I can't wait."

"Of course he's going to fry, partner," Paul stated. "He's going to get all that's coming to him and more. Justice will be served, same way it always is."

"It had better be," Dave snapped and he was quite prepared to carry on with his temper outburst until he caught Cathy's eye. She was giving him a soft look of understanding, telling him he had every right to be upset but that no amount of temper tantrums were going to bring Ruth back, so why didn't he just try and calm down? So, he did, in a flash, with a slight smile of acknowledgment that she was right.

Paul had witnessed the exchange and he stared at Cathy in amazement. "How did you do that?"

"Do what?" she asked in confusion.

"Get him to calm down like that?"

She looked back at Dave, having not been aware she was the one responsible for quieting him. "I don't know how I did it."

"Well, try and find out, please, because I've been trying for years to get him to stop flying off the handle at any given opportunity."

"Will you guys stop talking about me as if I'm not even here?" Dave said in exasperation. "Besides, I have every good reason to be annoyed because Ruth's murder shouldn't have happened. If Petcelli gets rid of people as easily as that, for the only reason being somebody has seen something they shouldn't have, then we could all be in bigger trouble than we think. We can't appear too inquisitive tonight for very obvious reasons. We've been playing it real careful all week not to get our covers blown and now we have to be *extra* careful. Since we want to get this case wrapped, we have to watch what we say and to whom we say it because we can't trust anyone in that place."

"We've already been doing all that," Paul said.

"I know, but tonight, we do it better. All of us. No exceptions." Dave suddenly caught a hold of Cathy's hand that she had just lifted towards him in a gesture of protest. "And no, I'm not standing on ceremony here, I just don't want a repeat performance of what happened to you last night, so stop looking at me like that, this is for your own best interests."

"But you made it sound that we can't look after ourselves," she said, "or that we don't know what to do."

Paul carefully hid a smirk and smiled innocently at Dave. "Talk your way out of that one, pal."

"I don't have to, I meant what I said." Dave arose and went over to pour himself another cup of coffee but he didn't return to the table right away and stood instead staring out the window. Another shower had just passed over, but the sun was struggling to come out again and probably would succeed until the next shower came along. After only a few moments, Dave turned around again, this time with a lop-sided grin on his face. "Okay, I'm sorry Cathy, Krista, maybe I did come on a bit strong there. It's just that news about Ruth has me a lot worried now because I don't want anything happening to either one of you. And I know you can look after yourself, Cathy – certainly you too, Krista - I never doubted that for a second, but it's like this, I, er, I'm not used to having a woman around who knows how to take care of herself." He paused and rolled his eyes. "What am I saying here? I'm not used to having a woman around, period. Anyway, am I off the hook yet? Please?"

Cathy chuckled softly. "Of course you are, just chalk this one up to experience and know to never say something like that to Krista or me ever again. Although..." Her eyes suddenly clouded over, "although I just wish poor Ruth had had someone like you looking out for her, it just hit me full in the face there that she's actually gone. I didn't get to talk to her too much but even though I hardly knew her, I still felt very sorry for her."

"I know what you mean, Cathy," Krista agreed sadly. "She always had this *needy* look about her, she wanted out of her lifestyle so bad and I think, given sufficient time, she could have got out... but she just didn't get the chance." She shivered in revulsion. "Three years younger than me and she's dead. Murdered and possibly raped and left with no dignity even in her death. What a terrible waste of a life."

Paul grabbed a hold of her hand and patted it in comfort. "What I saw of her, she was really pretty, she could have made it somewhere else as a dancer, or a model, she was out of place in the Blues Haven. Which echoes Dave's words rather well, I think. If Petcelli somehow figures out we're on to him, particularly you two girls, the first suspicious look he gives either one of you and you're both out of there. Now that we know what he's capable of, we don't want either one of you becoming his next victim. Are you with me on this one, Dave?"

"All the way, partner," Dave answered solemnly. "*All* the way."

CHAPTER THIRTY-FIVE

Later that night, Paul picked up Krista and Cathy to take them to the Blues Haven. The journey was passed in relative silence, none of them knew what the night would bring and it did no good to speculate so they chose to conserve their energy by remaining quiet.

As Paul pulled into the club's parking lot, a flash of car lights in his rearview mirror caught his eyes and momentarily blinded him. He wondered if it was the same car that he knew had been tailing him for the last few blocks and had now followed him in here and, instantly, his guard went up. But he knew he needn't have worried because when the car pulled up alongside his, he saw it was only Dave.

"Well timed, Big D," Paul said when they had all gotten out.

"Yeah, not bad." Dave smiled his greetings at Krista, then immediately pulled Cathy into his arms. "Take your lady friend inside, Cam," he advised lightly, not taking his eyes off Cathy's. "I want to say hello to *my* lady friend and I'd rather there wasn't an audience."

Paul grinned and looked like he was going to come off with a smart-ass response but he caught a warning look from Dave and instead, he put his arm around Krista's shoulders. "Come on, sweet-face, let's leave these two alone. See you inside guys, don't be *too* long. Hey, Kris, smell the testosterone in the..."

His voice faded as they walked away and, chuckling, Dave turned his attention back to what was obviously more important. "Hi," he said softly.

"Hi, yourself. You could have said that to me inside, you know."

"Maybe, but I wouldn't have been able to do this." He bent his head towards her and gave her a very long, slow, searching kiss and when he finally pulled his lips away from hers, it was evident he hadn't wanted to. He smiled faintly and held her close. "On the way over here just now, I suddenly realized I didn't get a chance to do that to you all day. I think I even broke a couple of speed limits to get here as quickly as possible in the hope that you had already arrived."

"That's naughty, I should get someone to issue you with a speeding ticket." But she was clearly delighted he had wanted to see her so quickly. "You can say hello to me like that anytime."

"Watch out, I might just hold you to that. Come on, we'd better get inside. But first, how's the head? And I want the truth."

"It's fine, really."

"Good, I'm glad. Did you remember to check your gun?"

"Yeah and I even brought along a spare clip, just in case. And no, I'm not too worried about what's going to happen tonight, seeing that was the next question out of your mouth."

"I'm doing it again, aren't I?" he admitted.

"You are, but really, it's okay, I think it's very sweet of you to be so concerned." She looked shyly up at him. "Did you mean it there?"

"Mean what?"

"About me being your lady friend?" She seemed a bit awkward but a whole lot cute to him and, laughing softly, he playfully kissed the tip of her nose.

"One thing you've got to learn about me, I don't say anything I don't mean, so yes, from here on in, and if it's all right with you, of course, I want you as my lady friend. I don't exactly go around kissing just anybody either, you know, so if that doesn't answer your question, then I don't know what will."

"And I'm the first in a long time?" she asked softly.

"Yes, a *very* long time." He wanted to tell her everything she might be curious about, he wanted to be totally up front with her, not keep anything about his past a secret from her, but he knew instinctively he had nothing to fear from her, that she wouldn't hold anything against him and maybe, just maybe, she would even understand why he had turned against women in the way he had chosen.

Each passing minute with her brought about a whole rush of new emotions for him and he couldn't wait to find out all that he was dying to know about her. But he knew he had plenty of time for that, he was in no hurry and he sensed that neither was she, they each mutually seemed to want to take everything slowly and not jeopardize anything by pushing each other too quickly. However, it was just so hard to know to take it slowly with her because, as he had already told her, she was working her way in under his skin all right and he was liking it more and more too.

He realized with a sudden jolt that she was not just in under his skin, she was also slowly tiptoeing her way into his heart, in a way that he actually welcomed. At that thought, he couldn't suppress a shiver of elation, which was only slightly marred by a brief feeling of trepidation. Old habits die hard, he reminded himself...

"Are you cold?" Cathy was looking at him curiously, wondering why he had gone quiet on her for a few moments, and then had shivered like that. "It's not really cold tonight, are you all right?"

He pulled himself back to reality with a faint smile and gently touched her cheek. "No, I'm not cold, I'm just enjoying the aftermath of that kiss." That much was certainly true, he couldn't get over how each kiss with her always left him wanting to beg for more. He gave her a chaste kiss on the cheek. "Come on, sweetie, let's go get this night over with - and by the way, thanks for keeping your hair down again."

"Only because you told me you liked it better that way." Linking her fingers through his, she led the way to the club.

No sooner had they stepped inside than a man wearing a tuxedo and a very mean expression approached them. He was tall, towering over Dave by at least five inches and he also outweighed him by a good forty pounds. If you were to meet him down a dark alleyway somewhere, he was definitely someone you would say "sir" to, then get out of his way as quickly as possible. He stood stiffly in front of Dave and Cathy and put his hand up to stop them from going any further.

"This is a private party," he informed them. "Unless you have an invitation, leave. Or come back in an hour when the bar opens for regular customers. But even then, don't hold your breath about being allowed in."

"We're not here for any party," Dave said calmly, "we're staff."

"Staff?" he produced a list of names from his inside breast pocket and read it over slowly. "Only two names unaccounted for, Dave Mitchell and Cathy Tanner. Any identification to prove who you are?"

Dave moved to produce his driving license but his real name was on it so it would instantly blow his cover. He pretended to search all through his pockets instead and quickly adapted a pained look. "I seem to have left my wallet at home. If you find Mr. Petcelli, he can vouch for us."

"Wait right here." They watched as he went over to Petcelli, who was standing at the end of the bar, and when Petcelli looked their way, then nodded, he came back over to them. "Okay, the boss says you're legit, go on through."

With a quick "see you later" to Cathy, Dave went behind the bar and helped Paul fill the cooler with beer bottles. "What's with the goon in the monkey suit?" he whispered.

"Look around you, Dave, practically everyone's in a monkey suit, even Petcelli, who also seems to be sweating bullets in a real nervous way. Feel the atmosphere and try telling me there's nothing different about the place."

Dave quickly glanced all around him and knew immediately what Paul meant. There was a sharp decline in the number of female clientele too, in fact, Dave could only see about half a dozen women milling around, all of whom were dressed to kill in glittery, formal evening wear.

One of the ladies suddenly caught his attention as she stood off to one side, chatting with a man old enough to be her father... only she was showing more than a daughterly interest in him. Gritting his teeth in annoyance, Dave quickly turned back to Paul.

"Uh oh, seems like we've got trouble."

"Who?" Paul looked over Dave's shoulder and scanned the room but he couldn't see anyone he recognized. "Who is it?"

"The bimbo at one o'clock, the one in the green, slinky number?"

There was a surge in the crowd but when everyone settled down again, Paul was able to pick out who Dave meant and he groaned. "Great, what the hell's *she* doing here? Shouldn't she be walking her usual beat over at Sixteenth and Vine?" He was referring to one of Bathville's red light areas, a great place to visit if you wanted to get lucky with one of the many prostitutes who strutted their stuff and promised their clientele a very good time, if they were willing to pay for services rendered. Paul and Dave had busted this particular lady of the night on more times than they cared to count, the last time being only about a month ago. Their faces were well known to her, which meant, as soon as she saw either one of them, she had every opportunity to get her own back on them by blowing their cover.

"Business must be bad," Dave remarked, "or else she's grown tired of turning tricks and doing blow jobs. Either way, we're still in trouble once she sees us and figures out we're here working undercover. Soon as Cathy comes over, I'm going to have to warn her to be ready, just in case Tahlulla decides to blow the whistle on us. Cathy can get the word to Krista."

Cathy, meanwhile, had just tried unsuccessfully to get into the changing room. She had been stopped by yet another bouncer who had told her that, following Mr. Petcelli's very strict orders, the changing room was out of bounds.

"But why?" she asked casually, "What's going on?"

Her wide-eyed innocent expression did nothing to soften the surly, suspicious expression of this particular bouncer as he stared indifferently down at her and ignored her question. "Arrangements have been made for you to get changed in the ladies' rest room," he informed her.

Feigning surprise, Cathy turned away without another word and went to join Krista in the rest room but before Cathy could say anything, Krista pointed to one of the stalls and put a finger over her mouth, indicating there was someone around. "Hey, Cathy," she greeted warmly, "how did it go with Dave?"

"Great!" Cathy shrugged out of her jacket and kept her tone light and conversational. "Wonder why we have to dress and undress in here tonight?"

"Search me, maybe they're painting the regular room and we'll be back into it tomorrow night."

At that, they heard the toilet flush and seconds later, Candy, the new dancer, came out of the stall. "Oh hi, Cathy," she gushed, "I've just met your friend here. Isn't it just neat that Kris is a dancer too?"

"Yeah, real neat. You two don't know how lucky you are to be getting a break every half hour. Poor me, I have to keep going." With a swift glance at Krista to warn her she was about to start asking a question or two, Cathy adapted a casual tone again. "You don't happen to know what's going on in here tonight, do you, Candy?"

Candy's baby blue eyes suddenly clouded over. "No, I don't. I asked Mr. Petcelli as soon as I came in but he just told me to mind my own business - and very rude he was too. All I did was -"

"It's okay, Candy," Krista interrupted smoothly, "Mr. Petcelli can be a bit abrupt at times. You'll soon learn not to ask him any questions at all." Which was the best piece of advice she could give for now and Candy nodded that she understood.

Cathy left Krista to give Candy as much underhanded advice as she could and went out to the bar to start her work. She looked around at the clientele, even admired the way most of the women were dressed, but tried not to appear too interested at the marked change in the paying customers. Showing even the slightest bit of interest and asking the wrong person about it could only lead to trouble from Petcelli.

The noise was the same as she'd had to endure all week, though. Everyone seemed to be talking at once, or laughing too loudly but she couldn't deny the charge in the atmosphere, the feeling of expectancy.... and for what, she couldn't wait to see.

Dave spotted her coming towards him but he saw Petcelli beckon her over before she even got half way across the floor. Petcelli said only a few words to her, then he called Dave over too.

"This is going to be interesting," Dave murmured to Paul then, fixing a smile on his face, he sauntered over to Petcelli and Cathy. "What's up, boss?" As soon as the question was asked, he stole a furtive glance around for Tahlulla but she seemed to have taken herself off somewhere, hopefully for good.

"I won't be needing you behind the bar tonight, Dave," Petcelli said, "it's not going to be busy in here tonight and Paul can handle the shift himself."

"Does that mean you want me to split?"

"No, far from it. I want you to do a little bit of waiting on tables tonight. I have a little, er, party going on in the function room, which is just off the changing room and you and Cathy here have been elected to serve drinks. All you have to do is keep your tray loaded with a selection of beer, wine, champagne and spirits. It's an open bar too, in case anyone should ask, so who knows? You just might make a lot of tips tonight, if you keep the drinks flowing. The bar will be stocked with drinks all night so that all you have to do is keep loading up when your tray is empty."

"Okay, sounds good. What kind of party is it?" Dave asked with very passable interest.

"You'll find out in about fifteen minutes. There's a fully stocked bar in there but you might have to come out here periodically for clean glasses." Petcelli suddenly smiled, but there was a very clear, dangerous warning behind the smile. "When you come out here to get glasses or whatever else you might need, you must not breathe a word of what is going on in the function room to anyone, and if you do, you'll be... fired. Immediately. Is that clear?"

"Sure, boss," Dave said, "but why?"

"Ask no questions and you'll not have to pay the penalty. Cathy, make sure you show plenty of leg and a lot of that tantalizing cleavage of yours tonight. And keep a smile on your face at all times."

Cathy nodded and did a remarkable job of not showing her outrage at Petcelli's sexist remark. Dave, who by this stage was quietly seething, also did a good job at keeping his cool. Petcelli walked away and she instantly squirmed in revulsion.

"I'll show him cleavage and leg all right," she spat, "and then I'll poke his beady little eyes out."

"Relax, sweetie. This is our last night, remember, you won't have to listen to anymore of his comments after tonight. Come on, let's go tell Paul we've been given the break we need in getting into the other bar."

Paul listened keenly when Dave filled him in on what Petcelli had ordered them to do. "Excellent," he said, nodding in approval. "First hand evidence at long last. Cathy, where are you going to keep your gun?"

"Oh my, I never thought of that." She looked herself up and down and couldn't restrain a grin. "There's definitely nowhere in this stupid costume I can hide it so I'll have to leave my bag handy somewhere so I can get to it in a hurry if need be."

Dave patted the small of his back. "My gun is right here, tucked safely beneath my shirt, so we'll be covered. Paul, you and Krista can await our signal and take it from there. And within the hour, this place should be closed down."

"Yeah, and not a moment too soon," Paul agreed. "Except

Tahlulla tries to interfere."

"Who's Tahlulla?" Cathy asked.

"A hooker. She's here tonight and she knows Dave and me. One sighting of either one of us and things could turn out a lot differently than any of us have planned. And with Dave going into the thick of things now, it's only going to be a matter of time before she sees him and recognizes him. Here's hoping she does the decent thing for once in her life and keeps her trap shut. Dave, you're going to have to make your move as quickly as possible once you get in there."

"Tell me something I don't know, bro. Cathy, I'll point her out to you and you can make sure you serve her all the time so I won't have to go anywhere near her."

"I can do that. You just make sure to keep your back turned to her at all times."

"Discretion is my middle name, so don't worry. Hey, what about Krista's gun? She's going to need some protection too."

"She gave me her gun before she went to get changed," Paul said. "I have it in a safe place."

"Let me guess, down the front of your trousers, right?" Cathy teased. "And here I was just thinking you were happy to see me."

Dave looked at her with a groan. "You little witch, that one's as old as the hills. Surely you can do better than that?"

"Usually I can but my mind is sort of distracted tonight, give me a chance to redeem myself."

Unaware to any of them, across the smoke-filled room, Tahlulla was observing their every move. She didn't know who Cathy was, of course, but she certainly knew Paul and Dave and she continued to watch them thoughtfully for another few minutes. "Well, well," she said to herself, "if it isn't my two very favorite officers of the law. Now, what oh what could those guys be doing in a joint like this, as if I didn't know?" With a smirk, she turned away and nearly collided with Krista, who was coming out of the ladies' room.

"I'm sorry," Krista offered, "I should watch where I'm going, huh?"

"That's okay," Tahlulla said amiably, then she noticed Krista's costume. "Do you work here, sister?"

"Yes, I do, I'm a dancer."

"How nice." Tahlulla looked her up and down and smiled. "With a body like that, you must earn yourself quite a lot in tips. And telephone numbers too from interested guys."

"I don't do badly in either department."

"Does your boyfriend mind you strutting your stuff behind his back? Assuming, of course, you have a boyfriend?"

"He does mind, but he works here too so he can keep an eye on me."

"He works here? How convenient. What does he do?"

"He works behind the bar. He's working tonight, as a matter of fact."

Tahlulla smiled again and Krista began to feel a bit uneasy under her not too discreet scrutiny. "Tall, dark and handsome is he?"

"Tall, *blond* and handsome, actually."

"I think blond guys are so cute, I really envy you." Tahlulla smiled her barracuda smile again and gestured in the direction of the bar. " Well, I'd better not keep you from your work. Take care, sister."

Krista watched her slink sexily away, puzzled as to why this stranger had been so friendly towards her, but having more important things to think about, Krista easily dismissed the incident from her mind. She had a few minutes before she had to start dancing and she wanted to have a few words with Paul, but she didn't get the chance because as soon as Petcelli saw her, he motioned to her to get up on stage right away. The bar had already been opened earlier than stated to regular customers by the look of things, but the numbers were few and far between, despite it being Friday night.

Five minutes later, he ordered Dave and Cathy to go into the other room. "And remember, you are not to discuss with anyone what you've seen." He looked at them meaningfully, then dropped his gaze to ogle Cathy's cleavage again. "Don't forget to show those babies off," he reminded her then, mercifully for him, he waddled away.

Cathy threw him a filthy look and continued to glare at him until he had disappeared from view. "Sexual harassment's another thing I want him charged with," she said coldly.

"And he will be, Cathy," Dave soothed. "Come on, grab a tray, fix a smile on your face - and let's go kick ass."

They soon discovered that the function room wasn't just "off" the changing room. To get to it, they had to go into the changing room, then through the door that had been kept mysteriously locked all week and then down a flight of steps. They hadn't even known a basement room the full size of the upper floor existed but at least it explained where Petcelli could hold a lot of illegal wheeling and dealings. When Dave and Cathy entered the function room, they darted a quick look around to take a mental stock of everything. The room was deceptively large, almost as large as the main bar area, and there were easily two hundred people milling around.

Their suspicions had been right all along, Petcelli was into gambling and already the poker, craps, roulette and black jack tables were fully occupied and people were standing waiting their turn at the numerous slot machines.

Dave whistled softly through his teeth. "Lookie here," he remarked dryly. "It's almost like being back home in Nevada." He turned his attention to the crowd, located Tahlulla and pointed her out to Cathy. "That's her, Cath, the redhead in the green dress."

"Leave her to me. Let's fill our trays and circulate."

Anytime Dave saw Tahlulla come his way, Cathy was always there to ward her off but then Cathy got stuck with a group of men who couldn't seem to decide what they wanted to drink and, trying to listen to their order, she could only watch in dismay as Tahlulla walked right over to Dave, tapped him on the shoulder and smiled winningly at him.

"Hello Sergeant Andrews," she purred. "Don't tell me you've finally seen the light and quit the force?"

Dave glanced quickly at Cathy, saw her plight as she gave him a helpless shrug and nodded briefly to her that it was all right, he would handle this accordingly. "Tahlulla, as I live and breathe. What's a nice hooker like you doing in a dive like this? Not turning enough tricks?"

"Even nice hookers can give themselves a night off once in a while. I saw your other half out in the other bar. Where there's one, there's always the other, which can only mean there's something cooking."

"I don't know what you mean," Dave said innocently. "Paul and I are just moonlighting here, trying to earn a little bit of extra cash, that's all. A cop's salary alone doesn't pay the bills these days. So, how's business?"

"Not bad, not bad at all." Tahlulla moved closer to him and placed a hand on his crotch, caressing him for all the world to see. "In fact, it's real good, big boy, so good I could offer you a freebie. Name what you want and it's yours, a hand job, a blow job, you want a quickie, old Tahlulla here can give it to you."

Dave grabbed her wrist and forced her hand away. "That's not nice, 'lulla, not nice at all," he scolded.

Her green eyes narrowed suspiciously. "Only a cop who's still on duty would turn down an offer like that," she goaded.

He laughed easily. "I told you, I'm just trying to earn a little extra money. Give it a rest."

"Hey, it's just so rare to find a man who's as well hung as you and it's always been a fantasy of mine to do it with a cop. You, Sergeant Andrews, you always have been my dream, my fantasy. Sometimes, when I'm entertaining a particularly boring client, I close my eyes and imagine it's you lying on top of me, emptying yourself into me. Paul's cute too and I wouldn't pass up an opportunity with him either, but you...Mmm, you're more my type. I could almost cream in my panties just by looking into those baby blues of yours. Would you like a little show? Watch as I bring myself off?"

"Not now, maybe some other time. What are you doing here anyway?"

"Xavier is a close, personal friend of mine and he invited me here tonight in return for a few favors." Her eyes narrowed again. "I take it he doesn't know you're a cop," she stated.

"Nope, and he's not going to know either."

"Which means there's definitely something cooking." She smiled cruelly. "Hmm, seems like it just might be payback time for old Tahlulla girl here." She backed slowly away, the same smile still on her face. "Maybe I'll cash in on it, maybe I won't. Keep guessing, sexy eyes."

Dave watched in defeat as she sauntered casually away, her hips swaying provocatively, her head held proudly high, drawing a lot of attention from several men with whom she flirted as easily as if she had been born to it. He saw Cathy was now free and he quickly beckoned her over. "We're in big trouble, Cathy, she's going to squeal, I just know it, so we're going to have to make our move. We have enough evidence now just by being in this room anyway, we can wrap this up right now. I'm going to try and make out our best line of attack here, you, in the meantime, make sure you don't let Tahlulla anywhere near Petcelli."

"I'll try. And oh, if she touches you again, I'll break her arm." With that, Cathy spun around and busied herself serving drinks again, leaving Dave staring after her in surprise, Tahlulla momentarily forgotten.

He smiled in amusement as he watched her throw Tahlulla a particularly nasty look as she passed her by. "Well, well," he murmured, "she can get jealous too. Interesting." He smirked to himself, then something occurred to him, only it was more a realization there was someone missing, someone who had been hovering around all night, playing a charming host. Petcelli.

Dave scanned all around the room but the fat little man was nowhere to be seen. He saw Cathy had a nearly empty tray and he hurried over to her before she could fill it up again.

"What's up?" she asked.

"Have you seen Petcelli?" he whispered.

"No, I was looking for him there but I can't find him. But Tahlulla hasn't been with him either. Maybe he's gone out to the other bar."

"Yeah, maybe." But Dave was starting to get a bad feeling, one that he always instinctively got when he sensed trouble. The warmth vanished from his eyes immediately and any relaxed nuances he may have been having were replaced instead by an alertness that would enable him to see everything and miss nothing. He felt as if someone was watching him from across the room and it only took a split second to see it was Tahlulla. Their eyes met and held and then, slowly smiling, she blew him a kiss. "*Bitch!*" he spat. "It's too late, she's already done it."

"Are you so sure?"

"Only going to be one way to find out." Dave set his tray down, coolly ignored someone who was trying to attract his attention for a drink order and strode purposefully over to Tahlulla.

CHAPTER THIRTY-SIX

As soon as Dave and Cathy had left for the other room, Paul leaned over the bar and fixed his eyes on Krista. People who had not been invited to the party had indeed been allowed to infiltrate the club, but the numbers were few and far between. It was slow going, but Paul didn't mind, he more or less had Krista all to himself like this and as soon as they wrapped things up, hopefully any time now, he was going to take her back to his place and this time, she was definitely going to be spending the night with him. He really didn't think his insistence that she do just that would put her off in the least.

Krista felt as if it was a waste of time dancing when there was only a handful of customers but she carried on with her duty, wishing Dave and Cathy would hurry up and get things under way. Ten seconds before she had started dancing, Paul had passed her a hastily scribbled note to tell her where Petcelli had sent their friends and all they had to do now was await their signal, but the signal seemed to be taking forever to arrive. It surprised her greatly when she caught a glimpse of the clock above the bar and saw she had only been on stage for about fifteen minutes. It had certainly felt a lot longer.

She felt Paul's eyes on her and she turned towards him. She couldn't fail to see the admiration and the lust on his face and, with a slow smile, she started dancing solely for him.

He watched her sexy moves in appreciation and the more he thought about taking her home with him, the more she seemed to read his mind and tantalized him even more. But his private performance was soon cut short when he saw Petcelli come waddling towards him and, hastily grabbing a rag, he straightened up and started wiping off the already spotlessly clean bar top.

Petcelli settled his bulk on to a barstool. "Bourbon rocks, Paul," he requested, "and take one for yourself at the same time."

Surprised at the gesture, Paul shook his head. "No thanks, Mr. Petcelli, I never touch the hard stuff, except on special occasions." *Very* special occasions, Paul was strictly a beer man, not that he thought the information was worth sharing with Petcelli.

"Suit yourself." Petcelli sipped on his drink, then turned to watch Krista for a few seconds. "Hot looking broad, your girlfriend," he remarked.

"She sure is, boss."

"Been going with her long?"

Paul flicked through his memory files to see if, on the day they had come for the interview at the club, had either he or Krista mentioned how long they had been going out together and, satisfied they hadn't, he gave a nonchalant shrug of his shoulders. "About three months now, I guess," he said smoothly.

"Serious, is it?"

Paul looked over at Krista and proudly puffed out his chest, a self-satisfied smirk on his face. "I like to think so," he boasted. "Who wouldn't be serious about a face and a body like that?" He hated having to talk cheaply about her like this, but right now, the situation seemed to call for it.

"Know what you mean," Petcelli agreed. "Where did you two meet?"

"At a gas station. I used to work the registers and stock the shelves and she came in one day to ask for directions. That was all it took."

"Lucky you." Petcelli glanced at his watch, then hoisted his bulk from the stool. "Keep my drink right here, I'll be back for it." He went over to Krista and led her to one side of the stage. "Take an extra ten minutes on your break, cookie," he said amiably. "Go spend some time with your boyfriend if you like, seeing it's not so busy - but don't forget to put on your robe, I don't want my customers may be getting jealous seeing you talking closely with another man."

"Thanks, Mr. Petcelli, I'll go get Candy right now."

"That's okay, she can come out at the regular time." He hadn't moved to let her past him yet, nor did it seem he was going to. "Say, how serious is it with you and Paul anyway?" he asked casually.

Hoping this wasn't his way of starting to put the moves on her, Krista forced a smile on her face. "Very serious."

"How long have you known him?"

"Not long, about three months, I suppose."

"Really? And where did you two meet?"

Krista glanced quickly over at Paul and saw he was watching this little exchange quite intently, but he was out of earshot and she inwardly groaned. They hadn't thought to concoct a believable story on their meeting and she sensed immediately they were in big trouble. "We met in a bar," she said, "I was there one night, with Cathy, and so was he. He offered to buy me a drink and we took it from there." It seemed like the most plausible scenario to pick, after all, thousands of men met thousands of women in bars all over the world, so why not her and Paul?

"And was it love at first sight?" Petcelli asked jovially.

"For me, yes."

"Nice to hear that sort of thing can still happen these days." He patted her shoulder with his sweaty palm. "Run along, cookie, I've got things to attend to." He watched Krista walk away, then returned to the bar. "Paul, come down to my office as soon as you've finished getting that order ready. Denise can set up her own drinks if I have to keep you longer than a few minutes."

Paul narrowed his eyes warily as soon as Petcelli walked away. He knew instinctively something was amiss and he wondered if it had anything to do with the conversation Petcelli had just had with Krista. Or maybe Tahlulla had spoken with him. Whatever it was, Paul was soon going to find out and he wished he could get a message to Dave and or Cathy.

Krista walked into the ladies' room and searched for her robe. Just as she pulled it on, a lady came out of one of the stalls and Krista recognized her immediately as being the woman she had accidentally bumped into on her way out to the stage earlier on. "Hello again," she greeted casually.

Tahlulla's green eyes gave Krista the once over yet again, then she smiled benignly. "Hello again, yourself," she purred. "Busy out there tonight?"

"No, not really." Krista began to feel uncomfortable under this stranger's cool scrutiny and she looked quickly around for Candy but she was nowhere to be seen, the ladies room was empty. She hastily tied the belt of her robe tightly around her waist and took a couple of steps backwards to the door. "Well, got to go," she announced cheerily, "I'm on my break and I want to spend some time with my boyfriend."

Tahlulla folded her arms across her ample bosom and arched a well-defined eyebrow. "Ah yes, he works here too. And you told me he's tall, blond and handsome. And like I told *you*, I think blond guys are really cute. If you're interested, I could show you where some action is."

"What sort of action?" Krista asked warily.

Tahlulla slowly circled her, looking her up and down and the interest in her eyes was not entirely lost on Krista. "You, me...and him, my place, any time you want. We could make our own sweet action, the three of us."

Krista didn't even try to disguise a shudder of revulsion at the implication of a three in a bed romp but, never having been one to raise her voice or display a temper, she easily kept her cool. "No thanks, that's really not our scene."

"Come on, don't be so virginal, be adventurous. Believe me, once you get used to the touch of another woman, a man's touch will never feel the same again. And I can guarantee your boyfriend will love you all the more for letting him live out what must be every man's fantasy - having two women at the same time."

"He's really not interested in that sort of thing. Neither am I."

"Why don't you at least think about it? There's no strings attached. You, me, him, one night. And if you like it, at least you'll know where to find me for the next time."

"No *thanks*," Krista said firmly. "Now please, excuse me." With that, she bade a hasty retreat, wanting to get as far away as possible from this bold, crude and presumptuous woman. It was the first time in her life another female had tried to hit on her but the novelty of that wore off after a mere split second and she squirmed in absolute disgust at the very thought of it.

Tahlulla remained in the ladies' room, laughing softly to herself.

After the first conversation with Krista, it hadn't taken much for her to figure out that Paul was the bartender boyfriend and it also hadn't taken much for Tahlulla to figure out too that Krista must be another cop working undercover. She had immediately told Petcelli that he had at least three police officers under his employment even before she had gone into the party and when he had received the news, and had found out who they were, he had informed her quite gleefully they would be taken care of accordingly.

She had enjoyed playing the little game with Dave after that, leading him to worry over whether she would tell Petcelli or not, when she had already done just that, and she had equally enjoyed this little scene with Krista. She loved getting the better of cops, it satisfied her no end, made her hot and ready for action.

Still laughing to herself, she returned to the party to do what she had come out for tonight and that was to win some money without having to lie on her back, her legs spread open, to get it.

As soon as she walked past the stage, Krista stopped and looked all around her in bewilderment. Paul was nowhere to be seen. Thinking he could maybe have just gone to the bathroom, she sat down at the bar, but when he still hadn't appeared after a good few minutes, she beckoned Denise over.

"Any idea where Paul is?" she asked.

"Yeah, the boss took him down to his office a little while ago. I was told to get my own orders so I don't know how long he's going to be."

"Oh, okay, I'll just wait here for him, I have thirty-five minutes to kill and I'm sure he won't be that long."

"I sure hope he won't be long too, I hate having to use the cash register, I'm always afraid of screwing up and if I make a mistake, there'll be hell to pay with the boss."

Krista tuned herself out to Denise's idle chitchat. She was starting to feel very uneasy but tried to keep her calm. She was just deliberating on how to get a message to Dave or Cathy when the bouncer who had stopped them on their way in earlier, approached her.

"Mr. Petcelli wants to see you in his office right now," he informed her.

"Why?"

"Something about your pay."

"My pay?"

"Yeah, Friday night's pay night. Weren't you told?"

"No, I wasn't."

"Whatever. Just come with me."

With a sinking sensation in the pit of her stomach, Krista arose and walked alongside the bouncer. He opened the office door for her and when she was hesitant to enter, he pushed her roughly inside.

It took only a second for her brain to acknowledge the scene that met her eyes and her first reaction was to scream in horror and protest.

But she refrained and stared coldly at Petcelli instead.

CHAPTER THIRTY-SEVEN

As soon as she had seen Dave coming towards her, his expression giving absolutely nothing away, but sensing she was in big trouble anyway, Tahlulla had bade a hasty exit to the ladies' room. After her little frolic with Krista, she had figured it would be safe to return to the party but as soon as she walked through the door, she felt her arm being grabbed by her left side and she was spun round to face a very angry Dave. She quickly adapted her come-on voice.

"Hey there, sexy eyes," she said. "Changed your mind about the freebie?"

"Shut up, Tahlulla." Dave was not impressed, that much was obvious as he positively glared at her. "What did you tell Petcelli?" he inquired coldly. When she stared apathetically back at him, he placed his hands on her shoulders and shook her. "What did you tell him, Tahlulla?"

"You're the cop, you figure it out," she answered smoothly.

"Did you tell him about Paul, me or the both of us?"

"What do *you* think?" she purred. "But okay, here's a clue. Who has busted me the most?"

"Paul," he admitted with a sigh.

"But *you've* busted me enough times too," she reminded him, toying with him and enjoying every moment of it.

"When did you tell Petcelli?"

She chuckled softly. "I really can't remember. Cross my thighs with silver and I might just get my memory back."

Growing impatient, he roughly pushed her away. "Once a whore, always a whore," he spat in contempt.

"Yeah, and once a pig, always a pig," she retorted icily.

"You're going down big time this time, lady," he informed her. "But if you want to save yourself a fortune in lost tricks, tell me what you've told Petcelli and I'll waive any charges you have coming to you. I'll even let you walk out of here Scot free, right now, no strings attached, if you tell me what I want to know."

"Tell me first what it is you're trying to nail Petcelli on."

"This little sha-bang that's going on right now, for starters. Also, drug dealing and, possibly at least five counts of murder. Enough said?"

"And you'll let me walk out of here if I tell you?" she asked, for the first time appearing co-operative.

"Right now, just like I promised."

Tahlulla may have been a high-class whore, but she was certainly no idiot, a cold, calculating businesswoman she could be through and through. "I ratted on Officer Cameron," she told him. "And of course, that hot little girlfriend of his. She's a cop too, isn't she?"

"Yeah, what was your first clue?" *Great*, he thought, *that's Krista in trouble now too.* "And when did you tell him?"

"Before I came into this party, at the start of the night."

Dave gritted his teeth. That had been over half an hour ago. "What did he say he was going to do to them?"

"He didn't."

"Tahlulla!" he warned.

"Okay, he just said he would take care of them. That's all he said, I promise you. Whore's honor."

He tried to assess if she was telling him the truth by looking into her eyes, but it didn't really matter if she was or not, she had told him more than enough and, if it was the truth, he didn't exactly have the time to stand here and exchange pleasantries with her. "Okay, get your fanny out of here. Don't speak one word to a single soul on your way out, don't even say good night, just go." He watched her slink away, not particularly caring he was letting her off so easily, he knew it would only be a matter of time before he ran into her again. He quickly beckoned Cathy over. "Time to get this show on the road," he said in a low voice. "We've been dragging our heels long enough."

"Where did Tahlulla go?"

"I let her go." He laid a hand on her arm. "Cathy, she told Petcelli about Paul and Krista and, although she didn't mention it, I'm sure she told him about me too."

"Oh no! Paul and Krista could be in a lot of danger, we have to help them!"

"Easy on, we also have to be careful." At her reluctance to obey his orders, and her obvious wish to go check on the well-being of Paul and Krista instead, he looked meaningfully into her eyes. "We *must* be careful, Cath. One slip up and Petcelli wins. I've noticed he has at least a half dozen bouncers floating around and, much as I'd just like to take each and every one of them out, we can't because there are too many innocent people around, so here's my plan..." He looked quickly around him, saw that most of the people in the room were too busy winning - or trying to win - to care what their friendly waiter and waitress were doing and he knew he and Cathy could very easily slip away when the time was right. "Because I can't trust Tahlulla, I can't afford to be on my own in case Petcelli's goons are waiting to jump me, so it's up to you to call for back-up, okay?" He stopped and instantly shook his head. "No, bad idea. If Petcelli knows Paul and Krista are cops, chances are he has put two and two together and has figured out you're one too because you all came in together on the very first day, very obviously friends. Damn, that wasn't one of our better ideas to do it that way, was it? But with you and Krista having the same accent, we really didn't have a lot of choice, it would have been too suspicious and -"

"Hurry up and decide what we're going to do, Dave," she interrupted impatiently. "Every second we stand here twiddling our thumbs only gives Petcelli more time to do what he wants with Paul and Krista."

"Do you think I don't know that?" Dave was getting anxious too but at the moment, they were in a bit of a bind, something they hadn't anticipated. What was supposed to have been an easy bust had turned into something far more serious... and all because of a whore called Tahlulla. "Okay, first, let's calm down here. Have you any sort of a plan?"

"Yes, and it's dead simple really. If you can let me use your mobile phone, I'll find a quiet area and call to request a backup. As soon as more officers arrive, we can go rescue Paul and Krista. Nothing can happen to either one of us in here, there are too many witnesses around, so I think we're safe. Once the back-up arrives, they can get rid of the bouncers, leaving us to get Petcelli."

"Good, Cathy, sometimes the most simple of plans can be the most effective." He pulled out his cell phone, hit the unlock button and checked to see if he had a signal down here in the bowels of the building. He had a couple of bars, good enough. "Here you go, baby, but -"

"I know, be careful." She flashed him a brief smile and went over to the side of the bar, which was the quietest area she could find right now.

*

Krista switched her gaze from Petcelli to Paul. "Are you okay?"

"Nope, I'm losing the circulation in my wrists, no big a deal really. Could be worse, could be my neck." As soon as Paul had walked into Petcelli's office, two bouncers had grabbed him, tied his hands behind his back and pushed him roughly into a chair, all before he'd had the time to realize what was happening. Paul hated surprise attacks, he totally loathed them, but usually his reflexes kicked in quickly enough to be able to do something about them. This time, his reflexes had let him down and he made a mental note never to let that happen again. A real master at keeping his cool, no matter the circumstances, he watched expressionlessly as Krista was tied up too and was forced to sit in the chair beside him. "Hey, never let me say any date with you isn't interesting, baby," he said to her.

"Shut up," Petcelli barked. "Troy, search the lady. Brad, watch him."

The bouncer called Troy moved towards Krista but Paul didn't want him anywhere near her and he quickly turned his attention back to Petcelli. "Use your head, man, your goons have already searched me and they found two guns, one which belongs to Kris. Look at what she's wearing, where is she going to hide a piece under that robe?"

Petcelli seemed to agree that Paul could be right and he clicked his fingers for Troy to retreat, which he did. Petcelli picked up one of the guns lying on his desk and looked at it with a lot of interest. "Pretty much police issue but still nice. What is it, a Glock, Gen4? Smooth action, no feed jam, takes, what, a 15-round magazine for that little bit of extra protection? Nice gun, Paul, real nice."

"How come you know so much about firearms?" Paul asked dryly.

"Served my country in the first Gulf War, way back in the early 90's when you were making your momma sorry you'd ever been born. Took a bullet myself, in the stomach. Since then, I've developed a keen interest in weapons."

"Didn't know bullets could make it through so much blubber."

"On the contrary, that was when I weighed a sprightly hundred and seventy. How many bad guys you shot down with this baby, Paul?"

"I really can't remember, I lost count after the first five or six."

"Is that all?"

"Yeah.... five or six *hundred*."

"Cute. Were you planning on using it on me tonight?"

"If the situation had called for it, yes, I would have, without even a second thought."

Krista was admiring Paul greatly for his nonchalance, he seemed so totally relaxed and she figured that if he could do it, so could she. "Paul, honey, when we get out of here tonight, will you massage my wrists for me? I see what you mean about losing the circulation."

He glanced at her in amusement. "Of course, I'll do that for you." He was proud of her, he didn't have to be too worried about her because she could obviously act as cool as he was.

"Shut *up*" Petcelli snapped again. "Kris Riley. That's not your real name, is it?"

Krista shook her head. "Nope."

"What's your real name?"

"Detective Krista Nolan," she said sweetly. She knew there was no point in pretending anymore, he obviously knew she and Paul were officers of the law, the fact he had taken them hostage like this was a dead give away. "Seeing we're getting to know one another better, what's yours?"

Petcelli ignored her and looked back at Paul. "And you are Detective Sergeant Paul Cameron."

"Seems like we can't get anything past you, Petcelli. Who told you anyway? No, let me guess... Tahlulla, right?"

"Who's Tahlulla?" Krista asked, then rolled her eyes in mock exasperation. "Yet *another* of your ex-girlfriends, Paul?"

"Not this time. Tahlulla's a true-blue hooker, busted her a couple of times. I'm sure you'll get to meet her before too long. Keeps offering me freebies, I may warn you, but don't worry, I keep turning her down. Seems like she may have the hots for me... my partner too, just to prove she ain't fickle. She's at the party tonight."

"I know who your partner is, Cameron, so you don't have to conceal his identity any longer," Petcelli smirked. "Dave Mitchell, aka Dave Andrews. Tahlulla told me I had at least three police officers under my care, at *least* three. I'm willing to bet there's another officer floating around, poking his - or of course *her* - nose into my business. I'm even willing to go all the way and bet it *is* a she. One of my business associates gave me a description of two detectives who came down to see him the other day, two detectives, a male and female. The description of the male sounded just like Dave Andrews, the female exactly like that cute little waitress with the cute little ass. Cathy, right? That was a nice touch saying she was from South Africa, real nice."

"You know, you're right on one thing, Petcelli," Paul said calmly.

"Only one thing?"

"Yeah, Cathy *does* have a cute little ass and you should know, you've patted it often enough."

"Always was one for a nice piece of tail." Petcelli suddenly heaved his bulk off the chair, walked out from behind his desk and came to stand directly in front of Krista. As she looked coolly up at him, trying to second-guess his next move, he placed his hands on his ample waistline and leaned over closer to her. "Any piece of tail, little lady, particularly one like yours. Stand up, give us a look at yourself."

She narrowed her eyes in derision and slowly shook her head. "Not on your life, Petcelli. I've had to exploit myself enough this week, thanks to you."

"How about I make you do as I say?" He moved to part her robe but she was more than ready for him.

"How about I have a better idea instead?" Before he could touch her further, she raised her foot and kicked him dead center in his crotch. She smirked in satisfaction when she heard him grunt, then double over and turn away from her.

The two bouncers moved towards her and the one called Brad lifted his hand in preparation to strike her but Paul would have none of that and was already prepared. He leapt out of his chair, neatly head-butted Brad, who fell to the floor like a stone, then, whirling round on one leg, Paul kicked the other bouncer on any part of his body he could make contact with. He got him square in the middle of his chest but, unfortunately, rather than just wind him, he couldn't do much damage.

Troy's fist connected brutally with Paul's jaw and he staggered back but before he could prepare himself for a return attack, out of the corner of his eye, he saw Petcelli grab a gun and point it directly under

Krista's chin.

"Sit down right now or else she bites a bullet," Petcelli warned.

"Don't do it, Petcelli. Don't do it."

"I hardly think you're in a position to give out orders, Detective Cameron. One more stunt like the two of you have just played and she's dead."

Paul looked helplessly at Krista, but her gaze back at him was completely unwavering, immediately calming him down again. She wasn't going to let her fear show, neither should he. Forcing a smile on his face, he gave an apathetic shrug of his shoulders. "Okay," he said lightly, "You win, Petcelli. For now."

"Shut up and sit down." Petcelli waited for Paul to take a seat, then signaled to Troy to stand behind Paul to make sure Paul couldn't move again. Petcelli took the gun away from Krista's head and pushed her roughly back to her seat. "You really are a dumb, stupid bitch, you know," he told her. "Kicking me like that has not only made me very angry but has also earned yourself a real hard time from here on in... and your lover boy is going to be the one paying the price for your stupidity. How do you like that idea?"

"It's a very good one," she acknowledged and, although outwardly she was still very calm, inwardly, her heart had started hammering nervously in her chest. "I suppose it means you're going to kill him and make me watch him die, something like that?"

"Yeah, something like that. Any objections?"

"Any number of them, yes, but I really don't want to tell you what they are. I mean, you've made it clear that I'm in big enough shit as it is so I don't want to antagonize you any further."

"Wise decision."

"Hey, before you kill me," Paul interrupted, "were you suspicious about us before Tahlulla told you about us?"

"Why's that important?"

"Because if I'm going down, when my Captain gives a eulogy at my funeral, I just want everyone to know what a fine undercover job I did on my last assignment. I'll rest easier in my grave knowing that."

"You crazy son of a bitch. But okay, in that case, no, I wasn't suspicious, not at all. Tahlulla drew me to your attention tonight and it seems I owe her big for this one. But to reaffirm what she had told me - she's a good friend but she *does* tend to spin tales now and then - I asked the two of you where you had met and you each told me different stories."

Paul and Krista glanced at each other. "What did you tell him?" he asked.

"I said we met in a bar. You?"

"At a gas station. Next time, we'll concoct a proper story."

"Yeah, next time let's say we met in a park or on the beach or someplace really romantic."

"There isn't going to *be* a next time," Petcelli reminded them.

"I wouldn't say that," Krista stated, "don't you know the good guys almost always win?"

Paul tuned himself out from what she was saying and let his eyes dart around the room, trying to find something of use that would at least help him get of his restraints. Brad was still lying on the floor but he was slowly starting to come to, which meant their odds had just worsened again. Paul cursed into himself and wished he could reach the knife style letter opener he had just spied lying on top of the desk, but even if he could have reached it without anyone seeing him, he wouldn't have been able to use it on his ropes because of the bouncer standing directly behind him.

He glanced up at the wall clock and estimated he and Krista had been in here for about fifteen minutes, twenty tops. That was far too long for his liking, Dave and Cathy should have figured by now there was something wrong. But then he reminded himself that Petcelli knew their true identities too which could only mean they were in grave danger now as well.

Dave watched Cathy speak into the phone then, when she hung up, she turned to him with a curt nod. He went over to her. "How long?"

"Ten minutes or sooner, I was guaranteed. I suppose we'd better keep working, I don't want to draw any more suspicion to us."

"Good idea." He watched as she grabbed her tray, forced a smile on her face and started circulating again and he couldn't help admire her greatly for her coolness when he knew she was really worried about Paul and Krista. He was too, of course, it wasn't exactly in his nature to just stand around doing nothing while his best friend was, in all likelihood, in great trouble. But sometimes, like now, the circumstances called for him to bide his time, so he carefully bit down his impatience.

Exactly seven minutes after Cathy's phone call, four uniformed police officers surprised everyone by suddenly barging into the function room. Everyone stood staring at everyone else, wondering what could be happening, but Dave deliberately wanted to wait a few minutes to put an end to their curiosity.

"Ladies and gentlemen, please," he called over the racket of the jangling slot machines, "if I may have your attention, I'll get back to you all in one moment." He went over to the nearest officer. "Hey, Joe, how many more men you got out there?"

"Four, Sarge, with another three units on their way. The boys are clearing the other bar and two bouncers have already been rounded up, just as Detective Edwards requested we do soon as we arrived. But I thought she said there were six bouncers to take care of first?"

"There are two in here, for sure. See the real mean looking guy over by the bar? He's one and so is that guy over by the nearest poker table. Petcelli must have the other two with him. Get these two out of here, I don't know if they're armed or not and they're making me nervous just by looking at them. And when I get nervous, I tend to get trigger happy. Catch my drift?"

"Loud and."

The two bouncers surrendered without much of a protest and Dave waited until two officers had escorted them from the room before he did anything to satisfy the partygoers' growing curiosity. Joe and another officer had started going around the room, with a police photographer following them, shooting pictures of the slot machines and roulette tables and anything else gambling related while the two officers ushered the crowd together.

Dave signaled to Cathy to come and stand beside him, which she did. "I am Detective Andrews of the Bathville P.D.," he announced loudly, "and this is Detective Edwards. The scene you have just witnessed is our first step in closing this place down. Tonight." As expected, an angry murmur started up and he had to raise his voice even higher to be heard. "The Blues Haven is operating this gambling party without the proper license, making this an entirely illegal operation. Because of that,

I'm sorry, but this party has to end right now."

"What do you mean, illegal?" Someone wanted to know. "We were invited here tonight under the indication we wouldn't be breaking any laws."

The naivety of some people never ceased to amaze Dave. "Whatever Mr Petcelli has chosen to tell you, it is obvious you have all been misinformed. We'll be taking a list of your names to keep on record and any further grievances you may have, you'll have to take up with Mr. Petcelli's attorney. After you give your names, you are free to go, but you will all be called to appear at the 7th precinct for questioning in the near future."

"But what about our winnings?" Someone else wanted to know.

"Any winnings... or losses, for that matter, again, you'll have to discuss with Mr. Petcelli's attorney." Dave beckoned Joe over. "Finish off here, will you, and make sure you use the proper procedure, I don't want any mistakes being made. Cathy and I are going to find Paul and Krista."

Cathy followed Dave out of the room but she stopped outside the ladies' room. "I'll only be a moment."

"You need to pee at a time like this?" he asked in surprise.

"Course not, but my bag's still in there.... with my gun in it."

Moments later, they entered the main bar area and Dave, who was leading the way, looked swiftly around him. Save for two officers, the only other person around was Denise, who was looking all around her in bewilderment. As soon as she saw Dave and Cathy, she ran over to them.

"What's with all the cops?" she wanted to know. "Did someone commit a crime?"

"Yeah, Petcelli sure did," Dave told her. "Look, Denise, you'd better split, things could get rough around here and I don't want - "

She peered up at him suspiciously, then at Cathy. "Are you two cops?"

"That's right," Cathy said. "Why don't you do as Dave suggested, huh?"

"I will, I -" Denise trailed off and suddenly buried her face in her hands. "Oh, I'm so glad something's being done about that man, he's had this coming for a long time and after what he did to Ruth, I -"

"What do you know about Ruth?" Dave interrupted sharply.

"I saw something happening in his office the other night. He was beating her around a bit and saying all kinds of threatening things to her, only I never knew what became of it because she disappeared almost immediately afterwards and I haven't seen her since. Is she...has she...is she okay?"

Cathy slowly shook her head. "No, Denise, I'm sorry, she's not okay. I'm afraid Ruth has been murdered."

Denise's slender fingers trembled over her mouth and she moaned softly. "Dear Lord, don't tell me."

"It's true, I'm sorry. Do you think you saw enough the other night to give a formal statement to us so we can tie her murder with Petcelli?"

"I don't know, Cathy, I'd like to...but won't I get into trouble for holding back information? I mean, I saw what happened and I should have gone to the police there and then but I was frightened because I know Petcelli saw me watching what he was doing."

"You're not in any kind of trouble, Denise, far from it. We know what Petcelli's capable of and we know you have only been trying to keep yourself from harm. Come down to the 7th precinct tomorrow, any time you like, and just ask for me, Detective Edwards, I'll be there to take your statement. In complete confidentiality too. We need all the help we can get in making sure Petcelli will go to jail for a very long time."

"Okay, Cathy, I'll be there. I promise."

"Good girl. Now go on, get out of here, and I'll see you tomorrow."

"Just one more thing, Denise," Dave said, "Do you know the whereabouts of Paul and Krista? And Petcelli too, for that matter."

"Yes, they're all down in his office, been there for about twenty minutes now, I think."

"As long as that, eh? Anyone else with them?"

"Yeah, Troy and that bouncer who stopped me on my way in tonight."

"Thanks, Denise, you've been a great help. See you tomorrow, sugar." Dave turned to Cathy, pulled out his gun, checked it was fully loaded and cautioned her to do the same with hers. "Okay, Cathy, time to put an end to this, are you ready?"

"As I'll ever be, only..." She stopped, looked down at her gun, then nervously towards Petcelli's office.

"Only what?"

"Only.... well, what if I have to shoot someone?"

"You've never shot anyone before." Dave said it as a statement, not as a question, and at her nod, he looked purposefully into her eyes. "Don't let it intimidate you, Cathy, not even a little. A gun is a cop's best friend and if it comes down to a cop getting shot or a bad guy getting shot, I'd rather it was the bad guy, every time. Just close your mind and imagine you're only shooting at a target in the practice range. I've seen you in action there and you're good, so just keep that in mind, okay? *If you have to shoot someone tonight – and don't forget, years and years can go by before a cop gets to pull his gun, never mind shoot his gun – I promise I will stay with you and talk to you and only when I know you're okay, I'll make you an appointment for tomorrow morning first thing with the Psychiatrist the Bathville Police Department uses for this very reason. Okay?"*

She nodded hesitantly. "Okay. Now come on, let's go."

He led the way towards Petcelli's office and they stood in position at each side of the door. They couldn't hear anything from within, which only added to their worry. Dave put a finger to his lips, telling her to remain quiet, then he pressed an ear to the door, listened for a few seconds, and nodded.

"I've got a voice," he whispered, "and it's Krista's, that accent is a dead giveaway. On three, we go in, me first, you cover me, just like you've been taught."

Cathy braced herself and, magically, her nerves disappeared as she felt the adrenaline flow through her body instead. At the final count, Dave delivered a sturdy kick to the door, sending it flying open, then he rushed into the room, Cathy right behind him.

CHAPTER THIRTY-EIGHT

The first thing Dave noticed was that Paul and Krista were incapable of doing anything to help, but the important thing was, at least they seemed unharmed. As startled as Petcelli and the two bouncers were at the sudden invasion, certainly, but still unharmed.

Checking on their wellbeing first, he didn't see Troy lunge towards the desk and grab up one of the guns but the movement did catch his eye and he turned swiftly towards it. Troy had already released the safety catch and was raising the gun in preparation to fire, but that was as far as he got because Dave, quick as lightening, fired off his own gun and the bullet penetrated Troy high in his right shoulder, shattering his collar bone. The force of the shot flung him backwards into the wall, but he didn't collapse, he stayed in a standing position, his eyes bulging in pain and surprise.

For a long moment, as the loud report seemed to remain suspended in the air and the smell of cordite permeated everyone's nostrils, no one moved. But Dave was still poised, ready to fire again, until he saw the gun slip unbidden from Troy's fingers. Troy sank to his knees, blood pouring from the open wound and blossoming like a red flower over the front of his white shirt, then he fell forward, unconscious. There was no bleeding in his back, therefore the bullet was still lodged somewhere in Troy's body.

Satisfied Troy was no longer an element of danger, Dave picked up the gun, put the safety back on and slipped it into the waistband of his pants. "Cathy, keep Petcelli and the other turkey covered. Paul, Krista, you both okay?"

"We're fine, pal," Paul said.

Dave moved behind Krista to untie her. "Hey, Kris, don't you just love this job?"

"Yeah, I do... I think."

"Of course, you do, it's so much fun." Dave rubbed her wrists for her, helping her get the circulation back, then, when she told him she was okay, he moved to untie Paul too. "Well partner, haven't I always told you I can't leave you alone for even a minute?"

Paul chuckled. "That you have."

Krista massaged her wrists a little more, all the while her eyes trained on Petcelli. Then she smirked. "Can I be the one who puts the handcuffs on Petcelli, Paul? Can I, please?"

"Not *can* I, *may* I," he corrected dryly, "and of course you may."

Cathy stared stonily at Petcelli, her gun leveled right at him. The other bouncer had backed off a bit, but he was watching everything and just waiting for the right moment to make his move. Mr. Petcelli had given him very strict orders to eliminate anybody who might come between him and getting what he wanted and he, Brad, intended on doing his best to obey Mr. Petcelli's instructions. Although relatively new to Petcelli's employment, Brad had been assured by Troy time and time again that Petcelli was very generous to anyone who followed instructions perfectly. Brad was anxious to prove just how well he could follow anything the boss told him to do and now seemed like the perfect opportunity for him to show off.

Dave turned to lift the other gun off the desk, but when he turned back to pass it over to Krista, and when Brad realized Dave was now blocking him from Cathy's line of vision, he saw his chance. In one slick movement, he grabbed the letter opener, bounded forward and sank it into

Dave's shoulder, right up the hilt.

Paul had seen it coming too late but because he hadn't even had the time to cry out to warn his partner, he moved forward to grab the gun Dave had dropped as soon as he had been stabbed, but before Paul could do anything, another shot was fired. When Paul looked up, Brad was lying on the floor beside Troy, and he turned to stare at Cathy in surprise.

"Well done, little dude!" he congratulated. "Good shot!"

Krista, on seeing the look of horror that had come over Cathy's face, but not knowing if it was because she had just shot somebody or because Dave had gotten hurt, quickly moved towards her. She took the gun off her and kept Petcelli covered.

"Go see how Dave is, Cath," she said softly, "I'll take care of this creep."

Dave had sunk to his knees, his lips set in a thin, grim line and Cathy and Paul quickly knelt beside him. "Dave... oh my God... are you all right?" she cried anxiously.

A film of perspiration had already appeared on his face, but he nodded. "I'm fine," he said slowly. "Paul, what's it looking like?"

Paul carefully examined the wound and grimaced. "Well, I could lie to you, of course, and tell you there's nothing much to worry about, but what the heck, I'll just tell you the truth. There's a three-inch blade making itself quite at home inside you, which means, soon as the sucker is removed, you're going to bleed a lot, need four or five stitches and possibly a tetanus jab too. Can't say anything about any internal damage of course, but it could be nasty if any nerves have been severed. Is that what you wanted to hear?"

Dave looked at Cathy and when he saw how concerned for him

she was, he forced a lop-sided grin on his face. "Not really, but it will do. Think you can get the blade out for me?"

"*No*, Dave!" Cathy said sharply, "Let a doctor do it, please, that's the proper way to get it done, under the right medical care."

Paul knew Dave wouldn't be concerned about something as trivial to him as the necessary first aid care and he moved to console her. "It's okay, Cathy, Dave's as tough as nails, don't tell me he hasn't told you that already? Yup, he's a tough old son of a bitch all right, aren't you, buddy boy?"

"That's me," Dave agreed. "Cathy, why don't you go find Joe, get him and a couple of the boys to take Petcelli away and to get an ambulance organized for our two friends lying on the floor here. Will you do that for me?"

"But I -"

"No buts, baby, okay? Just go, time's a-wasting and Krista's arm must be getting tired keeping that gun on our fat little friend here, so you'd be doing her a huge favor too."

Cathy knew full well that Dave was just trying to get rid of her to allow Paul to pull the knife out of him as soon as she disappeared, but he seemed adamant about getting his own way so, after a moment's deliberation, she reluctantly arose. "Okay, I'll go, seeing it's what you want." She gave his lips a swift kiss. "But I'll be right back."

Krista caught a hold of Cathy's hand as she passed her by, and squeezed it tightly. "He'll be fine, chum, don't worry." When Cathy departed, Krista turned her attention back to Petcelli, who had gone strangely quiet. "Didn't I tell you the good guys always win?" she goaded cheerfully. He stared at her in pure, unveiled hatred and, quite unperturbed, she stared calmly back. "Paul, before you do anything for Dave, run out to the bar and bring back some ice. As soon as you pull that knife out, apply the ice over the wound with some pressure, it will help stem the flow of blood."

"Aye, aye, doc. Dave, don't you dare move, I'll be back in two seconds." Paul returned to the bar and when he came back to the office, he had ice wrapped up in a towel and also a couple of extra towels that at least seemed clean and dry to soak up the blood. He tore Dave's shirt right up the back, saw he had his work cut out for him in getting the knife out as painlessly as possible and mentally braced himself. "Ready, partner?"

"Just do it, Paul. If it looks like I'm going to faint, make sure I don't bang my head on the way down and that I have a nice soft landing."

"At least if you bang your head, you'll be nowhere near your brain area so no need to worry."

"Ha ha, you're definitely not fun -" Which was when Paul delicately but efficiently and swiftly, pulled the knife from his shoulder and Dave ended his sentence with a loud gasp and an even louder profanity. "Jesus, son of a whore!" he hissed. "Man, that hurts."

"You're nothing but a wimp, Andrews," Paul teased, "a big baby. That's why you sent Cathy away, so she wouldn't see you cry over a little biddy knife wound." But then Paul saw Dave had paled considerably, that he even looked on the verge of passing out, and Paul cut the idle chitchat. "Hey, Dave, stay with me, partner. You okay?"

"Just peachy," Dave answered after a few moments. His whole world was gray and swimming and dangerously nauseating right now and he literally had to force himself to remain alert. "Yup, just peachy. Am I bleeding much?" He jerked away suddenly when he felt the ice touch his skin and he twisted his head around to try and see what was happening.

Paul pushed Dave's head away so he wouldn't see anything he shouldn't, and finished applying a makeshift dressing. "Sooner I get you to a doctor, the happier I will be. Think you can hold on for a while longer?"

"Course I can, just help me up, there's something I want to say to Petcelli before he's taken away and it's something you and Krista will be pleased to hear about too."

Krista glanced Dave's way, then beckoned Paul over. "Keep Petcelli covered, I'll give Dave a quick look over." She kneeled down beside Dave, checked his wound, reapplied the dressing more expertly and even took his pulse. She smiled. "No signs of shock, Dave, everything is as it should be, you'll be pleased to know."

"Hey, lady, I like your bedside manner, it's head and shoulders way above Paul's."

"Eighteen months of medical training taught me something. Come on, I'll help you up, if you feel yourself getting light-headed, don't be afraid to lean on me, I'm a lot stronger than I look."

Cathy returned just as Dave got to his feet and she moved quickly to help Krista and to help him. "How are you?"

He swayed slightly but he got his equilibrium back and smiled for Cathy's benefit. "I'm doing good, so good I was just going to let Paul and Krista know about that little piece of information Denise gave us."

Petcelli, who up until now still hadn't spoken a word, suddenly snapped back to attention. "Denise?" he repeated. "What about her? What did that bitch say?"

"He talks," Paul stated dryly. "Shut up, I liked it better when you played the strong, fat, silent type."

"What did Denise say?" Petcelli demanded again, his face as dark as thunder. "What did she say about me?"

"My oh my," Dave said, "I don't recall saying that Denise gave over information about *you*, but now that it's obvious you want to hear, I'm only going to say two words. Ruth O'Brien."

Petcelli flinched back. "What about *her*? She's dead, she was found..." He stopped and clamped his lips together.

"How did you know she's dead, Petcelli?" Dave asked coolly. "Her death hasn't been leaked to the media yet so nobody but the police and a handful of construction workers know that she's dead. I think it's time someone read this asshole his rights before he says something without his lawyer present. I somehow don't think he'll give up his right to remain silent unless he has his lawyer beside him holding his hand."

Paul gleefully quoted Petcelli his rights, then fished his handcuffs out of his back pocket. He turned to Krista and grinned. "I was going to use these to show you a whole new game later on tonight," he joked, "but it doesn't matter, we probably wouldn't have needed them anyway." He passed the cuffs over to her. "Here, we promised you could do the honors, so go for it."

Just as Krista clamped the cuffs on Petcelli's wrists, two police officers and a medical team arrived. Dave had his wound properly dressed but he was ordered, as he had feared, to get to the hospital as quickly as possible because he definitely needed stitches.

Petcelli was led away as soon as the bouncers were taken away on stretchers and the undercover part of Cathy and Krista's first case was now officially over. The exuberance they should have felt was only marred by Dave's injury, neither of them, particularly Cathy, would be happy until he was given full medical treatment.

Paul could see the worry in her eyes and he gave her a quick hug. "Take Dave down to the hospital, Cathy. I'll wait for Krista to get changed and we'll both see you down there, okay?"

"Sure. Dave, where are your car keys?"

"In my pocket, but I don't know if I want you driving my car or not."

"Why not?" she asked in surprise.

"Can you handle a car with five gears?"

"I drove a car with *six* gears, seven, if you want to include reverse too," she returned smartly. "You were with me when I got my new car, remember? The one that's a six speed?"

Dave looked at her in amusement. "Asked for that one, didn't I? But I've seen your driving too and you seem to like speeding. My car's not accustomed to being driven all that fast."

"I'm not the one who broke the speed limit trying to get here tonight," she reminded him and fished the car keys out of his pocket. "Come on, you're still bleeding and I want you to get all better."

"Does that mean you're going to kiss it better for me?" he asked hopefully.

She rolled her eyes. "I can see you're getting delirious so on that note, good bye, Paul, Krista, I'll take care of him and we'll see you later."

She put her arm around Dave's waist to escort him out to the car and, for the last time, walked out of the Blues Haven.

In the police unit that was taking Petcelli to jail, the prisoner was sitting uncomfortably in the back seat, his hands cuffed behind his back. The cummerbund of his tuxedo had popped open and his bow tie was loose, giving him a disheveled, drunken appearance.

But, despite his outward appearance, anyone who might have happened to look more closely at Xavier Petcelli would perhaps have stopped looking very quickly once they saw into his eyes.

There was nothing in them…nothing at all. No anger, no sorrow, no outrage, no guilt…nothing that should have been there at least. The only glimmer of emotion was that of someone on the brink of madness.

CHAPTER THIRTY-NINE

When Paul arrived at the office the next morning, he was surprised to see Dave was there too. "Hey, Big D," he greeted. "How's the shoulder? And I thought you were told to take it easy?"

Dave spun round in his chair to face his friend and shrugged out of his sling. "I *am* taking it easy, I'm only here to see how the interrogations go. You, Krista and Cathy will be doing most of the work."

"Hey, put that sling back on, it's to take the weight off your shoulder. Cathy nagged you to death about it last night, didn't she get through to you at all?"

"She did...sort of." With an over-exaggerated sigh, Dave put the sling back on, then he suddenly smiled. "She'll probably kill me for telling you this but on the way to the hospital last night, she cried real tears. For *me*. Can you believe it? She was so upset I had gotten hurt, it was really very touching and... well, I don't think any other woman has ever cried for me before. It was actually a real neat feeling."

"I'll bet it was. And it's real neat you and she seem to be getting closer and closer."

"It hasn't even been two days, Paul, give us a chance." But Dave couldn't keep a self-satisfied smirk from spreading across his face and he shrugged in admission "You're right though, it is neat."

"Of course, I'm right. And speaking of Cathy, I think she handled herself very well last night, in fact, both girls did. You should have seen Krista when she was brought into Petcelli's office and she saw that I had been captured. For a second, just a second, she looked like she was going to lose it, but she didn't and she was just so cool, it was like poetry in motion, man. Some of her one-liners greatly impressed me too, particularly when she pissed the hell out of Petcelli. I'm in love with a woman who's not only beautiful, charming, witty *and* great in bed - very great in bed...no, make that *amazingly* great in bed - but who's also cool, calm and totally collected when it comes right down to the nitty gritty."

"Uh huh." Dave nodded, then looked up past Paul's shoulder. "Hi Krista," he said innocently.

Paul whirled round and saw Krista standing in the doorway, the look on her face telling him she had heard every word he had just said. "Er, hi honey, been standing there long?"

"Long enough," she said dryly, "and thanks for all those compliments, but in future, keep our bedroom secrets to yourself."

"Hey, Dave's my best friend, I tell him everything, particularly if it's worth sharing and -"

"I'd quit while I was ahead if I was you, bro," Dave interrupted and gave Krista a wink. "Where's Cathy?"

"She's running a bit behind this morning, she's not feeling too good."

"Oh? What's wrong with her?"

"Nothing much, she just seems to be coming down with a real nasty cold. She'll be along in a little while. How's the shoulder?"

"Hurting like hell, but don't tell Cathy that, I'm trying to maintain a macho image with her."

"Good basis for a relationship, Dave," she teased. "Anyone taken a statement from Petcelli yet?"

"No, but you and I can go and see him right now, if you like," Paul said. "Dave, all right with you if I take Krista down to interrogation?"

One week ago, Dave would quite cheerfully have hit the roof at such a suggestion but this time, he only nodded his head. "Of course, it's all right, Krista needs the practice and who better than you to show her the ropes? I'm going to wait here for Cathy anyway and as soon as Denise comes, I'll help Cathy take her statement."

Paul and Krista went down to the interrogation room on the first floor and found Petcelli already there, waiting for them with his lawyer, Jeffrey Wilson. Petcelli had spent the night in the cells and he was anything but pleased about it if the sour expression on his face was anything to go by. But, even though no one else in the room knew it had even happened, at least the madness was gone from his eyes.

"Good morning, Mr. Petcelli," Krista greeted cheerfully. "Sleep well last night? I know I did, all tucked up in a nice, warm bed, nice soft pillows, it was awful hard to get up this morning, I can tell you, but it was actually worth it just so I could come in here and see you where you so rightfully belong."

"Eat shit, Nolan," Came the surly retort.

"That's no way to speak to a lady, Petcelli," Paul scolded.

Petcelli shifted his gaze to Paul. "Then *you* eat shit... and die."

"This is going to be fun," Krista remarked dryly to Paul.

Wilson stood up and leaned over the desk to address Paul and Krista. "My client has chosen not to answer any of your questions. He is pleading not guilty on all of your charges and wants to move for an arraignment date as soon as possible."

"Okay, if that's what he wants, but you've read the charges against him and surely even you can't believe he is innocent. Aside from the drug dealing and the gambling, both of which we now have enough evidence to prove he's guilty on, we're in the process of obtaining a statement from a witness who claims she saw Mr. Petcelli play a hand in the murder of a dancer who worked at the Blues Haven, the club he owned and operated."

Wilson stared calmly at Paul. "My client is well aware of the charges, as am I, Officer Cameron. None of us would be here right now if we weren't in accordance and I happen to think it's a waste of time us being here when my client is pleading not guilty and has the right to a fair trial to prove his innocence."

"I don't think it's a waste of time, Mr. Wilson," Paul said smoothly, "Detective Nolan and I have all the time in the world to sit here and shoot the breeze with you and your client, all the time in the world. We only have a couple of questions that need answering and seeing you are present, Mr. Wilson, here's one of them. Petcelli, did you kill Ruth O'Brien yourself or did you get one of your goons to do it?"

"That's two questions," Petcelli stated and wiped a thin line of sweat from his upper lip. "And no comment to either one."

"Convenient answer. Okay, try this one on for size. Are you responsible for the death of four other waitresses or dancers formerly in your employment, namely, Janine Garvey, Rachelle Sebar, Charlene Hadwell and Gloria Ho?" Paul knew this was a long shot, but just bringing up the names and getting Petcelli's initial reaction to them was why he was doing it.

A few seconds ticked by, then, his eyes narrowing and each hand clasped firmly into a fist, Petcelli said, "No comment."

Going by the body language alone, Petcelli may as well have yelled it out loud that he was responsible for the murders, but rather than bring it to Petcelli's attention that he knew he was as guilty as sin, Paul simply rolled his eyes as if exasperated. "How did I know you were going to say that? How long have you owned the Blues Haven?"

"Three years, you can check my lease."

"Don't worry, I will. Have you been running a gambling joint all that time?"

Petcelli smirked. "No comment."

"Surprise, surprise." Paul leaned back in his chair and casually examined his fingernails for a few moments. "You are aware that to run a gambling operation in your place of business in the Commonwealth of Massachusetts is illegal without a permit? A permit you have never applied for?"

"No comment."

Paul knew that if Dave had been here, lawyer or no lawyer present, injured shoulder or no injured shoulder, Petcelli's skull would have been making contact with the nearest wall by now. That was the way Dave liked to get results sometimes but Paul preferred the laid-back approach, it could prove to be just as unnerving. "Thank your lucky stars Detective Andrews isn't here right now, Petcelli," he said slowly, "he has a real mean, vicious temper, particularly when he comes across worms like you who try to wriggle out of telling the truth and hide instead behind a smoke screen of lawyers and easy, non-committal answers."

"I'll take that remark as concern for my wellbeing," Petcelli said smugly.

"Take it whatever way you please, I personally don't give a monkey's cojones. Oh, by the way, your records of employees are being passed to the IRS for further investigation. They'll be very interested to learn you've been scamming them for years now and since tax fraud is a federal offense, you're not just in big trouble with the cops, now you're also in big trouble with the Feds."

Wilson hastily scribbled something down on a sheet of paper, then looked up at Paul again. "What evidence do you have to prove that last statement, Sergeant?"

"It is required by law for an employer to take the necessary information on an employee as soon as he or she comes into his employment. Detective Edwards, who was also working on this case, found the so-called employment records in your client's filing cabinet in his office. There were very few social security numbers listed, no payroll book, nothing. What do you have to say to that, Mr. Petcelli? No, don't tell me, let me guess. *No comment*, right?"

Paul and Krista continued to ask questions for the next half an hour, each question only getting an unsatisfactory answer. Petcelli seemed to be getting more and more smug as each minute passed, but he clearly didn't know the damage had already been done, that his guilt was too obvious just by the perspiration on his face and the nervous failure to meet Paul or Krista's eyes when asked any given question.

In the end, frustrated but not showing it, they closed the interrogation.

"See you in court, Mr. Petcelli," Krista stated calmly and followed Paul out of the room after Petcelli had been taken away by the attending uniformed police officer, flanked by his now flustered lawyer. "If I hear "no comment" one more time, I think I'll scream."

"Yeah, you and me both. Let's go grab a coffee and join Dave and Cathy."

As they walked up the stairs, they met a couple of officers on their way down, who stopped and gave Krista a very appreciative once over. One of them even whistled.

"Hey, Cam, what you bringing this little lady in for? And does she have a sister?"

"Get out of here, Ernie," Paul said in annoyance. "Go on, go chase some bad guys or something."

Ernie smirked and folded his arms across his chest. "She sure is a sweet young thing, all right. She your latest conquest then? It's not fair you keeping all the good-looking broads to yourself, you should learn to share and share alike. She got a name?"

"Yeah, Detective Nolan. She's not my latest conquest, she's my last, and no, she doesn't have a sister. Now disappear."

"Oo, touch-y." And then, at Paul's menacing look, Ernie put his hat on and continued on down the stairs, but he was laughing merrily the whole way.

"*That's* the sort of remarks I was referring to," Paul said wistfully. "Did he bother you?"

"Not a bit, I rather enjoyed them actually. I like hearing I'm your "last conquest" and to show my appreciation, I'll stay with you tonight again." She paused and smiled sensuously. "If you want me to, of course."

"If I want? Baby, you don't even need to ask."

They found Cathy giving Dave's shoulder a look over when they arrived in the office moments later and Cathy glanced up at them. "Hello, you two, how did it go with our friend Petcelli?"

"It didn't, we got nowhere." Krista flopped down at her desk.

"Tell me how you're feeling? You sound terrible."

As if on cue, Cathy sneezed three times in a row. "I feel as bad as I sound then. Wonder what brought this on? You know I normally don't get sick, never mind get a cold. I could barely ask Denise any questions and Dave had to do most of the talking."

"Denise has been here already? Did you hear everything you wanted to?"

"Yup," Dave said brightly. "If all other charges somehow, miraculously, fall through, what Denise has told us is enough to send Petcelli away for a very *very* long time. And now that we've more or less got everything wrapped until the court appearance, all we have to do is tell Captain Hamilton the good news. Congratulations, ladies, you've completed your first case, and very well too, I might add. Paul and I are proud of you both."

"We had good teachers," Cathy said warmly, then sneezed again. "God, this is terrible, I can hardly breathe. I really should head home and lie down."

"I'll come with you," Dave said, "I don't like the idea of you being alone when you're feeling this bad. I can make you chicken soup and feed you cold remedies."

"Not all in the same bowl, I hope. But okay, follow me home then and nurse me back to health. Paul, Krista, good day, see you whenever."

"Take care, Cath," Krista said. "Keep warm. And if you need me, call me here, on my mobile, or on Paul's."

Cathy waved absently in her direction and left, Dave in tow. When she arrived at her apartment, she went right up to bed and after a few minutes had passed, Dave knocked softly on her door and entered her room. She was lying in bed, all bundled up and he laughed at her bemused expression as he sat down on the edge of her bed.

"Poor baby," he said. "Just can't handle the pressures of finishing your first case, huh?"

"I don't know and right now, I don't particularly care," she stated apathetically. "I usually don't get a cold, you know, I really don't."

"So you did this time, it happens. Do you want to go to sleep?"

"No, stay with me. Talk to me."

What he really wanted to do was crawl into bed beside her and just hold her but he knew that if he felt her body against his, he might only end up taking advantage of her and he didn't want to do that, particularly when she wasn't exactly feeling too good. "You know, you still look kinda cute, even when you have a cold," he said.

"Oh, I'm sure I do," she said dryly. She pulled her arm out from beneath the covers to rub her nose and he caught a glimpse of what seemed to be a very alluring nightgown. "What are you grinning at?" she asked suspiciously.

"Nothing," he said quickly and mentally pictured himself diving into a pool of freezing cold water. It didn't do the trick and he looked around the room for something to divert his attention. "That's a lot of books you have there," he stated, pointing to three shelves absolutely stuffed with hard covers and soft covers. "Mind if I take a look?"

"Go right ahead."

"I like to read too," he said as he picked out a few books at random and read the titles. Stephen King, John Le Carre, John Saul, so she liked horror and mystery stories. Interesting, he did too. She also seemed to like autobiographies and he was surprised to see a few books on the prophecies of Nostradamus and Jeanne Dixon. All these variations and not a romance novel in sight. "Can I borrow some of these?"

"Of course you can, take as many as you want. You can keep them too, or give them away after you've read them, if you like. I've got quite a few of them on my Kindle now."

"Thanks, I'll select them before I leave." Feeling it was now safe to be near her again, he sat back down beside her. "Why do you sleep in a king size bed?"

"Because I like to stretch out, lie diagonal sometimes, have as much space as I can in bed. I've been told I hog the covers too."

"Oh yeah? Who told you that?"

Cathy smiled in sudden embarrassment when she realized what she had just said. "Somebody I once knew," she said awkwardly. She looked like she was going to divulge further but at the last moment, she changed her mind. "Hey, you promised me you would feed me cold remedies," she said instead.

"So I did," he acknowledged. "Point me in the right direction and I'll have you one made in no time."

"You don't really have to look after me, Dave. I should be looking after you instead because you're the one with the injury. And speaking of which, I'm sorry for those tears last night. I didn't mean to make you feel uncomfortable."

He smiled gently. "You didn't. I was touched. It's nice to know somebody cares for me."

"I do," she said softly and looked directly into his eyes.

His smile slowly disappeared as he stared back at her and for a moment, he wished time would just stand still. He shrugged out of his sling and leaned over to give her a quick kiss but as soon as he felt his lips touching hers, he started kissing her urgently instead, not wanting it to end. With a soft moan, he pulled her towards him and moved his lips down to her throat as he gently peeled the bed covers away from her body so he could touch her. But although he desperately wanted to, he knew he shouldn't and he breathlessly pulled away. "Cathy, I - he said hoarsely, "I want -"

"They're in the medicine cabinet in the bathroom," she said softly, sensing his helplessness and wanting to put him at ease again. "The cold remedies."

He nodded and, without another word, he strode from the room. In the bathroom, he found the cold remedies but before he closed the cabinet door over, he scanned quickly over the other contents. A box of Tampax tampons, painkillers, cough medicine, eye make-up remover, face make-up, a packet of disposable lady's razors, cotton wool, bandages, Band-Aids and salve. Typically female contents and all vaguely reminiscent of what Terri had kept in their medicine cabinet during their brief union, only his stuff had been kept there too.

With practiced ease, he turned his mind away from his ex-wife, then, realizing examining the contents of a medicine cabinet in somebody else's house was a totally uncool thing to do, he closed the door and hurried downstairs.

While he waited for the kettle to boil, his mind kept returning to Cathy and the little incident in her bedroom just now. Nothing had really happened, he had just let himself get momentarily carried away, but it was all so crazy, she was stirring all kinds of emotions in him, new ones and old ones, safe ones and *very* dangerous ones and he shivered slightly when he realized he wanted to explore every one of these emotions as far as he could.

"But not today," he reminded himself. "It's not fair to Cathy with her feeling the way she is. Besides, I'm sure she'll have to have very strong feelings for someone before she'll let him anywhere near her, so forget it, Andrews, for now." So who had she been referring to when she had just said it was somebody she once knew who had told her she hogged all the covers? It didn't matter, whoever he had been, he must have been very special to her, and she to him, and at that thought, Dave felt an inexplicable, sudden stab of jealousy slice through his heart.

When he carried the hot drink upstairs a short while later, he was strangely subdued and all because he hadn't been able to justify his jealousy, but he forced a smile on his face, knocked softly on the bedroom door and entered. Cathy was sitting up this time but she was starting to look miserable and sorry for herself in the way that cold sufferers tend to do and the smile on his face became genuine.

"Drink all this up and you'll soon feel as good as new," he said.

"I'll only drink this if you put your sling back on," she challenged sternly and, knowing he wouldn't be let off so easily, he rolled his eyes in exasperation and dutifully did as she had requested. She sipped on her drink, peering at him periodically over the rising steam, her eyes narrowed thoughtfully. "You're not exactly accustomed to having a woman tell you what to do, are you?"

"Not really, but I could get used to it again, if only for a quiet life," he teased. "I happen to know that women are just born, natural nags so I learned to accept that a long time ago as a fact of life I just have to live with."

She smiled faintly but there was a strange light in her eyes, one that he couldn't understand. "Was Terri a nag too?" she asked softly.

He pulled back in surprise at her reference to his ex-wife. "I suppose she was, to a certain extent, but only if she didn't get her own way on something. I was only married to her for a very short space of time so I didn't get the chance to find out what she's really capable of."

"But you did love her, right?"

"I did," he admitted awkwardly, "or else I wouldn't have married her. But we were young, *too* young, I know now." He looked away but his expression was carefully blank and Cathy couldn't tell what was going through his mind. He obviously didn't like talking about Terri and she laced her fingers through his.

"I'm sorry, David," she said gently. "I didn't mean to pry, I'll change the subject."

He looked back at her and shrugged indifferently. "It's okay," he said quickly on seeing her remorse, "really, it's fine. That time of my life is firmly buried in the past and I can talk about it now without getting angry or even feeling hurt. Anything you want to know, just ask."

"I don't want to ask you anything, I want you to just tell me whatever you want. And if you don't want to, that's fine too."

But strangely, he did want to tell her and, after only a moment's hesitation, he started telling her everything about his ex-wife, how he had met her when he had been only seventeen and how he had fallen deeply and quickly for her, how he hadn't been able to wait to marry her and had done when he was eighteen and just out of high school. Cathy heard how Terri had been Dave's whole life, the very center of his universe, as he, he thought, had been the very center of hers. But after only six months of what he had believed to be wedded bliss, everything had changed in one fell swoop when he had walked into their bedroom one day and caught her in bed with another man, very obviously enjoying herself. He had walked out on her immediately, he hadn't waited for an explanation, hadn't bothered to pack a few clothes, hadn't even closed the front door behind him on his way out, he had just left.

"I was just so mad, Cathy," he stated. "I can't recall ever being so furious or so hurt in my entire life as I did right then and all I wanted to do was kill her or, at the very least, hurt her in the way she had hurt me. But I soon learned she wasn't worth it. I didn't see her again until our divorce and I haven't seen her since, nor do I ever want to. The wife I used to love is now a non-person in my eyes...." He paused and smiled vaguely, "and that's the way I want it to stay. I aborted her from my life and now I'm happy I did because if I'd stayed with her, I would never have become a cop, I would never have moved to the east coast and I would never have met Paul. I owe a lot to that guy, you know, he helped me through the first difficult months of the transition period, you know, the being divorced and three thousand miles away, so actually no longer being anywhere near my ex-wife and therefore not likely going to bump into her at the nearest convenience store anymore period, and then it all came easy again after that."

"You were so young, Dave, and I'm sorry you had such a rotten time thanks to her." Cathy felt like crying for him but she knew he didn't want either her tears or her sympathy so she swallowed the lump in her throat and forced a smile on her face. "Thank you for telling me about her."

"I'm glad I did," he said softly and he truly meant it, which sort of surprised him because she was still a relative stranger to him and he didn't exactly go spouting anything even remotely personal about himself to just anybody. But it wasn't lost on him either that Cathy was easy to talk to and he sensed that in talking to her so openly like this, they had just come one step closer to becoming more than just a new relationship, they were now becoming dear friends. "And now, young lady, that I have bored you enough with my life story, it's time for you to get some sleep - and no arguments, so don't look at me like that. Finish your drink, lie back and relax and when you wake up again, you'll feel tons better."

"If you insist, but please, don't leave me, stay with me. I mightn't fall asleep and I like your company so, will you stay with me?" She patted the bed beside her, hoping he wouldn't take the invitation the wrong way. All she wanted was to lie back and feel his arms around her but if she had only known that her suggestion was causing him all kinds of impure, lustful and totally delicious thoughts, she would have insisted instead that he leave.

He recognized, reluctantly, her innocent suggestion in the way it had been intended and steadfastly chased his impure thoughts away. But oh God, it felt so good to be having them at all. "Sure, I'll stay," he said warmly. He settled himself beside her, leaned against the headboard and, when he was comfortable enough that he wouldn't aggravate his shoulder, he pulled her into his arms.

Neither of them spoke anymore and when he carefully looked down at her a short while later, he saw she had, indeed, fallen asleep. Her breathing was a little raspy and congested, but she was at least lying peacefully, nestled snugly in his embrace.

With a contented sigh, he buried his face in her hair, enjoying the quiet and the tranquility and the feel of her in such proximity to him, a feeling, he knew, he could easily and quickly get used to.

CHAPTER FORTY

Cathy's cold hung around for a couple of days, but she didn't let it drag her down too much and she was able to carry on with her daily routine in her usual, cheerful style.

She was feeling too good about life in general, apart from the wonders and the joy and the expectations of her new relationship with Dave, she and Krista had received a high commendation from Captain Hamilton on how well they had handled their first case. He had even gone on to say how pleased and proud he was to have them on his team. His glowing praise meant just as much to them as Paul and Dave's had, but the girls knew not to let it go to their heads, they knew they still had a lot to learn and that what they had achieved so far was only a mere speck as to what still lay ahead.

At Petcelli's hearing, what should have been an open and shut case, proved to be anything but. When the charges were called against him, Petcelli's lawyer entered a plea of not guilty to each one. Although that had been expected, what was most surprising was the fact that as soon as the murder charges were called, with every single one of them, Petcelli held not a look of guilt or smugness on his face but one of complete and utter bewilderment, as if he honestly had no idea what he was on trial for murder for.

As each charge was called out, Jeffrey Wilson, Petcelli's lawyer, leaned over to his client, conferred with him for a couple of seconds and then would enter the not guilty plea. Wilson seemed slightly bewildered himself but also quite adamant that his client was as innocent as he was saying he was, despite the evidence presented against him.

When the fifth and final count of murder was called against him,

Petcelli amazed everyone present in the courtroom by suddenly and loudly breaking down into sobs of complete and utter dismay and fright.

"I don't know why you're trying to pin these murders on me," he managed to gulp, "I didn't do anything to those five girls, I swear I didn't, I never laid a finger on them, please believe me."

Paul and Dave glanced uneasily at one another. Petcelli's tears, although unnerving and totally unexpected, were also seemingly quite *genuine*. Tears could always be made to happen, especially if the actor was good enough, but the raw emotion behind Petcelli's could simply not be orchestrated.

The Judge seemed to be thinking the same thing because he asked Wilson to approach the bench, along with the District Attorney and after a few minutes of a conference, the Judge declared the hearing would continue in an hour's time, when Petcelli would hopefully have regained his composure.

Sitting in a coffee house half a block from the courthouse, Krista and Cathy were silent as they listened to Paul and Dave come up with new reasons for this latest turn of events.

"It just does not make sense," Paul said, not for the first time. "This is a completely different Petcelli than the one we saw last week at the club. It's almost like he's a completely different person, like a twin or something."

Cathy had just stirred more cream into her coffee and suddenly she looked up at Paul, her mouth open in surprise…and realization. "Oh dear God," she breathed. "Not a twin… Petcelli himself must be the crazy person that Herb guy was referring to. And didn't Gloria Ho, when she started to come out of her coma, say something, like "Petcelli, not

Petcelli"? That didn't make sense to any of us… until now… Petcelli's not a twin, but, perhaps… a schizophrenic?"

Krista, Dave and Paul stared at her for a long moment and then it was almost as if everything clicked into place for them too. "You think so?" Dave asked, although he wasn't really looking for acknowledgement. "Could it possibly be?"

"Best idea that came into my head today so far," Cathy said. But she was still shaking her head, still clearly not convinced that what they all seemed to know was right, was actually that – right.

"Okay, let me try and put this together again," Paul said and took a couple of seconds to sort it out in his head. "Petcelli really may not have actually physically killed those girls himself, but I can bet my last paycheck that he was the one responsible for their murder. I can also bet that his bodyguard, Troy Zellwig, will testify that Petcelli didn't kill the girls, but that whoever did, perhaps Zellwig himself, was only acting under Petcelli's orders. That would explain why Petcelli declared in court there that he didn't lay a finger on them. Technically, he's not lying… however, I do have to admit that his tears were just too… I don't know… *real.* I was watching his reaction closely when each charge was being called out and the only time he didn't seem bewildered was when the tax evasion, gambling and drug dealing charges were entered."

"Right," agreed Krista. "I was watching him too and although he didn't seem bewildered during those charges, and again despite the evidence against him, his whole demeanor changed soon as the Judge started calling out each victim's name. The other three charges are going to ensure he's put in jail for a very long time, perhaps as long as his natural life, why would he want to try and lessen the sentence by denying

murder charges? Massachusetts doesn't even have a death penalty so it's
not like he has that to fear."

"Hopefully he will have composed himself enough to let this
hearing continue without further interruption," Dave said. "His reaction
has certainly thrown us all for a loop and I'm anxious to get back in
control here."

The hearing got under way again and although still quite upset,
Petcelli at least managed to refrain from breaking down again. The
charges and pleas had all been entered and now the Judge started calling
on people to testify.

A number of people who had been at the party on the night
Petcelli's seemingly safe, sordid little world had come crashing down
around him, testified to the gambling that had taken place at The Blues
Haven and each person stressed they had been promised by Petcelli that
nothing illegal was taking place. The IRS representative proved that
Petcelli had never paid any employee income tax and then, as if to really
rub salt into Petcelli's wounds, The Blues Haven was not only closed
down, but a Health Inspector was called upon to give a report, the
building was declared a death trap and was ordered to be pulled down
immediately. And, to Krista and Cathy's immense delight, Denise,
Candy, Trixie and another girl from the club testified that Petcelli had
sexually harassed them repeatedly during their employment and those
charges were added to his ever-growing list. It was poetic justice indeed
for Krista and Cathy.

And then Troy Zellwig was called to the stand. He walked to the
front, still with his arm in a sling thanks to the mangled collarbone Dave's
bullet had caused, but even though he may still have been on heavy

medication, his eyes were clear and his testimony was to be entered as valid.

It came as no surprise that Troy had indeed been the actual murderer. It also came as no surprise that he had only been acting on Petcelli's instructions. Only two of the victims had parents present and as soon as they were aware they had at last got their daughter's murderer identified, they began to cry, silent tears of sorrow and hatred and pity and even relief, that now they could start mourning their daughter's death properly.

Troy's testimony only lasted about ten minutes and at the very end of it, he stole a glance Petcelli's way. No one saw them share a brief, conspiratorial nod.

Troy was ordered to be held over until his own hearing and, just as he was about to be laid away, all hell broke loose. Everything happened so quickly nobody really had time to react, least of all the bailiffs and security guards.

From inside his sling, Troy produced a semi-automatic machine gun. God alone only knew how he had managed to smuggle it through security but there would be time to think about that later. He took a balanced stance and started spraying bullets around the courtroom, maybe not meaning to hit anybody but killing two spectators outright and critically wounding three others nonetheless.

Paul grabbed Krista and threw her unto the ground, Dave did likewise with Cathy. They had had to check their guns with security so they had no means to protect themselves but that didn't stop them from raising above the benches every few seconds to see what was happening.

Troy seemed quite relaxed, walking towards Petcelli and firing the automatic all around the room. Petcelli flung his lawyer to one side and as soon as Troy was beside him, he let his bodyguard do his duty and cover him as far as the front door to the courthouse. Several security officers complied with Troy's instructions not to shoot and between the courtroom and the front door, no one else got killed or injured.

Paul and Dave, with Cathy and Krista right behind them, reached the front door just in time to see Petcelli get into a dark blue Ford Expedition SUV, being driven by someone Krista thought she recognized as being the bodyguard Cathy had shot when she and Paul were being held captive in Petcelli's office. His wound had only been superficial, apparently and they had all thought that at least until lunchtime that day, he had been in the hospital under police guard. They could only hope that nothing had happened to the police officer.

Troy kept Petcelli covered until he was safely down in the back seat of the powerful SUV and then, with one final spray of bullets to deter anyone from coming anywhere near them, Troy leapt into the vehicle and it sped off.

Dave was first to his feet and he sprinted forward. He was looking for the vehicle's license number but he quickly saw that the rear license plate was missing and he halted his sprint with a loud curse. The SUV was already a block and a half away, weaving in and out of the traffic.

Paul was on his cell phone, barking out to Captain Hamilton what had just happened, telling him everything he could think of, including the fact that there was no license plate to put an APB out on but he at least managed to give an accurate description of the vehicle, including the fact that the left rear wheel cover was missing.

The sound of approaching sirens, perhaps the paramedics, rang in their ears and then, when the shock of what had just happened hit home, the four of them stood breathlessly looking at one another, uncertain of their next move.

Three blocks away, the SUV stopped in an alleyway behind a Chinese restaurant. Brad, Troy and Petcelli got out and quickly transferred to a silver Toyota Camry. No one spoke, but their expressions were calm and smug.

Within twenty minutes, they were in an apartment on the outskirts of Bathville.

CHAPTER FORTY-ONE

The manhunt was on. Xavier Petcelli, Troy Zellwig and Brad
James were top of the list on Masschusetts' Most Wanted. Three days had
passed since the crazy stunt at the courthouse had been pulled and the
authorities were still no further forward in finding them.

Bathville didn't have a commercial airport but there were a few
private airfields in the area and within an hour of their escape, all airfields
were under tight surveillance. Logan International in Boston was alerted,
as well as several other airstrips within a 50-mile radius. Greyhound bus
terminals were placed under heavy guard and the major routes in and out
of the city, including the on and off ramps of the I-95 and I-93 were
patrolled round the clock.

As the original arresting officers, Paul, Dave, Cathy and Krista felt
duty bound to put more effort than any other law enforcement team into
finding the fugitives. Despite the added benefit of having the FBI
involved, they worked practically flat out in their search. The only event
they'd had to lift their spirits had been the discovery of the SUV that had
been abandoned behind the Chinese restaurant but they had found no
clues whatsoever after a thorough sweep inside and out.

Cathy had requested a copy of Petcelli's medical records but since
he had no known living relatives and only a few acquaintances, none of
who knew whom his Attending Physician was, finding his doctor had
been an arduous task in itself. But old-fashioned leg work, in the form of
physically calling each doctor listed in the yellow pages, resulted in
finding a Doctor Phillips who had treated Petcelli for close to twenty
years.

A sub poena to obtain the records was issued and when the

records were released, Cathy poured over them and read out the facts that they all already had suspected. Petcelli had been diagnosed with a type of schizophrenia, known in the medical field as undifferentiated subtype schizophrenia, over twenty years ago. After a hellish, bloody tour of Iraq, that had resulted in his gunshot to the stomach, his mental well-being had started a long downward spiral and through the remainder of the '90's, his mind started to show signs of subtle change. A new personality didn't exactly form, he didn't have hallucinations or delusions, rather he had periods of time when he didn't know what he was doing, nor would he ever remember that he had even lost time. Still able to function as fairly normal during those black outs was part of his illness and the only clue anyone would have that something was wrong would be the look in Petcelli's eyes, a look that was cold and calculating...and quite mad.

It was only when he had become a patient of Dr. Phillips that he was put on proper medication for him to live as near as normal a life as possible, as long as he remembered to take his daily recommended dosage. If he lapsed, his black out episodes could occur quite rapidly, but not always, sometimes a full day or two could pass before he would show any symptoms, providing he didn't take any medication in the meantime.

When he remembered to take his medication again, his dosage had to be strengthened until he was back to 'normal'. His illness was unstable, impossible to predict when it was going to strike without the medication and impossible to control without the medication at all. Although he really did try to take his medication regularly, when he became stressed or overworked, he just simply forgot all about it.

It was the promise he had made to his dying mother, the only person outside of Dr. Phillips who knew what was wrong with him, that he would continue to take the required medication and pay for any other medical treatment that came available as long as it was going to help him, that ensured he had hefty medical bills each month.

If he hadn't made the promise or if he hadn't become a patient of Dr. Phillips, perhaps Petcelli would have gone through the rest of his life on nothing but a killing spree. The 'crazy' person Herb had referred to had to be Petcelli because that was the night Ruth had witnessed the gambling party and too busy beforehand to remember to have taken his medication, Petcelli had panicked and gotten more than a little angry, enough that he had slipped into one of his schizophrenic moments soon as he'd seen her watching what was happening and had threatened to kill her.

Although he obviously hadn't, that night, any other time he was having one of his spells he would remember what she had seen and would threaten her any chance he could get.

The media or the police didn't know it but the exact same thing had happened with Gloria Ho only she had been attacked with the intention to kill almost straight away, simply because she had promised she was going to go to the police that very night and he could threaten all he wanted. Petcelli had wanted her to take her secret with her and he had indeed paid Troy $10,000 to finish the job he had begun on her.

As for Troy being able to smuggle the gun into the courthouse and past the tight security, it had been relatively simple for him. He'd had the gun stowed safely inside the sling that supported his arm and he told the guard that he had a metal pin in his arm so the machine would more than likely go off soon as he was scanned. When the guard went to physically frisk him, Troy merely grimaced in pain and said he couldn't move his arm yet. Afraid of hurting him and maybe inducing a lawsuit, and figuring a guy with an injured arm couldn't pose much of a threat anyway, the security guard had waved him through.

A week after the scene at the courthouse, Captain Hamilton ordered his team to take some time off, even if it was just an evening, to relax and do whatever they wanted as long as it had nothing to do with the case. He feared they were burning themselves out and he knew they needed the time to recharge their batteries.

Left with no choice, but figuring their Captain was right, Paul informed Krista he was taking her out for a romantic night of wining and dining. He didn't tell her where they were going but he did caution her to don her finest clothes, which was the only clue he was willing to give her.

Just as she finished applying the last of her make-up, she heard the doorbell ring and, knowing it could only be Paul, she felt a flutter of excitement at the prospect of seeing him again. Although they had spent most of the day in the station chasing up on several reported sightings of Petcelli, all of which were turning out to be like a reported sighting of Elvis, they really hadn't had much time together and certainly hadn't had any time to do any decent talking. She was missing him like crazy so she hurried to finish getting ready for him.

She stood back from the full-length mirror, gave herself a critical once over and decided she would do. She was wearing a linen jade green dress - it was her favorite color and also her favorite dress, Cathy had bought it for her for Christmas the year before and she hadn't had much of a chance to wear it. It was simply cut, with a short skirt, short sleeves and a round neck, but the simplicity of the style only served to make it a dress that could be worn anywhere for any type of occasion. All she could hope for was that Paul would like it.

She received her answer as soon as she walked into the living room and saw his reaction. He whistled slowly and appreciatively.

"Now I know why I couldn't wait to see you," he stated, "because baby, you look sensational."

She smiled shyly. "Thank you, and so do you." Which was a bit of an understatement, because in the navy suit, white shirt and navy tie with tiny little white polka dots on it that he was wearing, he looked good enough to eat. "Are you going to tell me where you're taking me yet?" she asked.

"Of course... I'm taking you... *out*. Which is all my lady needs to know, for now. Come on, your chariot awaits, reservations are for 7:30 and we'd better get a move on. Cathy, don't wait up, little dude."

"Which means, see you tomorrow because somehow I don't think you'll be home tonight, Krissie."

Krista smiled knowingly and gave her friend a swift kiss on the cheek. "See you, Cath."

Paul gave Cathy a kiss too and he was just about to escort Krista through the door when he paused. "Is Dave coming over to see you tonight, Cath? When I was speaking to him earlier, he was sort of vague about his plans."

"Then you know as much as I do, Paul, because I haven't spoken to him or seen him since this morning."

Paul and Krista looked at each other in bewilderment, then back at Cathy. "Er, Cathy, you two are getting along okay, aren't you? You didn't seem too happy at the mention of his name there and if he's done something -"

"Relax, Paul, everything's fine. We just decided the other day to take things slowly, that's all. Petcelli's disappearance is consuming too much of our time and we want to be clear of that before we can concentrate on ourselves."

"Are you sure?"

"Positive. We parted on really good terms today, I promise. Now you two run along, have fun and don't do anything I wouldn't."

"Famous last words," Krista teased. "Okay, chum, we're going."

Cathy closed the door after them and wandered into the kitchen to make herself a cup of coffee. She busied herself by watering the plants on the window ledge, but her stomach was empty and she decided that the best thing to fill it would be a slice of chocolate cake. Now that she'd put the sweet treat into her head, nothing could get it to leave and she knew she wouldn't be able to settle tonight without having some cake so, with nothing better to do, she started to make a cake and had just put the batter in the oven a short while later when the doorbell rang.

She hastily wiped her hands on a towel and went to answer it. She was surprised to see Dave standing on the doorstep and for an instant she wondered if maybe they'd made plans for the evening after all and she had forgotten about them.

"Hi, Cathy," he said, "Can I come in?"

She rolled her eyes in faint amusement and stepped back. "Of course you can, I'm sorry, I wasn't expecting to see you and I was just trying to remember if we had something planned for tonight."

"We didn't. Would you rather I didn't come over unannounced like this, that I phoned ahead first?" He followed her into the kitchen, not sure if she was annoyed with him, but her warm smile put him at ease again.

"You can come over anytime you want, I keep telling you that. Did you get your stitches out today?"

"Yes, I've been sewn back together and I'm as good as new."

"Good. I was going to call you later to see how you had made out but that won't be necessary now." Cathy poured him a cup of coffee and passed it over to him. "What's so funny?" She asked suspiciously when she realized he was laughing softly.

"You," he stated. "What have you been doing? Your cheek is all white."

She put her hand up to her face. "Oh. I was baking a cake."

"What did you do, bathe in the flour?" He gently wiped the flour away and was just about to give her a kiss hello when he suddenly looked at her with great interest. "Did you say you were baking a cake?"

"Uh huh."

"It wouldn't happen to be a chocolate cake by any chance?" he asked hopefully.

She chuckled. "Yes, as a matter of fact, it would and yes, you can have a piece as soon as it cools and I put the filling on it. Honestly, I'm beginning to wonder who has the biggest sweet tooth, you or Krista."

"Oh, Krista, for sure," he deadpanned. He watched her as she prepared the cream filling and he decided he liked seeing her at work in a domestic capacity like this. "What did you do all day? I'm sorry we didn't get to spend much time together at the station."

"We were like ships that pass in the night. You were busy doing one thing, I was busy doing another and still we're no further forward in finding our fugitives." She unclasped her hair that she had tied back when she'd been baking and ran her fingers through it, a vague look of apology on her face. "But no shop talk tonight, we have to relax, just like the Captain told us." She put her finger in the bowl, tasted the cream and frowned. She tasted it again. "Hmm."

"Hmm, what?"

"Does this taste sweet enough to you?" She dipped her finger into the cream again and, without even stopping to think about what she was doing, she put her finger up to his lips. It hit her too late that some men could take the action as a provocative come on but before she could pull her hand away, he grabbed her wrist and slowly sucked the tip of her finger and the cream into his mouth. She swallowed audibly. "Well?" was all she could say.

"I'm not sure," he answered evenly. "You try it again." This time, he dipped a finger in and held it up to her lips and, after only a moment's hesitation, she licked the cream off.

"Needs more sugar," she decided and hastily turned away, her cheeks flaming. That one simple gesture had set her pulse *racing* and she couldn't believe the intensity of it.

An awkward silence descended upon them, one that neither of them knew how to break and she kept her back to him as she washed up the dirty dishes, dried them and wiped clean the counter tops. She could feel his eyes boring right into her as she moved about and at last, she had the courage to face him. She smiled faintly but before she could say anything, he spoke first.

"Who taught you to bake?"

Surprise at the question calmed her down again and her smile became more comfortable. "I learned in Home Economics in school...and my mother taught me some too." She glanced at her watch. "Time to check the cake." She carefully opened the oven door and peered inside. "Rising beautifully," she stated and inwardly cringed at her choice of words. She hoped he wouldn't come back with a smart-ass answer and relaxed again when he didn't. "Not long now." She finished making the cream and this time tasted it herself, not wanting a repeat performance of the last time. "Soon as the cake comes out, we can go into the living room," she said.

Dave nodded slowly. "If you like." She had a tiny speck of cream on her bottom lip and all he wanted to do was lick it away and keep kissing her. At the very thought of that, alarm bells suddenly started sounding in his head but he hastily switched them all off and, without another word, he slid off the stool and in two easy strides, he was across the kitchen and standing directly in front of her. "This is crazy," he whispered. "I sense that you're suddenly afraid to be near me and I don't like that feeling at all. Are you afraid of me, Cathy? Are you?"

Her eyes carefully searched his and she slowly shook her head. "Not anymore," she said softly.

He sighed. "Good." He pulled her to him and kissed her as deeply and as hungrily as he dared, tasting the sweetness of her mouth and wanting her more and more and feeling his body trembling with longing for her. He couldn't halt his rising passion, he didn't even want to as their kiss grew even more intense and when she pulled her mouth away to catch her breath, he buried his lips at her throat and then, slowly, moved downwards.

They were each being carried along by the heat of the moment and she held his head to her breast, closing her eyes and moaning softly in pleasure as his fingers worked at unbuttoning her blouse. With a groan, he lifted her up, settled her on the counter, encircled her legs around his waist and pulled her to him.

She was just about to reach out to him when the timer for the oven went off, startling them at the same time as it jolted them back to reality. They stared at each other in bewilderment and shock.

Without a word, she leapt off the counter and hurried to turn the timer off but her senses were reeling, her head was spinning, her legs were totally numb and she nearly stumbled before she could reach the oven. She couldn't trust herself to speak, so she didn't.

He watched her as she put on oven mitts, lifted out two cakes and popped them out of the tins unto a cooling tray. "I, er, I'll leave if you want me to," he said softly.

She spun round to face him, genuinely surprised at his suggestion and at his obvious concern for her feelings, her heart ached with a very brief, very sudden but very real, feeling of love for him. It really only had lasted a moment but at least it hadn't scared her off. "But if you leave," she whispered shakily, "you won't get a piece of chocolate cake."

And at that exact moment, the strong feelings he had been fighting ever since he had held her in her bed when she'd been sick with the cold, won the battle and he knew he couldn't deny any longer how he really felt about her. "Okay, I'll stay," he said eventually, "but while we're waiting for the cake to cool, I think we should talk about what just happened, don't you?"

"What is there to talk about, Dave?" she asked as carelessly as possible. "You kissed me, you turned me on, I got carried away and then we were both saved by the bell, in a manner of speaking."

"But what if the timer hadn't gone off when it did? Would we have stopped anyway? *Could* we have stopped? I know I probably wouldn't have been able to because I was turned on too. Oh boy, was I ever?"

"I know, I could feel you," she murmured and shivered in delight. But then the seriousness of it all suddenly rammed home for her all the way as she started to come down from the high she had been riding ever since he had kissed her and touched her. "Dave, I don't know what's happening between us right now, I can't explain this to you or to myself. All I know is, I let you touch me and I let myself respond to you and I was willing to do anything you wanted me to do but usually...usually I like to wait for...well, I just like to wait."

"Until you love the person? And he loves you?" He hadn't meant to put her on the spot like that and he really wanted to tell her he was already half way there anyway, but he wasn't sure if this was the right moment.

"Yeah, something like that. I'm sorry, maybe I'm just old-fashioned, but that's just the way it is with me."

"Hey, it's a good quality so don't apologize."

She nodded, looking very pensive, then she gestured towards the living room. "Come on, let's go and sit down." And cool off a bit, she decided.

They sat down side-by-side on the sofa and for a while, neither of them spoke, they just collected their thoughts. He folded her hand into his. "You're very quiet, Cath, are you all right?"

"I'm fine, I was just thinking about...what just happened and I was also thinking that you're so incredibly sweet."

He looked at her in faint surprise. "How do you work that one out?"

"Because you just are, Dave, not every man would stop if they were as turned on as much as you said...as much as I could *feel*...you were. In fact, things could have turned very ugly very fast."

"I guess you're right," he mused, "but I've had years of practice at stopping myself in these sort of...circumstances." He smiled apologetically for his choice of words. "But now that I've calmed down some, and have had time to think about it, I think I could have stopped myself just now, with you, because it all comes down to respect. I happen to respect you, dear lady. A lot. I wouldn't push you into doing something you didn't want to do."

"But that's just it, Dave, I *did* want to. And I'm sort of surprised at myself that I was willing to just let you...willing to let myself...well, you know." Cathy lowered her eyes, feeling a bit awkward at talking so intimately with him. This was the first time this sort of conversation had taken place between them and she felt a bit out of her depth. But she needn't have worried too much because he seemed to understand and he put his arm around her.

"I know," he said softly. "But don't be surprised anymore. I used to be able to turn away from any woman I was ever with without even giving her a second thought, but ever since you first kissed me - and I'm referring to our first kiss that Thursday night outside the club - my will power has managed to fall by the wayside. In fact, the number of cold showers I've had to take because of you..." He chuckled as he recalled that he wasn't exactly joking. "Anyway, that's the truth, you kiss me, I get so turned on... and it's a beautiful feeling."

Cathy suddenly sat up stiffly and looked at him in bewilderment. "Wait a minute, are you telling me I can turn you on with just one kiss?"

"Are you kidding me?" he cried in astonishment. And then he saw something in her eyes he was beginning to recognize all too well now: her insecurities. He wanted to do something, or at least say something, that would help her overcome these insecurities and maybe at the same time, he could make her feel good about herself. "It's not just your kisses that are a turn on to me, Cathy, everything about you is...and I do mean *everything*."

"Oh yeah?" she asked dubiously.

"Yeah. And I want to tell you a mere few of those things."

"But Dave, it's really not necessary."

"It's okay, I don't want you to feel uncomfortable, I just want you to hear the truth, so here goes." He closed his eyes, rested his lips on her cheek for a moment and inhaled deeply. "From the very start, your smell has turned me on, you smell so damned good... clean, fresh...musky...my favorite scent on a woman. I've even fantasized about your scent and before you might start to think I'm some sort of weirdo, I'm really not." He leaned back and carefully looked over her whole face, as if deciding which part of it he could talk about first. "Do you know your smile can turn me on too? The way your mouth turns up at the corners, that tiny little dimple that sometimes appears on your right cheek, it's so cute. You have a lovely smile, Cath, and as long as you keep smiling at me, that's all I want." He looked her slowly up and down, she had so many attributes, he wanted to take stock of them and tell her about each and every one. He could see she was becoming more than a little awkward because of his words so far but he wanted to get through to her just how special a person she was to him. "Your walk happens to be a major turn on too, you know, the way you walk across a room, your hips swaying in the way they do...all natural too, your walk, I know, is anything but a put-on. Even the very way you talk, I love hearing how you form your words in that kooky accent of yours, it's just so neat. But you want to know what turns me on the most about you? It's easily your eyes. Cathy, they are just so incredible...absolutely breathtaking, I only know I've never seen eyes quite like them before. But it's not even just that they're gorgeous, it's the way you use them, the way you look at people with them, openly and directly, and when you look at *me*, my heart all but stops. Anyway, I could go on all night about you, and I very happily would too, but something tells me you don't want to hear anymore. Am I right?"

"You are." Cathy shifted uncomfortably, feeling her cheeks burning with embarrassment.

"Why don't you want to hear anymore?"

"Because I just don't. I'm just not used to hearing such glowing praise about me, that's all. Krista yes, me, no."

"Krista is a real stunner," he acknowledged, "but no more or no less than you. I know she has a lot going for her but whatever it is she may lack in, I'm sure you make up for."

"Krista doesn't lack in anything, except a will power when it comes to food. Pity help Paul tonight, that's all I can say, I hope he brought plenty of money with him because he's going to need it."

"Hey, how did the conversation suddenly turn around to Paul and Krista? We were talking about *you*, remember?"

"Yeah, well, as far as I'm concerned, the conversation's going nowhere. But thank you for the nice things you said about me."

"*Thank you?*" he repeated in astonishment. "You said that as if you were thanking me for giving you a gift you didn't particularly like but were pretending that you did."

"I'm sorry," she said meekly, "but like I said, I'm not exactly accustomed to hearing so many compliments about me at the same time. I just can't handle them."

"Well, you'd better get used to them because you'll be hearing a lot more from now on." Dave decided she needed a time out for a while, she was still clearly uncomfortable so he smoothly changed the subject. "Any beer in the refrigerator?"

"No, sorry, neither Krista nor I drink much beer but we've been meaning to get some in for you and Paul."

"Okay, no problem. Any chance the cake would be cooled enough to eat yet?"

"Only going to be one way to find out. I'll be right back."

He watched her rise and walk away and it wasn't lost on him that she seemed very relieved to be getting away from him. He just could not understand how such a beautiful girl, who was so strong willed, could have so many stupid, unnecessary insecurities about herself but he was determined to get to the bottom of them.

Cathy didn't return for nearly fifteen minutes but she came bearing goodies in the form of two slices of chocolate cake and two mugs of freshly brewed coffee. She set the tray down and grinned. "It's ready, I only took so long because I had to melt chocolate to put in the filling. Do you want the big piece or the wee piece?"

"The big piece, naturally." He tipped her a wink and tucked heartily into his cake. "Mmm," he mumbled, "this is the stuff dreams are made of. I'm a firm believer in the old saying that the way to a man's heart is through his stomach and baby, with cake like this, my heart is yours."

She looked at him in faint amusement. She felt totally relaxed in his company again, the silence between them as they ate their cake was companionable and the episode in the kitchen earlier now seemed like nothing more than a memory.

After Dave had polished off two slices of cake, he stretched lazily and put his feet up on the sofa. "I feel quite at home here," he announced happily. "I feel like I've been coming here for years and years and not just a few weeks. Mind if I move right in?"

"Krista might have something to say about that," Cathy answered with a soft chuckle.

"How would she ever know anything about it? She's hardly ever here now anyway, except for a change of clothes. Paul keeps her otherwise engaged."

"That much is true." Cathy wanted to stretch out beside him but she was suddenly afraid to in case she wouldn't be able to trust herself to keep her hands off him. She decided to take the chance anyway and nestled in alongside him, taking him completely by surprise. "Is this okay?" she whispered.

"Sure," he said after a few moments, although he wasn't really sure if it was or not. They lay like that for quite a while, not talking, just enjoying being together. He stroked her long, soft hair, breathing in her musky scent again and feeling quite contented. "Cathy?" he said suddenly, making her jump when he broke the silence.

"What?"

"Are these curls of yours natural?"

"Yeah, every last one of them. They're awful and I hate them."

"You shouldn't because they're beautiful. And so are you."

Cathy shifted slightly so she could look up into his face. "I wish you would stop saying that."

"Why should I? It's true. And I never say anything unless I mean it, remember? Why do you lack confidence in yourself?"

She pushed herself up and sat up straight to glare at him. "I don't," she snapped.

He quickly sat up beside her, unperturbed by her quick temper. "You do. Even Paul noticed it."

"Good for him." She looked moodily away. "Just change the subject," she advised.

Dave deliberated, then patted her knee. "Okay, I'm sorry, I didn't mean to make you angry."

She nodded. "I'm sorry too, I didn't mean to fly off the handle like that." She looked back at him and gave him a brief smile. "It's my biggest fault."

"Mine too."

"I know," she agreed.

"Then we're very alike after all. Paul was quite right, I probably have a lot more in common with you than I first thought."

"Maybe. Can you make chocolate cake too?"

"Nope," he said, and grinned impishly. "Why do you think I keep hanging around here for?"

"*Not* just for the chocolate cake, I hope!"

"No, definitely not for the cake." He smiled faintly. "There's a lot more for me here than just the cake." He felt like he wanted to kiss her again and because she seemed to read his mind, the atmosphere between them suddenly shifted to a high level of intensity. He hesitated for just a moment then, putting his hands on her shoulders, he pulled her gently towards him. His eyes drilled right into hers, making her heart race in anticipation at the yearning she could see. They kissed deeply and he felt himself rising for her all over again and he wanted to tell her it was all right, he loved her, he really truly did, he would never take advantage of her, but he was afraid to speak in case she mistook his words of love for words of lust, words spoken only in the heat of the moment, for the moment.

Dave broke away first, panting heavily. "I knew that wasn't such a good idea," he said hoarsely, "because now I want you more than ever, Cathy, I want to make love to you...over and over...and because I can't, I think I should go." He stood up in preparation to leave, convincing himself he was doing the right thing, at least for her sake. "I'll see you tomorrow."

Left with little choice but to let him go, Cathy nodded, planted a chaste kiss on his cheek and silently escorted him to the door. She sat down heavily on the stairs after he had left, feeling her heart sink as, unbidden and certainly unwarranted, she managed to persuade herself that her relationship with Dave was already over before it had barely even gotten off the ground.

CHAPTER FORTY-TWO

The next morning found Cathy sitting at her desk in work, reading a two-day old newspaper and trying to take her mind off Dave. She had come into work really early, mainly to get out of an empty apartment where the silence had stifled her and where she felt as if the walls were closing in around her.

After Dave had left her the evening before, she had dragged herself up to the bathroom, ran a steaming hot bath and had tried to soak away her tensions, but it hadn't worked and she had crawled into bed immediately afterwards, feeling sorry for herself and wishing Dave would just come back. But he hadn't, no great surprise really, and when she had finally managed to fall asleep, around 2:00, she had only dreamt about him, a deep, intense dream of strong sexual undertones that had jolted her awake, reaching out to him, calling his name and wanting him to feed the burning throb in her groin that he had caused… only to feel a tremendous let down when her senses had returned to normal and she realized she was lying alone.

She was nervous about facing him, which was another reason why she had come into work early, to give herself time to settle herself before Dave arrived. She knew he usually came in around 7:00 so she had another fifteen minutes or so to collect herself.

Krista and Paul came breezing in five minutes later. "There you are, Cath," Krista said cheerfully. "I thought I would have seen you at home but I must have just missed you."

"Yeah, must have." Cathy smiled vaguely and had to force herself to act normal. "So, where did you two go last night?"

"I took my beautiful lady to a place called The Seaview Manor,"

Paul said as he flopped down at his desk. "It's a little place along Route 7 and it overlooks, surprise, the ocean. After a superb meal, we went dancing, then back to my place for a nightcap."

Cathy grinned. "Must have been some nightcap, seeing you didn't come home last night, Krissie. But it sounds like you had fun."

"We did. What did you do last night?"

"I baked a cake."

"Goodie, I'll get a piece when I go home tonight. Did Dave come over?"

It was a fairly innocent question but Cathy couldn't keep a sharp edge from her voice. "Yes he did, if you must know."

Krista and Paul glanced at each other in surprise. "What happened, Cathy?" he asked carefully. "You don't seem too pleased about something. Did you two have a fight?"

"No, we didn't. Honest."

"Then what is it?" Krista was swiftly growing concerned, particularly when she couldn't read anything into Cathy's expression.

"It's nothing, Kris, really and truly, it's nothing. If there was something wrong, I would tell you, you know that."

"I know you normally would but for some reason, I get the impression you're holding something back this time. So, what happened?"

Paul narrowed his eyes thoughtfully as he listened to Krista try and pump Cathy for information that Cathy was very obviously unwilling to share. He hadn't spoken to Dave since the previous afternoon so Paul couldn't even begin to guess what was wrong, but, like Krista, he was determined to find out.

When Dave arrived a few minutes later, he paused in the doorway for a moment, his eyes on Cathy and nobody else. She seemed terribly unhappy this morning and he knew that he was the one responsible for her unhappiness, making him want to just take her in his arms and make it all better for her.

"Hello, people," he greeted and walked on in. "How's it going?"

Cathy jumped at the sound of his voice and turned to face him. He looked so handsome this morning, a little tired looking, maybe, but still so damned handsome and, for once, she actually resented it. But his looks weren't his fault, she reminded herself and she quickly looked away, her heart hammering in her chest.

Paul immediately sensed the distinct tension between Dave and Cathy, as did Krista, which underlined all the more there was something very definitely wrong. "Going good, partner," he said cheerfully. "Were you at the gym this morning?"

"No, unfortunately. I wanted to go but I was advised to refrain from strenuous exercise for a few days after getting my stitches out." Dave sat down and wished Cathy would at least look at him but she seemed engrossed in a pile of faxes that had come through since they'd left the office the evening before and whether it was just a ruse to deliberately ignore him, he couldn't tell.

Paul watched him watching Cathy and decided the two of them needed to be alone for a while, so he stood up. "Come on, Kris, let's go get the coffee and donuts this morning."

Krista understood perfectly why he had suggested they should leave and she quickly arose from behind her desk. "Good idea. Thanks to you, I missed breakfast this morning and my stomach's beginning to think my throat's been cut."

Dave waited for her and Paul to leave, then he sat down at Krista's desk, beside Cathy. "How are you doing, love?" he asked softly.

"Fine, thanks," she murmured, her eyes still fixed on one of the faxes. "You?"

"I'd feel a lot better if I knew you weren't so angry and disappointed with me."

Genuine surprise at his statement at last prompted her to look at him. "I'm neither angry nor disappointed with you, Dave, far from it. Why should I be?"

"Because things got a little bit out of control last night and I didn't exactly handle it accordingly. I just ran out on you, leaving you all alone and, I'm sure, confused, and I'm really sorry."

"No need to be sorry," she stated matter of factly.

"Well, I am. After I left you, I drove around for ages afterwards, wanting to go back to you but we both knew that if I had returned, we would only have ended up doing something I'm not sure you're really ready for. When I finally got home, I drank a beer or two and then went to the phone a hundred times to call you."

"Why didn't you?"

"Because I was afraid to in case I would hear something in your voice that would make me come running back to you." Dave paused as he saw her turn away from him and lower her eyes, but he pressed on anyway. "Look, Cathy, what I want to say is this. Last night was unreal for me. I experienced feelings for you, and not just the sexual ones, that I haven't felt for anyone in a long time. But as I lay in bed last night, thinking of you, I wondered why I should be having these feelings at all because, really, I don't know anything about you, other than where you're from and that you have a quick temper similar to my own. If we're to continue seeing one another - and I want that more than anything - I want to find out everything about you, I want to discover the real you, know your likes and dislikes, find out what makes you laugh.... even what makes you cry, just everything." He studied her profile, wishing she would look at him again, he couldn't even be sure if she had really been listening or if she had managed to tune herself out. Then he saw her lift her gaze, a faint smile playing at the corner of her mouth and he knew he had managed to get through to her at least a little bit. "What do you say, Cathy?"

"I say...." She looked back at him and, with one swift glance into his eyes, she saw how genuinely worried about her he was and how much he wanted to continue with the relationship. "I say, I feel so stupid now, I had managed to convince myself that you would come in here this morning and tell me you no longer wanted to see me again, except on a professional basis, of course. I was dreading seeing you again because I thought you would totally ignore me - or just talk to me long enough to tell me it was good bye."

"Thought wrong then, didn't you? I know we agreed to take things slowly, but it's sort of hard for me to do that now when I want to spend as much time with you as I possibly can. I wasn't teasing you there when I said I was experiencing feelings I haven't had in a long time, which is why I want to find out as much about you as I can." It was the closest Dave had come to telling her he was falling in love with her but she didn't seem to be aware that he had chosen to take the easy way out as she blew a huge sigh of relief.

"Okay, you can find out as much as you want to about me, but you might be pretty disappointed, I'm a very boring person, you know."

"Somehow, I doubt that. Tonight, after we wrap up here, and assuming we have no new leads to go on that will have us working until midnight, it's going to be just you and me. We can go for something to eat, or go for a drink, even take in a movie if you prefer, anything you want to do, just name it."

"I'll think about it," she said with a chuckle. "I'll want to go home first and change so if you can come and pick me up, we'll take it from there."

"Sounds like a plan." He smiled into her eyes, then figured it would be safe to venture on a kiss, so he leaned over towards her but, just as she offered her lips to him, he paused. "Can you trust me with a kiss this time?"

"Can you trust *me*?" she teased.

"I don't know, as long as you're not going to be tempted to jump my bones or something."

Cathy gurgled happily, which made him laugh too and, just as they engaged in a not too cautious kiss, Paul and Krista arrived back.

"Well, well, lookie here," Paul said dryly. "Can't leave these two alone for even five minutes. Dave, Cathy, I'm shocked... no, I'm *appalled*, at what I've just witnessed. Don't you know that kissing full on the mouth like that makes a perfect breeding ground for all types of horrible, nasty bacteria?"

Dave rolled his eyes in amusement, tipped Cathy a wink, and then neatly flipped Paul the finger. "Up yours, pal."

"Right back at you, Andrews." But Paul was secretly relieved that whatever it was that had been bothering Dave and Cathy seemed to have been resolved and, catching Krista's eye, they shared a knowing smile.

*

As far as work was concerned, it was to go down in history as a non-day, a day were nothing happened other than they received an appropriate amount of faxes, emails and phone calls concerning Petcelli and his bodyguards. No leads whatsoever arose from the correspondence and for the first time since it had all begun, they were happy to leave work knowing other police teams and the FBI were still working round the clock and getting the same results they were.

A rainstorm had swept over Bathville late that afternoon, bringing with it gusting winds and, later, thunder and lightning. The storm showed no sign of abating at 7:00 as Dave drove towards Cathy's and when he got out of the car, by the time it took for him to run the short distance to her front door, he was soaked through.

Cathy ushered him quickly inside. "Oh my goodness!" she exclaimed, "you're drenched. Get that jacket off you before you catch your death."

Before he did take his jacket off, he brought his hand from behind his back and extended to her a single, long-stemmed, perfect red rose. "For you, pretty lady."

Taken aback, she shyly took it from him and inhaled its sweet fragrance. "Thank you, Dave, roses are my favorite flower," she said softly. "I'll just go put this in water, okay?"

He shrugged out of his jacket, hung it over the newel of the banister and followed her into the kitchen. She had just put the rose into a bud vase and he watched as she smelled it again before setting the vase carefully on the windowsill. She seemed delighted at his simple gift, which was good enough for him.

"Looks good," he said. "I had to shield it from the wind on the way in from the car and I nearly lost it."

"I'm glad you didn't. It's beautiful, and thank you."

"My pleasure. You decided yet what you want to do tonight?"

Cathy turned back to the window and peered outside. "No sign of the storm letting up, is there?" In answer to her question, she saw a huge streak of forked lightning brighten up the whole sky and it was followed seconds later by a loud clap of thunder. "Guess not."

"The weathermen said that the winds are gusting up to sixty miles an hour, there are trees down all over the place."

"Sounds pretty bad. Hope Krista made it over to Paul's all right."

"I'm sure she did. So, what do you want to do?"

"I think I want to stay right here, I don't want for us to have to go out in that weather."

He looked at her inquisitively. "Are you afraid of the storm?"

"On the contrary, I love stormy weather and the windier it is, the better. I don't like lightning, though, especially forked lightning, it can do so much damage, but the thunder doesn't bother me. Do you mind if we stay in?"

He wasn't sure if she was testing the waters with him so he decided to take it she wasn't. "The weather *is* kinda bad," he acknowledged slowly, "and since I want to find out all about you, where better than in the comfort of your own home?"

Realizing by the tone of his voice he was really uncertain about what she had intended as a fairly innocent suggestion, Cathy smiled awkwardly and tried to come up with something neutral to say. "Have you eaten yet?"

"Just a sandwich around 5:00. I wasn't sure if you wanted to go out for something to eat or not."

"Oh, in that case you must be starved. Can I make you something a bit more substantial than a sandwich?" She moved towards the refrigerator, but he stopped her.

"No, you don't need to do that, if I get hungry later on, I can order a pizza or some Chinese food. One thing I would appreciate though, would be a towel for my hair, I'm dripping all over your nice, clean kitchen floor."

"I'm sorry," she said and hurriedly reached into a drawer for a clean towel.

After he was dried off somewhat, they went into the living room and sat down. He declined her offer of putting on some music and at first, they just talked a little bit of small talk but that didn't last long because Dave wanted to set the ball rolling in getting her to open out to him.

"Okay, young lady, that's it, you needn't think you're going to get out of this because I'm putting you in the spotlight right now. I will just ask you questions off the top of my head, and you answer them at your will. Any objections?"

"Will you take my rose away if I object?"

"Most definitely."

"Sly move, Andrews, you leave me with no choice." She chuckled happily and curled her legs up underneath herself to at least make herself comfortable.

"Okay, here goes... from the top...."

Over the next little while, he found out that she hated being called Catherine, that her middle name was Laura, after her maternal grandmother, her date of birth was June the sixth, 1991, which made her a Gemini, prone to mood swings but with a devil-may-care attitude about life. Her favorite color was blue, she loved most types of music, excluding only jazz, country and western, rap, and heavy metal and, to his surprise, she declared a passion for classical music, especially Beethoven and Chopin. She told him she could cook as well as she could bake, her specialty being anything made with pasta and that if there was one thing she truly hated, it was an untidy, unclean house.

After telling him all that, she looked at him with a hopeful smile. "Is that enough for now?"

"Oh no, you're not getting off the hook so easily. I have yet to hear all about your family, your life in Ireland. What made you decide to join the police? What are your pet dislikes? Have you any hidden talents hidden beneath that gorgeous body of yours I should know about?" Dave had seen her automatically stiffen as soon as he had mentioned her family and for a brief moment, there had been a very distinct coldness in her eyes. "Well?" he prompted when she seemed reluctant to talk to him this time.

"My life in Northern Ireland was probably as normal as your life in the States," she said eventually. "I went to school, grew up, never did drugs, had my first alcoholic drink when I was seventeen, enjoyed an average social life, went on holiday to places like Greece, Spain and Italy, I've been all over the United Kingdom too, except for Wales. I met Krista when I was nineteen going on twenty, moved in with her and her parents when I was twenty going on twenty-one and I talked Krista into pulling out of University to join up in the police with me. I loved the work, it was just something I had always wanted to do, ever since I was a young girl."

"Is it true that police work over there is very dangerous?"

"Oh yes, very, not just police work either, but any type of security work. But I've been assured by older people in the force that I used to work with that today's police are a lot safer than they were, say, 20 years ago."

"All I had ever heard about your country were the bullets and the bombings and the unnecessary murders but I'm sure it's a very beautiful place too. In fact, I would love to see it as it really is, through my own eyes and not through the jaded eyes of the media."

"You'd love it," she enthused, "not just Belfast, but the whole country. It's so beautiful and so green, you might never want to leave."

"I'd be prepared to take my chances."

She grabbed a cushion and hugged it to her, her eyes shining brightly at the mention of her homeland. Then she returned to telling him about herself, how the only thing she could really pride herself in was having an excellent memory, that she hated countries, especially her own, being torn apart by religious differences or racism. How she hated spiders and most insects, that she deplored foul language, the depletion of the ozone layer and the pollution of the oceans.

The more she talked, the more relaxed she was becoming, until he prompted her that she had yet to tell him of her family. He saw her shift uncomfortably, dart her eyes nervously around the room until she lowered her gaze and hugged the cushion more tightly to her.

"Cathy...what...?" Dave was confused to this sudden turn around and, by the look of it, he knew he had hit a raw nerve. He recalled

Krista's words to him from a few days ago, how she had explained that a lot of Cathy's insecurities and earlier problems - whatever *they* might be - had been caused by her family and he wondered if he should push the issue. "What's wrong?"

She impatiently threw the cushion to one side and sat on the very edge of the sofa, her eyes troubled and angry. She seemed to be struggling to calm down again and he waited as patiently as he could for her to say something. "I'm sorry, Dave," she murmured, "I was hoping you wouldn't ask me about them."

"I don't mean to pry," he said carefully, "but why won't you tell me about them?"

"Because they're not worth wasting any breath over," she stated hotly.

"Okay, simmer down, I'm sorry, I didn't mean to make you angry." He was inwardly shocked at her performance, but he was also concerned, but before he could say anything else, she spoke first.

"Much as I'd like to pretend I have no family, unfortunately, I do. I have a mother, a stepfather and a stepsister and my real father is God knows where, if he's even still alive. I should have mentioned them when I was talking about my major dislikes there because that's the category they most definitely belong in." She looked at him over her shoulder and her eyes were cool and clear with honesty. "And I'm not even ashamed to admit that I hate them because they deserve it. Krista's the only family I have now and that's fine by me because she's all I want."

He couldn't take his eyes off hers and he didn't know whether to be appalled at her admission or to admire her for her honesty. "I'm sure what you've told me is perfectly justifiable, Cathy," he said softly.

"It is, trust me. Please, just don't mention them again." She looked moodily away. "Anything else you want to know?"

Sensing that he should really bring this conversation to a close, Dave put a relaxed smile on his face. "Just one more thing. Tell me the one thing in this whole world that you love the most."

"Oh, that's an easy one to answer. I absolutely adore children. I want to have at least three kids by the time I'm thirty, then try for another couple during my thirties because it's always been my dream to have a large family of my own someday."

"Really? That's very interesting. I'm impressed."

"No need to be impressed, it's just the truth."

"In that case, tell me just *one* more of what you love the most?"

"Okay...*one* more and that's it. I love listening to the wind when I'm tucked into a nice warm bed but I love it even more when I'm walking by the sea on a windy day. I love being by the ocean and it's my dream in life to have a home overlooking the ocean, raising my gaggle of kids." She stopped and turned to him with hope in her eyes. "Don't you think we've talked enough about me? You must be bored to tears hearing me spout non-stop about myself like this and if you keep asking me questions, you're not going to be surprised anymore about me because you'll already know everything there is to know."

"Okay, if you want to stop, we'll stop, but I'm *not* bored to tears, far from it. In fact, I could sit here all night just hearing all about you."

"But why?" she asked critically. "I'm really nothing special."

"Oh, but you *are* special..." he said softly and caught in a breath, ".... to me."

Dave couldn't have stunned her any better if he had hit her with a sledgehammer and all she could do was stare at him. "*What* did you just say?" she whispered.

"I said, you're special, Cathy, and make that *very* special. To me." He waited expectantly for her response, hoping and praying he hadn't gone too far.

Cathy repeated the words silently to herself, her lips moving slowly over each syllable, her eyes wide in wonder. She put her shaking hands up to her face. "Oh my, and only a very short while ago, I wasn't sure if you even liked me or not and now.... now you're saying I'm special to you?"

Being a man who believed in going for what he considered to be right, Dave nodded slowly. Then, with his heart in his eyes, he plunged right in with what he really wanted to say. "Not only are you special to me but I think... no, I *know*, I'm falling in love with you, Cathy."

Cathy leapt off the sofa and stood in the middle of the living room, her senses reeling. She couldn't look at Dave, she was too scared to, in case she saw something in his eyes that told her he had only been joking. She knew he was waiting for some sort of response but she didn't know what to say just yet, or even what to do and then she did something totally unexpected to either of them and something completely out of character.

She burst into tears.

CHAPTER FORTY-THREE

The wind rattled and shook the windowpane and thunder boomed deafeningly overhead. The storm just was not willing to let up, but Dave heard neither the wind nor the crashing thunder, all he could hear were Cathy's gentle sobs, his eyes fixated on the subtle shaking of her shoulders.

In alarm, he sprang up beside her. Without a word, he folded her into his arms and held her and it was only when her tears had subsided somewhat that he let himself speak. "Cathy, I'm sorry," he whispered, "I'm sorry, I put you on the spot and I didn't mean to. I didn't mean to make you cry."

Cathy rested her head against his chest and with his arms around her like this, she suddenly felt very safe and protected from the outside world and she knew that she had nothing to fear anymore, from anyone. She was as surprised at her tears as Dave was, she was very embarrassed about them too, it truly wasn't her style to just break down into tears like that, but they had just happened, nothing she could do about them and they were the least of her worries right now anyway. "Why did you say that, Dave?" she asked softly.

"Because I wanted to and I meant it and I've been wanting to say it for quite a while now." He closed his eyes and kissed the top of her head. Her hair felt silky soft against his lips, and smelled of coconuts. "I apologize for upsetting you like that but I won't apologize for speaking the truth. I love you, Cathy, so much, and you're the first woman I've said that to since Terri."

She felt her eyes well up again but this time, she managed to blink the tears away. "But how can you say you love me when you really don't know me? I may have answered all those questions you asked me about myself, but they were really only trivial things, surface things, you don't know the *real* me."

"Yes, I do," he argued gently. He tilted her chin up with his forefinger to force her to look at him, which she did, then he placed a hand at her heart. "I know you have a warm, caring heart, which tells me a lot about the real you. You appreciate small gifts, like a simple red rose, which tells me about the real you. You are completely honest and I know you would never willingly hurt me, which tells me even more about the real you. You are a strong-willed, fiery and yet very vulnerable woman and I know you're a lady who goes after what she wants and yet won't step on anyone else's toes to get it. I know you have very strict morals, about a lot of things and I know I can trust you with my life. All that and still more tells me enough about the real you, they're all the important things. If I thought for one minute I was wrong about any of them, I would walk out the door right now but I know I'm right so I'm not going anywhere. You are the sweetest person I have ever met and I'm proud to say that I love you." All the time he had been talking, he hadn't taken his eyes off hers in the hope that she would see he was telling her the truth. It felt good to have finally told her how he felt and her tears had only succeeded in touching him deeply, making him love her even more. "I'm not asking you to love me in return, Cathy, I wouldn't do that to you, but if it ever happens, then you'll only make me the happiest man in the world. I just want you to know that it's enough for me now that I love you."

Her heart was hammering in her chest by now and she wondered if maybe he could feel it because he hadn't taken his hand away yet. With all his words still ringing in his ears, her eyes searched the face of this man whom she had positively detested since the very first day they had met, who had detested her just as much in return and yet who was now standing here in her living room telling her he loved her. She shivered slightly at the beautiful absurdity of it all.

"Nobody has ever said such lovely things about me before," she said, "and actually said them as if they were true."

"Which they were, which they are. I love a woman who is as dedicated to her job as I am and who also knows how to take care of herself. I love a woman who isn't afraid of speaking her mind and I love a woman who can stand up to me and my temper. I've never come across anyone quite like you before, a woman who cannot be intimidated by me. Not that I'm saying I take pride in the fact I can easily intimidate people, but I know it's the way I can be sometimes. But while we were talking there and you were telling me about yourself, do you want to know what really clinched it for me? The way your eyes lit up when you talked about having a large family someday. So many women these days are nothing but career minded, it's so rare to hear a woman actually say she wants a lot of children. I'm an only child, see, and I hated growing up alone so I always promised myself I would have a large family of my own one day too. You see, we really *do* have a lot in common, we both want what's important out of life."

Cathy reached out and touched his cheek. "It's nice to know that, Dave, it truly is. But please, stop saying so many nice things about me, you might give me a swollen head."

"Now why do I believe that to be an impossibility? So, my beautiful lady, now that I've bared my soul to you, how do you feel?"

"Strange," she admitted, "but grateful." She screwed up her nose in disgust. "No, that's a very poor choice of words. I'm touched, Dave, completely touched. I've been under the impression, ever since we met, that you're a very deep person who doesn't like expressing himself verbally much, seems like I was wrong about you being the strong, silent type when it concerns you speaking your mind. Paul told me that you're a very complex person, and maybe you are to some degree, but some of the things you've just said to me, I can see you for what you really are. And I like what I see."

He looked at her suspiciously. "Why do I get the feeling there's a 'but' at the end of that?"

"There's not," she said quickly, "really there's not. You have so many fine qualities and I like finding them out one at a time, they're always a welcome surprise. It's not just that you're gorgeous to look at either.... I could lose myself just by looking into your eyes...but I like it that you're not one of those good-looking males who like to preen themselves in front of a mirror or shop window, with a comb in one hand and their ego in the other and who are as shallow as a kiddy's play pond. There's a hell of a lot more to you than just good looks and a great body and I find your inner qualities are just as... no, make that *more* appealing."

Cathy had just said something to him no other woman ever had, even Terri, *especially* Terri. His ex-wife had been in love with him partly for his looks and she had never tired of displaying him to her friends just so she could show off what a handsome boyfriend and, later, husband she had. He hadn't liked being shown off like a prize horse but he had been young and not as wise as he was now. And now he had a woman who liked him for the sort of person he really was, the person underneath the skin.

"Hey, *I* could get the swollen head here," he teased. "Keep talking that talk, lady, it's music to my ears - and very good for my ego too." Dave badly wanted to kiss her now, but he didn't dare because a little voice inside his head insisted on telling him how risky it could become and the last thing he wanted was a repeat performance of the evening before.

But he was saved further dilemma when a loud crash sounded overhead, inside the house, and they both looked up at the ceiling.

"That's Krista's room," she announced, "something must have fallen over. I'll be right back."

He waited for her to come downstairs again, which a few minutes later, she did. "Everything okay?"

"Oh yeah. She left a window open, just a wee bit, but a gust of wind managed to blow over one of her medical books and also a couple of ornaments and -" She stopped and frowned when she felt something warm trickling down her hand. "Oh *no!*" she exclaimed in annoyance. "Look." She showed her left hand to him, which was covered in blood. "One of the ornaments got broken, I must have cut myself when I picked up the pieces."

Dave, after a quick look to inspect the damage, escorted her promptly into the kitchen. He held her hand under the cold water for a few minutes and when most of the blood was washed away, he examined the cut again. "Oh my goodness, I don't believe this," he suddenly exclaimed in horror.

"What?" she asked uncertainly.

"Doesn't this hurt at all?"

"Just stings a bit, that's about it."

"B-But you should see how deep the cut is, it should *mega* hurt."

"Let me see," she said impatiently.

He quickly shielded her hand with his own. "I don't think that's such a good idea, Cath. Once you see it, you might want to faint. I know *I* do - and I've got a really strong stomach."

"Dave, I'm sure you're exaggerating, just let me see my hand, please."

He looked at her in distress then, with a quick peek at her cut again, he slowly took his hand away. "Okay, but don't say I didn't warn you. Don't worry, I'll catch you if I think you're going to faint."

Undeterred, she looked at the palm of her hand, then back up at him to see that he had adopted a purely innocent expression. "It's the tiniest wee cut in the whole wide world," she stated dryly.

"It is?" He looked at her suspiciously, then at her hand again. "Well, will you look at that, so it is. All that blood really threw me, you know, it was so easy to make a mistake."

"Your ruse to get me worried didn't work, you mean. Going to faint, indeed! I happen to bleed a lot, even with the little cuts like this one. Now, if you want to make yourself really useful, pass me a piece of paper towel." She shook her head in fond amusement but before she could take the piece of paper towel from him, he turned his attention back to her hand.

"Let me," he said and gently wiped away the last of her blood. He didn't stop until he was satisfied the bleeding wasn't going to start again, then he planted a delicate, soft kiss on her palm. "There," he said, "all better. Feel okay?"

Her hand could have been hanging on by a thread and a prayer by now, for all Cathy could have cared, she had been too busy enjoying the feel of his fingers as they had gently and tenderly looked after her very minor injury and it hit her all at once, and no longer as any great surprise, that she was beginning to recognize what her feelings for this man before her really meant. She knew now what she must do, and it shouldn't be all that difficult because he had already made her feel more than special. In a way, he had even placed the ball in her court.

Taking in a deep breath and letting it out slowly, she said, "It feels fine, Dave. And I love you."

He jerked his head up and looked at her in astonishment. "E-Excuse me?" he stammered. "Wh-What did you just say?"

She eyed him as calmly as she could. "I said, it feels fine. And I love you."

His astonishment swiftly turned to shock and all he could do was stare at her, knowing his ears could only be playing tricks on him. When he came to his senses, somewhat, he realized she was looking at him curiously, her head tilted slightly to one side and he knew she was waiting for him to say something. "You do?" His words came out in a croak and he swallowed quickly. And then it hit home all the way, his heart started beating again and a smile spread slowly over his face. "You *do*. And you're quite sure about this?"

"More sure than I've ever been about anything in my entire life. I should have told you when you told me, only I think I was in a state of shock. Now I'm not...well, not as much anyway, which is how I've managed to tell you. I'm sorry I kept it from you, it won't happen again." She smiled, happy that she had told him and even happier that she seemed to have made him happy too.

Dave was looking at her in a state of wonder now. "You're sorry?" he repeated. "You've just told me you love me and you say you're sorry you kept it from me? You have absolutely nothing to apologize for, sweetheart, absolutely nothing. If you still hadn't told me five years from now, I wouldn't have cared, as long as I could still continue to be with you." He grew very serious as he reached out to caress her cheek. "This is incredible news, baby, just incredible. And to think I could have passed all this up - and very nearly did with the way I treated you when you first arrived in this country. This would not have happened if we had chosen to continue with our vendetta against one another."

Cathy nodded and earnestly searched his eyes. "It's true too," she whispered, "I love you."

He pulled her into his arms and just held her close and all he knew was he didn't want to let her go. Ever.

As the wind and the rain continued to rattle furiously against the windowpane, they held on to each other for a very long time. Nothing could have made this night any more perfect for him, absolutely nothing.

But when Cathy suddenly pulled out of his arms and looked steadily up at him, it seemed that she had a different idea in mind, one that set his heart beating faster in his chest if he was reading her right.

"What's wrong?" he asked carefully.

"Nothing. I was just thinking how much I would love a kiss right now."

"A kiss? I think that could easily be arranged." He slowly bent his head towards hers and as soon as their lips met, he felt a tingle spread over his whole body. With each passing moment, he kissed her more intensely, wanting her more than ever now as he felt the heady sensations of the first stirrings of fire in his groin. Almost two long years of sexual depravation and pent-up sexual frustrations had finally reached a peak and all he knew now was, tonight, they were going to be released.

But he still had Cathy to consider, despite her obvious signals maybe this was still too soon for her and she might want to wait a while. With a low groan of remorse, he tore his mouth away from hers.

"What's wrong?" Cathy asked breathlessly.

"Nothing, I…" He closed his eyes in pleasure at the feel of her lips on his throat, licking him, sucking lightly on his skin. "You don't have to do this, you know, not if you don't want to."

Her eyes were dark with desire for him as she looked up at him. "Ssh," she murmured and kissed his neck. "It's okay."

He grabbed a handful of her hair at the base of her neck and forced her to look at him again. "But we don't have to do this, not tonight, not if -"

"Shut up," she requested and slowly unbuttoned his shirt all the way down to the top of his jeans, planting a trail of soft kisses across his chest as she worked her way downwards.

Almost at the point of no return now, Dave tried one last time to postpone what he really knew was only going to happen anyway. "We can…huh…we can still wait, you know, until -"

"Shut *up*," she said again, impatiently, and moved her attention to his belt. "Jesus, *men*!" With slightly shaking fingers, she unbuckled his belt… and jumped slightly when the phone rang.

They both turned to look at it in irritation. "Do you want to get that?" he asked on the third ring.

"The machine will pick it up," she answered and turned back to his belt again and just as she slipped it out of the clasp, they heard the machine click on, the introductory message left by Krista to please leave a message at the beep and a second after that, Paul's voice came over the speaker.

"Hey, guys," he said, "I was really hoping to have caught you." By the sound of it, he was on his cell phone, but he was also speaking in hushed tones and Dave frowned over at the answering machine, just distracted enough by Paul's voice to have heard something in it he didn't quite like. Without thinking, he grabbed a hold of Cathy's hand and stilled its movement on his body. "If you get this message within five minutes…" There was a pause, then "It's just about ten of eight now, it's just to let you…."

Dave bounded over to the phone. Something was up, he knew it. He picked up the receiver. "Yo, Paul, we're here."

"Dave! Thank goodness. Listen, get down to…." Paul's next words were blocked out by a loud burst of static, presumably caused by the storm, and the next thing Dave heard was, "…. Krista's inside."

"Come back?" Dave requested.

Paul had heard the static too and he hunched down lower in the front seat of his car. "I said, get down to the 7-11 on corner of Lucy Street and Deerling Boulevard. I've just seen Troy Zellwig and Xavier Petcelli enter, but Krista's inside. Unarmed."

Aware Cathy was looking at him for an explanation, Dave nodded. "Backup?"

"Already requested. But you're just as close."

"On our way." Dave hung up and looked grimly at Cathy. The passion of a few moments before was all but forgotten about as she watched him buckle up his belt and button his shirt again. "We have to go, sweetie. Don't jump to conclusions, but Krista may be in danger."

It was all she needed to hear to get her moving.

CHAPTER FORTY-FOUR

As they sped off in Dave's car, he could only fill Cathy in with the little Paul had told him. She didn't ask too many questions but although she seemed alarmed for Krista's safety, at least she didn't seem on the verge of panic.

Lucy Street and Deerling Boulevard were about fifteen minutes from Cathy's apartment. The storm had kept a lot of people indoors tonight because the traffic was scant and he was able to complete the journey in less than ten minutes.

He slowed the Camaro down to a crawl and saw Paul's Mustang parked outside. There were two other cars in the small lot, a Camry and a dark colored Sonata. He couldn't see directly into the store, thanks to the many posters up on the windows advertising ware like 2 liters of Pepsi products at only $1.39, Twinkies $2.49, Doral cigarettes $5.79 + tax, coffee to go 80c, Doritos, all flavors, 79c and All Detergent $3.19.

"Can't see a damned thing!" Cathy exclaimed in exasperation. The store was to their left and she had twisted round in her seat as he had passed it. "Can't even see Paul in his car."

Meaning to do a circle of the block, Dave signaled left and turned down Lucy Street. There were two huge dumpsters beside the convenience store, one labeled "Cardboard Only", the other without a label and just as Dave started to accelerate to get down to the next intersection, Paul leapt out from behind the dumpster nearest the street.

Dave spotted him immediately and pulled the car in beside the dumpster. He got out of the car, looking at Paul for an explanation.

Paul beckoned them to come to the corner of the building so he could see the main door again. "Krista expressed a desire for some chocolate chip ice cream," he started, "and because the Shop 'n' Save close to my place was in darkness when I got there, I'm guessing because of the storm, I came here because I know this convenience store usually has pretty good deals. Krista got out of the car and as soon as she entered the store, the Camry pulled up alongside me. I saw Petcelli and Zellwig get out and as soon as it registered it was actually them, I called for backup, then called you. The backup arrived a couple of minutes before you did and, under my instructions, the three units are on the other side of the building, lights and sirens off. The FBI is apparently on its way, with the same instructions. Captain Hamilton called me five minutes ago too, he has the God damned SWAT team ready, if we need them. So far, it hasn't turned into a hostage situation so hopefully we won't have to bring them in."

Dave quickly checked his gun was loaded and he peeked around the side of the building. There was absolutely no movement. Not even another car had pulled up. "Any idea who's in the Sonata?"

"It was there when I arrived. Could be the store clerk's." A flash of lightning lit up Paul's features momentarily. The rain had still been pouring down steadily and he was soaked to the skin. He looked worried, but he also looked primed and ready for action. "Your gun loaded too, little dude?" he asked Cathy.

She nodded. "Checked it in the car on the way here."

"I wanted to take them both out soon as I saw them," Paul said. "But, of course, I couldn't. And by the time I would have gotten out of the car to warn them to halt, they would have been inside the store anyway. I just wish I could see inside, I don't like not knowing what's up with Krista."

"Does she have her gun with her?" Cathy asked. She knew that when she was off duty, Krista carried her gun in her purse. On duty, she wore a holster under her jacket or sometimes even a waist holster. Krista also had an off-duty revolver, which she carried tucked inside an ankle holster under her sock. Cathy didn't think Krista had the latter on her, not if she'd just been going round to visit Paul and had her regular gun in her purse. Cathy also didn't think that if Krista had gone into the store to make one purchase that she would have carried her purse with her, that she would just have taken her wallet out and into the store with her.

Paul too knew how Krista carried her guns and he solemnly shook his head. "It's in her purse, which is on the floor in the car."

Dave got down on one knee and peered round the side of the building again. He wished the posters advertising the specials this week were on the outside so that he could just rip them all down but of course, they weren't. However, the posters weren't covering every square inch of the window, in fact, there were quite a few gaps that, if he was very careful, he could go up to them and be able to see inside the store.

Without a word to either Paul or Cathy, he quickly crept forward and looked through the first gap. He couldn't see anything except the back of a person in a green smock. He couldn't even tell if the person was male or female. Crawling sideways, he looked through the next gap in the posters and saw the person in the green smock again, only this time more in profile. He could see it was female and a very terrified one at that. She was maybe in her mid-twenties, with bleached blonde hair and tired circles under her eyes. Dave followed her line of vision and saw Troy standing a few feet before her, a gun aimed right at her. He could see Troy's mouth moving but he couldn't hear the words coming past his lips.

Moving sideways again, he was able to see down an aisle… and his heart gave a jolt of alarm. Petcelli had a gun too, only he had his aimed right under Krista' chin. Although clearly unhurt, and seemingly quite calm too, Dave didn't like the gun being in such proximity to any part of Krista' body. He went back to Paul and Cathy and told them what he had seen.

Cathy set her lips in a grim, hard line. "If he touches her, so help me God, he's a dead man," she announced coldly.

Paul looked down at her. "Sorry, Cath, you'd have to get past me first." He locked gazes with Dave. "Okay, buddy boy, time's a-wasting here, don't you think? Any bright ideas?"

Dave knew how anxious Paul was to get this over with and he closed his eyes briefly in acknowledgement. "Did you have one of the backups stake the back entrance?"

"Of course. Want to try and get in that way?"

"Thinking about it. But what if as we're going round there, they decide to leave through the front entrance, taking Krista with them?"

"One of us will have to stay here and keep watch," Paul said. They both looked at Cathy. "You up for it, Cathy?"

"If it means saving Krista, I'm up for anything."

"How many walkie talkies you got in your car?" Paul asked Dave.

"Two, I think. But I don't recommend using them, especially if we make it inside from the back. If Troy and Petcelli are still in the store, one burst of static caused by the lightning and they'll hear us."

Paul cursed under his breath. It looked like they were going to have to go in blind and hope the element of surprise was all it would take to bring Petcelli and Zellwig down. If they could time their getting into the building to the claps of thunder, that would at least give them some noise cover. Only thing was, the storm seemed to be abating, which meant the times between the thunderclaps were going to be longer.

Cathy blinked the rainwater from her eyes and glanced briefly around the side of the building. A car had just pulled up and an elderly gentleman got out. With a click of irritation, she sprinted over to him, keeping as below the level of the window as she could. She pulled out her badge. "Sorry, sir," she told the startled man and saw him pale when he saw her gun. *God,* she thought, *I scared the bejesus out of him, hope I haven't sent him into cardiac failure.* "Don't worry, sir," she said quickly, "I'm a cop, as you can see by my badge. You can't go into the store just yet, we have a…er, we have a bit of a situation going on. Please get back into your car and drive away."

At least the man was obliging because without another word, except something about "Crazy terrorists!" mumbled under his breath, he got into his car and pulled away.

Cathy went back to Paul and Dave. "That was close. One of us would have to stay here anyway, just to stop other members of the public from trying to get in."

"Time's a-wasting." Paul said again, more vehemently this time. "We gotta get a move on."

Cathy was just about to ask for instructions when a gentle ringing of a bell caught her attention. She turned towards it and recognized it as being the type of bell stores use to warn the clerk someone has either entered or exited the building. "Oh shit, something's happening," she said and ducked quickly back out of sight.

Dave looked quickly round the side. "They're coming out," he whispered. "All four of them, including the clerk. Paul?"

"If they believed that Krista and I truly were romantically involved, they will have assumed by now that I could be here too," Paul whispered back, "They might even have remembered or recognized my car from when I took it to the club, so they'll be looking for me. Unless they threatened her and she told them outright, of course, then they know for sure I'm here. Knowing I'm a cop, they will be ready to fight me off so here's the plan…"

Once explained, although not the *best* of plans, it was still the only one they had. After a brief glance to see what was happening, it looked like Petcelli and Zellwig were going to take Krista and the store clerk with them and Dave knew they had precious little time to start acting on it.

CHAPTER FORTY-FIVE

Zellwig was leading, holding the terrified store clerk close to him, with his gun tilted up under her chin. Petcelli was right behind him, his left arm around Krista's neck in a stranglehold, his right hand holding the gun at her temple.

Paul stepped from the side of the building into the open. His gun was raised and pointing directly at Petcelli. Paul's face was outwardly calm, only the sharp blue of his eyes foretold his murderous intent.

It was Zellwig who noticed Paul first and, with a smug smile, he turned himself and the clerk towards him. "Well, well, we meet again, Officer Cameron," he said, using the clerk as a human shield. Paul noticed for the first time that Zellwig was holding the girl *and* the gun with his left arm and hand, which meant his damaged collarbone was still an issue for him. Paul knew from past observations alone that Troy was predominantly right-handed.

"Drop the gun and let her go, Zellwig," Paul ordered. "You too, Petcelli. You okay, Krista?"

"Getting wet but otherwise fine," she said. But the look in her eyes was pleading with him to please hurry up and get this over and done with.

Petcelli swung towards Paul, making Krista wince when his arm dug into her neck. He didn't take the gun away from her head. "You're doing it again, Cameron, you're giving orders when you're in no position to give them. I knew that if this lovely lady was here that you had to be too, I'm glad I followed my instinct, even when she told me she was here on her own." Without taking his eyes from Paul, Petcelli barked an order to Zellwig. "Troy, get that bitch into the car and start the engine. We'll be with you in a moment."

Paul had been worried about the fact that they had two weapons to his one. If Zellwig was getting into the car, even though he would still have his gun ready for action, at least it improved Paul's odds slightly with having Zellwig further away and working with only one good arm. Paul passed a silent communication with his eyes to Krista. *Can you take him?* He asked her. *No!* came her frantic reply and she looked quickly down at the gun to indicate why. Paul nodded. "If you let her go, Petcelli, right now, no one will -"

"Oh shut up, Cameron, how stupid do you think I am? Don't bother wasting your breath trying to negotiate. We were in that store for at least fifteen minutes. I'm sure you saw Troy and me getting out of the car and going inside. Are you going to tell me that during that time, you didn't call for backup? And that it isn't already here?"

Paul switched his gun to his left hand, keeping it steadily aimed at Petcelli's head. "No, I wasn't trying -"

"Shut up. Wherever the backup is, get rid of it." Petcelli pressed the gun firmly against Krista's head. "Now!"

Left with no choice, Paul went to the other side of the building. Twenty feet back towards a fence that bordered a private house the three police units were sitting. Engines and lights were all off but the six uniformed officers were all standing outside the vehicles. They stiffened soon as they saw Paul, who was nothing but a back-lit figure coming towards them and then, the nearer he got to them and his features became more distinguishable, they were able to relax slightly when they realized who it was.

"You guys have got to take off," Paul said. "Radio Captain

Hamilton and let them know I've just given you instructions to leave. Also, make sure the Feds don't get here, certainly not within the next ten minutes. Tell Captain Hamilton I'm doing what I can but if it comes to it, Krista and the store clerk will be taken hostage without us being able to stop it. Their vehicle is a silver four door Toyota Camry, perhaps a 2014 model, license plate is a Massachusetts Spirit of America, 293386. Zellwig and Petcelli are both dressed in blue jeans and dark jackets, Petcelli's has a Bruins logo on the breast, Zellwig's is plain. Both are armed and obviously dangerous. I'm not here alone, guys, Detectives Andrews and Edwards are here, only neither of the fugitives knows that. Take off now, okay? Block off all intersections and wait for further instructions."

Paul went back round to the front entrance. He had only been gone a minute and he knew he had given Petcelli ample time to make a break for it but he also knew that Cathy at least would have stopped that from happening. He had to hope that Dave was almost in position by now too. He was somewhat surprised to see that Petcelli was still in the same position and that Zellwig was sitting in the driving seat of the car, doing nothing but waiting for Petcelli's next instructions.

Why *hadn't* Petcelli tried to make a break for it? Paul couldn't help but wonder. But it took him only a second to figure it out. Petcelli was so smug and so certain he was going to win this, he wanted to play with Paul a little while longer. He was enjoying this too much, which snapped Paul's patience.

Petcelli waited for the third cruiser to drive slowly by and he smirked at Paul. "Good boy," he patronized. "*Now* we can talk negotiations."

This was the real point where Paul's plan was going to come into effect. Cathy would be waiting to assist on his right, Dave would come up on his left, from where the cruisers had been parked. All he had to do now was wait for the precise moment to distract Petcelli enough to get him to either drop the gun or at least take its aim from Krista.

"Negotiations about what?" Paul asked flippantly.

Petcelli started for a second but composed himself quickly. He laughed indulgently. "Oh, naughty boy. Nearly got me there. You going to back off and let me take your lovely lady away with me or do I have to shoot you first?"

"Not necessary," Paul said, stepping slightly more in front of Petcelli. "I would, however, advise you to drop your gun right now, Xavier."

"Why would I want to do that?"

"Because of her," Paul said, nodding at Cathy, who had crept stealthily up behind Petcelli from his blind side and before Petcelli could turn around, Cathy had her gun pressed against Petcelli's temple.

"*TROY!*" Petcelli roared, even as he felt Paul try to pry the gun from his fingers. But when he stole a glance at the car, he saw Dave leaning into the driver side window and a second later, open the door and pull Troy roughly out, obviously not caring that he was hurting the collarbone he had damaged in the first place. He pushed Troy to his knees on the ground and, still mindless of the collarbone, grabbed Troy's arms behind his back and handcuffed him.

The next moments passed in a whirlwind, making it difficult for the events that happened seem real, never mind have one of them put them in chronological order later.

Because of the rain Paul's fingers hadn't been able to find purchase on the barrel of the gun and with Petcelli trying to pull it out of his way, it didn't help his quest. Paul did the only thing he could at the moment and that was he grabbed Krista and pulled her out of the fat little man's arms.

Petcelli, surprisingly agile for a man of his bulk, slammed his head back and head-butted Cathy neatly on the forehead. Dave had had his gun trained on Troy but he was watching everything that was going on and soon as he saw Cathy was reeling, he raised his gun just as Petcelli raised his and fired it immediately. Petcelli went flying into the wall of the convenience store and he slumped slowly to the ground, leaving a trail of blood behind him on the wall as he fell.

Petcelli's forefinger had convulsed reflexively after the bullet impact and his gun went off. At first it was thought that the shot went wild but a movement caught Dave's eye and when he looked down, he saw Troy had fallen backwards, his upper body bent at an impossible angle because he'd been on his knees, which were still underneath him. It was then that Dave saw the dead, dull stare in Troy's open eyes, which should have at least blinked automatically at the raindrops falling into them and a small black hole dead center in Troy's forehead.

Petcelli's bullet hadn't gone wild after all.

Krista ran over to Petcelli and felt at his neck for a carotid pulse. She felt nothing and bent to listen for a breath from his nostrils and mouth. Still getting nothing, she checked the pulse again and then stood up. There was nothing she could do for him. Petcelli was dead.

Paul had run to the Camry to check on the store clerk. She was shivering and shaking and clearly in shock but she was otherwise unhurt and was at least able to speak coherently. Paul was grateful she hadn't gone into hysterics. After Petcelli and Zellwig were taken away, he would get her statement, as well as call her boss and have him or her arrange for shift relief.

Dave ran over to Cathy. She was looking towards Krista as she checked on Petcelli and she smiled tiredly at Dave. "Everything happened so quickly there," she stated unnecessarily.

He looked at her in concern. "I saw him head butt you, are you okay?"

Her eyes fixed on Petcelli, she nodded slowly. "Yeah, I'm fine. Wish I could say the same for our friend down there."

"Too bad, it was him or one of us." He briefly squeezed her hand and then smiled into her eyes. "Hey, what is it with you and head injuries anyway?" he teased.

"Don't know. The baddies just seem to automatically know where my soft parts are."

Krista was wiping off her hands and she came over to them. She saw Paul was busy with the store clerk and she gave Cathy and Dave a hug. "All this for chocolate chip ice cream. Still trying to decide if it was a good thing or a bad thing that we came out tonight to get some."

Dave looked over at Petcelli's body. "With all those poor women, including Ruth O'Brien, he had killed, I think it was a good thing," he said softly.

Helping the store clerk inside to the dry and warmth of the store, they sat her down behind her counter and placed the phone in front of her. "Call your boss," Paul told her, "and let me talk to him."

While Paul took care of that, Dave got on his cell phone and called the Coroner's office to come and pick up two bodies. They were to be held at the morgue pending an autopsy if requested by the court and then to be released for burial. Dave then called Captain Hamilton and told him what had happened, as much as he could relate during the last few minutes when everything had gone down so quickly.

"Yeah, they're both dead, Cap," Dave said. "Self-defense as far as shooting Petcelli was concerned and accidental shooting on Zellwig's half. Give us the night to sleep on it, Cap, we'll probably have more information after a good night's sleep."

Captain Hamilton knew Dave wasn't trying to stonewall him, he believed his detective when he said everything had happened too quickly to yet get a handle on it. "Fair enough, Andrews. And what about the other fugitive, Brad James?"

"I'll call for a tow truck and have the Camry taken down to the station. We'll go over it with a fine toothcomb, see if there's something that has an address of where they were staying. If it does, then we'll stake out the place and hopefully have him within 24 hours. If not, we'll just keep looking until we find him." Dave glanced over at Krista, caught her eye and grinned. "And oh, you can thank Detective Nolan's sweet tooth for getting the bad guys tonight, Cap. Next time you see her, you'd better have a pint of chocolate chip ice cream to give her as a thank you."

"Is *that* how you guys found them? Because of *chocolate chip ice cream?*"

Dave chuckled. "Yup. Krista can explain all when you see her. Anything else you need to know for now Bob or can we call it a night once the bodies are taken away?"

"Go ahead, call it a night. I'll radio the uniforms, tell them to follow the bodies to the morgue. Just have Paul finish getting a statement from the store clerk and I'll see you guys bright and early tomorrow morning." The Captain paused. "Chocolate chip ice cream indeed," he said in amazement. "Good night, detective."

Dave swiped his finger over his cell phone to lock it and then pocketed it. "Except for Brad James and his whereabouts, mission accomplished. Paul, Krista, the Captain said to finish getting the statement from the clerk and once the bodies are taken away, we can call it a night."

"Good to hear," Paul said, spooning a third sugar into a Styrofoam cup of hot tea he was planning on giving to the clerk. "You and Cathy don't have to wait around, Krista and I can take it from here, if you like."

Dave looked over at Cathy. She was in profile and not listening to the conversation as she gently stroked the clerk's back in an attempt to calm her. He thought of what Cathy and he had been doing prior to receiving Paul's phone call and he just about managed to conceal a shiver of pleasure. "Sure, partner, if that's okay."

Paul followed his line of vision, saw the look he gave Cathy and he grinned. "Get outta here," he coaxed. "See yas!"

Dave and Cathy bade their farewells and he started to drive them back to Cathy's place. The journey was passed in relative silence, except for the drumming of the rain on the roof and the windshield and the steady rhythm of the wipers. He pulled into a parking slot right beside Cathy's car, turned off the engine and the lights and waited for Cathy to make the next move.

She smiled awkwardly. "Well now, alone at last."

He reached over and pushed back a strand of her hair from her cheek. "Hey, we can certainly call it a night right now, if you like," he said softly. "What we were doing earlier…before… well, it can wait until it feels right again, if you like."

She pondered for a few moments and then she sighed heavily. "Would you really mind, Dave? I feel so dirty and sweaty and we're both soaked through, would you mind if we took this up again… another time?"

He barely managed to hide his disappointment but he nodded quickly. "Another time it will be, baby. Guaranteed. You're right, we're soaked, I don't want you getting a relapse from that cold and I really should go get changed too."

She leaned over and kissed him softly on the mouth. She had seen his disappointment, brief as it had been, and she felt bad, but the timing was just all off now, it no longer felt spontaneous and she knew that if they were both to go inside, that it would only end up feeling awkward. "I'm sorry, Dave."

"No need to be. See you tomorrow?"

She nodded and got out of the car. He waited until he'd seen her disappear safely inside her apartment and then, clamping down his disappointment as best as he could, he pulled away into the night.

CHAPTER FORTY-SIX

New England has unpredictable weather all year round but especially in spring. The storm of the day before had done nothing to dispel the heavy rain clouds and even the thunder and lightning, which had long since tracked out to somewhere over the Atlantic, had not broken the unseasonable muggy temperatures. The weathermen, almost apologetically, could only forecast the chance of another thunderstorm later that day and, hopefully, a few days of a dry spell afterwards.

The rain pelted against the windowpane of Captain Hamilton's office but inside, he was beaming at his four best detectives. He had just received yet another congratulatory phone call, this time from the Mayor of Boston, commending his team on finding 2 of Massachusetts's 3 most wanted, thereby helping restore safety to the streets again.

"I haven't had the heart to tell anyone this all happened just because you wanted chocolate chip ice cream, Krista," the Captain chuckled. "I really don't know how well it would be received with the higher-ups and I don't know if they would see the funny side of it or not."

Krista had the good grace to blush. She didn't want her sweet tooth to become legendary when she hadn't even been in the country six weeks. "Let's just keep it our little secret," she advised.

The Captain was about to crack another comment aimed at her but the ringing of his phone again interrupted him. He picked it up. "Yes? Yes, this is he." He listened to the caller for a couple of minutes, scribbling words down and punctuating the call with monosyllabic replies of his own. Then he hung up. "That was Officer Barnett. He followed up on the address printed on the registration found in the Camry's glove compartment." He leaned back on his chair and clasped his hands behind his head, his eyes sparkling in triumph and good humor. "Brad James was arrested five minutes ago, guys. He gave up without a fight and is on his way to jail even as we speak. That's it, the case is closed."

"Not until we get our paperwork done, right?" Paul said with a groan. He knew the drill only too well.

"Right," the Captain agreed. "So, if you make a good start on it today, I'll give you all a day off when it's all done. Sound like a deal?"

In good spirits, they returned to their desks and started to the task on hand. Dave wanted to concentrate on his work but he kept looking over at Cathy and he couldn't stop thinking about the events of the evening before in her apartment. He had told her he loved her. She had told him the same thing. They had ended up *nearly* having sex... and probably would have if it hadn't been for Paul's call.

He hadn't even told Paul yet how far his feelings for Cathy had progressed and he had a pretty good idea that she hadn't told Krista yet either. He certainly hadn't told Paul about the near-sex episode either, he didn't think it was fair to Cathy and he certainly didn't think she would approve.

But she had just been so god damned *hot* last night. Absolutely wanton, no inhibitions whatsoever... even taking the initiative and turning his body to fire everywhere she had touched him. *God,* he thought, *careful or you'll have to adjust the little guy and in work that's a* tres *uncool thing to do. Okay, so the little guy ain't so little right now, but just put him back to sleep...* He was at least grateful his lower body was safely under his desk at the moment and he willed himself to calm down.

Cathy couldn't help but pick up on his vibes and it only took a few moments for her to feel the same way he was feeling. There was no denying the sexual tension between them and as the day progressed, it only got worse. If Paul and Krista noticed, they certainly weren't saying anything but, to give Dave and Cathy their dues, they did at least manage to remain professional and to even do what work was expected of them.

At close of day, Dave came over to Cathy and helped her on with her jacket. He leaned forward and licked her earlobe, causing her to shiver slightly. "Your place, around 7:00?" he murmured.

"Definitely." She turned to him with a smile and then gave him a soft but swift kiss on his mouth. "Krista has told me that Paul's taking her for dinner somewhere. We'll be quite alone."

"Good."

7:00 couldn't come quickly enough for Dave. He had gone home and taken a quick shower, as well as given his face a run over with his razor. He applied only a splash of musky cologne, had dressed in black jeans and a freshly laundered sky blue button-down knit top and had left his apartment with ample time to get to Cathy's.

The weathermen had been right, a thunderstorm that had been brewing since late afternoon finally unleashed its fury and it promised to be even more severe than the one of the previous evening. The only difference was the wind, although strong, wasn't threatening to reach gale force this time.

Cathy answered his knock almost immediately, as if she had been waiting right beside the door for his arrival. In truth she had been watering her plants at the kitchen window and had seen him hurry up the path to get out of the rain and she had quickly gone to open the door for him.

"Hey, beautiful," he greeted and, just as he had done the

previous evening, he took from behind his back another long stemmed perfect red rose. "Just because," he said softly.

She smiled and took the rose from him to put in a bud vase. While she was taking care of that, she gave him a towel to dry his hair and then they were able to give each other a proper greeting. He pulled her into his arms and hugged her tightly, his hands roaming possessively over her back and down towards her buttocks.

Cathy was almost mirroring his movements on his back and just as she was about to ask him if he'd eaten, she was silenced by him putting his mouth on hers and kissing her hungrily.

Oh God *how I want this man!* She thought and she knew that it was almost as if they had stepped back in time to the previous evening, that they hadn't had a twenty-four-hour interruption. This was as spontaneous as it was going to get and it certainly felt right, they didn't have to ask if it was what the other wanted because they knew it was.

They had been driving each other crazy all day with subtle looks and gentle, brief caresses and it was about all either of them could take by now. She was ready for him and had been since that morning.

Knowing she didn't have to hold back any longer, she unbuckled his belt, undid his top button then, slowly, eased his zipper down. She deliberately didn't touch him, she just looked at him and tried unsuccessfully to conceal a shiver of pure pleasure.

He reached out to her again and placed his hands on her shoulders, his mouth seeking out hers as he pulled her to him. He kissed her greedily and moved his hand down to her upper thigh. She was wearing a skirt tonight, one that came down to mid-calf, and he impatiently hitched one side of the skirt up. He smoothed his hand up her leg, fondled the firm curve of her buttock, and then emitted a soft curse.

"Why do women have to wear so many layers of clothing?" he said hoarsely, in reference to her slip, her hose and her panties.

"Take them off," she instructed breathlessly, "just take them off and make love to me."

Dave sank to his knees and slowly peeled her underwear down, his lips leaving a trail of hot kisses from her inner thighs down to her ankles and then back up again. He caught the intoxicating scent of her sex and could feel her heat even without touching her. He wanted to take her right now, but he wanted to at least *try* to wait as well, to give her the chance to be as ready as he was, so he stood up and started to unbutton her blouse but his reservation to wait soon fell by the wayside when he felt her hand on his crotch. He emitted a deep, guttural sigh and let his attention be deliciously distracted for a moment by the gentle but oh so heavenly pressure of her fingers as she caressed him.

It was almost more than his poor, sex-starved body could handle by now and with a swift glance into her eyes, he groaned softly, picked her up and encircled his waist with her legs.

"Cathy, I'm sorry," he murmured, "I have to..."

"So do it," she ordered urgently, "I don't care where, just do it."

He laid her carefully on the floor and he took her as slowly as he could. It seemed a bit wild and a bit crazy to him to be making love to her for the very first time right slap bang in the middle of her kitchen floor, both of them still with most of their clothes on, but then, he only had to remind himself, she was a wild and beautifully crazy woman, so maybe it wasn't so unusual after all.

It seemed that within no time at all he felt her tense beneath him and the hard, wonderful spasms of her body were enough for him to let his moans mingle with hers. Neither of them held back in sharing their pleasure with the other and when it was all over, Dave smiled at her, then rested his head above her shoulder, feeling like he had just come home after a long, lonesome journey.

Neither of them could speak, neither of them even wanted to in case it would break the spell and they enjoyed the silence as they got their breath back.

"You're delicious, Cathy," he murmured in her ear.

"You're spectacular," she whispered back, then giggled softly. "And well worth the wait."

"Oh yeah?" He chuckled with her and raised himself up so he could see her face. Her eyes were tender and clear as she looked at him with a slight smile playing at the corner of her mouth and he pushed back a lock of hair from her cheek. "It's been a very long wait for me," he said, "and now I know what I was waiting for." He reluctantly pulled out of her, made himself presentable, then helped her to her feet. He folded her into a tight embrace, not wanting to let her go. "I love you, baby," he said solemnly. "I just love you."

"And I you."

"Good." He turned his head towards the window and frowned. "Still storming out," he remarked.

"I think we managed to cook up our own storm in here," she purred and kissed his neck. Her whole body was still tingling all over with the afterglow of their lovemaking and she only knew she couldn't wait for him to take her again. She shivered slightly in anticipation and contented herself in the meantime with just having his arms around her.

"I've never made love on the kitchen floor before," she suddenly announced, then blushed deeply, as if she was a bit embarrassed by this admission.

He smiled, loving her for her innocence as much as for her passion. "You should make a wish then."

"I will and I'll let you know later if it comes true." With a teasing smile, she stooped to pick up her discarded underwear but she suddenly seemed a bit distracted and she looked at him pensively. "Dave, this is for real, isn't it? I mean, all that we're feeling for each other, it *is* for real, it's not just a passing thing, is it?"

Dave sensed her always-underlying vulnerability again and he quickly pulled her back into his arms. "It's real all right, it's definitely real."

Relief washed over her and she nodded. "Thank you because I don't like to be used, I've been used enough in the past and I would die if I was to be used by you too."

"Hey, I would never use you, Cathy, never. I've used enough women in my time, that's one of the reasons why I stopped seeing them, so I couldn't do it again. Please believe me on that score because it's true."

"I believe you. And to prove that I believe you, I want to tell you what I'd like to do right now, if, of course, you're up to it."

He couldn't fail to see a mischievous twinkle in her eye and he looked at her with great interest. "What would you like to do?"

"I'd like to go up to my bedroom...with you...and get naked. All the way naked, this time." She turned away and threw him a seductive look over her shoulder. "But like I said, only if you're up to it."

Dave felt a stirring in his groin all over again and he slowly nodded. "Oh yes, I'm up to it all right. Lead the way."

They took their time undressing one another as they sat on the edge of her bed, neither of them wanting to hurry it and wanting instead to draw as much pleasure as they could from this second encounter.

Cathy fell in love with Dave's body as soon as she saw what he had to offer. His chest was firm, with a smattering of dark hairs that trailed down to his navel, his forearms and upper arms were strong and muscular, his stomach was flat and trim and his legs and buttocks hard and powerful.

"Oh *my*," she stated in unabashed wonder and roamed her eyes covetously over his whole body. "Have I just died and gone to heaven?"

He smiled in way of an answer and took off the last piece of her clothing. Now it was his turn to stare in awe at the sight of her completely naked like this. She was small framed but beautifully proportioned, with generous curves but with no hint of excess fat anywhere on her perfect body and, reaching out, he smoothed his hands possessively over her soft skin. "And you, my love.... you are so beautiful."

Their love making this time was slow and completely sensuous as they each discovered what turned the other on. Dave soon learned that Cathy was a very willing and adept partner, she soon learned he was a totally unselfish lover, who wanted to please as much as he was being pleased. He took her again only when he was assured she was more than ready for him and it was only when he heard her call out his name and tense beneath him was he willing to submit to his own powerful release.

Cathy sighed in contentment when he settled down beside her and pulled her into his arms. She nestled her head comfortably against his shoulder, hearing the steady rhythm of his heart gradually slow down to a more normal beat. "I hope you realize I'll be expecting this sort of treatment from you every time we make love," she told him breathlessly.

He smiled and reached out to wipe away a trickle of sweat from between her breasts. "Could be arranged."

She gave him a slow smile and when she rested her head back against his chest, he saw her steal a glance at the bedside clock. It wasn't even 8:30 yet, the night was still young, only she didn't want the night to end at all.

Dave seemed to read her mind as he watched her eyes cloud over and he came to a swift decision he had already been toying with. "I'm not going anywhere tonight, Cathy," he said softly, "not if you don't want me to. I want to stay right here with you."

She brightened immediately on hearing that and she hungrily kissed his neck. "Good, because I was wondering how I could discreetly leave you so I could get my handcuffs and cuff you to the bed."

"You're a funny lady," he stated and playfully kissed her nose.

Chuckling, she raised herself up on one elbow and unashamedly displayed her nakedness to him. "Are you hungry yet?"

"Depends what for," he said lightly, trying not to leer at her beautiful breasts. "For food, yes, for you, definitely yes."

"The food wins, I'm afraid because I'm starved too. You can have me for dessert if you like."

"I could go for that," he agreed.

"Good. What would you like?"

"How does pizza sound? We could order it and get it delivered."

"Sounds fine to me, I love pizza. If you don't want to look it up on your cell phone, there's a phone book in the drawer underneath the phone, you call the order through while I go to the bathroom. I don't mind what toppings you get, I'll eat anything."

Dave watched her slide out of bed and he raised his eyes in appreciation at the sight of her body again. When Cathy returned a few minutes later, he had already phoned the pizza order through and he threw back the covers for her to get in beside him.

"Half an hour for it to get here," he informed her. "My wallet's in my jacket pocket for when it comes."

"That's all right, I'll pay for it."

"Nope, *I'll* pay for it," he argued.

"I will."

They bantered back and forth for a few moments, until he grabbed her and silenced her by kissing her on the mouth. "Do you ever take no for an answer?" he teased.

"Of course not."

"Witch." He looked at her happily. "Make sure you cover yourself up when you answer the door to the delivery boy. I don't want him getting more than his tip."

"With *my* money, I can give him pretty much what I want," she flashed right back at him.

He groaned and threw his hands up in defeat. "Okay, buy the god damned pizza. But the next meal's on me."

"Deal. But you might be sorry."

"I'll take my chances." He pulled her towards him so he could hold her close again. He just couldn't get enough of having her body next to his, she was warm and soft and fit perfectly against him.

They each settled into a light, contented doze and were awoken a while later by the sound of the doorbell. Cathy leapt out of bed, grabbed her robe and hurried downstairs to answer it. It was the expected pizza and, knowing full well what was going through the young deliveryman's mind at her unkempt appearance, she quickly paid him and closed the door. She grabbed a couple of drinks from the refrigerator, a couple of plates and some napkins and hurried back up to Dave.

"It's stopped raining," she informed him, "and I haven't heard any more thunder so the storm must have passed. And you should have seen the look on that guy's face when I opened the door to him, if looks could undress, I'd be naked."

"Lady, you are," Dave said dryly, "underneath that itsy bitsy robe."

"It covers the essentials."

"Just about."

They tucked into the pizza with a lot of enthusiasm and polished it off within ten minutes. Dave lay back and patted his stomach in contentment. "Can't understand how I worked up such an appetite," he said innocently. "Isn't there something about the weather, that if it's storming out, you develop an amazing appetite?"

"Isn't there something about Americans that they can do rude gestures like this?" she retorted and flipped him the finger.

"Good one," he acknowledged. "Did you get enough?"

"Pizza or sex?"

"You choose," he said lazily.

"It will have to be the pizza then because the sex is now on hold until after an hour has passed. No strenuous exercise on a full stomach."

Cathy positioned herself in his arms and they lay in a companionable silence for a while. She felt like pinching herself she felt so good, she couldn't believe how well things had gone for them and she smiled. Dave's thoughts about her were erratic but out of nowhere, he started thinking about how sexy she was and he couldn't help but think that a woman who was this sexy could have so many insecurities and be vulnerable about a lot of things. The vulnerability jolted a memory into his head and he looked down at her to ask her something. "Cath, remember the night we all were at that nightclub, the night you and Krista got your badges? Do you remember the guy who tried to hit on you?"

"Yes, what about him?"

"After he left, what did you mean when you said you're not used to guys trying to touch for you?"

"Trying to touch is the same thing as trying to hit."

"I know that, that's not what I meant. How come you're not used to guys hitting on you?"

"I'm just not," she said awkwardly.

"Are you kidding me here?" Dave wasn't sure if she was and one look at her eyes soon told him she wasn't. He quickly adopted a casual approach. "With your looks and your body, I figured it would be the other way around, that you'd be sick to death of guys trying to hit on you."

"There haven't been that many, Dave, just a few really. But as I recall, I didn't handle that particular guy on that particular night very well. I usually do a lot better than that but I usually have more time to think about my actions and what I want to say."

Totally baffled now, Dave had to find out what she meant. "You usually have more time? I think you'd better explain that one, Cathy."

"It's quite simple really, once you stop and think about it. Krista's the one who gets all the guys hitting on her, not me. Once they find out she's not interested, that's when they turn their attention to me, by which time I have thought up a suitable retort to tell them to buzz off. Because this guy started in on me straight away, I didn't have time to collect myself, hence that rather embarrassing situation that followed."

It wasn't really the explanation Dave had been expecting but it made sense, although it saddened him that Cathy had managed to make herself out to be second best to Krista. At that precise moment, he made a solemn promise to himself that he would do everything in his power to make Cathy feel like the most important person in the world and never feel like second best again. "If I hadn't stepped in when I did, do you think you could have dealt with the guy yourself?"

"Probably. Maybe I should have thrown my drink at him instead."

"Yeah, could have saved my pants for me."

"Don't remind me about that," she groaned, "please, I can still see the look on your face when I threw that drink at you. I thought you were going to murder me, or at the very least, punch me right on the jaw."

"Hey," he said sharply, "I've never hit a woman in my entire life, nor do I ever intend to, particularly the woman I love."

"Even if it's warranted?"

"Nothing warrants a man hitting a woman, nothing. I may be a hot-tempered asshole at times but I would never take my temper out on a lady."

"Even if you were pushed to the limit?"

"Especially if I was pushed to the limit. That's when I would get up and walk away."

"That's really good to hear." She kissed him on the mouth, then snuggled in against him again. "Dave, why didn't your parents give you brothers or sisters?" she asked suddenly.

It was an unusual question, but he didn't mind answering it. "Because they didn't like children," he stated.

She bolted upright and stared at him in shock. "Then why did they have you?"

"Beats me but they did, and here I am." His eyes twinkled at her but she was very clearly horrified at his statement and he moved to try and calm her down. "It's no big a deal, Cathy, I told you I'm an only child and that's because my parents really don't like children. I grew up in a loveless home and that's just the way it was for me."

"But why? Were they poor or something?"

He rolled his eyes in amusement. "On the contrary. My father is fifty years old and is a multi-millionaire… in fact, last I heard, a *multi, multi*-millionaire."

Cathy recoiled as if she had just been slapped and for an instant, she even looked as if she was going to jump out of bed and run from the room, but she didn't. "A m-millionaire?" she repeated.

"Yup, that's what I said. Big whoopee, huh? He has all the money in the world, can buy whatever he wants and yet the one thing he can get and give for free, he refuses to give to me. Even if love was something you could buy, he still wouldn't be prepared to buy any for his only son and heir."

"Heir? You mean the money's yours?" The news was getting worse, she now looked like she was going to pass out and he stroked her bare thigh to try and settle her.

"Yes, it will be mine, eventually, and I say big whoopee to that too. I don't want the money, I don't need the money, but I'm going to get it anyway. But I already know what I'm going to do with it when I get it and that's give at least ninety-five per cent of it away to charity. I didn't mean to sound so blunt in telling you, particularly when it seems to have upset you, but I really don't care about the money. I come from a rich family, so what?"

"So what? I'll tell you so what! People might think I'm only going out with you because I'm after your money." Now she looked like she was going to cry and Dave began to get a little alarmed.

"Hey, baby, you feel in love with me before I told you about the money and besides, only two other people over here - Paul and Captain Hamilton - know about my background so I really don't think you have anything to fear about what other people are going to say."

"But that's not the point, I just wish you had told me sooner."

"Would it have made a difference?"

"I don't know...it's just... it's just... Oh, I just don't know, Dave, this news has just about knocked me for six. Do you have much money now?"

"I suppose, but only because I just got paid yesterday. And I suppose the twenty thousand dollars I got as a twenty-seventh birthday gift from the old man last October helped bump up my bank balance. But a good chunk of that's gone now, I bought my car with some of the money and paid off six months on Paul's car loan - not that he knows about it, I'm keeping it as a surprise for him, so please don't tell him. We both opted to have our own personal vehicles, rather than have the department supply them and I just didn't feel right buying my car outright and watching my partner have to make payments each month. Anyway, I don't get a cash gift like that from my father every birthday, or even at Christmas time, I only get it when it appears my father has gotten a surge of guilt so tries to buy me off. In fact, that was the first substantial amount I've received from him since my divorce and since my father thought I had blackened the Andrews name, it's taken him nearly ten years to even remotely forgive me. I wrote him a thank you note and politely asked him not to send me a money gift ever again. There's no love lost between us, or with my mother, and it suits me fine."

Cathy nodded, still clearly trying to come to terms with it all. "Why don't you get along?"

"Any number of reasons. I'd be the first to admit I have a strong will and from the very first time I realized how strong willed I can be, I've used it to my advantage. Being rich, my parents wanted to send me to the best schools in the country but I didn't want any of that so I rebelled and insisted I be sent to a public school, just like anyone else, where I would get just as good an education. After many tantrums, I got my wish. My father owns a couple of hotels in Las Vegas and one in Reno. He always wanted me to go into the hotel business with him but since that wasn't what *I* wanted to do with my life, I rebelled against that as well. And telling him what I wanted to do was the most satisfying thing I've ever told anyone, if only to see the look on his face. After I had made my intentions perfectly clear, I toyed very heavily with the idea of becoming a mechanic, cars always have been my first love. I was always at my happiest working on them, fixing them up, tuning the engines, whatever. And then one day, not long after I left Terri - I had just turned nineteen at the time - I found myself standing outside the Police Academy. And that was that, I became a cop. My father hit the roof when he heard about the career I had chosen, he threatened to write me out of his will but since he knew that was what I wanted anyway, he retracted that decision. Since I definitely wasn't going into the hotel business with him, he hasn't been able to forgive me. He didn't come to my graduation and he's barely spoken two words to me since. He couldn't even bring himself to congratulate me when I was offered the chance to come out east as a Detective, even though it was an almost unheard-of opportunity."

"Because you were so young?"

"Exactly. But that was all Captain Hamilton's doing, he masterminded the idea of bringing in young cops to work as detectives, as you know, or else you wouldn't be here. I owe it all to Bob for having the faith and trust in me that he did. At least *he* supported me."

"I'm glad he did. But I still can't understand why your own parents can't love their own and only child. It just doesn't make sense."

"Look, Cathy, my parents don't even know the true meaning of the word love. They only love the money, their business and each other, certainly not me because I didn't fit into what they wanted in their lifestyle. Horrible as that may be to hear, it's not so horrible for me to have to say it. I was brought up by nannies, housekeepers and servants, a few of who I know loved me, but I've basically been on my own since I've been old enough to walk and really, I've accepted it. I accepted it a long time ago."

Dave had been speaking so nonchalantly, Cathy truly believed he had accepted it, but she felt so sorry for him and this time, she did start to cry, soft tears that filled her eyes and trickled slowly down her cheeks. "It *is* horrible," she managed to gulp. "You may have had everything while you were growing up but you never had the greatest gift of all and it's so terribly sad. How can you be so forgiving and so generous?"

"Because I wanted to make sure I would never be anything like my parents," he replied easily.

"You're such a sweet person, David, you deserve a whole lot better than what they could ever have given you."

He gently wiped away her tears, sorry that he had made her cry but feeling touched that the tears were, again, for him. "That's why it doesn't matter to me. Two of the most important people in the world to me love me now and accept me for who I am and that's enough for me. Paul and you are my family now, and Krista too, if she wants to be included and I couldn't ask for anything better."

Cathy threw her arms around him and hugged him fiercely. "I *do* love you, Dave, with all my heart."

"Then that's all I want to hear. Please don't cry anymore, I didn't tell you this to extract any sympathy from you." He hugged her back, feeling somewhat relieved that he had told her about his past. The money he stood to inherit was still a very long time in the future, his parents were both in peak physical condition and, barring an untimely fatal accident, Dave would more than likely be near retirement age, or beyond, before he received any money. But at least dollar signs hadn't appeared in Cathy's eyes at the very first mention of it, if anything, it had only unnerved her, which made him grateful that he knew she could love him for being him and not because of his fortune. He wanted to lighten the mood so he gently pushed her back and looked into her eyes. "Can I make a suggestion here?"

"Sure," she said, with a last swipe at her tears.

"I feel sort of hot and sticky, why don't we go take a shower or a bath together. It's been so long since I've had the pleasure of doing something like that with a woman and I would really like to. Do you mind?"

"Of course not," she said gleefully, "but let's make it a bath, that way you can talk to me some more. You run down to the kitchen with the pizza box and dirty dishes and I'll go run the bath right now. And oh, while you're downstairs, look in the fridge, I remembered to buy some beer so help yourself."

They enjoyed a long, luxurious bath together and Cathy was the one who asked him a lot of questions this time. She found out his middle name was Anthony, which was, ironically, his father's name, that he loved sports of any kind, especially hockey and baseball, he liked to relax by watching *The Three Stooges* movies, or by reading anything he could get his hands on, or by going to watch Paul play his hockey games. He confessed modestly to being the best marksman in the precinct, an honor he clearly didn't like having, but he had accepted the responsibility. He loved classical music too, like her, only his preference was Mozart and then, clearly bored about talking about himself, he started to keep her amused with a few stories from his early days as a cop.

He had her total attention the whole time, but she had been driving him crazy sitting facing him like this, totally nude, her hair piled high on her head and falling around her face in wet, cute little ringlets. And the way she had been holding the sponge and smoothing it absently over her body hadn't exactly helped matters either.

He felt himself rise for her all over again and he wasn't even a bit ashamed or bashful to show her as he leaned over to kiss her deeply. He jumped out of the tub, dried himself off quickly, plucked her out of the water, wrapped her up in the towel and dried her too. He loosened her hair, shook it free and carried her back to the bedroom, where he laid her gently on the bed and made slow, delicious love to her.

Afterwards, he held her in his arms and let her fall asleep as he watched over her. That incredible hair of hers was fanned out over the pillow and he raked his fingers through it, feeling its soft, silky texture.

"I love you, Cathy," he murmured, even though she was asleep and couldn't hear him. "I really love you."

And just before he fell asleep too, he knew something magical had happened tonight. He had found the woman he wanted to spend the rest of his life with.

CHAPTER FORTY-SEVEN

Dave was the first to awaken in the morning and he waited patiently for Cathy to awaken too, which she did, about fifteen minutes after him. She opened one sleepy eye, looked up at him and let a slow smile spread over her face.

"Morning, sweetheart," she whispered.

"Morning back." He thought she looked beautiful first thing in the morning, soft and warm and totally desirable and he quickly pulled her towards him for a cuddle. "You feel so good," he murmured lazily.

"So do you," she replied in contentment. "Did you sleep okay?"

"Like a log. Is it all right if I take a shower?"

"Only if you'll let me join you. You know, I could get quite used to waking up in the morning and finding you lying beside me. It's the best feeling in the world."

"I'll bear that in mind for tomorrow morning, then." He glanced at her in sudden alarm, he was being presumptuous. "Er, that is, if it's okay with you, of course."

"Need you even ask?" She chuckled happily and reluctantly slid out of bed. "I've got to go to the bathroom so I'll start the shower and you can join me when you're ready, okay?"

When he stepped in under the steaming hot water a couple of minutes later, he tried to hold back from touching her but his willpower lasted all of five seconds and when he reached out to her, it was obvious to both of them just how much he wanted her. He couldn't seem to get enough of her, nor she of him, and it was quite some time before they were able to finish their shower and go back to the bedroom.

They got dressed, something neither of them seemed to want to do because it meant they would have to wait a while before they would be together again.

"Can we play hooky today?" Cathy asked hopefully.

"Don't I wish? Come on, love, there'll be plenty of times for us to be together, don't look so unhappy." But he was unhappy too, his feelings for her were just so strong and he had to struggle to get some cheer into his voice. "What are you making for breakfast?"

"Anything you want. How do you like your eggs done?"

"Over easy, scrambled, whatever. I should warn you I like to eat a big breakfast in case I have to skip lunch. Come on, I'll help you." He followed her downstairs, fondling her bottom the whole way and making her laugh.

"Didn't you get enough of me?" she teased as she lifted some eggs and bacon from the refrigerator.

"Nope, never." He kissed her and looked at her inquisitively. "Where did you learn to kiss like this anyway? Oh, don't tell me, the Edwards School of Charm?"

"No, Girl Scouts," she said innocently.

"Yeah, right. Something tells me you were never in the Girl Scouts."

They moved around the kitchen, doing this or that to prepare the breakfast and it was almost as if they had been living together for years, they worked with the practiced ease of a long-time couple.

Just as they sat down to start their breakfast, Paul and Krista pulled up outside. The sun was splitting the trees this morning, almost as if the storm of the night before had never existed, but Paul wasn't thinking about the weather right now as he slowly got out of his car and stared at something that had grabbed his attention as soon as he had parked.

"What's wrong?" Krista asked and followed his line of vision. "Is that Dave's car?"

"It sure is. Wonder what he's doing here so early?" He went over to the vehicle and laid a hand on the hood. "Well, well, the engine's cold," he stated dryly, "which can only mean one thing. Come on, I'm dying to find out if I'm right, aren't you?"

Krista inserted her key in the door lock and as she stepped inside, she called out, "Cathy?"

"In here, Kris," came her voice from the kitchen.

Paul and Krista went and stood at the kitchen doorway and they looked expectantly at their friends. "What's all this?" he asked casually. "Dave, what are you doing here?"

"Having breakfast," Dave replied innocently. "What does it look like?"

"Coffee, anyone?" Cathy asked brightly. "I made a full pot."

Paul didn't say a word as he poured himself and Krista a cup of coffee, put milk in the cups, passed hers over to her and sat down at the table, beside Cathy and directly facing Dave. "Nice weather outside," he stated.

"Sure is a fine day," Dave agreed. "Some storm last night, huh?"

"I'll say." Paul raised his cup to his mouth, took a quick sip and turned to Cathy. He looked her over a bit critically. "You seem mighty tired this morning, sweetie. Didn't you sleep good?"

"I slept fine, Paul." Cathy glanced at Dave, smiled, and resumed her eating.

Paul turned his attention back to Dave, who, on seeing the wicked glint in Paul's eyes, prepared himself for a barrage of abuse. "You must have been up at the crack of dawn this morning, Big D."

"How do you work that one out?"

"Your car engine's cold, which means you've been here for quite a while."

"Damned good detective work, Paul. Ever think of taking that line of work up professionally?"

"Toyed with the idea, yes. Say, how long have you and I known each other?"

"Four years, I believe, this coming June."

"That's right, four years. Long time."

"Yes, long time. What's your point here?"

Krista looked on in carefully concealed amusement. Paul really didn't have to ask any questions, it was blatantly obvious to anyone that Cathy and Dave had spent the night together. He, for one, was looking like the proverbial cat that had swallowed the canary and as for Cathy, there was a look of such contentment in her eyes that Krista had never witnessed before.

"My point is," Paul continued, "in all that time, I've never known you to leave the house in the morning without shaving first."

Dave scratched at his telltale stubble and grinned. "Two for two, Cam-man."

"Thank you, I know."

Cathy chuckled softly, knowing exactly where this conversation was heading. She looked over at Krista. "You're very quiet this morning, chum."

"Nothing to worry about, Cath, I'm just drinking my coffee, minding my own business." And dying to find out what Paul was going to say next to get either Dave or Cathy to admit to what they'd been up to.

"Why didn't you shave then?" Paul asked.

"Don't have any razor blades. No shaving cream either."

"Yes you do, I was with you in the drugstore the other day when you bought some cream *and* new blades. Did you lose them or something?"

"Nope."

"Get them stolen on you?"

Dave smiled. "Nope, again."

"Didn't bring them with you then."

"When?"

"Last night, when you came over here."

"Why should I have to bring shaving stuff with me? Cathy has her own razor, I'm sure of it, so why would I have needed to bring mine?"

"Good question." Paul set his cup down, realizing he was just going to have to be blunt about it. "Look me square in the eye, Andrews, and tell me you didn't stay here last night."

Dave leveled his gaze with Paul's and said quite calmly, "I didn't stay here last night. And you want to know something else?"

"Yeah, you're lying."

"Three for three, my man, I'm impressed." Dave grinned. "Why didn't you just ask me outright instead of going through all that bullshit about shaving and razors?"

"Because I wanted to see if you were man enough to 'fess up first." Paul turned back to Cathy, his face suddenly troubled and full of concern. "Tell me the truth, little dude. Did he do something terrible to you? Like take you against your will or something? Because if he did, I'll haul his ass down to the slammer so fast, his head will spin. Did he?"

"He didn't do anything terrible to me, Paul," she soothed. "In fact..." She paused and looked at Dave, her eyes twinkling mischievously. "...If you really must know, I think I had the most incredible, wonderful night of my life last night."

Paul immediately pretended to gag and pushed his coffee away in disgust. "Please, I've just eaten breakfast, I don't think I want to hear anymore."

"Serves you right for being so nosy," Dave said. "But for your added information..." It was his turn to pause and he locked his gaze with Cathy's, his eyes shining with happiness. "...I happen to have fallen in love with your little dude," he continued softly. "I love her very much, but that's not even the best part, the best part is that she loves me too. Am I a lucky guy or am I a lucky guy?"

Paul instantly dropped the teasing, he had just heard exactly what he had wanted to hear and he couldn't have been more pleased for his friend. He reached over and thumped him on the shoulder. "Great news, Dave, I'm really happy for you. Now maybe you'll listen to me more often when I tell you what I know to be true."

"Shouldn't have to listen to you too many times then because you don't know too many things to be true."

"Seems I got lucky this time, you jerk."

"If you say so." Dave smiled at him and winked at Cathy. "How much did you pay him in advance to say so many nice things about yourself to me, love?"

"Not too much, he comes cheap."

Krista couldn't take her eyes off Cathy as she watched her friend receive, accept and return a kiss from across the table from Dave and Krista couldn't contain her happiness much longer. "Good for you that this has happened, Cathy - no, good for the *both* of you." And then, as was to be expected from her, she gave Cathy and Dave a big hug each.

"Seems Billy was very prophetic after all," Cathy remarked when they had all settled down again.

"He sure was," Krista agreed. "Although I think even he couldn't have seen this happening so fast."

"Who's Billy?" Paul asked.

"Our ex-boss, in Belfast, Detective Inspector Billy Clarke. When we knew we were being accepted into Captain Hamilton's program and therefore would be moving to the States, he told us we were going to fall in love with Americans eventually. I think I'll send him a nice long email and tell him he was right."

"Good idea, Kris," Cathy agreed as she picked up her plate, carried it over to the sink and started to wash the dishes.

Paul watched Dave carry his plate over too, grab a drying cloth to help her and then slip his arm possessively around her for a quick cuddle. Paul hadn't seen Dave look this happy or so at peace with himself since.... well, since never, Paul had to acknowledge, and it was great to see. It was a rare novelty too to see Dave be so open with his affections towards a female, which meant that he truly did have strong feelings for her and the light in Cathy's eyes, as she looked up at him after he had whispered something in her ear, confirmed that she had just as strong feelings for him.

Krista reached over the table and squeezed Paul's hand. "Don't they look great together?" she whispered.

He smiled and turned his attention back to the lady he was in love with and would be forever. "Awesome, sweet-face, totally awesome."

Paul knew that something important had officially started between all four of them, not just two separate love affairs or two separate friendships, but a very strong, single friendship, one that was based on compatibility, mutual trust and undying respect and one that could only continue to grow and never flounder. He grinned broadly and slipped his hand over Krista's. Life was good.

The phone rang and because Dave was the one nearest to it, he answered it. "Morning, Cap," he said brightly, as soon as he heard who it was.

"Andrews? What the hell are you doing there at this time of the morning?"

"Having breakfast with Cathy," he said sweetly. "Why do you ask?"

The Captain groaned into himself at the tone of Dave's voice. *Oh Christ,* he thought, *it's happened again, there must be something in the water....* "Never mind. Paul and Krista there too?"

"We're all here. Why?"

"Just wondering when one or all of you were deciding to come into work, that's all. Sorry to bust up your little party but in case you weren't aware, there's crime happening on the streets, there are drug pushers to be caught, murder weapons to be found...I could go on but I'm sure you get the message. If that's not clear enough for you, let me put it another way. Get your sorry asses down here! Pronto!"

"Certainly, sir, anything for you, sir," Dave said happily and hung up before the Captain could give him new orders. "Remind me to remind him he promised us a day off if we finish our paper work. He is requesting the pleasure of our company so it seems like we have to hustle. Oh well, another day, another dollar. Paul, your car or mine? Or would you rather travel with Krista?"

"Either way, doesn't matter to me."

After a round of kisses and hugs and promises to "see you at the station", they parted company.

The first day of the rest of their lives had started and nobody knew what the future was going to bring their way. Nobody knew that a lot of troubled times lay ahead, for all four of them. Nobody knew anything of the difficult road Fate was going to lead them down sometimes, when their friendships would be pushed to the limit and tested far beyond the bounds of fairness. Nobody knew that good times lay ahead too, as was to be expected through this journey called Life but one thing they did know was they would be going through it all together and, for right now at least, life couldn't be any better.

It was too bad that they had no way of knowing that, at that very moment in Ossining, New York, in Sing Sing Correctional Facility, an inmate was studying a picture of Paul. If they had known what he was thinking, they would have been able to prepare for, and maybe even prevent, the events of the near future. The inmate had been studying the picture and several others of Paul, for years, using Paul's image to turn dislike into loathing and working out ways to execute a plan of revenge. With his release imminent, it wasn't going to be too much longer to put the plan into motion...

THE END

ACKNOWLEDGEMENTS

I have encountered many friends and acquaintances who, once they knew what I do for a hobby, were quick to offer a hand, or encouragement, or a pep talk or whatever they thought I needed. I couldn't have done this without any of you, no matter how small a role you might have played.

To Mr Daniel Diehl, my first ever editor… I have taken your notes and suggestions to heart and thank you immensely for your patience and guidance. Just know that I won't be able to hear 'Fairytale of New York' by the Pogues without thinking about you.

To my brother Barrie Edgar and to Peninsula Print for the cover. Extraordinary work and done without having to burn the midnight oil after all. Ok, sort of makes up for all the time you used to get me into trouble when we were kids.

To Dr Monika Gooz, my best and dearest friend, who has believed in me from the start and is the only person to have read the first book in its latest version and still loved it. Any medical input you have given me has been invaluable, and your support and encouragement will never be forgotten.

Honourable mentions have to go to Jon Rodgers in Summerville, SC, for giving me police procedural pointers; to Dr DeAnna Baker-Frost for advice on medical terms and for supporting me from the get go; to

Diana and Colin Leitch – all that photocopying and medical advice and patience and encouragement, way back when, you were the best and I'm pretty sure Andy and Colin are looking down now on "Issy" with a smile on their face; to my sister-in-law Freda Edgar for taking the time to read the first three books when they were in a totally unpolished state; To Lisa Elder for the many photos and patience. To my mates at work: Stacey, Bernie, Martine, Sarah, and Sharon, for being interested and supportive enough to let me spout on (and on) about this first novel.

To my mum Norah, my dad Randal and my sister Shirley for being the best parents and sister a girl could wish for. I wanted to make you proud and I hope that I have.

And, of course, my darling husband, Mark Kravetz. I couldn't have done this without you, you know that. I can never thank you enough for helping me fulfil my dreams. This one's for you, baby.

NOTE FROM THE AUTHOR

"Murder Is Just the Beginning" can be enjoyed as a stand-alone work, yet it is the first installment in the crime thriller Bathville Books series, a series of eight exciting books with the last book concluding with a thrilling ending.

If you enjoyed this book, it would be fantastic if you could leave a review and let other readers know. Sincere thanks.

For a taste of what you will find in book two, here is the first chapter. "The Revenge" is available right now on Amazon, iBooks, nook, and Smashwords.

"THE REVENGE"

CHAPTER ONE

The prison doors slammed shut, dividing the line between freedom and confinement with a loud crash that echoed and re-echoed around the boundary walls and the courtyards of the prison building. A group of five men walked slowly, almost hesitantly, towards a waiting ancient school bus that would transport them to the bus depot in Ossining, New York. Sing Sing Correctional Facility now loomed behind them and not one of them looked back as they boarded the bus that would take them away from what had been, for some of them, home for many years.

One of the inmates who had just been released looked slowly around him with cold, slate gray eyes, his expression completely emotionless as he tasted for the first time in five years the feeling of liberty.

He allowed himself only a few minutes of pleasure at the realization he was, finally, free, then, once settled on the public transportation, his mind immediately turned to the plan that he had been harboring and nurturing ever since he had been imprisoned.

Zooming south along Saw Mill River Parkway, and then onto NY-9A, the trees and buildings and other vehicles passed in a blur. He could have dozed, he could have read, he could have watched the scenery, but he didn't want to do anything, he just wanted to concentrate on his plan. Traffic was uncharacteristically light because within the hour, he was waiting to be served in a bank in downtown Manhattan, New York.

When he approached the teller, his request was simple enough: He wanted to reopen his accounts that had been frozen for so long and then close them all by drawing out his money. After obtaining the necessary ID, the teller punched his name into her computer, a slightly bored expression on her face as she expected to see a balance of maybe a few hundred dollars splash across her monitor. But what she saw instead shook her out of her disinterested stance into one of shock.

"But, sir, you have over fourteen million dollars in your account. Are you sure you want to draw out every penny?" She spoke with a nasal New Jersey accent, her red hair had been teased and permed to within an inch of its life and her thirty eight year old body had been poured into a skirt suit more befitting a ripe and svelte teenager. She was trying to maintain a professional air but she had obviously been thrown off guard.

Her customer stared calmly back at her, trying not to appear impatient. He shifted his gaze down to her cleavage and decided her bosom was just begging to be released from a blouse that was two sizes too small, but he didn't care what she looked like, he thought the female body was an art in itself, with all its wildly different shapes, forms and sizes. After five years, he was more than anxious for some sweet female company but he couldn't allow himself the pleasure of even thinking about that right now, he had a lot to take care of first.

His eyes went up to meet hers again and he smiled. "Yes, every red cent. If it's a problem, maybe I could speak with the manager?"

The teller balked a bit, feeling momentarily intimidated under this middle-aged man's cool, gray stare. He didn't look the type of person who could have so much money, his clothes were wrinkled and a bit out of date, she could catch a faint whiff of body odor and his thinning gray hair desperately needed a trim at the back. But then, she reminded herself, this was New York City, where eccentrics rich or poor crowded the streets day and night, so really, she shouldn't be so surprised.

She gave him a curt nod. "One moment, please."

He watched her walk away and tap softly on the door of the manager's office. He observed her rather animated conversation with the manager through the glass partition, saw them both look, as discreetly as possible, his way and then, after a few moments, the manager merely nodded.

Twenty-five minutes later, he stood out in the street again and breathed in the crisp, autumn air. How he loved New York in the fall and how he had missed the hustle and bustle of the city he had been born and raised in and had lived in for most of his fifty five year old life.

And now he was going to have to leave it again, after only a short visit, but what he had in mind was worth leaving his beloved city for. He had the ready cash he needed, in unmarked hundred, fifty and twenty dollar bills, carefully stowed in a money belt tied securely around his waist, and the balance of his account in a cashier's check tucked safely into his wallet, now all he had to do was make a few phone calls and he would be on his way to getting what he wanted.

He took one last look around him, wishing he didn't have to leave just yet, but he knew he would be back some day very soon, once his plan had been carried out and executed to perfection.

Yes, he decided, freedom tasted very sweet today indeed. Especially when it was sprinkled with all his newly restored riches.

ABOUT THE AUTHOR

I was born and raised in Northern Ireland, near Belfast. I emigrated to Canada in my mid 20's and while there, started writing. My day time job was as a   medical secretary to various health care professionals, but my spare time was dedicated to my writing. I lived in Canada for 12 years and during that time had almost completed seven novels in a series. After living at home for a year, I moved to the United States and continued my career as a medical secretary. My writing was shelved for just a little while during my time in the States but, since my return to Northern Ireland upon my husband's retirement six years ago, I have been able to resume my hobby and complete the seventh novel. I currently work full time within the Education Authority and dedicate as much time as possible to my family and my writing.

Printed in Great Britain
by Amazon

36560771R00310